A MAN FOR *Others*

Slainte

KEVIN COUHIG

A MAN FOR OTHERS

This is strictly a work of fiction. All of the characters and events are entirely from the imagination of the author and any resemblance to actual people, places and events is coincidental and unintended. Belturbet is a wonderful town filled with terrific people. Nothing described in this book happened there.

The only exception to this is the character Caoihme (pronounced Kee Va.) I met her one night in Galway. Her words helped heal my heart, she pointed me home and then she disappeared. She remains real to me to this day.

Print ISBN: 978-1-66787-266-7
eBook ISBN: 978-1-66787-267-4

DEDICATION

For

Claire

ACKNOWLEDGEMENTS

The author gratefully acknowledges the support of his editor and advisors: Claire Strombeck, Mark Couhig, Rob Couhig, Missy Couhig, Jim Odom, Owen Kemp, Katherine Ward, Noelle and Sam Leblanc and my wonderful wife, Claire. Thanks to them for their advice and encouragement.

I also want to thank Lt. (Ret) Julie Ann Jones of the NOPD, Richard Stalder former Secretary of the Louisiana Department of Corrections, attorney Arthur Lemann and West Feliciana Clerk of Court Stewart Hughes, for explaining and helping me understand the police, Corrections Department and judicial system procedures. Jason Berry spent hours and much effort to help me make this better. Their help was invaluable. The mistakes are mine alone.

CONTENTS

"Come away, O human child!
To the waters and the wild
With a faery, hand in hand
For the world's more full of weeping
than you can understand."

– "*The Stolen Child*" – WB Yeats

PROLOGUE

The young curly-haired boy kicked the football against the low stone wall of the bridge crossing a tributary of the Boyne River. Ice covered the roadway and icicles hung from the edges of the stones where the water had started to drip then froze instead. The sky was grey and dark, and the air much colder than normal for Ireland, even in the dead of winter. Big snowflakes fell intermittently. Still, the boy continued kicking the ball.

Standing quietly on the other side of the bridge, I could hear him mumbling to himself, "Practice makes permanent … Practice makes permanent …" in time to the ball rebounding back to his foot, before he'd kick it again, trying to hit the exact same spot on the wall.

He was a beautiful, slender young boy, no more than eight years old. And although he was intent on his practice, he was smiling, laughing to himself. I could see what happiness is supposed to look like in a child of his age. His curly black hair held the snowflakes as they fell, and then, as they melted, the moisture ran down his face, his cheeks turning bright red.

Knowing what was about to happen, how it would test his character and set the course of his life, made me wonder about the life we faeries lead. When I looked back on this moment, I was grateful to be there at the beginning.

He miskicked the ball and it ricocheted off a stone, then bounced against his shin, cleared the low wall, and fell down toward the bank of the river. He glanced around sheepishly and finally noticed me standing there. His face was flushed with embarrassment.

"You'd better get down there quickly," I said. He stared at me until I said again, "The ball—don't you want to retrieve it?"

With that, he ran to the edge of the bridge and stepped around the buttress and climbed carefully down the side of the bank that ran along the river. He used the stones embedded in the bank to steady himself as he climbed down to retrieve the ball which had lodged near the water's edge.

Much of the ground had begun to accumulate small patches of snow, and the river's banks had ice formed amid its rocky shores. The water was deep under the bridge and the swift current struck the larger boulders in the stream with force. The water broke into waves as the stream ran past the boulders.

As foretold, I saw Brendan Keane march over the bridge, followed by his beleaguered wife, Bridget, and their six children. Bridget clutched the youngest baby in her arms and the other five trailed behind her in descending order of age. Little Peter had seen the ball fly over the edge and the toddler stopped to peer over the stone wall. As the rest of the Keane family continued in their attempt to stay up with their Da, young Peter climbed up the wall to see where the ball went.

Bridget turned back to check on her family just as Peter stood up on the bridge wall. Her scream was so piercing that the startled boy lost his balance and fell to his knees. For a moment, it looked like he would be able to recover his balance on all fours, but, as he landed, the ice on top of the wall caused him to slide slowly toward the outside edge of the wall. His tiny fingers grasped but could find no purchase.

I watched them as the Keane family looked on in horror. Young Peter slid off the wall and fell toward the river ten feet below. The last image we had was his terrified face falling past the top edge of the stone wall.

The Keane family ran to the wall and looked below, where Peter had fallen into the middle of the stream. His limp body bubbled to the surface, pinned in the swift current to one of the big stones midstream.

On the shore, we saw the young boy staring at the body, terror in his face.

He took off his jacket and his boots and ran into the river, dancing to protect his feet amid the stones and icy water. Reaching the deeper water, he swam with a strength surprising in a boy so young and lithe, we saw him reach Peter, still pinned against the rock, his head was below the rushing water, his body askew. The young boy pushed him up along the rock until his head popped out of the water. He cradled Peter's neck, pulled him in, and struggled to swim toward shore. He swam with one arm, clutching Peter with the other.

He reached the shallow part of the river near the bank and dragged Peter to shore. Brendan Keane scrambled down the bank and picked up his son in his arms. Laying him carefully on his back, he did compression on his chest and blew into his mouth while holding the toddler's nose. After several attempts, Peter coughed and began to breathe.

Brendan Keane lifted the boy again, hugging him tightly as he climbed back up the bank of the river, then handed Peter to his mum as she handed off the baby to her oldest daughter. She turned to the boy and said, "Ah, Robby, we are eternally grateful for what you done, lad. You saved little Petey."

The boy stood shivering as he put on his coat and slid his soaking wet feet into his boots, his ball now tucked under his arm.

"Ah, Mr Keane saved him. I was just there to get him out the water. Thank goodness that woman got me down the bank when she did."

"Who is that?" asked Mrs Keane.

They all looked around for me, but I'd already faded into the background—as we faeries often do when our work is done.

BELTURBET, IRELAND

1974

CHAPTER 1

Belturbet is a small Irish town parallel to a tributary of the River Boyne where so much Irish history has played out in battle over the centuries. Slightly shabby houses and stores lined a main street that traversed the town completely. Belturbet appeared to have as many pubs as people, but the Three Horses was its most popular.

Molly Coughlan owned the Three Horses pub and ran it with an iron fist. She knew most people in town agreed that Robert Emmet Coogan was the best Belturbet had on offer. Nearly everyone in the town had recognized him as special since the day he had rescued young Peter Keane nearly a decade ago.

The street rose at each end of town and fell in its middle. Flowerboxes filled every window as if those could cover the underlying madness.

At the northern end of town, the two churches tethered to each of its warring factions seemed to glare at each other across the street corner next to the post office. It was a community rife with bitterness and religious discord, a town torn by The Troubles between Protestants and Catholics.

Despite those differences, Molly would put money on the fact that people on both sides of the divide would agree that Robby Coogan was the brightest light pointing to the future.

Robby was now slightly over six feet tall with dark curly hair and blue eyes that promised much yet revealed very little. His chiseled face was imbued with kindness and a gentle nature that only disappeared on the football ground. There, he revealed a fierce countenance that no one would see in an ordinary encounter.

Molly had heard many women admit to one another in the pub that it was this fierceness that made him a regular part of their fantasy life. She'd smile to herself watching these women of Belturbet make a sign of the cross when Robby would pass them on the street. Often, their faces were filled with a combination of hopeful joy, lust, and shame. Younger women even had trouble speaking to him in an ordinary manner, mumbling and stuttering in an unaccustomed way, some avoiding eye contact altogether.

Despite the general agreement as to his bright future, arguments raged daily in Molly's pub as to the path Robby should choose for his future. Most people in Belturbet felt pride and a sense of loss knowing that the town couldn't hold him for itself. "Oh, if he would just stay, the leadership he could provide, what a bright future we could have. He might be the one to make it all work," they would often mutter to Molly over a pint.

As was known to most, Robby was facing an immediate decision.

Men generally fell on the side of Robby becoming a professional footballer. They knew that eventually he could lead Ireland to the World Cup. Belturbet's women, however, would snort derisively at this suggestion from the men.

On Wednesday and Sunday evenings, they would gather in the Three Horses and listen to Robby's musical gift on the guitar, his melodic voice bringing forth the poetic lyrics he wrote. The women knew that he would someday command stages around the world to countless adoring fans. Women knew, because they adored him. "He's already a more magical musician than his pa, Mike," they told one another.

Mike had taught every one of their children music for years and was himself known for his gentleness and musical talent. Visiting musicians from around the world detoured through Belturbet to visit Mike, and he would invite them to join joyous musical sessions for the public. For many years, Mike had held forth at the Three Horses on Wednesday and Sunday evenings, and was loved by all. The townsfolk would mutter to Molly while watching Mike's set, "Just putting up with Maeve all these years, the man is a saint." He brought their children, his students, into the public performance on Wednesdays, filling each with a love for music that their parents knew would never die. Molly would look back on those evenings as the most peacefully joyous times in the town's history.

To Molly, Mike summed up his wife, Maeve, as "a brilliant shot". Mike's words were subtly intended to indicate that she was as powerful with her words as with actual weapons. Molly had heard the whispers that Maeve was deeply involved with the Provos of the Irish Republican Army and its more dangerous activities.

One rumor had her as the training officer of the IRA, teaching new members in the use of weapons and the construction of bombs. Not many had the nerve to take on Maeve when she held forth on the divide. So the townsfolk were grateful that Maeve seemed of late to be quieter and less visible in the Troubles.

In the heat and shadows of the Three Horses pub, the lunchtime argument took on new force. That afternoon, Robby was playing for the local side against its nearby rivals. It was rumored that Liverpool would have scouts in attendance who were intent on offering Robby a place in the club with an eye toward the first team in the near future.

The darkness inside the Three Horses was pierced by a glow emanating through the bay window facing Main Street, Belturbet's principal street of commerce. The stone fireplace with its small fire burning filled the room with a peaty flavor that did well to smother the lasting odor of last night's beer spills. Amid the dark wood of the benches, booths, and walls decorated primarily with beer and stout ads, the window provided regulars with a glowing light and a bright view into the light mist in the heart of Belturbet that day.

The pub was occupied mostly by men having lunch and stout. Molly tolerated no talk of religion or the Troubles. Given the nature of her clientele, she realized that arguments were in the ordinary course of life in Ireland, but she did remarkably well at keeping those arguments focused on sport, art, and literature. It didn't hurt that most of the men were afraid of her wicked tongue. Many had felt the lash, deciding it wasn't really worth it to break Molly's rules.

"I'm just saying dey wouldn't be coming here just for nothing—dey obviously have real intent," said John McGuire, a tall, ascetically thin, self-acknowledged expert at everything. "Dey'll know real quality when dey see it. This boy has everything. He can boss a midfield like no one around. And with that pace—brilliant." McGuire looked at the group of men at the bar as if to challenge anyone to disagree.

"All right, I'll grant you that's true around here, but English professionals are another thing altogether," said his companion, Phil Beatty. "Sure and all, he's a real talent, tremendous pace and an eye for goal, but that's competing with local lads, not da big fellas. Today's derby will be a good test. The Dundalk side have got that brilliant lad in midfield, so, fair play to Robby, he'll have to give it a real go."

Not ordinarily a man of emotion, John McGuire appeared to Molly to have tears welling in his eyes when he added, "Can ye just imagine him molded by the hands of Shankly and playing alongside Keegan and Clemence and Hughes? We'll be singing his praises forever and a day. All of County Cavan will be covered in glory for having brought forth such a rare talent."

"And doesn't she just think he hung the moon," said Molly, looking into the fog and drawing their attention to the object of their discussion. At that moment, Robby Coogan was seen on the street carrying his younger sister, Caroline, whirling around his shoulders. The little redheaded was pulling his cap, squirming and laughing with a look of joy on her face that was brighter than the glow coming through the window into the dark gloom of the pub.

Phil Beatty's attention was drawn to the small boy tailing behind the pair, football boots much too large for him slung around his neck. The boy was staring at his brother, Robby, with undisguised worship, a look of awe on his face. "That Padraig has so much to live up to, it isn't fair," he muttered, before adding, a bit louder, "I wish that radical bastard would leave Robby the hell alone." Drawing a glare from Molly, Phil dipped his head and paid special attention to his Guinness, but he couldn't help himself from saying, "There's nothing holy about dat bastard."

Just a moment before, Robby had stopped to speak with Father Mulkey, who had emerged from the post office across from the Three Horses. The short, portly priest was dressed in a black cassock with wooden rosary beads hanging from his waist. The fringe of white hair surrounded a bald head that appeared too large to fit his body. He was gesticulating to Robby and his red face seemed especially spirited.

Most would have bet that Mulkey was working hard on Robby, to remind him of some duty as an altar boy. The Coogans were known throughout County Cavan as a deeply religious family, father and mother attending church nearly every day. Father Mulkey had made it clear to all that he saw in Robby the kind of leadership the Church needed in constant supply.

Molly and Father Mulkey had grown up together, and Mulkey's family was as deeply ingrained in the ongoing conflict for Irish independence as it was with the Catholic Church. Molly remembered Mulkey's pa once saying that "belief in Catholicism and the war for Independence were soldiering in the same cause." Shortly thereafter, Mulkey's father had been found beaten to death in a back alley of the town. Most of the locals believed he had been killed by British soldiers to send a message.

Molly was hoping that the conversation wasn't concerning some serious and dangerous idea. For reasons she couldn't understand, watching Mulkey and Robby together filled her heart with dread.

CHAPTER 2

Phil Beatty reached his post inside the football ground as the modest crowd began to find their seats for the match. Beatty was short, overweight, and hampered by a left leg shorter than the right, necessitating use of a special shoe to correct his balance. Despite his infirmity, he was constantly on the move and constantly on alert to signs of danger.

The recent spate of bombings in the border region of the Republic and Northern Ireland made the threat uppermost in his mind. Phil's training and experience as a member of the Garda made him especially wary of any events where a large number of people gathered with their guard down. Today's match brought a measure of excitement to the community as the Cavan team was playing its rivals from County Louth. Phil knew it could also provide a break in the vigilance needed under the current threat.

Phil walked to the back side of the concrete seating to look into the areas behind the stands. He discovered only small boys playing a pickup game of keepy-up with a small football. A quick check of the toilets and wandering through the crowd had left Beatty feeling more comfortable. There were very few of the local troublemakers here, but to Phil they weren't looking for more than the competition on the field.

The teams were on the pitch knocking the ball around and stretching. The field was patchy and rough from its multiple use with the other sports favored by local boys. The local team uniforms of blue-and-yellow-striped shirts and socks were matched by scarves worn by many of the thirty or so fans on the sidelines and nearly two hundred more in the concrete stands.

The visiting team dressed in red were matched by the scarves on the hundred or so fans who had traveled to watch the match. The excitement from the small crowd in the concrete stands was palpable, as most were aware that today's match would leave the team that won leading the Ireland county league at a critical point in the season.

Added to the excitement was the appearance of two representatives of Liverpool Football Club, who were standing midway up the stands to catch a clearer view of the action. They were there to evaluate several of the boys on both sides. Fifteen- and sixteen-year-old boys were at the right age to sign a full professional contract, and there were two or three boys they were known to have their eyes on. After the match, they planned to visit with those boys if they thought they might have a future with Liverpool.

It was a typical soft day in Ireland. The fog had lifted and had been replaced by a light rain. The pitch lights were on, despite the early hour in the afternoon. Robby Coogan approached the center circle, where he was joined by the referee, two linesmen, and a stocky lad named Billy O'Shea who captained the other side.

Robby and Billy eyed each other warily as they went through the ritual of the referee flipping a coin and telling them of his desire for a clean match. Billy knew that if he could keep Robby quiet during the match, the Louth side would have a better chance to take the game and the lead in the league. For his part, Robby seldom worried about an opponent. After years of competing against Billy, he recognized him as one of the most talented players in Ireland, but knew he had been successful against him in the past.

The Cavan team started brightly. Crisp passing and strong tackles meant that, for the first fifteen minutes, they controlled play and kept possession for long stretches of time. The possession didn't, however, result in much in the way of scoring chances. It seemed that at every opportunity, Billy O'Shea made one fierce tackle after another to stop quality approaches to goal. The half ended 0–0.

Along the sideline during the second half, Phil Beatty and John McGuire and several other men were shouting encouragement to the locals. John was increasingly nervous as each attack by Cavan was rebuffed, saying, "Lord, I hope that dis isn't another of dem where we dominate and dominate, then give up the one-off break."

As if directed by McGuire's fear, Billy O'Shea won the ball at midfield, slalomed through defenders, and accelerated all the way into the penalty area, where he fired a shot into the roof of the net for a one-goal lead for Louth. A massive groan went up from the home crowd and many hung their heads at the prospect of a home loss.

Billy trotted back toward the midfield with the ball in his hands, and Phil noticed him saying something to Robby, in an attempt to needle the local in front of his home crowd. Robby responded by grabbing the ball from Billy and placing it on the midfield for the kickoff. What Phil couldn't see was Robby saying to Billy, "You'll fecking regret that, you fecking wanker. You are gonna wish you'd never opened your mouth, not about me maw …"

Five minutes later, Billy was waiting to receive a high ball, with his eyes up, tracking the flight of the ball. Just as the ball cradled against Billy's chest, Robby Coogan ran into him full tilt from the side. Billy flew off the ground before he tumbled down to the field, where he lay gasping for air. The referee ran over, reaching for his pocket. Some wondered out loud whether it was a yellow or red card which would result in Robby being ejected, while others worried that Billy might not be able to get up. Robby innocently looked at the referee, saying, "Sorry, sir, never saw him. Ball watching, I'm afraid." The referee showed a yellow card to Robby and play continued.

For long periods of time, the game stayed mostly in midfield, with each side getting no clear chances. Just as the home crowd resigned itself to a disappointing loss, Robby appeared to rise to a new level physically. He was all over the pitch, winning ball after ball, and making concise passes into the area. But he was repeatedly let down by his teammates, who couldn't finish their chances. It seemed that every time a chance was created by Robby, Billy was there to block the shot or win the ball.

"Well, Robby owns this game now. 'Tis only a matter of time," said John McGuire to his friends along the sideline. "Fecking genius is what he is."

Phil Beatty agreed, suddenly realizing that perhaps John was right that Robby had what it took to go to the professional level. He turned to look at the Liverpool men and knew that they were as excited as the home crowd by what they were seeing. Turning back to John, he said, "If that Billy weren't so damn good, this game would already be done."

As the ball rose and bent toward the goal area from a corner kick, Robby rose "like he had a feckin' step-ladder", according to John's later description at the Three Horses. He headed the ball toward goal. Miraculously, the goalkeeper got a hand on it and it bounded off the top bar and back over Robby's head.

Later, people who were there—and many who weren't—all described it the same way. As both teams scrambled in panic mode, time seemed to slow down only for Robby. He turned his body as the ball flew over his shoulder away from goal. Taking the ball out of the air with his left foot, he brought it down gently, slid the ball between his legs to allow him to turn and face goal, then smashed home to tie the game and keep Cavan in the hunt for the championship.

"Legendary", it was labeled by John McGuire when he later took up residence on his stool at the Three Horses.

After the match, Billy O'Shea trotted up to Robby and the crowd watched as Robby extended his hand. Billy hesitated and finally grabbed Robby's hand, saying, "Robby, that goal was ... was true magic."

Robby grinned, put his arm around Billy's shoulders, and replied, "Well, hell, Billy, it was always going to take a bit of magic to get past you. Well done." Billy glared then relaxed a bit realizing that Robby was not completely sincere in his praise.

The boys continued shaking hands and talking with the other players when they were finally approached by the two men who had come over from Liverpool.

"Quite a match, boys," said the taller of the two. He moved with the grace of an athlete and had a face that showed the effects of a life spent in the elements, craggy skin with hooded eyes. As he pulled his long coat closer to his body and rewrapped his red scarf, the man said, "You two lads did a fine job out there today—you both showed real promise and skill." Phil watched as both Billy and Robby looked in awe at the two men.

"Ah, thanks, but we've both played better than this," said Billy, while Robby just looked dumbstruck.

The smaller of the two men moved closer to the boys and said, "Perhaps you boys could ask your folks to meet with us in a bit for a discussion on your futures?"

CHAPTER 3

The small ivy-covered stone cottage where the Coogan family lived on the edge of town was filled with excessive amounts of heat, music, and conversation on a normal day. The small front room contained stuffed furnishings facing a stone hearth with a roaring peat fire. Maeve and Mike had scurried around for nearly an hour straightening pillows, sweeping up in front of the hearth, and preparing biscuits and tea to serve to the visitors.

While going through the preparations, each had made it clear that they disagreed on the hoped-for outcome. During the conversation with the Liverpool visitors Mike had been embarrassed by Maeve's behavior, her comments were condescending about football as a choice for a young man of Robby's talents.

The men left after offering to bring Robby over to Liverpool and indicating that they would be making a written offer in the near future.

Robby, for his part, sat quietly and asked few questions. That left it to Maeve to lead the interrogation. Despite her viewpoint, Maeve had later admitted to Mike she had been impressed with the men and their manner of laying out the opportunity they wanted to provide to Robby. It briefly left her wondering whether she should be open to this path for Robby to follow.

The Coogan family's back garden of several acres had a gentle slope down to the river to the west. It was bordered by a field filled with sheep on one side and Northern Ireland to the northeast. Robby was kicking a ball with Padraig as darkness approached.

“Robby, Robby, Robby, teach me that move you done today.” Padraig was visibly shaking, looking at his brother as if he were facing God Himself. Padraig was still wildly excited, the men from Liverpool having left just minutes earlier.

“Paddy, come over here.” Robby leaned against the stone fence and his brother came trotting up to him. “Listen. I know that you’re excited by the men who were here earlier. Okay, so am I. Calm down lad.

When I make this decision, it’ll lasting consequences for everyone and not just for me. It looks like fun and the men we met were fine fellows, but it will affect my whole life.

So right now, I’m trying to understand what God would want me to do. See, boys like us are lucky. We have good parents, and choices of how to serve God so that heaven awaits us when we’re done. That’s the most important thing to keep in mind.” Robby smiled at Padraig and said, “Let’s play a little more keepy-up and then we can go have our tea.”

Sitting in the light edging toward night amid the crystal air, Robby felt a shiver run through his body. In a moment that would haunt him for the rest of his life, he stared down at his brother’s glowing face as Padraig hugged and told him, “I know how lucky I am to have a family like ours, and to have you as my brother.”

Robby sat and watched Paddy juggling the ball and laughing, before turning to go into the house, knowing that the discussion with his parents would continue after his brother and sister had gone to bed. Robby knew that his pa wanted him to pursue a career in music but would be happy for him whatever he chose. His ma was another matter entirely. Maeve thought football was for children. She made no bones about her belief that life was intended to be more serious than chasing a ball around a field. For that matter, she also had a vague disdain for music as a career. Robby made up his mind to listen to both parents, then pray to make the right decision for himself and his family.

Robby walked through the house to the bedroom he shared with Padraig. His younger sister, Caroline, had a separate room at the end of the hall.

As was often the case, Caroline's room was currently filled with several young male IRA soldiers. They had been staying quiet and out of sight during the visit earlier with the men from Liverpool. Mostly younger than you might expect, dressed in scruffy clothing, their filthy appearance and the odor of smoke and musty dirt that filled the room gave them the appearance of criminals hiding from the law. Which was exactly what they were—the law being north of the border that was the property line of the Coogans' back garden.

Caroline's room was decorated with lace, pink walls and white-trim windows, but had on various occasions also served as a respite for Northern Ireland prison escapees who simply stepped over the border that was the backyard property line of the Coogan household. It was a peculiar aspect of policework in Ireland that male Garda were not permitted to enter a young woman's bedroom for inspection unless accompanied by a female officer. Since there were no female Garda in Belturbet, Caroline's bedroom served perfectly as a bunk room for IRA trainees and other visitors seeking anonymity.

Caroline, as with most nights, was going to sleep on a small divan in her parents' room. Her mind was reeling, filled with happiness and dread in equal measure. She liked football, but she worshipped her brother Robby. When the gentlemen left, she realized that Robby would likely be leaving for England soon. The men had offered to bring him over for training and maybe to sign a contract. She was so happy that Robby would get the chance to play for Liverpool, but knew she would no longer have him as part of her life on a daily basis, and that made her sad.

Maeve came into the room to tell Caroline good night. Kneeling next to the divan, she kissed her daughter on the forehead and gently asked her about her prayers. "Of course, Ma, I wouldn't miss my prayers. I said a special prayer for Robby, for Da, Paddy, and for you as well. Do you think Robby will go to play football?"

"Time and God will decide that, Caroline," said Maeve distantly. "Go to sleep now."

The small cottage had only one room that was sacrosanct—Mike's musical room. No one entered without permission. Maeve emerged from Caroline's room, knocked, and asked Mike if she could join him.

"So, are you happy about what's gone on here tonight?" she said.

Mike was used to the fierce and domineering tone of his wife's conversations. She tended to speak in directives and with a contempt for others' opinions that grated on him. He carefully put his guitar in its case, using the time to consider his answer and the direction his response would take the discussion. "Well, if you are asking whether I'm happy about those lads in Caroline's room again, the answer is the same as always. No, I'm not happy to have our family constantly dragged into your war. It endangers our children and our life here, and its likely real danger with no useful purpose." Mike always knew that putting Maeve on the defensive meant that she would strike back fiercely.

Maeve folded her arms across her ample bosom and glared at Mike. "You know that's not at all what I'm asking about. But just to remind you again, there are no neutrals now. We either have to fight for our future or give in to these bastards who have robbed us of our land, our lives, and freedom for generations. Do you forget that they killed both your father and mine? That they banned our religion for so long? That they took your grandfather's farm? And for what? Because we want to keep to our own beliefs? Mike, you know we aren't fully human to them, so they don't want us to have a right to choose our own way of governing."

Mike said nothing, just gazed calmly at Maeve until he could see that she was cooling off and likely to actually hear what he had to say. "And that's what I think we should allow Robby to do—make his own choices. You know he has so many gifts from God. That can make choice more difficult, not less. He has that command of people, those musical gifts that I can only dream of having, but he is a young man who must make his own choices of how to fulfill God's promise."

"But, Jesus, Mike, football? That's no way to become the man God, you, or I intended him to be." The look on her face was pained. "He could be a great political leader, but I could live with him being a priest or," she snorted, "even a musician."

Mike winced, before he rose from his chair and stepped across the room to Maeve, putting his arms around her gently.

"Football is not very different from what I do with my music. The best some of us can do is try to make people happy in a miserable world." Mike nuzzled his face into Maeve's neck and whispered, "We can't all be as strong as you. Besides, I don't see him having the determination to be a footballer. I think he tends, like you, to look at this as child's play. We just have to see what he decides."

Maeve shrugged off Mike's embrace and turned for the door, saying over her shoulder, "I have a few things to discuss with the men, then perhaps we can have a longer discussion with Robby."

Mike watched the determined way she walked out of the room, and once again realized that he would forever remain a peripheral aspect of her life.

CHAPTER 4

Maeve walked into Caroline's room to a fetid and feral atmosphere, laced with anger and hatred. The contrast of the atmosphere of the room filled with dolls and stuffed animals, the pink walls and frilly curtains and bed ruffles, couldn't be starker.

Father Mulkey and five bearded and dirty men of various ages were sitting on the bed and chairs, and leaning against the wall. One of the men against the far wall, his face pocked with wild beard patches and what looked like splotchy gunpowder burns, was Bobby O'Brien. He had recently escaped the Belfast jail in the cover of night after spending months in solitary confinement. O'Brien was used by the IRA principally as an explosives expert, though he had also killed using other methods regularly.

Bobby was florid faced from anger, haranguing the other men in a cruel and condescending way. "About what I'd expect from a bunch of tin fecking soldiers. We are in a war and people are supposed to die in war. Da notion that we can do what needs doing without killing is fecking stupid."

Father Mulkey looked to Maeve for help before responding, "Bobby, we do recognize that there may be the odd death along the way, but only when needed, and it's not necessary at this juncture. The goal here is to send a message to those who ought to be with us that it's a dangerous game to play to play footsie with our enemies. If we fall into our anger and make revenge our goal, we will lose locals from our cause."

Maeve looked slowly at each man until they returned her gaze.

"We have a good plan," she said. "It will send the right message to our Prime Minister and any other politicians who want to play on both sides. We know that he has supported us in the past, even helping to provide some of the weapons we carry today. So, the problem isn't that he's alive, the problem is that his political ambition may have gotten in the way of his loyalty."

She walked across the room and stood with her face within inches of O'Brien. "Bobby, we can all understand and respect your anger, and we admire your commitment. I personally know that revenge can be satisfying in the right circumstances. But, Bobby, you, of all people, are smart enough to know that if we follow down the same path our dads and grandads took, we will end up in the same place. We aren't looking to kill PMHaughey at this time. If you can't get on board with our plan, then go back to Belfast."

O'Brien's visage faded from anger to dread. He didn't acknowledge Maeve's statement in any way, but simply leaned against the wall and stared at her without malice or promise.

Maeve knew that this was as close to a commitment as she could expect, so she turned to other men and said, "Father Mulkey, have you confirmed his meeting and its purpose?"

"A local lad who travels with Haughey spoke with me yesterday. He told me that Himself will be in town this coming Thursday. He will meet his counterpart from Belfast to discuss ways to reduce tension, and—this is the worrying part—including having the Government share information about what were termed 'people of interest'. This may include many of our friends. Perhaps Haughey thinks that it will help him to overcome his difficulties from the trial and restore him to good graces with the Taoiseach."

"Meeting time and place?" said Maeve.

"We've confirmed that the meeting will be held in the post office building on Main Street so that he can slip in quietly that morning. Me friend at the post office confirmed the room is reserved then. They will be using a first-floor office of the postmaster. If he follows his normal schedule, that means he'll be arriving around ten am. My man says that he has another political engagement in Cavan at noon, so the meeting is expected to be about an hour."

Maeve walked over to Bobby and quietly spoke to him. "Do you have the materials needed?"

"Enough to blow a hole in the feckin' street and everything near it."

"Well, we won't be needing all of that. Will you put the package together in the way we discussed? We want it loud, but not particularly destructive. Can you make the car jump without destroying the street or the area? We'd like it to appear that the explosion was rather a dud."

"Sure, I can do it, but I still think the fecker would be better off dead. If he's willing to betray us here and now, he'll do it again."

Maeve put her arm around Bobby's shoulders and looked him in the eye. "Well, there's a part of me that agrees with you. However, we have to take the long view here. He could be useful to us again. Now, since you men need to be seen elsewhere, Father will take care of having the car delivered early that morning on Thursday. Bobby, you go on up to Galway. What I need you to do is have the car ready on Wednesday night. Leave the car on Dominick Street next to the Galway Arms. No later than eleven pm, leave the key on the front tire and someone will take over from there." Maeve gave O'Brien a look that could peel paint. "Bobby, make sure the timer is set to go off at exactly ten forty-five the next morning."

Turning to the others, she said, "You men can grab some kip, but make sure you are gone by daylight. Get out of town no later than Wednesday. You're going to want to be seen publicly Wednesday night and all day Thursday, but as far away as you can get. And please, when you go in and out, even to smoke or take a walk from here, continue to use the tunnel in the closet. It's best if Mike and the children don't know who and how many of you are here."

As she was leaving, she said to Father Mulkey, “Father, please come back after leaving through the tunnel. Our family has a personal matter on which we could use some of your good advice. Please, stay for tea.”

After Maeve left the room, the men looked at Bobby to judge his reaction. Father Mulkey, especially, watched him carefully. He had known Bobby for years and understood that it wasn’t feigned anger that caused O’Brien to propose murder. “Bobby,” he said, “we’re all reading out of the same book now, aren’t we?”

“Of course we are, Father. I understand the strategy, though I think it’s foolish ta believe anything useful ever comes from a politician. Put it down ta a lack of trust. I have a car ta get ready.” With that, Bobby went into Caroline’s closet, out the door behind the clothes, and into the tunnel. He was followed by Liam Connolly, a slender, dirty man, whose job it was to keep an eye on Bobby.

Father Mulkey spoke to the remaining men: “Listen to what she said and make sure you’re all gone by Wednesday and visible somewhere else on Thursday. And, for God’s sake, don’t rely on one another to verify you were somewhere else.”

CHAPTER 5

Robby, feeling very much in the middle, sat at the small wooden table in the kitchen with his parents on either side. Maeve had already made it clear that she thought the notion of going to England and pursuing a footballing career would be a waste. She finished her comments looking directly at Rob and saying, "You have a chance to be important and have a lasting impact on our people. For a man like you, with your talents, it would be a waste to spend your life playing a child's game."

Robby surprised himself by reacting angrily, "Ma, suppose it's just my way of learning more about myself, about life in general? Come on, I'm still young. Shouldn't I have a chance to try things before I set off on a specific path?"

"Fair play, Robby. Perhaps I'm in more of a hurry than is needed, but if you go in that direction, it can turn out that suddenly it's five or ten years from now, and you look up and realize that it's been time wasted. You'll have abandoned your education, you'll have little time for your music, and those footballers look to be an ignorant crowd overall," said Maeve.

Robby loved his mother despite her overbearing demeanor and rigid ways, but he admired his father's gentle nature and innate kindness. He turned to his pa, hoping for some wisdom that would help in his decision.

Rob listened carefully as Mike said, "Rob, you are a boy of many gifts, and though your ma and I love you and take pride in who you are, those gifts come from God and God alone. The joy you bring people with your sport and your music is worthwhile in itself. What you must choose is a path that you believe God would want you to take. None of us know for certain what God has in mind for us. I think you should take a few days and pray. Open up your heart and mind, and then, whatever your decision, you will know that you've entered into it in the right spirit."

There was a quiet knock of the back door to the kitchen. Maeve got up and opened the door to Father Mulkey, who was smiling broadly as he entered the house with a small basket in hand. "Well, I've brought some chocolate biscuits, as I know we've got serious business here, and a good biscuit is always needed when serious business is at hand." He smiled at Robby and plopped his plump frame in the seat across from Robby.

"Thank you for coming, Father, would you care for tea?" said Maeve. She walked over to the counter and poured a cup of tea, returning to the table to place the cup in front of the priest, who nodded his thanks.

"That's lovely, Maeve," said Father Mulkey. Turning to Robby, he asked, "So, where are we? Is the conversation entirely about football and music, or are there any other considerations for your future?"

Robby was unable to look directly at Father Mulkey as he said, "Yeah, thanks for coming, Father. My da was just telling me that what I need to do is take a few days for prayer before deciding whether to accept the offer from Liverpool." He shifted uncomfortably in his chair, as if indicating that he wasn't sure what to say next.

Father Mulkey nodded thoughtfully and said, "That's always a good way to go about considering an important question. Do you mind if I lay out another possibility for you to consider? I've always thought you a remarkable boy with intelligence, character, and wonderful leadership ability."

"Thank you, Father," Robby said quietly, while continuing to shift back and forth in his chair, as though he couldn't quite get comfortable.

"Let's consider that your talents may be larger than football or music for that matter. God gives each of us talents so that we may serve others. I've seen your commitment to God in your service nearly daily as an acolyte. While there is nothing wrong with choosing entertainment or sport as a career, perhaps there is something larger you may want to consider. In addition to those talents, you have a piety that can bring comfort and belief to those in need throughout the community.

Robby looked wide-eyed at Father Mulkey, stammering, "What do you mean, Father?"

"Ireland, Robby, Ireland. Perhaps you can become a man who serves his God and country in a leadership role to help us finally be a truly free people. It would require further education and more experience, but our future could be bright if only our young would be able to remain and help us build that future. We need young people like you."

Robby was stunned. He had never considered that his future held any type of path other than football or music. Now he wondered if his commitment to God might require him to serve in the manner laid out by Father Mulkey.

Father Mulkey continued, "When I left secondary school, there were fifty-two people who graduated with me. How many are in Ireland today? Two, including myself, and both of us priests. The rest have immigrated to the US, Australia, England even. How can we take our proper place in the world if we lose our best?"

"Do you think I should be a priest then, Father?" Robby said, his voice quivering. Despite his deep faith in God, he was afraid of the commitment Father Mulkey might be asking him to make.

Father Mulkey looked directly at Robby, as though his mother and father weren't in the room, before saying, "Not necessarily, Robby. That option is open to you but, as important, our country cries out for leadership in the areas of economics, law, and politics to get the oppressive boot of England off our neck. For centuries, we have been kept from many basic rights that we should enjoy. This creates an anger that spreads through our country and to the north, resulting from our long history of oppression. The Troubles come from that anger. We need smart and committed leadership to make our way as a country and to reunite us with our brethren in the north and then to bring new prosperity to our country."

Father Mulkey sipped his tea and stood, then began to pace the room as he spoke: "All areas of leadership will require you to continue your education, and I can arrange for you to receive that further education if you so desire. You are a natural leader with a gift with words. That can serve more than just yourself or your poetic and musical interests. What I'd like you to do is make that part of your consideration in the next few days, and if it interests you, we can visit further on this opportunity and the direction your education should take."

Mike stood abruptly and said, "We have until the weekend to let the fellows from Liverpool know your decision, so why don't you take a few days to consider and we will revisit this on Friday. Father, will you come back then for more discussion?" Without waiting for an answer, Mike left the kitchen with his head down.

Robby watched as Maeve gave a very satisfied look to Father Mulkey and said, "That sounds like an excellent idea. Robby, does that suit you?"

"Sure, Mum," said Robby who was relieved to end the discussion unresolved.

Father Mulkey snapped his fingers as though he'd just remembered something and said, "Robby, can you give me a hand with a matter while you're doing your thinking? I need to have a car brought back from Galway on Wednesday night? I have to be there earlier that day, but the car won't be available until later. Would you ride over with me and could I ask you to drive the car I'm picking up back for me then?"

"Sure, Father, just let me know what time you want to leave," said Robby. Truly, he was happy to be at the end of the conversation, and made to follow Mike out of the kitchen.

Maeve, her face bright red, turned to Father Mulkey when they were alone, and said, "You cannot bring him into this, you eejit. What can you be thinking! He's just a boy."

"Maeve, no harm will come to anyone of it, and when he realizes what has happened and his part in it, he may understand that his childhood is over and that there are other commitments a man must make. That is the next step toward achieving the greatness which you and I believe is his destiny. I meant what I said about Robby. His talents will be wasted in football and music, but God requires us at times to give guidance in subtle ways." Father Mulkey picked up a biscuit and nibbled on it while he returned Maeve's malevolent stare.

CHAPTER 6

Molly stared through the window of the Three Horses as if caught in a dream. She loved staring through the window out onto the street in the time before it got busy for lunch. Today, the weather was bright and cloudless, which gave her an unusual view of the people walking, parking their cars, and the Garda patrolling the main street in town.

Turning slowly and sitting on a stool at the corner of the bar, she looked throughout the main dining area of the pub to make sure that all was ready for the doors to open. The woven rope ceiling, the nautical lights, and the wood-covered walls lent the feeling to many that this was their second home, while the fireplace across from the bar gave off a smoky peat scent that reminded Molly of the aroma of a fine Irish whiskey.

Robby opened the door and stuck his head in, saying, "Morning to ya, Molly. Can I have a word with ya?" He gave Molly a hug and said, "So, I wanted to let you know that it'll just be Da tonight as I've got to help Father Mulkey with something over in Galway. I won't be back in time.'

As Robby walked over toward Molly, she realized how disappointed she was that Robby wasn't going to play that evening. She knew that with his impending decision, his days of playing Wednesdays would be coming to an end. "Well, sure, Robby, that's fine. Although I'm gonna miss that beautiful voice tonight. We were looking forward to it—it won't seem like a proper Wednesday without you here."

Robby must have heard the disappointment in Molly's tone because he said, "Well, perhaps I can make that up to you. I'm bringing my guitar with me, so I'll take a look at writing a tune for you, if you'd approve of that."

"Sure, that'd be lovely, Robby. I hope it'll be a happy song." Molly reached over and gave Robby another hug. "Get on with ya—you don't want to keep a priest waiting and I see Father has just pulled over out front." Once again, Molly realized what a special person Robby was. She had no doubt that Robby would return with a beautifully crafted song that she would cherish long after he left for Liverpool.

Robby got into the passenger side of Father Mulkey's car, holding his guitar case on his lap.

"And what is that for, Robby?" asked Father Mulkey.

"Well, Father, I've heard that a musician can make a few pence busking on the streets of Galway, and I intend to see if that is true tonight." Robby had known Father Mulkey his entire life and often served as an acolyte for Mass. He also knew that there was more to the priest than his service to God. Just as Robby understood Father Mulkey's commitment to the priesthood, he knew that Father Mulkey also was a dedicated servant of a Republican Ireland. The priest's commitment often was believed to include service to the IRA alongside Robby's ma.

"Well, we had best get along with ourselves, Robby. It's a long way to Galway and I want to make a stop and show you what I consider the most beautiful place in Ireland for contemplation of the type you're facing with this decision ahead of you."

They rode in silence for a while until Robby got his guitar out of the case and started picking out some notes while humming along.

After a few moments of Robby's playing, Father Mulkey said, "Now where do you think those beautiful notes come from, Robby? Is that a song I should be familiar with, do you think?"

Robby continued playing and said, "Ah, no, Father, I promised Molly I'd try to write a song for her since I'll be missing tonight at the pub. I don't really know where these melodies come from when I'm trying to put something together. I just hear them in my head and try to make some sense of what I'm hearing. My da has taught me a lot about the structure of music, so I know it has to have some logical order and be almost mathematical without spoiling the beauty."

"What about the words, Robby? How do they come about?" Father Mulkey kept his eyes on the road, but Robby could tell he was truly curious in the way most non-musical people were about the process of crafting a song.

Robby said, while continuing to play softly, "Well, for me it starts in my heart with an idea that centers on how I feel about something. Molly asked me to make it a happy song, so the music has to feel happy in its cadence and tempo, and then the words come from an idea about what makes a person happy."

"And what do you think makes people happy, Robby? How do you pick that out?"

"Ah, I'm still pretty young, so I think that my songs need to be simple, since I've so little experience in the world. Mostly, I try to get in there about how things make you feel, like a new person in your life or an event or day that seems special to you at the time. My friends think I'm too soft in my music—they love the rock 'n roll. Of course I do too, but to be completely honest, I have trouble with all that, as it puts me at odds with how I sometimes feel about life."

Father Mulkey stopped the car to turn onto a connecting road and looked at Robby before making the turn. "And how do you feel about life, Robby?"

For a long time, Robby looked like he might not have heard the question before finally answering in a quiet voice, "I'm confused right now, Father. I don't really know what to do, and yet it is time to decide some important things. I've prayed and prayed, and unlike the music, no answer or direction seems to come into me head or my heart."

"Robby, sometimes God answers our prayers by not answering at all. He is letting us make up our own minds. Perhaps it would help to first understand who you intend to serve in your life. Is it God, yourself, your country, or what? That will help you to build a framework on which to construct your decision. Now, I've seen that you are deeply religious and pay homage to God in your everyday life. Have you considered becoming a priest?"

Turning in his seat, Robby said, "Yes, Father, I have done so. But it's not for me. I admire greatly men who are priests, but it appears only half a life for someone like me who wants to have children of his own and a wife to share that life. I want to have lots of kiddos and give them the same happy childhood me ma and da have given me. I suppose you cannot do that and be a priest too," he said with a laugh.

"Well, no, Robby, that's not part of God's present plan," said Father Mulkey, though he joined in Robby's laughter.

Robby continued, "It seems most folks want me to go to Liverpool and give that a try. A part of me desperately wants to do that. It sure looks like fun and all, but I think there may be too much of Ma in me. I'd say I like fun as much as the next fella, but I don't think it would be the truth. I love to play football, and hope it'll always be part of my life, but I don't know if I could really make the life that I want doing that. It also appears to me that the boys who make it in football want only football, and it drives them every day. I don't think that's how I am, so it probably won't work for me for long. I may try it for a bit, though, and gain some experience in life that way."

Father Mulkey was slowing the car and waited for an oncoming car to pass, then took a right onto a small lane that dipped below the main road into a small valley to the right. The road was narrow and winding, so Father Mulkey paid strict attention to his driving. When they came to a straight part of the lane, Robby asked where they were headed.

Father Mulkey said to Robby, "Have you read much of Yeats in your school work?"

Robby said, "Ah, yeah! He's my favorite."

"Well, Robby, if you remember the poem 'Stolen Child', it references the area we are approaching, the falls of Glen Car. There is a beautiful waterfall there where I love to sit and pray. Join me there and we will pray for you to make a good decision."

CHAPTER 7

The melodic sound of the cascading water and the dappled sunlight striking the waterfall was soothing, just as the priest had promised. The tree cover and stony hillside provided a place of perfect peace. Robby rested on a stone and prayed for answers, while Father Mulkey walked further up the hill toward the water, which seemed as though it were tumbling out of the hill itself. It was the perfect place to have a conversation with God. When it appeared Robby was finished praying, Father Mulkey made a sign of the cross, then rose from his resting area on a flat portion of the hill overlooking the waterfall, and beckoned to Robby to follow him to the path that led them back down the hill to the carpark.

As they were scrambling through the woods and down the hill from the waterfall, Robby seemed to unleash something that he had been holding back. "Father, when you asked me whether I had considered being a priest, I left something out in my answer." He hesitated for a long time before continuing, "I'm sorry if this sounds arrogant ... For a long time, I have felt that God has a special calling for me. I know that he has blessed me with some talent in football and music, but a part of me thinks that he sees those only as tools for me to be effective in some special purpose that I don't yet understand." He paused and cleared his throat. "I believe that it has something to do with children, perhaps as a teacher. I want to serve God, but am very afraid that, if I make an unwise choice with my life, I will have wasted the talents God gave me, and I will fail Him. Father, there is nothing more important to me than to be useful to God and man."

Father Mulkey, rather than answering immediately, continued down the dirt path toward the car. The morning had shone sunlight not often seen for such an extended period in that part of Ireland. The slight, cool breeze pushed a light mist through the exposed roots of the trees on the hill to the waterfall. The hike felt mystical in a way that only Ireland can produce. That feeling heightened Father Mulkey's sense of how important this moment might be for Robby's future.

He settled into the car, then turned to wait. Robby scrambled in, before picking up his guitar and beginning to strum. Only then did Father Mulkey say, "I know exactly how you feel about that, Robby. I, too, have felt often that God intended me to do more than just serve him as a priest." He let a few moments pass, then said in a quiet voice, "I suppose you've heard the rumors about my service in the IRA, have you now?"

Robby visibly stirred due to this unexpected turn in the conversation. "Ah, Father, I don't pay much attention to the politics. I've also heard those rumors about my own ma. I know that she is very active in the politics, if not the fighting. I've seen the fellows from the north who come round on the sly."

Father Mulkey turned in his seat to face Robby directly, saying, "Well, those rumors are true, Robby. Both me and your mother are Republican in our leanings and we match our beliefs with our actions." When he saw in Robby's reaction no sign of shock or outrage, he continued, "You know that both of your grandfathers and my father were all killed by British soldiers, don't you?"

"Sure, Father. Ma and Da have told me the stories and I know that what's happened to Ireland is wrong—it feels very painful for us as Catholics and Irishmen. It leaves us feeling that we do not have control over our own lives."

"That is because we do not have control, nor will we until we grab it for ourselves … Robby, would you be willing to help in the effort to right that wrong?" asked Father Mulkey.

"What can someone like me do, Father? Of course I'd like to help, but I'm not trained as a soldier and really don't fancy the idea of killing, even in a just cause. Maybe I'm too soft to be of use in this war."

Father Mulkey started the car. As he began to pull back onto the road, he said, "Robby, each of us can contribute in a manner that uses who we are and our skills to help in our cause. You will be someone who looks above the fray so you won't be suspected of participation. That's why we chose you for this mission."

The car remained quiet until they completed the rise to the main road and Father Mulkey turned right onto the road to Galway.

The bright sunshine warmed the car considerably and Robby let the window down to allow some air to refresh the vehicle before clearing this throat and asking, "What do you mean by mission, Father?"

"Robby, I asked you to join me today so that you can bring a car back to Belturbet tonight. I won't go into what's in the car, but you should know that it involves a bit of danger. It's also better if you don't know what's in the car that you will be delivering. You'll pick the car up outside the Galway Inn on Dominick by the bridge. I'll show you where it will be when we get to Galway. You should pick it up at any time after midnight and drive it back to Belturbet. Make sure that you drive around a bit and that no one is out and about. You'll be arriving around two or three am, so no one is likely to be out at that time. I want you to park the car on the side street by the Post Office, right there on the corner. Be patient and make sure that no one is around before you park the car, and that no one sees you when you get out of the car. You should leave your guitar somewhere else before you drop off the car and go pick it up on your walk home." Father Mulkey reached in his pocket and retrieved a pair of cotton gloves. "Shove these in your pocket and make sure that you wear them the entire time you are in contact with or inside the car. Once you have delivered the car, you should walk home and, to the degree you can, avoid seeing anyone along the way."

He slowed the car and turned to Robby, saying, “This is one of those times where you can be useful to man, as you’ve expressed the desire to do.”

CHAPTER 8

The night air was cool and damp, yet the streets of Galway were full of people on their way to and from their evening engagements. Many groups were popping into restaurants and pubs, their happiness seeming to carry them along in waves. Robby had been wandering around the area for a while, feeling he was the only person alone in the city.

He felt confused but proud of the assignment given to him by Father Mulkey. It offered him a way to be useful in a cause he believed in and wanted to support. Whether this would be a one-off, or was a gateway to further involvement, he didn't know.

He found a spot near the bridge in front of one of the more popular pubs. He took his guitar out, rested on a step nearby, and began to play, singing some of his more popular songs from his Wednesdays at the Three Horses. At first people continued walking by while slowing to listen, then small groups of two or more would stop to hear him complete a song. Often, they would applaud and drop coins or bills in the guitar case in appreciation.

As the crowds ebbed and there was a quiet on the street, Robby saw a young woman, dressed as a waitress, with black curly hair and cerulean-blue eyes come out of the pub. She was dancing slowly and twirling, laughing while carrying a glass of beer. She stopped and placed the beer on the step next to him with a curtsey.

Looking into his eyes, she said, "Well done, Rob, your music is as beautiful as you are."

Robby was stunned. He knew that he had never met her, but her name flowed off his lips with a sweetness he would savor for the rest of his life. "You are Caoimhe, aren't you? I've dreamed of you many times …"

"As I have you, Rob. I'm so happy to finally have met you."

Caoimhe sat next to Robby on the step and touched his hand on the frets of the guitar pushing them gently away. "Let's play this together." And they played a melody that Robby had heard in his head for a long time, but they played it in a time that changed the song from harsh and demanding to sweet yet desperate. When they reached the end, Caoimhe leaned into Robby and kissed him. Robby thought, *I hope that this will be the last thing I remember on this earth—your face and that kiss.*

Caoimhe stood, brushed off her uniform and, said, "I'm going to go inside now to finish my shift. I wish we could have spent more time together."

As she turned to go back to the pub, she said, "I hope you don't—" But then she stopped speaking, and disappeared into the pub.

"Well, there is your answer, Father … This is where songs come from, the glorious mysteries of life," Robby murmured to himself. Many times he had imagined this moment and the questions it would answer.

He played the melody that had haunted him for such a long time, finally learning the words such that the melody made sense.

Caoimhe came from the mist

An island faery out west

Dancing and laughing

And filling my heart

The day that I knew

I could be

I would be

True

Eyes from the ocean

Black curly hair

Like her island, solved mystery

When her gaze met my stare

The day that I knew

I could be

I would be

True

Robby wrote the lyrics on a sheet of paper from his guitar case so that he could show them to Molly on his return to Belturbet. For the first time in his life, Robby's heart was full to bursting with a feeling so strong it left him dizzy. He couldn't wait to bring Caoimhe home so his family get to know her. And in turn, he yearned to learn more about her and meet her family. Suddenly, his future made sense to him no matter what path he chose.

Liam Connolly was frightened. In the dim light of the garage where he and Bobby O'Brien had been working on the car they were to deliver that night, O'Brien had scarcely ceased cursing and muttering.

Liam knew that Bobby was a man steeped in violence and few idle threats. Most of the muttering sounded threatening, so he had kept his distance, smoking cigarettes one after the other in a corner of the garage.

Liam was often asked by his mates about working with O'Brien. He joked with them that it made him no more nervous that when we awoke in the bed of some woman he barely knew and wondered if her husband would be coming home soon. As he explained it, *"You never know when that sort of situation can go badly wrong, but you're certain that eventually it will."*

Liam was caught in a trap. He knew that O'Brien was deliberately violating the order to make sure that the bomb wasn't massive. He had watched Bobby load more explosives than would be needed by a factor of three. And he knew the leadership would hold him at least partially responsible and this was, to him, completely unfair.

"If they are so right and powerful, then they should know better than to let Bobby loose on something as delicate as this," he muttered under his breath.

"What was that? What did you feckin' say?" asked Bobby.

"Well, I noticed that we might have overloaded the boot with explosives, is all. Weren't we told to make the bomb only to make the car jump a bit?"

"Feck 'em. I don't make bombs to make cars jump. I make bombs to kill traitorous bastards." Bobby walked over and stood right in front of Liam, with a glare that looked like it came straight from hell. "What are you going to do about it, you little turd? I'm after killin' tonight and I don't mind adding you to the pile."

Liam backed away quickly. Putting his hands in front of his face, he said, "No, no, I'm just after saying that we might have a squabble with some of the leadership, is all."

"Well, feck 'em. Now get off your arse and go bring this car down to the spot in front of the Galway Inn. Leave the key on the front tire. If you're thinking of crossing me on this, remember, I know where you live. More important, I know where your ma lives." With that, O'Brien threw the keys at Liam and stormed out of the garage.

The night got colder and the mist turned to rain, but Robby waited and waited as more people abandoned the pub and headed home. Finally, Robby could wait no longer. He picked up his guitar and walked into the nearly empty pub.

The bartender saw him and said, "Young fella, that's some lovely music you've played for us out there tonight. It made me glad the smokers keep the door open. I don't usually encourage this street business, but I enjoyed myself tonight. Let me draw you a stout on the house."

Robby said, "Thanks, but I've only come in to see if Caoimhe will be getting off any time soon."

The bartender looked puzzled. "And who is this Caoimhe you're looking for?"

Now it was Robby who was confused. "Bright young woman who was a waitress here tonight. I met her out on the street earlier. Dark hair, blue eyes?"

"Well, it looks like someone is having you on, lad. There's no one like that working here tonight. For a while, we did have a girl by that name and of that nature—I believe she was from one the islands. Left months ago. Said she had to go looking for a man named Rob, something about some trouble. Like a lot of them from them islands, she seemed a bit too mystical in her approach for my taste. Lovely girl, though."

Robby returned to his seat on the step, mulling over whether he had actually met Caoimhe. Was she real? A faery? Or a creation of his imagination? Whatever she was, he knew that his feelings were real. He opened his guitar case and retrieved the lyrics, reading over them again. Yes, his feelings were real. He folded the page and wrote a note to Molly so that he could get Padraig to drop them off at the Three Horses before lunch the next day.

Though the rain had stopped entirely, it continued to get colder, and Robby stuck his hands in his coat pockets, where he found the gloves given to him earlier by Father Mulkey. It was time to go and bring the car to Belturbet.

CHAPTER 9

Molly was at peace with her world. She sat near the window of the Three Horses adding sugar and cream to her cup of tea. She stirred her tea, then blew on it a bit, while savoring the morning light streaming through the window from Main Street. The cook had come out from the kitchen and they had gone over the menu; the tables were set; no suppliers were expected before lunch; and Molly was looking forward to a few minutes of peace and quiet before the rush expected during lunch service.

When she later sat down with Phil Beatty, clutching a piece of paper, lips quivering, heart pounding, all she could say over and over again was, "Well and truly broken …" It took Phil some time to realize she was describing her own heart.

Eventually, she was able to tell Phil Beatty what had happened. "I first saw Padraig and Caroline skipping down the street near the post office. They were hand in hand, laughing in the way that children do. At first, I thought that the distortion and scrambling of their bodies and limbs was due to the glass in the window. Then the noise hit and it was so fierce, the windows here rattled and the street seemed to disintegrate …

"The car parked to the side of the post office seemed to come apart and fly into the sky. Then," she said, her voice cracking, "I realized the flying mess also was filled with bits of the children. Legs, arms, their bodies." She broke down and cried so fiercely that Phil was concerned she might do damage to herself. He held her in his arms, and she just sobbed and seemed scarcely able to breathe.

"Molly, oh, Molly. Let go of it, girl … Molly, I don't like asking, but please finish. We need as much information as possible to see if we can find justice. We cannot bring those beautiful children back but we must find justice for them."

After a long time, Molly got control of her body and straightened up, shrugging off Phil's grasp. "Then I ran outside," she said, "Caroline was across the street and Paddy was nearer to me, so I reached him first. His body was so mangled, I wouldn't have known him, as his face was a bloody mess. One of his arms was gone. The other hand was grasping this." She clutched a piece of paper that had handwriting on it. Most of the note was gone, but the remaining piece read:

I could be

I would be

True

Eyes like oceans

Black curly hair

Taking the paper from Molly, and straightening the seared edges, Phil said, "It looks like a poem of some sort …"

"Lyrics, more likely. Robby said he was writing a song he wanted to share with me. I've been sitting here thinking that when he hears what happened, Robby will blame himself for sending them along with the lyrics. My God, life can be so cruel. Poor Mike and Maeve. Losing two children …"

When she hesitated, fear filled her eyes,

"Ah, Jesus, Phil, what will this do to Robby?"

BOSTON, USA

JANUARY, 1975

*"For there must be guilt somewhere—
whether in the sentence of the court, or in the
catastrophes posterity must determine."*

– Robert Emmet – Speech From The Dock

CHAPTER 10

Rob Coogan had spent much of the past year disoriented and lost. Days went by with no meaningful interaction with other people. He spent hours playing pain-filled melodies on his guitar, his inner voice praying for help, for peace, for death.

Walking the dark, gray streets of Back Bay, he was invisible to those he passed. To him, they were ghosts who walked by without notice. When his brain worked at all, it drove him to wonder if he and his mind had been permanently separated.

Late into the night, sleep would not come and he sat on the wooden floor of his room braiding metal guitar wires into rosaries. The standard five decades of beads, twisting the wires into barbs like those used to keep animals from passage, barbs that dug into his fingers while he said continuous novenas and tried to understand. Still, his pain did not recede.

Sadness seemed to drag him daily into a marshy darkness from which he hoped to never emerge. He thought often of ending his misery, visions of himself hanging with one of his guitar wire rosaries around his neck, a chair overturned below him, in his sparse room with only a lightbulb flickering overhead. This was one of his everyday rituals.

Only his lingering faith kept him from acting on his desire to end his misery.

A man-child, not quite eighteen, he spent most of his time living silently by himself in his dorm room in Linden Hall. The tilted floors, quirky angled walls, and smoky odor of the room spoke of its past as a hotel and its current use as a dorm for young musicians.

The renovated hotel's neighborhood consisted primarily of pizza parlors, late-night hookers plying their sad wares, bodegas, and other converted buildings that made up the remainder of the campus at the Berklee College of Music.

His dorm room was just an empty chamber where Rob's thoughts bounced like old doors banging in the wind. The groans emanating from nearby Fenway Park when the Red Sox collapsed at the end of the summer had brought more misery to the area, but Rob barely noticed.

Since arriving, Rob had barely eaten. His body was thin, his face gaunt. He prayed constantly. His dialogue with God was repetitive and driven by guilt: "God, I know that I am irredeemable and that I will burn in hell for all eternity. Please show me the way to use the life you have given me to provide comfort to others, especially children, so that I may use the time left to me to reduce the suffering of others." He repeated this prayer to himself constantly. Though he attended mass every day, he no longer took communion. He had not attended confession since that day in Belturbet.

In his own mind, he was beyond redemption.

In the aftermath of the tragedy, Rob's parents and Father Mulkey had agreed that Rob should leave Belturbet, knowing that guilt and its signs might make him subject to more attention than was good for anyone.

Maeve had been torn in half by the loss of her children and her bitterness at the British enemy which "had brought this to my family". She blamed the deaths on the Cause which had ruled her since British soldiers had executed her father in the street of Belfast. Despite her anguish, she chose to refocus on the Cause once again, telling Mike, "If my life is to mean anything, I must press on." She did not even take note of the hurt that was Mike's involuntary response to this comment.

Mike had set aside his own pain, focusing on Rob. He knew that Rob had no future in Ireland. He felt that a life in music might help to repair some of the tremendous pain he could see in his son.

Mike had contacted Hilton Baines who had traveled through Ireland the previous summer, spending a few weeks with the Coogan family. Hilton was a guitar instructor associated with the Berklee College of Music in Boston. He had been much impressed with Rob's talent on guitar and his songwriting when they had played together in the cool gloom of the Three Horses. Hilton had seen the audience's reaction and was clear in his belief that wider audiences would have the same response to Rob's genius.

With Hilton's help, Mike had been able to get Rob into Berklee, and Rob had left for the States shortly after the funerals, joining the class in early January. Hilton had arranged an audition to gauge the reaction of the faculty, who was unanimous that Rob should enter the singer/songwriter and guitar curriculum.

Though Mike wrote to him weekly, Rob rarely wrote back. When he did write, they were letters of facts, containing nothing meaningful. Mike's worry increased with each passing day. Knowing Rob's flair for the written language, the dry letters he received caused Mike's worry to increase.

Several months had passed with no word at all from Rob.

Hilton Baines loved his students and they venerated him. Like many great teachers, he had a special affinity for those who were more talented than he in his area of study. The students affectionately called his small classroom the "gnome room", which was an apt description of Hilton's appearance. Short and rotund with a monk's fringe of hair, his looks were offset by a happiness that shone from his eyes constantly.

The classroom reflected his love for guitarists, with posters of Jimmy Hendrix, BB King, George Harrison, and Carlos Santana lining the walls alongside pictures of the great classical guitarists, Vahdah Olcott-Bickford, Alice Artzt, and, his favorite, the Argentinian Maria Luisa Anido.

Though he was an accomplished guitarist himself, Hilton's one true love was for songwriters who translated human feelings into poetic lyrics. In this area, he knew that he did not have the gift; he also knew he had never had a student as talented as Rob.

As class finished early one morning and the students began to pack up their instruments and drift away, the phone in his office rang.

Hilton settled into his small desk chair and lifted the phone. "Hello, Hilton here."

"Hilton, it's Mike Coogan."

There was a brief pause as neither man knew how to dig into the conversation to come.

"So, I'm just calling to check on Robby. I haven't heard a thing from him for a while and just wanted to see how me boy is doing."

"Rob is doing well in class," said Hilton. "People admire him here, but we are all concerned that he seems to suffer greatly." Hilton Baines knew that many musicians use their suffering to inspire their greatest stretches of creativity, but he recognized that this was deep-seated pain. His concern for Rob, and by extension, for Mike, led him to say, "Losing his brother and sister seems to have emptied him out. He goes to class, does sessions with others in his class, but there is very little in the way of socializing with others." He hesitated, before saying, "Unfortunately, I don't see any improvement and I would be misleading you if I didn't say that I'm very concerned."

"Ah, I worried that might be the case," said Mike, "Do you think I should come over for a visit?"

Hilton breathed a sigh of relief, then said, "Yes, I do. As soon as possible."

CHAPTER 11

In late February, Rob was walking down Hemenway Avenue on an overcast and frigid Boston day. The wind whipped through his jacket, delivering a blast of cold that caused him to shudder. He hurried along because he did not want to be late for his Ear Training class.

Walking with his head bowed, Rob's mind was filled with prayer and anguish in equal measure. As he navigated the turn from Hemenway to the Commonwealth street crossing, he saw her out of the corner of his eye. Caoimhe. She was leaning against a column in front of the old Sherry Hotel building. Her lithe body was bouncing as if to keep warm through dance, her entire being glowing in the dour light. Her curly black hair was waving in the wind and the ocean-blue eyes stared at Rob with compassion so deep it warmed him against the day.

"Caoimhe, is it really you?"

Caoimhe held her hand up as if to push Rob away. "Rob, we only have a few minutes, so please listen. I tried to warn you even though I knew then, as now, how your life and mine play out. We faeries are sometimes cursed with The Sight. I thought I could change things, thought we would have more time and then … Ah, Rob. All my life I was waiting for you and thinking I could change what was going to happen." The oceans opened and her tears fell like Irish Sea waves crashing.

Rob stepped forward, his heart beating fast and painfully. He wrapped his arms around her, saying, "Caoimhe, it was me. I knew what I was doing. I knew that someone might get hurt. I wanted to help. To be a real soldier.

It went so wrong. I killed them, Caoimhe. My own beautiful Padraig and Caroline. I took their breath, their future. They were only children. It was brutal. We buried them in parts."

Through her sobs, Caoimhe struggled to say, "Rob, like me, you cannot change or fix anything in the past. Soon, you will find a way to fight some of the evil that haunts children throughout the world. This will be your life's work. You may not have the happiest of lives, but the work you will do will make the world a better place for others."

She kissed him gently on the cheek, and whispered in his ear, "Is tú mo ghrá, anamchara", then slipped around the building column and faded from view.

Rob stood still, tears streaming down his cheeks, before slumping down on the concrete sidewalk in a heap. Hearing Caoimhe tell him she loved him, calling him her soul mate embedded the first warmth in Rob's body since the burials.

His body ached with the pain that had occupied his mind for over a year as if tearing his flesh trying to get out. Finally, Rob turned his head when he noticed a classmate named Jim Olson looking strangely at him as if to say, *Are you mad?*

Grace Garland Interview Recorded Transcript

New Orleans *Times Picayune*

June, 2005

Jim Olson: *I had seen him before in class and in some of the rehearsal halls. I knew he was a terrific guitar player. Everyone at Berklee was a music lunatic in some form or other. Rob was one of those that pissed you off because you knew that you would never be that good, no matter how much work you put in.*

He was what all the students at Berklee called a "real player". Those guys came to school and then went. Some came back to finish; some didn't. Rob was the real thing. Everybody knew it. During that first year, we called him the "genius ghost". He dazzled everyone in class but had never joined the groups that formed to practice and learn from one another in the rehearsal rooms at the school.

The real players end up traveling—forming or joining a rock 'n roll band. That worked out for some of us. For most, it didn't, and they would come back to school or move on to a different career. Lots of talent there at Berklee. Rob was it. The real player. A brilliant composer of songs. Music and lyrics. Unreal talent.

Boston's where my band came together. I have what the fucking critics called an "interesting" rock voice and I'm a pretty good performance guitar player. But—and here's my secret—all of my recordings have a studio musician on lead guitar because I just don't have the creativity needed. And I'm not solid enough technically for recording. Once the records are made, with practice, I can replicate the part well enough for live performance. My looks, voice, and performance qualities along with great songs and great musicians in the band made us a headliner in the late '70s through the early '80s. We got the glory, and Rob got a big chunk of the royalties—pretty sure he made a couple of million from his songwriting, just from our band.

See, those songs you still hear from our band, golden oldies from the '70s, Rob wrote four of them, including our number-one single from 1977, "True". Two others stayed way up in the charts and are still played a lot today on the oldies channels.

Musicians often tell one another that if you are blessed with a number-one song, you better hope you love it because you are going to play it every night for the rest of your fucking life. Well, I love that record. Late at night when I've indulged a bit too much, it can still make me feel it hard.

I wish I could tell you that I played the guitar riffs and solos on that first album, but that was Rob. He was playing with us when the record execs first heard that song. They really, really wanted Rob to be in the band. But he had no interest and couldn't be convinced, no matter what they threw at him. We were lucky to get him in the studio for the recording and he got the publishing rights to his songs. The label guys kept going to Rob for songs and studio work during the '70s and early '80s.

Later, we recorded our third album at the Studio in the Country in Bogalusa, Louisiana. We wanted some horns and nowhere has better horns than New Orleans. Rob was living down there and doing a lot of studio work. Rob wrote two of those songs, including "Belief", and played all of our guitar leads. Just the other day, I was listening to a new band's recent hit on the radio and I knew right away that Rob was the guitar player in the studio on that record. Notes that drip tears. Amazing dude.

Nothing I have read about Rob these days is a complete surprise. I knew he was deeply religious. At school, all of us knew he went to church every day. This was in a music college environment where most of us partied as hard as we practiced. Gonna-be, wannabe rock stars. Lots of weed, acid, coke, and booze.

Not Rob. Straight shooter, the most upstanding guy I ever met. We heard that his little brother and sister had been killed by a bomb right before he came to school. Life fucks us all over in one way or another, and Rob certainly has had more than his fair share. You could see it in his face and feel it in his music.

I was just walking down Broadway towards class one day when he appeared to have slipped on the ice and fallen in a real tumble. He just sat there, staring at a concrete column. Looked like he was talking to someone, but no one was there. He must have knocked himself silly. Looked like he was carrying on a conversation, pauses and everything.

But what I remember best is that it was the only time I've ever seen him cry. No sound, just tears rolling down his cheeks in a steady stream.

It was the luckiest day of my life.

Jim Olson, a slender young man with a classically beautiful face and blond hair in what was then called a "Beatles cut", was the only classmate Rob had talked to for more than five minutes during his time in Boston. He bent over Rob's slumped form and said, "Rob, you okay? You look like you've seen a ghost."

Rob looked up from the sidewalk, dazed. After a few moments, when he appeared to gather himself, he said, "Ah, sure, Jim. Just talking to myself and almost ran into the column. Was lost in thought ..." Rob used the sleeve on his jacket to wipe the tears from his eyes and face.

Jim pretended not to notice.

Jim helped him up and patted him on the back as a thought occurred to him. "Hey, Rob, a few of us are going to play together tonight and we'd like to have you join in with us. Thinking about playing some rock 'n roll. We really need a good guitar. You interested? We've got a rehearsal hall reserved for eight—all night if we want." They began to walk together toward class. It appeared to Jim that Rob appeared reluctant so, putting his arm around Rob's shoulder, Jim continued, "We've got some really good people. Bob Maxwell, you know, drummer?"

Rob shook his head and said, "Don't think so, but we may have met."

As they entered the building, Jim said, "How about Timmy Tanner, fantastic on the keyboard? He's a local guy, plays on Sundays at St Celia right around the corner. He's not at Berklee, but plays in a local rock band as well."

Rob looked at Jim and said, "Skinny black-haired fellow? I think I've seen him play at the church during mass."

"Yeah, that's him. What do you say?"

Rob hesitated, eyes vacant as if lost in thought. Then seeming to come back to reality, he said, "Uh, sure, okay, I'll be there ..."

"Right on. It'll be cool," said Jim as he turned down the hall to his class.

He left Rob wondering why he had agreed and what he was getting into.

CHAPTER 12

The rehearsal room was a friendly space with soft carpet and acoustic tile ceilings which produced a warm and harmonious sound. It was filled with pianos, drum sets, and guitars perched on guitar stands.

After playing together for several hours, the boys had appeared to Rob to be quite good musicians, particularly Bob Maxwell, who set down a solid beat, Jim Olson, the vocalist, and Timmy Tanner, a keyboard player with fantastic chops.

Near the end of the session, Jim had asked Rob if he had any songs that he had written which they might like. After thinking about it for a moment, Rob played the song he had written for Caoimhe back in Ireland—a song he now called "True".

He'd played it softly, singing the lyrics for the first time since the night he had met Caoimhe and the song had been written. The lyrics now held a melancholy voice and the guitar notes deepened the pain. He was so engrossed in the music, he was unaware of the rest of the band in the hall until near the end of the song. Lifting his eyes from his guitar to the room, he realized that Timmy's younger brother, Jeff, had walked right up next to him. Jeff, Jim, and Timmy were staring with slack-jawed faces that each held a look of awe.

The eight-year-old boy waited until Rob finished and said, "No fucking way you wrote that song."

Timmy leapt from behind the keyboard and grabbed the kidby the ear, twisting it roughly. "Shut the fuck up, Jeff." He pushed Jeff away, saying, "I told you he was the best—these guys have been talking about him for weeks."

Timmy turned to Rob and put his hand on his shoulder. Leaning in, he said, "Sorry about that—he's usually a good kid but we are worried about him. He hasn't been himself lately, filled with an anger. We don't know where it comes from."

Rob put his guitar down and walked over to where Jeff had wandered to the corner of the practice room rubbing his ear. He sat cross-legged on the floor next to the boy. As Rob stared at Jeff, he realized that he saw the kind of pain that didn't come from the twist of an ear but from inside, deep down in the young boy's heart. It was accompanied by fear that darkened Jeff's eyes to nearly black.

"Hey, you okay?" asked Rob.

His eyes leaking little tears, Jeff pulled his head out of his chest and sneered at Rob. "You don't care, so don't fucking pretend you do." With that, Jeff jumped to his feet and left the practice room with a glance at his brother. "Heading home, Tim, as if you care."

Rob knew that he did not really know Jeff or Timmy, but recognized that the pain in Jeff was something serious and deep-seated. He felt a kinship with the boy and wished that he could do something to help. He returned to his chair and spoke with Timmy for a while about what had happened. Timmy lit a cigarette, before offering one to Rob, and they sat smoking and talking quietly for a few minutes.

Later, Rob left the rehearsal hall when the drinking and pot-smoking seemed to become the emphasis of the evening. He had enjoyed playing with Jim Olson and his friends, but thought he would finish his night in church.

Rob knelt in a middle pew in St Cecilia church. Nestled among the other buildings of Berklee College, St Cecilia felt like a part of the urban campus. The beauty of the church wasn't lost on him, but yielded little comfort. As he fingered the guitar-string rosary, saying his prayers, his eyes wandered from the statue of St Pius on the right side of the sanctuary to the various naves and arches of the church adorned with images of Mary. It was quiet, with only the flickering light of the candles and light leaking through the door to the sacristy providing illumination. Rob's head was bowed nearly to his chest, which meant he was invisible to any others entering the church at this late hour.

He thought again of his vision of Caoimhe earlier that day. Rob believed that she had physically been present with him that day. Why she had materialized, he didn't understand, but he thought over and over about her message to him. He begged Mother Mary to help him understand the message and to make sense of his life. What had Caoimhe meant that he was to bring comfort to children? What was his role in life to make that happen?

Rob was startled to hear voices coming from the sacristy. In the many nights he'd spent here at St. Cecilia, he'd never seen anyone here this late. Only during mass and in early evening would he run into others on their way to services or confession.

He straightened slightly and saw shadows moving in the light coming from the sacristy. Hearing what sounded like whimpers of pain, he strained to hear more.

"Father, no, please, no ..." It was the sound of a young voice filled with terror and pain.

"Now, son, this is what God wants of you," said an older voice, filled with self-satisfied authority. "You must learn to put yourself in the service of God?"

"Please Father, No! I don't want to do this."

"But this is a special service you do for God. It is our way of becoming one with each other and the Lord."

Rob couldn't believe what he was hearing. He knew that he must do something, so he rose from the pew and strode toward the sacristy. Crossing the altar in the darkened room he tripped on a riser and landed on both knees, as if coming to a position of prayer. His knees connected with the wood in a loud thump.

"Who is there?" came the older voice from the sacristy.

Rob rose and continued walking toward the sacristy door. "What is going on there?" he said.

At that moment, Jeff Tanner came out of the sacristy door with the look of a feral animal on his face. He saw Rob and in a painful silent terror he ran down the risers on the altar and through to the aisle, exiting the church.

A priest then came out of the sacristy, straightening his cassock and smoothing it down to its fall line. He was short with silver hair and a hawk-like nose that made the shadows on his face look threatening. He had a look of consternation on his face and his cassock, despite being smoothed down, revealed an erection.

The priest said, "You really shouldn't be in the church this late. What are you doing here?"

It was then that Rob's questions, his prayers, were answered for him.

What was he doing here had been the central question he had tried to answer ever since the explosion had killed Padraig and Caroline. Now he knew.

"Excuse me, Father, but I came for confession."

The priest cleared his throat, seemingly relieved, and said, "Well, we aren't in hours for confession right now, but I think I can make an exception for you. Come along." With that, the priest strutted down the risers and to the right aisle, where the confession booths flanked the aisle of the church. He opened the middle wooden door on the confessional and sat waiting for Rob to enter one of the booths for the penitents.

Rob slowly walked toward the confessional. For the first time, he knew. He knew what Caoimhe had meant. Reaching the confessional, he opened the middle door and, taking his guitar string rosary from his pocket, he looked into the surprised eyes of the priest.

"I think you are confused, Father. It's not me who will be making confession." He grabbed the priest by the shoulders, spun him to face the back wall of the confessional, and held his hands together while slipping the rosary over the priest's neck. "It's your time to make peace with God."

Whether they were to protest or confess, the words of the priest were cut off into a gargle as the rosary tightened around his neck. Rob placed his knee into the lower back of the priest, and, with steady pressure, the rosary bit into the flesh and cut off the priest's supply of oxygen. Soon, he quit struggling for breath and slumped back into his chair in the confessional.

Finally, Rob knew why he was here.

CHAPTER 13

Rob woke unburdened. Rolling out of bed, he realized that he had slept his first dreamless sleep since living through the nightmare in Belturbet. Grabbing his rosary from the nightstand, he looked at the caked blood on the guitar string barbs of his rosary with wonder. He ran his fingers over the barbs, thinking that perhaps he should be feeling sorrow and shame. Instead, he felt as if his life had begun again.

Rob now knew his mission with a clarity he hadn't felt at any time in his life. Rising from the bed, he walked into the bathroom and began to wash the blood from his rosary. As the chunks of scabbed blood stained the water pink and swirled into the drain at the bottom of the sink, Rob smiled and began to pray St Patrick's Prayer.

May the Strength of God Pilot us

May the Power of God preserve us

May the Wisdom of God instruct us

May the way of God direct us

May the shield of God defend us

May the host of God guard us

Against the snares of the evil ones

Against the temptations of the world

Rob knew now that his life would be dedicated to help God guard against the snares of the evil ones. To protect the children as Caoimhe had foretold in her vision.

After patting the rosary dry on a towel in the bathroom, he returned to his bed, where he pulled on his bellbottom jeans, and placed his rosary in the pocket, before putting on a clean T-shirt. As he bent to pick up his boots there was a knock on the door. It startled Rob—the first time anyonehad knocked on his dorm room door since he had moved in the year before. For a moment, Rob felt panic, but it was quickly replaced with a calmness that came from knowing that what he had done was right and just. He would open the door to reveal whatever faced him, safe in this knowledge.

He was shocked to see his father, Mike, and Hilton Baines faces drawn with worry. Throwing his arms around Mike, Rob wept as he hugged his father fiercely. "Ah, Da, it's so good to see ya." Releasing his grip, he indicated that the two men should enter the room.

Hilton Baines patted Rob on the shoulder and said, "Well, Rob, I just wanted to let your dad know where your room was … I'll leave you to it." With that, he turned and retreated down the hall.

Grace Garland Interview Recorded Transcript

New Orleans *Times Picayune*

June, 2005

Timmy Tran: *My brother, Jeff, lived a tortured life. We didn't know why until right at the end.*

He travelled with us during the '70s and '80s as a sound man. Set up and ran sound at all of our shows. He was really good, too. Worked his ass off, always ready on time, could make any venue sound great, big or small. We had a big budget for equipment and he loved buying and using the new stuff. He came up with sounds that really enhanced the shows. His mix was always right on.

It was funny, but whenever we were in the studio and Rob was working with us, they were very close. They'd go off and they spent a lot of time together. I was into myself, thinking I was the big star and all, but I was a little jealous of how close they were. I tried with Jeff, but I really didn't have any effect. No one did, except Rob.

Jeff would be better for a while after seeing Rob, but sooner or later he'd start to slip back. Bad, bad, really awful alcohol problem. Then there were lots of drugs around, so he was heavy into that as well. Very self-destructive. We nearly lost him a couple of times on tour.

My parents were very solid and religious, and none of understood where this came from—you know, what his demons were or why he was so fucked up. Maybe we should have guessed. When the priest got killed at St. Cecilia, Jeff refused to go to the funeral. We all thought he was just upset because he was so close to Father O'Neil. Fucking hell…

His relationship with Rob makes more sense to me now. Apparently Rob protected him in the only way he knew how. But Rob couldn't fix what had already happened.

Those bastards destroyed a lot of lives, and not just those they hurt directly. My parents endured pain their whole lives. They died in pain over Jeff. I know we are supposed to forgive, but some things aren't really forgivable. I only know that I loved Jeff and I love Rob.

Mike Coogan sat next to Rob on the bed in his dorm room with a sadness that was palpable. "Son, how are you really doing? Your ma and I are really worried about you. We haven't heard from you in so long, and your letters, when they come, sound like you're lost."

Rob rose from the bed, sat in his desk chair facing the bed, and said, "Da, to be honest, it's been a struggle. For most of the time here, I've felt as if in a dream—or, better said, a nightmare." Reaching into his pocket, he felt the barbs of his rosary and continued, "But I'm better now, truly." He saw the relief in Mike's face.

Mike sat with his arms across his legs as if in a crouch. Without looking up, he asked Rob, "Do you want to talk about what happened? And what has or could make it better?"

When Mike began to sob quietly, Rob returned to the bed and put his arm around his father's shoulders. "Da, I have prayed and prayed to understand why it happened. I don't think we will ever know. We know that God has a plan for us, and what has helped me a bit is to realize that I might not ever know why …

"I asked Ma once why she was so committed. I knew she was a Provo, even though she never said so. All of us heard that from others. That she was a real feckin' soldier. One day right before the bombing, I'd asked her why, why are we drawn into this struggle? Why is it up to us? See, I knew she also believed in God with all her heart and I couldn't get the two to match up."

Mike shifted away from Rob, saying, "Your ma is an incredible woman. Difficult, demanding, but extraordinarily loyal to God, her family, and wedded to the Republican cause. To be honest, it's causing me to back away from her a fair bit. She went through a period of tremendous pain after Caroline and Padraig were …" Mike began to quake with sobs. He covered his face with his hands, then said, "And now, by God, she's back at it."

Rob rose from the bed and walked to the window, gazing out into the dark winter of Boston. "She told me that it wasn't a conflict with her belief in God, but a reinforcement of that faith.

"'How can fighting injustice be against God's will?' she asked me. We talked about the Sunday that the Brits shot those thirteen unarmed people up in Derry. Then the bastards lied about it. She told me about your pa and hers, our lands taken, them killed. I asked her if God would want us to harm others in pursuit of worldly goals, and she told me something I'll never forget. She said, 'Our life, our freedom, our will, is a gift from God. Allowing any government or person to take it from us is a repudiation of that gift.'"

CHAPTER 14

After walking under the night sky, Mike Coogan sat quietly, stirring and sipping his tea in a booth in a small coffee shop he had found on the street between his hotel and Rob's dorm. The sun was not yet up, the Boston winter misty and cold. The coffee shop, though warm and filled with the smells of breakfast, sausage and bacon, and baking biscuits and waffles, was thinly scattered with people—some on their way to work, others, less reputable in appearance and employment, on their way home.

Mike had felt comforted by his visit the day before with Rob. Apparently something had happened to him recently that had lifted his spirits and set him back on a more positive path. Yet, Mike had slept fitfully the night before. The effects of travel? More likely the disquieting interruption of his dreams.

Mike knew he could only describe them as dreams to others, but for Mike these mystical experiences and the actions that they set in motion had become the core of his reality. Beyond his family, these were what had given his life true meaning. What allowed him to connect with God in a meaningful way. To serve Him. A secret he had never shared with anyone, not even Maeve. He'd always feared that Maeve would make fun of his dreams and they were too precious to him to risk allowing that to happen.

Over many years, often while he was in his music room and strumming his guitar or quietly listening to music, the remembrance of the stories told by his ma would guide his actions. It was if those stories, captured in his memories, would come back to him in the form of dreams and talk to him in muted tones. The dreams would describe what path Mike should follow.

Mike had now grown old; his life was nearly done. His own children were gone, his wife distracted, and the road ahead for him looked bare and lonely. There would be only his music, prayer, and the wait.

Last night, when sleep would not come, his ma had appeared on the edge of his bed, her face leathery and lined by the sun and the wind and a difficult life. Her hair was silver, flecked with strands of pure white, yet still long, wavy, and full. Her dark blue eyes were now rheumy with tears or age, of which he was not certain.

"Michael, it is the time for others to do our work, to carry on your legacy with the children," she'd said to him. "I have one last request. Please share with our Robby the history of Oileán Na Bpáistí and its role in God's work."

As Mike sat in the coffee shop, sipping at his cooling tea, he remembered when his mother had told him the story of Oileán Na Bpáistí off the coast of western Ireland. That was when she had recruited him to a cause he had willingly joined and would never regret.

Last night, Mike had felt her warm hands hold his head as a mother holds her new born, her eyes filled with warmth, gratitude, and love. She'd seemed to become younger and was once again the young mother of those many years ago. Then she'd become a swirling mist, her image less defined as it had risen toward the ceiling and drifted away.

Moving backward in time in his memory, Mike recalled learning from his ma that faeries often need the help of what she called "real people" to perform their work.

For Mike, this work had started after he and Maeve had married, when doubt about his union had first emerged. He loved and admired Maeve, but her fierceness had begun to scare him more and more. It caused him to wonder if she would ever see their family as her true priority. Sadly, time had proven that nothing meant more to Maeve than the independence of Ireland and a re-joining of the North with the Republic.

Shortly after Rob was born, she had gone back to her work with the IRA and the beginning of the Provos. It was then that Mike had realized that she would love him and their family but that "higher principles", as she described them, would always come first in her loyalties.

Mike had looked toward years of loneliness, cast adrift by Maeve's choices. So, instead, he had decided to focus on the happiness of his children. On his music. Until his first dream when his life had become purposeful and important.

When Mike was young, his father had been brutally killed by British soldiers. Afterward, there were many nights when his mam had struggled to feed her children. She would place meagre portions before them each night in the smoky kitchen of their tiny cottage. Mike and his brothers and sisters would pretend not to notice that she gave herself almost nothing to eat. When one of the younger children would offer to share their food, Mam would always say, "Well, I don't want to be a fatso now, do I?", pushing away the offering.

For the children, she attempted to replace nutrition with entertainment, to feed their minds with stories of redemption and revenge and glory. She would then fill the smoky air with tales of the faeries.

Mike wished now, with the job at hand, that he had told those stories more often to his own children.

Mike had learned from his mam that providing a safe haven for damaged children was the principal work of the faeries of Oileán Na Bpáistí, Children's Island. The island where the faeries gave these children a place to restore their souls, preparing them to join God.

The faeries, as is their natural way and soon after establishing the island, realized that they might also be able to stop some of this behaviour, to protect some children whose souls had not yet been damaged.

To keep the sinners from repeating their sins.

For Mike, it was protecting others from the damage the evil caused. Seeking the evil ones out, praying for them and sometimes sending them to whatever judgement they faced at the hands of God. Mike had done this work for the children most of his adult life.

Over a dozen times through the years he had intervened on behalf of what he had come to think of as The Children, sparing untold numbers from the damage to them that would have been caused by those who sought to cause them pain.

In that way, his life had become fuller and more satisfying despite the disappointment of his marriage to Maeve.

The waitress placed the plate in front of Mike and the smells of bacon and the hot coffee as she refilled his cup brought Mike back from his reverie. As he saw the sun peeking through the gloom of night he decided to finish his breakfast quickly and continue on his way to see Robby. He wanted to make sure that Robby knew the story of Children's Island as was told to him by his own mum.

CHAPTER 15

When his father knocked on Rob's door that morning, gone was the jaunty knock he was known for, now replaced by the light tapping of the timid. As he opened the door, Rob could see his father was not well. Mike was perspiring and pale. Rob helped his father lie down in his small dormitory bed, propping him up with pillows.

As Rob wiped his father's face with a cool, wet cloth, he said, "Da, I think we should get a doctor to come and take a look."

"Ah, I don't think that will be needed, Robby. I'm just a bit winded from the lack of sleep and the walk over here in the weather."

"But you're pale as a ghost. Are you in pain?"

Mike said, "No more than the usual for an old man like me." Grinning, he said, "You know an old fella once told me that getting old was like frying the bacon naked. You don't know where it's going to hurt, but it'll hurt you somewhere." When Rob smiled, Mike said, "I'm so happy to see you, lad. I've missed you something fierce. What a lovely man you're turning out to be. I spoke with Hilton a short while ago and he was worried about you terribly. I was so hoping that a visit would help you in some way to deal with … the god awful tragedy we are all suffering."

"What of Mam?" Rob asked. "Why didn't she come with ya?"

"Ah, well. You know your ma. Said she had a bit of business to attend to and, though she'd love to see you, thought you and me might have a better visit without her here." Mike groaned and shifted his body, seeking a more comfortable alignment. "I think she still suffers from the guilt and really can't face you yet."

Rob watched as his father clutched his left shoulder. Mike's face was covered with sweat.

"Da, I'm going to go down the hall to call for a doctor for you."

Mike opened his eyes and looked at the outline of his son through a haze as Rob left the room. He realized that he must tell Rob. Time was running out for him.

Rob returned and sat on the edge of the bed. Mike could only vaguely make out his form as his vision grew increasingly hazy. Grabbing Rob's hand, he told him to listen and asked him not to interrupt.

Mike squinted painfully to try to see Rob and judge his reactions as he began talking. "I learned of this from me mam. Many people would consider it a myth, but I believe it with all me heart. Back in the mist of time, God looked on what he had created. He became troubled with the realization that his great gift of free will was being used by his enemies for evil. Man, you see, could be corrupted and would use his free will to place his own interests above that of God, focusing on this world rather than the next. Them with evil intent abused the most important gift God had bestowed on Man—free will. Of course, there are many who still use their free will to help others and to live out God's hope for us. Sadly, others do not.

"Of the things God saw that troubled him most? Some children are abused and mistreated so early and to such a degree it damages their souls, making it difficult for them seek reconciliation with and become one with God in his heavenly Kingdom.

"Across the world, God called upon what we call in Ireland faeries. They are known by other names around the world. He gave these faeries mystical powers to help Man … Well, and sometimes to test us and put us back on the path, which as you know can be needed by all of us. One of the gifts faeries bring is to help us understand how we must love and help one another. To remind us of the power and glory that awaits those who cherish life and provide for the happiness of others.

"I remember hearing them words from your Gran, sittin' at that old table with a different broken chair for each of us." Mike's look made it appear he was staring into space and, truly, he could no longer see Robby.

Mike wiped his face with the bedcover and shifted in the bed once again. His eyes lost even more focus and he stared up at the ceiling while holding Rob's hand tightly. His breath came in gasps as he continued. "Robby, have you ever heard of Oileán Na Bpáistí. Children's Island? No, of course you haven't … I neglected to tell you this story before.

"Well, the Irish nearby say it is somewhere off the coast of Ireland near Galway. In the middle of the Irish Sea, it's where the Gulf stream crashes against the arctic blasts. It is told that it is a place constantly surrounded by these arctic misty winds. The circling winds threaten any unwelcome visitors and hold them at bay. Children's Island, lost in a swirling mist in the Irish Sea, is a special and magical place.

"Inside the mist, the sun always shines and the winds are cool. The rains, needed to keep food plentiful, generally fall at night. Beautiful sunny days and cool nights. Waterfalls and rainbows everywhere and plenty of flat stones on which to contemplate and learn, to visit and to pray.

"It is here that these children are brought by the faeries. To repair their souls. To prepare them for an eternity in heaven. To repair the damaged souls of the children who come to the island," said Mike, with tears running down his face. He couldn't see Rob, but he had to trust his son was listening. "Now I haven't seen it myself, but I'm given to understand that at some points in time there are thousands of these poor children on the island.

"Of course it doesn't exist in a physical sense such that we can go for a visit. It isn't in or of this world, but placed somewhere along the path to

Heaven. Similar to how the nuns described Purgatory. Except there is no sin for the children to be forgiven. Only the sins against them that need repairing. A way station to prepare each damaged soul for its further journey along the path to eternity with God. I think you'll agree that is a lovely thing that God has given these children …

"Now the fairies knew that evil remains in those who cause the suffering of these children. They keep at it as long as they are alive. As Mam told me, the fairies can do wonderful things for man, but they can be quite ferocious if they are cross. The evil ones who constantly fill up the island make them very cross indeed."

Mike took a deep but shaky breath, before saying, "So that's all I know about that. Last night in a dream, your gran came to me and asked me to tell you the story of Children's Island. Now that is done as well."

Suddenly Mike's eyes closed and his breath became shorter and raspier. His jaw became slack and saliva dripped from the corner of his mouth as his head lolled to the side. Rob pulled Mike up into his arms, then lay him on his back, flat against the bed. "Breathe, Da, breathe," he said as tears rolled down his cheeks.

Mike's eyes opened suddenly. He looked at Rob, and in a voice now clear and strong, he said, "I've had a wonderful life, Rob. I had the love of your ma, you three wonderful children, me music … And helping so many, many children."

As Mike's voice grew softer and his eyes closed, Rob could hear him murmuring an Act of Contrition. Then he was quiet and still.

The door opened and the school's doctor came bustling through. He quickly removed his stethoscope from his bag and listened to Mike's chest. Turning to Rob, he shook his head sadly.

THE DENTIST'S WIFE

My brother tells me I am a professional Irishman. His comment implies I pretend to be something I'm not. I think you will admit we all do this on occasion. We hide our true selves behind edifices constructed with an eye toward protecting ourselves from the judgement of others.

I have spent a relatively long life collecting great jokes and sad stories. I tell the jokes and mostly keep the sad stories to myself.

Now I tell you this, the saddest of all my stories, to tear down the construction behind which I hide. Perhaps to help me understand what happened to me—what set me on this path. More important is for me to find out whether I will follow this tortured path to its logical conclusion.

Early in my life, I was like most young men in a hurry. I only vaguely understood emotions and, then, only in theory. Not really in any place in the heart that mattered, that defined my existence and became a permanent part of my soul.

Then I lived this tale. It placed me at the center of true evil and its lasting consequences. Evil that enters our lives, stays embedded within our families, and has consequences for generations.

It left me with a sadness so deep and haunting that even now, years later, when the details have faded, the pain visits late at night and my body feels as if it is on fire. I become consumed with a desire to take action, to rectify something reason says should be left buried in the past.

What I have tried to do is erase these thoughts from my brain. Yet, like most men of my generation, I don't really accept that some things can't be fixed, and my heart pushes me forward.

In quiet moments in the middle of the night, I feel there is only one act that will quench the fire. Revenge. Real and visceral and bloody. A defining event. Who I was before, and then forever who I will be after.

I have fought this desire as I will no longer be the man I wanted to be when I was young—when I viewed sadness as an emotion momentary or vague, and when I thought right and wrong were simple and concrete.

We need to recognize that each of us confronts evil in our own way. Most of us are cowards, whether we acknowledge it or not. When we consider it at all, we prefer to rely on some vague institution or some other individual to protect us from the ravages of evil. It feels safer and is less revealing to us of our true nature. I know those who only hope for justice aren't picky about the details as long as they aren't directly involved.

The horror of justice is often in the details.

The Dentist's Wife is the story that broke my heart.

When I met her, she was in her early twenties and I was too old for her.

Recently divorced, with a thriving law practice, I was intent on having as much fun as possible. And we did. I met her on a co-ed softball team and was instantly attracted to her. She was athletic and smart and the funniest person I'd ever met. We laughed and built happy stories together with an ever-widening circle of friends.

She was reluctant but I was persistent. I ultimately won her over with the music we loved and all manner of jokes featuring Irishmen, penguins, and various other species walking into a bar.

I believe she saw in me a kind heart. I knew right away that she was for me. She knew how much I loved her and that I made her feel safe, if only occasionally. After a few years, she gave in and said yes.

Even then, I knew she had a wall that I wasn't to acknowledge and which I was never permitted to look behind. I was aware of the distance, but it didn't concern me. In fact, it was exactly what I was looking for because it meant I was permitted to have my own private space. I spent inordinate amounts of time on my legal and political career. I was able to do so without guilt or guile.

Later, when it began to unravel, the wall she had built over a lifetime tumbled down. She crumbled. For long stretches of time each day, she was almost catatonic. Her skin was blotched as if her body temperature couldn't be contained. She cried all day. Every day. For weeks. Then months.

We went to therapy and she began to open up. I wish I could say that I was entirely supportive, but this isn't one of my happy stories. Over a long period of time, and with help, she was able to tell me what had happened. She wanted to tell it. I realized now that I pushed her away, really didn't want to hear. I didn't want to live through it myself. It hurt too much.

With each word she said, I began to be haunted with a vision of revenge in the name of justice. Or was that justice in the name of revenge? I'm not completely certain. I only know that my search for justice has become the defining question of my life, of who I am as a man.

Like most who deal with trauma, her life had a before and after. In her before, she was four and half years old and about to go to preschool for the first time.

She was freckle-faced, curly-haired, wiry, an energetic tomboy with an uncontrollable cowlick in the middle of her bangs. She loved to ride bikes and would play outside with her dogs, exploring the countryside until late every afternoon.

She was a happy child who ran everywhere. Her father would watch her bounding across the pasture and just laugh. She flittered about and ran so much he called her "Running Bird", or just "Bird".

Her father was always on the go, developing a new business. Her mother's family was from the same town where they lived. Her mother worked occasionally in her brother's office where he was a veterinarian with a wide-ranging practice. Looking back, it is clear that her mother was suffering from some distress during this period, drifting through life, detached and distracted. Bird's mother was gone often to see and tend to her own mother.

The town was an idyllic-looking, relatively small town in the middle of the country. Her family were well-known and played an active role in the town's life. They lived outside of town in the country in a beautiful home in a peaceful setting. If the town sounds too perfect, that's what people saw on the surface. Few were aware of the evil that resided beneath the facade.

When she started pre-school, a friend of her mother's, whom Bird told me she thought of only as the Dentist's Wife, offered to help out the family by taking her to and from school.

Bird really liked the Dentist's Wife. She had glossy black hair with dark eyes and a classically sculpted face. The Dentist's Wife looked to Bird like a princess grown into a queen.

She bought her a doll which Bird loved instantly. The Dentist's Wife said they would keep the doll at her home and they could go there to play with the doll after school. The Dentist's Wife also had two beautiful Irish Setters, one she named after Bird.

After Bird's first day of school, the Dentist's Wife took her home to visit the doll and to play with the puppies. She asked Bird if she thought she was pretty. Bird told her yes, she did. Bird asked the Dentist's Wife if she thought Bird was pretty. Something in the Dentist's Wife's response scared Bird. She became wild-eyed and off-kilter, noticeable even to a child.

You shouldn't remember your first day of school for what happened next. This was to become Bird's after.

Bird is wearing a beautiful dress of bright blue with a white collar and trim. Her hair had been fussed over that morning and she looks the image of a young happy child on the way to a new adventure.

As Bird skips happily toward the house, she hears a sound that she has never heard before. She sees a bird fly by and into a flowering bush, landing with a flourish near the path. The bird begins chirping a beautiful sound that Bird later learns is the call of a whippoorwill. As they reached the Dentist's Wife's home, the whippoorwill suddenly stops singing.

Bird is playing with the doll on the big antique four-poster bed when the Dentist's Wife grabs her from behind, pinning her on the bed. At first, Bird is confused. Then her fear turns into terror as the Dentist's Wife punches her stomach, holding her and not letting her go despite Bird's pleas and screams. Then, The Dentist's Wife's face glazes over with an almost gleeful look. She removes Bird's clothes and then she rapes and sodomizes Bird, using her fingers and objects. It is very painful and Bird screams repeatedly.

Standing, the Dentist's Wife rubs herself against Bird, holding her like a rag doll and using her as an object of her own madness. She begins to dance and mumble. It appears to Bird as though she were talking to someone in the room, though no one is there. All Bird really understands is the pain and the terror that fills her body, spreading like poison.

The Dentist's Wife delights in the pain she causes and is excited by the terror she inflicts. The look on the Dentist's Wife's face grows even more crazed and haunting as the agony continues. It is an image that becomes seared in Bird's psyche. An image that will haunt her, at odd times during the day and in the middle of the night, every day for the rest of her life.

In many ways, the actions and the image of the Dentist's Wife controlled Bird's life from that day forward. Her childhood ended with this onslaught of terror.

Later, as she was cleaning Bird's injuries and putting her clothes back on, the Dentist's Wife made it clear to Bird that she was not to tell what had happened. She was told that if she said anything, her family would all die. The Dentist's Wife promised to kill her father, her mother, the dogs, and then promised she would kill Bird last after making her watch as she slaughtered her family.

In the words of the Dentist's Wife, "Little girls who tell and cry are not permitted to have dolls or pets and their families will all die and end up in hell. Only you can keep your family alive."

Once she returned home, Bird did not know what to do. She cried at all hours of the day and could not sleep. She became impacted and couldn't go to the bathroom. She became more and more frightened. She was four and a half years old.

She would be forty-five now ... I know that the fear never left her.

I later learned that this action is best described as "soul murder". It renders a child unable to process life in any way that can be described as normal. There is apparently a subset of child predators to whom soul murder is the ultimate goal. I'm given to understand that in the era of the internet, these particularly evil practitioners even trade images of the acts that destroy a child's soul.

This fills me with a rage that I know I will be unable to control.

Bird told her mother that the Dentist's Wife scared her and that she didn't want to ride with her from school. She cried and complained that her fingernails were too long and scared her. Bird's distracted mother thought her daughter was just shy.

But Bird was unable to tell anyone the full truth of what was happening to her. She was frozen with fear. Somehow, she came to believe that because she had told the Dentist's Wife that she thought she was pretty, Bird deserved what was happening to her.

This torment continued regularly for the entire school year. Bird lived in constant terror that someone would find out and terrible things would happen to her family and her pets and her friends.

Only on occasion could she go away in her mind, drifting off to a place where she felt safe, peaceful. In that quiet place, she could still hear the whip-poorwill, the last moment that defined the before part of her life.

She locked away the terrible things that were happening to her. She began to put her sadness and terror into little boxes in her mind. At nearly five years old, she only knew that if she could keep secrets, her family would remain safe.

On the last day of the school year, the Dentist's Wife picked up Bird from school. Bird's eyes now appeared dead and she rarely smiled. The Dentist's Wife asked Bird if she wanted to visit the puppies after going past the store. Bird knew better than to say no.

When they arrived at the Dentist's Wife's house, they carried groceries into the kitchen and she sat Bird on the counter while she put away the groceries. Bird relaxed for just a moment and the Dentist's Wife came from behind her and roughly pushed her off the counter. She tore her lip and blood splattered everywhere. When Bird looked up, the Dentist's Wife was laughing maniacally and uncontrollably. This image is what she would see in her dreams for the rest of her life.

In my bedroom, I have a clock that chimes the sound of a different bird on each hour. I had the clock fixed a few years ago so that after ten at night, it only chimes the sound of a whippoorwill.

Sometimes it helps.

ALABAMA

1979–1985

During one of my adolescent arguments with my mother, I fought furiously for my belief that kindness and thoughtfulness are exculpatory virtues of the lazy and ambitionless—me, in other words. My mother disagreed, saying, "Kindness and thoughtfulness are lovely attributes, to be sure. But they are not virtues."

You can rely on the kind and the thoughtful to provide comfort when times are difficult, and to lend a restful shoulder when such is needed. But when you need—when you really need—an ASSHOLE, in capital letters, a flaming, withering son of a bitch, thoughtful and kindly people will always let you down. No, for that you need someone steeped in anger, and in righteousness (in its best sense). What you need, in other words, is a real son of a bitch.

– Theodore Dawes

CHAPTER 16

It was a glorious day for Rob Coogan. Speeding along in his open-air Jeep, the drive on Highway 190 near Mobile felt like he was slaloming into a new future.

Having recently graduated from Berklee in Boston, Rob reflected on how, despite losing his father while there, his time in Boston had changed the arc of his life in so many positive ways. He'd left Boston filled with purpose in his goal to serve God in his work with children. At the recommendation of Hilton Baines, Rob was attending Spring Hill College, planning to get a further degree in Education to accompany his musical training at Berklee.

The rare lack of humidity left blue skies with air purified and washed by the gulf breezes. The crystal-blue sky provided a stunning backdrop to the coastline home of Dr Theodore Dawes. The unique gulf-washed, hurricane-bent look of the live oak trees lining the driveway from the shore road led visitors to expect, then see, a traditional southern mansion on the drive to the house. The Spanish Moss hanging like wisps of smoke led the way down a gravel driveway to a circular parking area in front. Columns and wide porches with floor-to-ceiling doors framed by hurricane shutters completed the look of genteel Southern style.

The front porch was filled with comfortable chairs, long benches with cushions of multiple colors, scattered toys, bikes, and soccer balls. A cloth-covered table held a Scrabble game seemingly in progress, then abandoned to the elements. One look and you knew a family that loved one another lived in this home.

Jumping from his Jeep and walking briskly to the side door, Rob Coogan entered the house through the kitchen. Glancing into the living room, he stepped down quietly into the warmest and most welcoming room he'd ever seen. Theodore Dawes half lay across an enormous dark brown leather couch. He was facing a television playing taped reruns of soccer from around the world. Doc Dawes stretched his massive arms, rubbed his bald dome and then his eyes, playfully pretending to come out of a deep sleep.

Doc was an imposing figure. A full two inches over six feet with a body formed through intense physical exertion to become the Senior Powerlifting Champion of Alabama—as he liked to point out, "for five years in a row, next year will be six". His dark rather piercing eyes were juxtaposed with his warm grin which perpetually spread sunshine. Laughter was what you were most likely to hear in his presence. That's what had led him to his successful practice of psychiatry. He'd combined his broad and deep intellect with an easy-going personality in one-on-one situations. People trusted him. More importantly, they liked him, and they respected him as a man of principle. Almost invariably, they enjoyed being in his presence.

As Rob settled into one of the several comfortable leather chairs facing both the television and the couch on which Dawes rested, Rob said, "Doc, I want to thank you again for letting me stay with you while I settle a bit. I'm sorry it's gone on longer than we thought. It's always tough to find a spot to live and to get acquainted with my surroundings. I'm liking this area, though. It's warmer than any place I've ever lived."

"Well, Rob, it's not as though you aren't earning your keep. With a house this big, we're not likely to run out of room. The soccer practices you do for the club are the best I've seen. The boys are really excited. They look like they're really picking things up quickly. I am grateful to Hilton for putting us together."

"Ah, I'm having a bit of fun myself," Rob said. He knew that the standard of the boys he was teaching was well below what he was used to, but wanted to keep them encouraged. It was the parents who worried Rob. They all seemed to combine lack of knowledge about the sport with an absolute certainty that their boy was a potential star. While he wanted to encourage the boys, he sought to do so in an honest way. He saw some conflict in his future over that.

"What's that on the telly?" Rob said, turning to face the television.

"Just *100 Great Goals*, once again." Doc sighed. "We are really starved for soccer on TV around here. I'm sure that I've seen every tape I have fifty times." Doc stood up and moved to the chair next to Rob's . "The kids and Patty love having you here. We just hope that you're comfortable and feel part of the family. Hilton told me that you've had some real trauma in your life, and if you don't mind my saying so, sometimes I can see it in your face and your demeanor. If it ever suits you, I'm here to talk, but really more to listen." Dawes shifted his attention directly to Rob, and his eyes lent a kindness to the words.

Something in that moment caught Rob in a way he hadn't felt since leaving Belturbet for Boston—like there might be some real happiness in his future. He realized that he already felt a real connection with Theodore Dawes. The doctor's gentle goading of his own children revealed his competitive yet loving nature. The open way in which he expressed love for his wife, Patty, was something that Rob hadn't seen before in his own life. It lent a sweetness to Doc's character that had drawn Rob in more and more in the weeks since his arrival.

"There are things I haven't spoken of that it might be a bit much to ask of you to hear," said Rob quietly. "Not even sure that I could make myself say out it loud, the things that are troubling me."

Doctor Dawes reached over and turned down the television. With a faux fierce visage then breaking into a grin, then laughing out loud, Doc sat back in the sofa and, facing Rob, he said, "Give me a dollar."

"Give you what?"

"A dollar—reach in your pocket and give me a dollar. Then you are my patient and everything we say is protected and confidential." Doc laughed again.

Leaning over his knees with his hand folded as if in prayer, he said, "Asshole lawyers on TV always ask for a dollar from their clients they think may have something to hide so they are protected from having to disclose whatever they learn. As a physician, I don't really have to charge you to give you legal status as my patient, but I've always wanted to use that line." Once again, Doc laughed, which helped Rob to relax. "You know that I had to be trained as a physician first and continue my studies to become a psychiatrist. I like the feeling it gives me about myself that I can help people deal with whatever traumatized them. And almost everyone has something. In order to do what we do, psychiatrists sometimes have to maintain confidences that are beyond the reach of the law."

Rob removed his wallet and took a single bill from it, handing the bill to Dawes. Grinning, he said, "Well I guess this is like the church then. I think what I really need most is to go to secular confession." Looking somewhat chagrined, he said, "I haven't been to the real thing in a fair bit of time."

Doc Dawes grinned. "Then you've come to the right place, Rob. I trained to be a priest as a younger man."

Rob was startled. He could feel his body tense. Suddenly he didn't want to confide in the Doc any more.

A banging sound coming from the back door announced the entrance of what Doc called "Patty and the Brood"—two girls and three boys combining into a bundle of energy and noise. Doc always added, "Swirling around the center of our universe." The first child to enter the room, Marcelle, looked at Doc and said, "Dad, more soccer? Jeez, don't you think of anything else?" With that, the slender teenager tossed her long dark hair in a practiced move and turned to Rob with her hands on her hips. "So, did you?" she challenged Rob.

Rob sat up slowly in the easy chair, and frowned. "Did I? What is it you're asking?"

Marcelle walked over to face Rob. "I have a friend at school who says you wrote 'True'. That it's you playing the guitar on the record. I told her no way—there is no way you'd be camping out in our house if that were true."

As she was issuing her challenge, her three brothers, baby sister, and mother, Patty, entered the room. "Marcelle, you're being rude," said Patty. "You should never be rude to a guest. Rob isn't who you should be challenging on this; it's your friend who made the story up." Patty walked over to Rob and shifted the throw pillow behind him to make him more comfortable, tousling his hair as she said, "Sorry for that, Rob." She snorted. "Teenagers."

A voice breaking with the effects of adolescence came from behind the sofa: "Besides, if he wrote that song, he'd be in the band. No way he'd be down here working with our soccer club." Louis, the oldest boy, loved arguing with his older sister.

Rob looked at the family with a deep appreciation for the love with which they filled their home. After his years alone in Boston, the home of Doc, Patty, and the Brood filled him with a warmth that he vaguely recalled from his own childhood.

With a pout and arms akimbo, Marcelle asked again. "Well, did you write it? 'True'? "That would mean you know the band. Do you know ..." She hesitated. "Jim Olson, like, uh ... personally?".

Rob said. "Guilty, I'm afraid. I met the boys while I was at Berklee and they liked a couple of my tunes."

Grace Garland Interview Transcript

New Orleans *Times Picayune*

June, 2005

Marcelle Dawes: *Of course I was in love with him; all of the girls were. Sure, we were attracted to his physical beauty and talent, but what got me in a place no one has ever touched before or since was that he was the sweetest man I ever met. My brothers thought he was a god. Apparently, he was as good at soccer as with the guitar. His lyrics are like the poetry of my life.*

The years he spent with us and my dad's obsession filled those boys with a love of that game that just grows and grows. All of the grandkids play now, too. Sometimes I think that all they and my dad care about is football. Oh, and especially Liverpool. "Red for Life"—their common motto. They cry more every time "You'll Never Walk Alone" plays before a match than they even did at my wedding when Rob played and sang to me and my husband. There wasn't a dry eye in the house when that took place.

Of course, after a few years of living with us, he finished his degree at Spring Hill. After that, he moved to New Orleans to do more with his music and to teach high school and work with some soccer club there. As he was driving away, I sat in the kitchen with my mother and cried for hours. We both cried. My mother thought of him as one of her sons.

Often, over the years, we'd go together and see him play live at some of the local bars and restaurants and he was truly phenomenal.

What I remember most is when he used to play and sing to us on my parents' porch for hours. Christmas, Thanksgiving, and Fourth of July were mandatory, but lots of Sunday meals late after church and the soccer was over, we'd sit and listen as the sun went down.

He was in great demand from the record labels for studio work and I could see why. His guitar playing was unique, like he played an instrument that held more magic in it than anyone else. He made a lot of money from his songwriting and studio work, so I suppose it made sense to buy a place closer to the music scene in New Orleans. But he kept teaching school and coaching soccer. It seemed like every year his team would be in the State Championship game. He made the Jesuits on Bank Street very happy.

Back when I was at LSU, he'd let me and my friends stay in his house on Esplanade back of the Quarter. You may imagine it raised my star in the sorority. We would sit, talk, drink, and smoke on the enormous staircase that rose from the street to his front door. Years later, we would joke we were the sashaying ladies immortalized in song.

The absolute highlight of my college years was the night he dedicated "True" to me at Tipitina's. Every girl with me was green.

Of course, all those girls loved him, too. He'd always put a big food spread and beer stash in the fridge for us when we would invade his place in New Orleans. He wouldn't stay there when we were in residence. I asked him why, once, and he said, "Respect. It's something you should always have for others but, as important, for yourself." Jeez, an Irish Southern gentleman, I guess that's what he is.

Does what you are telling me he may have done make sense? On a certain level, of course it does. He is so fiercely loyal. I said he was sweet, but I never thought of him as soft. I watched him at his soccer practices and during the games. He was tough as a cob, and many times I thought he was too hard on the boys. If something needed doing, he'd do it. If something needed saying, he'd say it. No question. When I asked my dad about how tough Rob was on the boys, Dad told me that sometimes in life you need a SOB.

Rob had collapsed into one of the many wicker chairs on the porch watching Doc smoke his third cigar of the day. Doc made the rituals surrounding his cigar smoking a central element of his habit. First, he carefully removed the cigar from the wrapper, then removed the label, which he folded and placed in his shirt pocket. Then he produced a cutter from his pants pocket and very precisely snipped the tip, testing the flow of air. Finally, he flicked open his lighter and snapped it to engage the light. Holding the flame away from the tip, he sucked the flame toward the cigar and took several puffs to light it fully.

Sitting back in his chair, he looked through the cloud of smoke at Rob and said, "Well, aren't you full of surprises? I wonder why Hilton didn't mention your accomplishments. He only said you had a great background in soccer and might help teach the boys. I figured you were looking to combine teaching music and coaching soccer, and that's why you chose Spring Hill."

Ignoring the question, Rob said, "Well, Doc, you and your family are so kind to me, after being in Boston which is a rather cold place to be on your own." Laughing quietly, he realized that Doc was someone he could trust said, "Your offer to take my secular confession is something I'd like to consider. Getting some bits off my chest might be something I've needed for a while."

Doc took a deep draft off his cigar, releasing the smoke with a satisfied sigh, and said,

"Of course, you could always go to St Agnes and do a real confession."

The cloud of smoke drifting on the breeze through the porch momentarily shrouded Rob as he answered, seemingly from a place far away, "No. No, I don't think I'm ready for that. May never be."

CHAPTER 17

Beltonville Middle School no longer had children in its classrooms. The School Board had repurposed the building as an administrative center four years ago. Instead, the buildings were occupied by educational bureaucrats during school hours.

As with many schools in Alabama, its most prominent physical facility was what formerly had served as the home to its football team, the Badgers. For several years, the field had fallen into disrepair after the school's abandonment as a teaching facility. Doc Dawes had then worked to make the facility the home of the Alabama Hurricane Soccer Club—the club of which Doc was also the driving force.

After considerable wrangling with local politicians, Doc had secured a lease on the facility. Now the facility was where the Hurricanes practiced during the week and played matches on the weekend. Parents and others had been pulled into the project, constructing goals, resurfacing and maintaining the field, and building small sided fields for younger kids and for practices.

Every afternoon, as the bureaucrats left for home, the parking lot would refill with parents dropping off and picking up their children for soccer practice. Many stayed behind to watch from the somewhat rickety wooden stands that remained along the sideline of the main field. The stands had the atmosphere of a convivial church picnic. Groups of moms traded stories of their days and gave one another support in determining the right way to respond to the challenge of raising children in the modern world. Fathers tended to want to be closer to the action, watching from the sidelines, and the children went through their paces. As night fell, the lights came on and the moms and dads left with the younger children, but practices for the older teams would often continue until nearly ten at night.

Hurricane Park became a place where parents watched their children grow up, where friendships were formed, and where rivalries played out on a regular basis. In many ways, Doc considered it his greatest sporting achievement. Particularly after he brought Rob Coogan in as Director of Coaching.

Rob focused on the older boys' and girls' teams on an individual basis, but he ran technical training for the younger ages, and outlined practice plans with every team's coach in the club. Doc could already see the improvement in the quality of instruction once Rob began working with the parent coaches who struggled due to their own lack of experience with the game.

Tonight, Doc was angry, beside himself with concern for the mecca he had created. For the second time in the past week, he had seen two patients assigned to him by local judges as an element of their probation. Doc knew that the two elderly brothers had no meaningful connection to any child or family engaged in the club. He knew why they would show up and watch practice from under a tree on the far side of the facility. He also knew that their presence violated their probation.

Doc had intended to confront them earlier in the week when he had first seen them lurking, but they had drifted away prior to the end of practice and he had missed them. He knew that he would see them at their next therapy session. This time, he decided not to wait until the end of practice, and to confront the brothers directly and immediately.

Disengaging himself from the conversation amid the crowd of parents in the stands, he walked slowly around to the field to the grove of pine trees lining the far side of the facility. As Doc rounded the corner of the field near the corner flag, he saw that the brothers had become aware of his presence and were moving away as quickly as possible. Breaking into a jog, Doc called to them in his authoritarian voice, "Hold it right there." Approaching the two men, he said, "Just what the hell do you think you're doing here. You're not allowed near gatherings of children. You know that. If I report this, you'll be back in jail."

Jed Billings, the oldest of two brothers, approached Doc nervously and said, "Dr Dawes, we are just watching our niece at her practice. We mean no harm. Do you have children here? We didn't know you were a soccer guy."

"Which child is your niece?" said Doc. "I'm unaware of your having any relatives in the area. That wasn't covered in your file."

"Well, she's really just our neighbor, but we consider her family. Little Lily over there with the young girls," Jed said with a look that made Doc's skin crawl.

Jed's brother, Randy, ran his hand through his balding gray hair, his face covered with sweat. "Doc, we are going. Won't be back. We meant no harm. Please don't misinterpret this today."

Doc now understood why the precocious Lily exhibited a highly sexualized nature for a young girl of eleven. He'd often wondered what trauma was bringing this aberrant behavior out in the young girl. For weeks, he had been trying to figure out a way to intervene with Lily's single mother. Turning to the Billings now, he said, "Well, we will see, but I will have to report this to the authorities at the probation office. Now get the hell out of here and don't ever, ever come near this place again."

As he turned away from the Billings, Doc came face to face with Rob, whose eyes were bathed in concern.

"Doc, are you doing okay?" said Rob. "Are those fellows causing some trouble? What was that about Lily?"

"Rob, I think I've got it handled for now. Get back at it and we will talk about it later."

But, looking at the concern on Rob's face, he knew that the questions would have to be answered.

Patty finished up her kitchen duty after a late supper that evening, then wandered from the kitchen to the den and plopped down in Doc's lap. Doc knew she would have noticed how unnaturally quiet he had been through the meal, letting the chaos surround him without his usual running commentary.

Wrapping his neck in her rather plump arms, she kissed him and whispered in his ear, "What's going on? You aren't at all yourself."

With a deep sign and holding her tight, Doc said, "Patty, sometimes what I have chosen to do for a living is more than I can bear. I know as a psychiatrist that I'm supposed to believe that I can make a difference in every one of my patients. Sometimes I have to face it that some of them are just the embodiment of evil.

"Right now, I'm wrestling with how to handle a potential threat I see being created by two of my patients. The hardest part is that I shouldn't discuss the particulars with anyone, not even you, love."

Patty wriggled out of his lap. Leaning over to kiss his forehead, she said, "Teddy, you are the dearest and best man I know. You'll figure out what must be done. But please don't believe that you are responsible for everything and everyone's happiness. That's just foolish and stressful for no reason."

With that, Patty walked around the room picking up cushions, straightening chairs and lamps, and preparing the room for the next day's onslaught. Then she walked to the stairs and yelled to the children, "Everybody, time to finish up homework, say your prayers, and get ready for bed."

Doc leaned over and removed one of his prized cigars from the humidor. Checking his pocket for a lighter and cigar clip, he went through the door to the formal living room and continued out the front door to his rocking chair on the front porch. As with most nights, Rob was sitting on the cushions of a restored church pew strumming his guitar, filling the night with soothing music. Listening to Rob play while singing quietly, Doc realized once again that Rob's presence added so much value to his life and family.

"Rob, what's that song? Don't think I've heard it before. It's beautiful."

"Ah, just a new bit I'm doing for some friends. They have a new record due and they are going in to the studio over in Bogalusa next month. I told them I'd let them hear a few new tunes when my songs are closer to ready. Which they are not—can't really get the hook right so far. Ready or not, they'll be coming by this weekend, so I've got to get busy." Putting the guitar down and placing a sheet of paper covered with thoughts and chords in his pocket, Rob looked at Doc and asked, "What was that at the fields tonight? You looked furious at those fellas. Is it something I might be able to help you with?"

Doc finished his ritual lighting of the cigar. After releasing the first satisfying exhalation of pungent smoke, he leaned forward, saying, "I was just telling Patty that my profession is really frustrating sometimes. Those are some really dangerous bastards. They shouldn't be around children. Never. And here we were having a really pleasant evening with all that laughter and fun, and seeing them was like feeling a hot blast of evil enter a place I love so much. In many ways, my job makes me feel helpless to actually combat the evil that the job reveals to me all the time."

Rob stared at Doc, then hesitantly asked, "So they are pedos, are they?"

"Well, Rob, they are patients of mine under court-ordered treatment, so I cannot comment on the specifics of what they tell me. But the public record is clear. They've been released from prison where they were serving time for abusing children."

"Is that something that can be cured? Can you keep them from doing it again? That's something I've always wanted to know."

"Well, that's the sixty-four-thousand-dollar question, isn't it? Lots of back and forth on that in the psychiatric journals. In my experience, the more dangerous a pedophile is, the more likely they are to keep doing it. It seems to be an obsession that grows in strength over time, and ultimately it controls every thought and action of the individual. Then, very damn little can stop them other than prison. Or death." Leaning back in his chair, Doc exhaled a large cloud of smoke and added, "Dying really works."

Doc watched as Rob removed his rosary from his pocket and began fingering it. He looked far away, his lips mouthing what seemed to Doc to be a prayer, an incantation against evil.

CHAPTER 18

At mid-morning, the Dawes home was preternaturally quiet, devoid of its usual chaos. As was his custom, daybreak had found Doc on the way to the gym for his workout and then on to his office in town. Then the children left for school. Shortly thereafter Patty, left for a local coffee shop for her book club meeting.

Rob knew Doc kept patient files in a small wooden file case next to the desk in his home office. He felt only mild guilt when he took the opportunity to enter Doc's office and look through the files for two names. Fortunately, the two files were side by side and contained both the names and address for each patient.

Reviewing the files confirmed his belief. He also learned that the brothers lived together and ran their business outside of the small town of Bentonville. Apparently, they made a living by raising bees and selling the honey at local stores and markets. Looking up the address, Rob noted that it was an isolated road not far from the practice facility.

Rob's Jeep trailed a cloud of dust as it traveled the long gravel road off the main highway from Bentonville toward Mobile. Reacher Road was lined with ancient mobile homes and small houses on small acreage lots. A few of the houses were neat and well-kept, but many were dilapidated. Yards littered with the detritus gathered in a life of poverty in the South. Abandoned tractors, broken bicycles, and sacks of garbage revealed the loss of hope that was the center point of the lives playing out inside many of the houses. For Rob it illustrated the difference from the poverty of rural Ireland and what he was witnessing here. The Irish seemed angry and sought to place blame where those trapped in poverty here seemed immersed in despair.

Hanging from the turn signal was one of the handmade rosaries which Rob regularly used to say his prayers while driving.

Three miles down the road, Rob slowed to look for an address when his attention was drawn to a hand-lettered sign promising Local Honey for Sale. Turning into a driveway barely wide enough to pass through, surrounded by privet hedges and trees on either side, he pulled past a small ramshackle house. Then, noting a directional sign next to the driveway, he drove past it fifty yards or so to a small tin building. The building sat near a collection of what appeared to be twenty or thirty beehives. Two men with bee protection clothing working among the hives glanced up as Rob pulled his Jeep to a stop next to the building.

"Is it safe for me to be out here?" Rob asked as he exited the Jeep. Holding up a small bag, he said, "I'm interested in some honey."

The taller of the two men responded, "They won't sting you over there. Why don't you go into that building and I'll join you in a moment."

Rob entered the door, finding himself in a small room in the front of the building. The walls were lined with shelves packed with honey containers of various sizes. A small metal desk with two chairs was set in a corner. The top of the desk was littered with papers, invoices, and a small calculator. He walked over and looked through an open door to a larger room filled with equipment used in the honey business and stacks of what looked to be empty hives and boxes of containers on pallets.

He turned as Jed Billings came into the room and said, "This is quite a setup you've got here. What's all that gear back there used for? I don't know much about bees. You think you have time to show it to me and explain how all this works?"

Randy Billings methodically placed frames of brood, drawn comb and honey into an empty hive box. Then he carefully reached in his shirt pocket and removed a small plastic container with a new queen inside. He placed it carefully between two of the frames to complete the creation of a new productive hive. The bees on the frame he transferred would, over the next few days, eat the candy filling the tube and release the queen. By that time he bees would be accustomed to the scent of that particular queen and accept her. The mated queen would begin her lifelong work of laying eggs to build and maintain a productive hive.

Randy loved the almost omnipotent feeling of control over the bee collective that putting this puzzle together brought him. He particularly enjoyed the dominance as nearly all of the bees were female. As he and Jed often discussed, it was that feeling of control and power that made all of their work and their hobby special to them.

He lifted the now complete hive and placed it on top of the crossties used to keep the hive off the ground.

His exertion and the warmth of the day brought sweat to cascade down his face. Removing this beekeeper bonnet, he wiped his face on his sleeve. Turning to look at the small office and work building, Randy realized that Jed had been inside the building for a long time. He wondered whether he should go check on him and the customer. Something about the young man was familiar but Randy couldn't remember where he'd seen him before.

Just at that moment, Rob stuck his head out the door of the small building and yelled, " I think something has happened to your brother, please come see. He may need help."

Rob shut the door and stood outside it as Randy quickly walked toward the building. "He is in the back room."

As Randy reached for the door knob with his left hand, he felt Rob grab his right hand and twist it behind his back with force. As he attempted to wriggle free Rob shoved him against the door frame, grabbed his left hand off the frame of the door and twisted it behind his back. A rope was slipped over both hands and pulled tight.

Locking the door to the building from the inside, Rob turned back to face the Billings brothers. They sat facing each other in the two chairs in the unairconditioned showroom office. The brothers faces were filled with fury and rivulets of sweat poured down their faces.

Hands tied together behind the chairs their feet were roped together and a final rope around their waists, binding them to the chairs.

Rob half sat on the desk he reached into the bag he'd carried with his supplies and removed a pair of gloves. He looked intently at the two brothers with a look of pain and pity. He was filled once again with a sense of duty.

"Now is the time to make your peace with God." He said, reaching into his pocket and removing his rosary. "I will pray with you before you go."

MOBILE TIMES

TWO ELDERLY BROTHERS FOUND MURDERED

Local brothers Randy and Jed Billings were found murdered late Friday afternoon in a small storage building used by their beekeeping business on Reacher Road. Bentonville Police Chief Samuel Fercassi told the *Mobile Times* that the two brothers appear to have been garroted after being tied in two chairs facing each other. "Definitely a lot of anger in whoever murdered them two."

A local man, Sidney Bailey, told this reporter that he did chores for the brothers and discovered the bodies when he went to pick up his check. "Whoever did it nearly tore old Jed's head clean off. Looked to me like they must have used a hack saw. I don't guess I'll ever get my money now."

Police are asking anyone who saw anything suspicious to call and promised to follow up on any leads.

CHAPTER 19

Rob sat quietly in the family room surrounded by the Dawes family. He knew it would be normal to feel guilt for the actions he had taken the night before. But he didn't. It was as if his guilt from the deaths of his brother and sister and his role in their deaths had made him immune to the guilt he should feel for carrying out what he considered God's will.

Instead, his killing the two brothers the previous day filled him with a feeling of quiet appreciation for the purpose of his life. He thought of Caoimhe and his heart swelled with joy. He knew that more children would not have to face the limbo of Children's Island or the pain on the path there. He hoped that she would come to see him soon so that he could feel his purpose refilled.

In his heart, he knew that he was beyond redemption and that his purpose in life now was to save and protect The Children from evil as best he could. He would face the consequences of his actions when the time came and hoped that he could do so with gratitude for the gift of purpose that God had bestowed on him.

When he had returned to his room the previous night, he had washed his rosary and watched the bloody water circle the drain before the water became clear. His momentary feelings of doubt did not last as long as the water remained mixed with blood. His conscience was as clear as the water when he was done.

He looked at the Dawes family with awe. Doc and Patty were playing Scrabble with Marcelle and Louis. The baby was playing and gurgling in the playpen next to Patty, and the boys were running around the front yard kicking a ball and yelling "gooaaaal" every few minutes.

As he was strumming his guitar and working on lyrics for a new song, Rob raised his eyes from the fretboard and stared into the eyes of Doc Dawes. Doc averted his eyes quickly but remained focused on the question in his mind.

"It is too a word," Marcelle shouted at Louis.

"Nope, it isn't," Louis responded. "I challenge."

Marcelle picked up the dictionary and thumbed through the pages as Doc and Patty rolled their eyes and Louis folded his arms and stuck out his chin.

Marcelle licked her finger and began thumbing through the pages one at a time looking for her word. Finally, she said, "Ahah!" With a look of triumph at Louis, she read, "Felkin, f-e-l-k-i-n, an adjective used to modify the color of light."

For a brief moment Louis looked dejected and then he said, "Let me see."

Closing the dictionary, Marcelle said, "What? I told you what it said."

Louis reached for the dictionary as Marcelle attempted to slide it out of his range. He leaned over quickly and grabbed it from under her hand. Standing, he looked through the dictionary and said, "As Dad says, trust people but cut the cards."

After opening the dictionary and shuffling through the pages, Louis looked at Marcelle and said, "Okay, I see what's in here. I'm done for tonight, think I'll go up and study before bed." With that, he leaned over and kissed Patty on the forehead and headed through the front door.

Marcelle looked crestfallen. Turning to her father, she said, "It was just a joke."

Doc was putting the pieces and the board away. He looked at Marcelle and said, "Marcelle, Louis knows that, but no one likes to be taken advantage of, so being honest counts all the time. Probably time for all of you to go finish your homework and hit the hay." He knew his words were rather harsh, but he tempered his advice with a kind smile.

Patty stood up and gave Doc a kiss on the forehead, then walked to the railing of the front porch and yelled at the boys to come in for bed. "Tell your father goodnight on your way in, boys, as I'm sure he is going to foul the air with one of his cigars." She patted his shoulder as she followed Marcelle back into the house and the two younger boys scrambled up the stairs and leapt into his lap.

Doc faux-wrestled with the boys and gave each of them a kiss, then sent them on their way. Now he was left alone with Rob on the suddenly quiet porch. Standing, he walked to the railing and leaned over to gaze upward at the star filled night sky. Taking a cigar from his pocket, he went through his ritual and watched the first cloud of smoke as it rose into the air, obscured the sky, and filled the porch with a pungent scent. Then Doc walked over to the rocking chair near Rob, and sat down, puffing his guitar in time to Rob's strumming. He felt at peace and reluctant to have the conversation that he knew he needed to have.

Finally, Doc said, "Did you hear about what happened to the two men from the soccer field the other night? My patients ..."

Rob stopped playing and looking wide-eyed at Doc. "What happened?"

"Seems someone killed both of them. They were found at their place. Both dead." When Rob didn't respond, Doc continued, "It appears they were strangled."

Rob sat quietly for several minutes and seemed deep in thought. Finally, he responded in a manner that Doc would remember vividly and think about often: "And how do you feel about that?"

It was a question that Doc used often in his practice. A question intended to get someone to expand on what they were talking about. Often used to get them to reveal deeper thoughts and worries that he sought to bring to the surface. How strange to have the question put to him.

"Well, Rob, killing people is a terrible thing."

"Is it now? Always? Don't people often get killed in righteous conflicts such as war? And didn't you say that those fellows were some very bad people?"

Doc slowly rocked in his chair and thought about what Rob was saying. He knew that the two brothers had committed truly horrific acts and likely deserved their fate.

What he was concerned about was whether he had unwittingly played a role in their demise. He realized that he didn't know what lay at the heart of Rob's problems and wondered whether Rob had taken clues that he did not mean to leave in his path.

"Are you suggesting that killing someone like those brothers would be justified?" Doc asked Rob gently.

After hesitating briefly, Rob said in almost a whisper, "I'm only saying that sometimes life doesn't turn out well for those who bring evil into the world and that I, for one, don't lose any sleep over them types being gone from this earth. Out of the way, so to speak."

"Rob, perhaps it's time for us to have that secular confession we talked about before." Doc looked carefully at Rob, searching his demeanor for clues to his thinking. "Remember that I was trained to be a priest and that I consider what we talk about protected from disclosure to the law under my doctor patient confidentiality."

Rob's head drooped against his chest. When he raised his eyes to face Doc squarely, Doc looked at a different man. Fierce, defiant with a look that showed no hesitation or doubt.

Doc wondered what he was getting into when he said, "Go on, son, tell me about it."

NIGHTMARES COLLIDE

This is how Bird's nightmare became mine. How the evil visited upon her translated to a blight on my soul that drives me with a fury which grows and grows each passing year. Much of this story I learned from her as we unsuccessfully sought to keep the evil from destroying her life. It began to destroy mine.

When that first school year was over there were no more opportunities for the Dentist's Wife to continue the abuse. Still, little Bird hated her town and was always scared. She kept her mind almost entirely occupied with identifying where terror would come from next.

The next few years were difficult. She was unable to focus on her school work, and she was so quiet and distant that she was misdiagnosed as having a learning disability despite being very intelligent. Occasionally she would see the Dentist's Wife driving by or at other people's homes, and would become even more frightened. Late at night, she would become so terrified that she would take her blanket and sleep on the floor outside her parents' room.

She continued to blame herself and to think that this evil had happened to her because something was wrong with her. From the moment the Dentist's Wife started to torture, torment, and abuse her, the abuse had controlled her life. She became frightened, secretive, and private. Others, including her family, confused her behavior with being shy.

For the next few years, she grew up in fear. She hated what had happened to her. She thought that she deserved it because she liked girls. She prayed to God to let her not be scared any more. She was lonely and isolated, even from her family. She had no one to help her deal with what had happened.

And then one day when she was ten, her family moved to a new town, a new start for everyone, including her. She was almost happy; she almost felt safe. She made friends in the neighborhood and enjoyed her new environment. She began to believe that she had a chance to be normal and happy. Toward the end of the first year in the new town, she and her brother went to spend a week with her grandmother.

When they returned, everything had changed once again.

It felt like being pushed off the counter top.

Despite living in the same new town, they had been moved to an entirely different house and neighborhood. No explanations were given, but the atmosphere became quieter and tension lingered on a permanent basis.

Then her family began to attend a fundamentalist church.

Her mother worshiped the charismatic leader of the Ministry for Christ Church, Reverend Jim Vilas. Reverend Vilas was tall, with a shock of pure white, very carefully styled hair. He was tall and wore expensive suits. His powerful voice and the certainty of his teachings seemed to her mother to be a direct answer to her unspoken prayers for direction in a life that seemed rootless.

The services were filled with music and the teachings were judgmental and forceful. Bird's mother threw herself into the teachings and activities of the church. The whole family was made to participate in lessons, classes for kids, and other activities, in addition to attending church for hours each Sunday.

By now, Bird was certain she liked girls, in the same way her girlfriends liked boys. Although it felt normal to her, she believed that she must keep this a secret. In fact, she even decided that she must never act on her desires as it would bring more evil to her life, the kind that had happened to her with the Dentist's Wife.

Reverend Vilas's sermons reinforced her feeling that she was evil and sinful. She believed that she was a very bad person, undeserving of a peaceful and productive life. She felt that even God had abandoned her. Her loneliness became more intense.

Inside the activities of the church, she made a friend named Cherry. They had so much in common, including their lack of enthusiasm for the church and its teachings. Cherry was funny and liked to make fun of the church, often referring to its leader as "the Right Reverend Bent-Jim". Bird developed a crush on Cherry, especially enjoying being with her friend at the church camp they attended.

Then one day at the camp, a younger girl made a public accusation of Bird's feelings for Cherry, labeling it sinful ... evil. Bird went home and told her parents that she would never go to the camp again. She also never spoke to Cherry again.

During this time, the dynamic of her family changed. Her father began to suffer financial losses and had two heart attacks in rapid succession. Her older brother began to rebel and, when called to task on his drug use, attempted suicide. Bird found her brother along with the empty pill container, and her parents brought him to the hospital, leaving Bird at home alone for most of the night.

From the moment her parents returned with her brother, the family's attention centered on her brother's struggles. There was no room for the Bird's problems and behavior. She became a caregiver and more invisible inside her own family each day.

In her dreams, she continued to be visited by the Dentist's Wife. Unlike many victims who bury the memories, she retained and regularly revisited the physical torment and terror. Her fear, loneliness, isolation, and self-hatred grew. She tried to fall asleep by hearing the whippoorwill in her dreams, instead being visited by a vision of the Dentist's Wife and her maniacal laughter.

During the remainder of her middle-school years, she knew that she needed someone to help her. She started writing a journal in which she recorded her feelings and revealed her thoughts about her sexuality. Then she left it in a place for her mother to find.

It soon became obvious that her mother had read the journal, but she did not discuss its contents with Bird. Instead, she left religious tracts in her room, which made Bird feel abnormal and sinful. It confirmed to Bird that she, herself, was evil, as she had suspected all along.

Finally, Bird's isolation was complete.

Her only remaining alternative was to never, ever acknowledge her feelings and her sense of what had happened to her, and who she was, even to herself. She began to control her pain and only let it out on rare occasions and only when no one else could witness the terror, sadness, self-loathing, and loneliness she experienced every day.

During the remainder of her high-school years, her wariness and need to hide who she was meant that she could not risk having girlfriends and she wasn't comfortable enough with boys. She simply avoided deeper relationships altogether, despite the occasional inquiry from her mother. The junior and senior prom were her only two dates during high school, and she spent most of her time being the confidant to her friends and the caregiver to her family.

Bird attended a small community college with several of her high-school friends. She knew that she desperately wanted to fit in, and thus developed a friendship with a boy. He was funny, and fun to be around. It made her more a part of the crowd, and all of her friends saw her as "normal".

She dated several boys yet never felt connected to them. Despite being highly intelligent, she did poorly in school. She failed almost everything, often appearing to fail on purpose. Her mind was so hyper-vigilant to danger and being exposed that it left no room for purposeful work.

Her father died and she retreated even further. Losing what felt like her last loving connection, she gave up on finding understanding or happiness or any sense of peace.

Finally, she acknowledged to herself that she was gay. That made her hate herself and feel responsible for the evil that had happened to her.

Eventually, we met. I was an older guy who made her feel safe. She knew that I loved her madly and she liked my kindness. I made her feel safer, more secure. She came to love me, although she knew that she was not "in love" with me.

For a number of years, we lived a relatively happy and simple life in a house filled with dogs, cats, our friends, and my family. She was busy teaching children; I was busy with the law and politics.

But she hated being dishonest. And she began to hate herself even more for her deception. Her desire to live an authentic life free of fear and dishonesty became overpowering in its intensity.

We built a weekend house in the country. This tranquil space reminded her of where she was tormented by the Dentist's Wife and the fear and the dreams intensified.

I found her on the couch one night when returning from a day in court. No lights in the house, no music, no movement at all. I thought she had fallen asleep. It took hours before I could get even a word out of her. Then the dam opened and she began to tell me this story.

We spent months and months in therapy. Sometimes I would believe that she could recover and resume a normal life, perhaps even with me. Every day when I would come home was different and challenging. She spent most of her time in the dark. No music. Staring into nothingness. Crying often. Speaking very little.

Then I came home one day and she was gone. Again, I thought she was asleep. Curled up on that same couch with the blanket she'd slept with as a child. Frozen on her face was a look of torment and sadness so haunting that, remembering it now, years later, still makes me weep.

She left the note under the empty bottle that had held the pills.

I can't force myself to share the note with you, but I still read it every day.

NEW ORLEANS

2001–2003

A Man for Others

St Ignatius Loyola

CHAPTER 20

Uptown is an elegant but rather staid part of New Orleans. Its streets are lined with massive homes, the people within those homes protected by wrought-iron gates and fences, as well as the privileges of wealth afforded to them by the city and its power structure.

The streets look as though they were bombed repeatedly during World War II and have yet to be fixed. This inept and benign government neglect has the benefit of keeping the speed of traffic through the neighborhoods to a crawl. Live oak trees over a hundred years old line many of those streets.

Century-old houses remodeled three or four times with the principal requirement that they be more functional without giving away that they've been remodeled line the side streets. Most have gardens which are filled with impeccable landscaping and flowers that fill the air with sweet fragrances that hang in the humidity like pungent perfumes.

Henry Clay Avenue, in the heart of Uptown, is best known for a sign painted and repainted on the street in the middle of its intersection with Garfield Street. Irregular letters spell out "Drunk Zone" to warn oncoming traffic of the presence of the DKE fraternity house on the corner opposite Tim Noland's house.

Tim Noland was one of the few defenders of the fraternity in the neighborhood. As he admitted often, "They are the only neighbor that behave more badly than me." Uptown New Orleans society venerates conformity yet pretends to welcome eccentricities. That pretense goes only so far. For most of his neighbors, Tim Noland was well over the line. In true New Orleans style, the complaints were spoken often yet politely, and couched in humor.

When weekends came along and both corner houses were in full party mode, the neighbors resented and complained about Tim Noland most for, as they said, "Most DKEs eventually outgrow their bad behavior and become leaders in the community". The Drunk Zone was regularly a passageway for visitors to parties on both sides to pass back and forth in a swirl of noise and laughter.

Tim Noland kept a thriving business for associates in his law firm, serving as an intermediary between the DWI and drug arrests of the young trustafarians and their parents. The youngsters were interested in tweaking their parents' sensibilities. The parents only cared that there would be no permanent record that left college with the arrestees.

Tim Noland himself had once prowled the halls of the DKE House during his time at Tulane Law School. He'd left Georgetown University without a degree due to an accident during his junior year abroad. Spending a few months in the hospital had left him hours short of his degree. Despite that failing, he'd had sufficient hours and an outstanding academic record, and was duly admitted to Tulane Law School. Since Georgetown had not permitted fraternities, he'd felt duty-bound to be a DKE pledge as a first-year law student, to "broaden his experience".

Tim Noland became legendary as DKE's social chairman. He once convinced the Irish Channel Marching Club to modify its St Patrick's Day route and do an unscheduled stop at the DKE house. The stop lasted four hours and ultimately resulted in nine arrests.

To this, day there is a plaque in the DKE house honoring its then-house-mother, Millie Johnson. Her defense, as the police arrived in force and were attempting to require the parade to move along, is immortalized on the plaque in the entrance hall: "One thing you gentlemens should know, there ain't a actual schedule to a N'awlins parade. And ain't none needed neither."

During one of the many suspensions of the fraternity by Tulane University, Millie was relocated by Tim Noland to become housemother in his new home across the street. She often said, "Ain't a hell of a lot different than before, 'cept da pay is better." Over the years, any woman who co-occupied "her" house for any length of time, including both of Tim Noland's wives, was treated kindly and welcomed with affection by Millie. But each was warned, "Oh, hell naw, you ain't cooking on my stove."

Despite having thrown himself headlong into the fraternity life, Tim Noland had distinguished himself at Tulane Law School. An editor of the Law Review and graduating with Order of the Coif honors, he finished second in his law school class. Upon graduation, he surprised one and all by ignoring the offers from the white shoe firms. Instead, he settled in with an ancient single practitioner in the area of criminal law, Milton Reese. Within three years, Reese died. Tim Noland had since run his own practice. He replenished it regularly with bright young associates, many of whom went on to distinguished careers.

Tim Noland's intellect and broad knowledge of finance and accounting had led him to become the preeminent criminal lawyer in the state, particularly in the area of white-collar crime. His trial skills meant he was in huge demand on personal injury cases that actually went to trial. His practice in this area was fed regularly by lawyers whose principal skill was signing clients and offering to settle. When settlement was not offered, they turned the actual trial over to Tim Noland, who often won outrageous sums for the client. Tim Noland had served on the panel of lawyers who ultimately settled the tobacco case for the State of Louisiana. A settlement which had left him a very wealthy man.

Despite this, his expressed preference was defending, as he put it, "real, hard-working criminals who admit that they are criminals, at least to me. Oh, and they have to be able to pay. Either in cold hard cash or publicity—either is coin of the realm to me." This is where his wheeler-dealer skills came to the fore.

Grace Garland loved the kaleidoscopic rainbow of moving colors created when the morning sun pierced the crystals hanging from an immense chandelier in the two-story open stairwell leading from the second-floor bedrooms to the large living area in Tim Noland's home. Her slender frame literally raced down the stairwell as the dance of light and colors sought to overcome her frustration. Last night had not gone well.

Reaching the bottom of the stairs, she turned toward the kitchen, the epicenter of Tim Noland's home. She found Millie at her stove. Pots were covering all burners on the stove. The smell of chicory coffee and baked goods improved her mood considerably.

Millie looked briefly at Grace, turned, and retrieved a cup and saucer which she filled with coffee and hot milk from one of the pots on the stove. Placing the coffee on the table in front of Grace, she said, "You want some eggs or juice, Gracie girl?"

Blowing over the top of the cup, Grace said, "What I'd really like, Millie, is some of your famous St Bernard Parish advice. But yeah, eggs would be nice."

Millie turned her rather impressively large frame toward Grace and said, "How 'bout a quick Benedict?"

"Ooh, that would be fantastic, Millie, but you don't have to go to this much trouble for me. I have to get to the paper pretty soon."

Millie popped four English muffins in the toaster, grabbed a small jar from the refrigerator, turned back toward the stove, and began the process of assembling Eggs Benedict.

She placed two plates covered with Eggs Benedict, one in front of Grace and one for herself, across the broad natural wood table that dominated the center of the kitchen. Pots of jam and honey fought for space among the newspapers and magazines strewn across the table.

Plopping down in the chair opposite Grace, Millie appeared to say a silent prayer. Then her thick pale right arm completed the sign of the cross, knife already in hand. She cut one of the eggs on her plate and took a bite, moaning with satisfaction. "Someday I'm going to quit eatin' all this foolishness. Prolly right after I get wider that I am tall. Uh oh, too late." she laughed.

They sat in silence eating until Grace asked quietly, "It's over, isn't it, Millie?"

After hesitating briefly, Millie seemed to choose honesty. "Well, Gracie girl, the part where you were pretending about being together forever is over for sure." Moving around the table and putting an arm around Grace's shoulders, she continued, "Tim, he likes his ladies, and he's honest and mostly kind to 'em, but he just don't seem to be able to hold it together with none no more. So you gots to decide whether you want to move on to dat 'just friends' part. Some can, some can't. For me, I hope you can, 'cause his friends never stop coming round and I love you, baby girl."

After a brisk walk down Henry Clay to the neutral ground on St Charles Avenue, Grace reviewed her notes on a story she was on her way to cover. She waited for the streetcar that would carry her downtown to work.

Stepping onto the streetcar, she settled into her seat, realizing that no longer riding down St Charles to work with Tim might be what she would miss most of the relationship now ending. The streetcar in New Orleans was a popular tourist experience, and many of its visitors piled into the cars later in the day. Earlier in the day, as the steamy heat rose in New Orleans, it was the preferred mode of a commute to the CBD for many along its route. Memories of those trips with Tim, where he was widely recognized and seemed to entertain the entire car full of passengers brought a smile to her face.

Knowing how much sadness Tim carried, and watching him switch on and off so often had left her confused. Once, when she had asked him about this ability, he had jokingly reminded her that "the key to the legal business is sincerity. Once I learned to fake that, the rest came easy". When he recognized that this answer had made her laugh and repelled her in equal measure, they had had a long serious discussion. He'd admitted that his jokes and acting ability were something he worked on seriously. In his typically lawyerly fashion, he'd said, "First, because it's important to be skillful in anything I do in my profession. Second, because in the ordinary practice of law it is about convincing people and that is easier if they like you. Finally, it's because I can never forget that my clients need me to do my best for them. Many are desperate." After some hesitation he added, "But, to be completely honest, it's more important to me that others like me than that I like myself. So being a phony on occasion is part of the deal."

Grace knew herself well. Despite vague hopes, she had always known that her time with Tim would come to an end. He was older and damaged in a way she could not really understand. She also recognized that her own ambitions left little room for others to be first in her own life. She prided herself on truth being uppermost, whatever the cost. "Reporter first" was what she reminded herself often.

It was how she had met Tim, and grown to know and love him.

CHAPTER 21

Nearly a year earlier, Grace was sitting in her small apartment on a Friday night watching the local news. The news promos had promised that it would cover the live return at the airport of a man accused of kidnapping a child in Baton Rouge.

The man had been coaching the child in some martial art when the parents had discovered that he was abusing the child. He had lured the child into his car and driven to California. The boy had been lost for several weeks until an anonymous tip had led the police in California to recover the child and arrest his kidnapper. It was a news sensation and Grace was trying to figure an angle to report on the case. She had done some research and met with people who knew the family in preparation for a meeting with her editor to pitch her story.

She was settling into the sofa when the news anchor announced, "After the break, we'll be going live to the airport, where our reporter, Phil Benton, will be on hand to show us the arrival of accused child molester, Dillon Antoine."

Grace moved quickly to the kitchen and poured more wine into her glass and was looking through her mail on the countertop when the news returned. The anchor segued to the live shot in the airport. Turning to watch, Grace saw a young, thin, bearded young man with a receding hairline in handcuffs and shackles shuffling through the gate, two Sheriff's Deputies holding his elbow on each side.

Leaning against a phone booth in the left corner of the screen was a man in a baseball hat hunched over as if he were on the phone and blocking out the sounds to hear his call. As Antoine walked nearly level to the man, he turned completely, stuck his hand holding a pistol to Antoine's head, and fired.

Evident on the screen amid the cacophony and jerky motion of the camera, the far side of Antoine's head spread out in a rapidly widening cone of blood and bone. Antoine collapsed out of the arms of the deputies and crumpled to the floor. The Deputy closest to the shooter turned and, with a look of anguish and astonishment, was clearly heard over the reporter's feed to say, "Ah, Jesus, Bobby why?"

Bobby Manthis, it turned out, was the abused boy's father.

By the next morning, Grace had convinced her editor to assign her to the story, knowing that readers would all be wanting the answer to the Deputy's question. She realized that the story would now turn to what would happen to the father and she wanted to follow that to its conclusion.

The initial sensation of this story died rather quickly. Bobby was in jail for less than a week before being released on bail. There was only mild and scattered outrage that the bail was set at a level rather low for such a serious offense.

Tim Noland, Bobby's lawyer, provided a compelling argument to the judge and later to reporters: "Well, it's not likely that Bobby Manthis will do that again. Whether it was a moment of madness or with intent, it simply isn't a situation that will recur, and thus he doesn't represent an ongoing danger to the community. What's left for us now is to discuss whether we go to trial and what the proper punishment is for a father who sought to protect his son and his family. I expect that we will meet with the prosecution and see what can be worked out."

A month later, Bobby Manthis went into court and pled guilty to manslaughter. He was sentenced to five years in jail which was suspended. He was also placed on probation and ordered to have mental health treatment for six months. In all, he spent less than a week in jail.

For her follow-up to the story, Grace had been able to get Tim Noland to agree to an interview. Part of the interview and some information he provided her, he required to be off the record. Under the headline, "A Man for Others", she described Tim's role in the Manthis case.

In her piece, Grace described Tim Noland as a product of Jesuit High School and Georgetown University, both Jesuit institutions. "A Man for Others" is an expression which is attributed to St Ignatius of Loyola, the founder of the Jesuit Order. Tim Noland revealed that being imbued with that philosophy by the Jesuits during high school and college had led to his dedication to those in trouble.

During the interview, Tim had very specifically told her, off the record, of the terrible abuse that the boy had suffered and the damage it had already caused the Manthis family. He acknowledged that the District Attorney was deeply moved by that evidence. Despite that, the DA had been prepared to go forward with a trial. What had changed the DA's mind is when Tim Noland had laid out his trial strategy to the DA. It is highly unusual for a trial attorney to give his strategy to his potential opponent. Tim Noland described it as a risk, but an acceptable one.

Tim Noland told the DA of his willingness to use what in the South is called the "He Needed Killing" strategy, technically called "jury nullification". Jury nullification requires a very skilled trial lawyer, as it is not permitted by rules of the court. Essentially, defense counsel must build a case against the actions of the victim of the crime, which results in a jury ignoring evidence when rendering the verdict. Tim Noland had shown graphic evidence of abuse to the DA that he was prepared to show to a jury. He was prepared to ask them what each of them would do if it was their child who had been abused in that manner.

The DA, as an elected official, realized he was in a no-win position. He was going to be required to prosecute someone with whom even the people in his own office admitted they sympathized.

Recognizing that in the skilled hands of Tim Noland, jury nullification was a winning hand, the DA folded. The really interesting part? Almost no one complained.

Two days after her article ran, Grace had gotten a phone call from Tim Noland asking her to join him at the Bon Ton for lunch. Very little of their conversation had revolved around the case. Instead, they had spent the time discussing their lives, and revealing themselves and their individual ambitions and frailties.

Seven hours later, they had found themselves walking hand in hand as sunset cast its spell on Audubon Park. After walking quietly for several minutes from the shaded path near the park's lagoon onto Prytania Street, they were surprised by the loud barking and excited behavior of a brown-and-white mixed-breed dog lunging against the cast-iron fence.

Grace was startled and leaned into Tim for protection. "Ah, don't worry, that's just my buddy, Buster," Tim had said as he walked over to reach a hand over the iron fence. The dog immediately stopped barking, and alternately slobbered on and rubbed the top of his head against Tim's hand.

Turning back and walking up to Grace, he placed a hand on each shoulder and looked at Grace as if searching for similar kindness. Then they agreed with a look and slowly joined hands to make their way back to Tim Noland's house.

It had been the beginning of one of the best years in Grace's life. Now it was coming to an end.

As Grace stepped off the streetcar at its Bayonne Street stop for the short walk to One Shell Square, she realized that it needed to be over. She was reassured by Millie's words that it could end in friendship. Tim Noland would always be an interesting, challenging friend. Mostly good memories, now just part of her life. She decided that she would tell him later at lunch.

CHAPTER 22

Lisa Sanders placed the phone in its cradle on her desk outside the office of Jay Giles on the thirty-fourth floor of One Shell Square. Surrounded by file cabinets and modular wooden furniture, Lisa was, as the name partner's paralegal, perched in the center of the activity of a very prosperous plaintiff's law firm.

The firm was best known for its advertising slogan: "G, H & B—With You All the Way". The slogan was seemingly on every other billboard along I-10 through New Orleans. Featuring an annoyingly corny musical jingle, the advertisement was played regularly during the news on the local tv and radio channels.

Lisa knew she might have to scramble to get everything organized and assignments handed out to the clerical pool before heading out for the walk to Galatoire's to stand in line. She was looking forward to her favorite part of the week, the bacchanal, which was Galatoire's on a Friday afternoon in New Orleans. That no reservations were taken at Galatoire's meant that someone had to be in line early to secure a table. Many in the line would be stand-ins sent by law firms, businesses, and judges to hold a place in the line.

The phone call with Grace had been upsetting, but had seemed inevitable to Lisa for some time. After commiserating with Grace briefly, they had agreed to continue the discussion in the line waiting to be admitted for lunch.

Giles was the lead partner in Giles, Hampton and Benson. He was also Lisa's part-time lover. Lately, Lisa felt that she had been relegated to a booty call in Giles's list. The affair, which had started two years ago during an out-of-town trial, had then blossomed quickly into full-blown passion. Over the past year it had now settled into comfortable and disquieting in equal measures. She knew that Grace's fate was her own. Perhaps this was the impetus she needed to stop what she knew was her own destructive behavior.

At thirty, Lisa knew that she was attractive, though most people thought she would be underestimating her own beauty using that term. Long black curly hair, green-blue eyes on a near-perfect face, with a lithe and athletic body. Tennis and long early-morning runs kept her fit. She was smart, funny, and ambitious, which were the characteristics that matched her well with her best friend, Grace. They shared everything about their lives and kept each other centered.

Perhaps it's time for me to start over as well, she thought. Time was passing for both of them and they had discussed whether it was time, as Grace described it, "to put away foolish things".

She heard the loud voice long before the shadow of Jay Giles fell onto her desk.

"Good morning, beautiful Lisa," Giles said, leaning over her desk, not looking into her face, but his attention drawn further down to the opening in her silk blouse.

"Jesus, Jay, is subtlety completely beyond you?" Lisa responded with a half frown, half smile.

"Ah, apologies, my sweet. But appreciating all of your gifts, your intellect, that beautiful face, your fierce loyalty, and your love, I'm still drawn like a fourteen-year-old boy to your beautiful bosom. As a bee to honey. Sweet, sweet honey, it is. My sincerest apologies." With a bow and a mischievous grin, he stood up straight, presenting his cufflinks and smoothing his suit.

Jay's rather corpulent body was stuffed in a handcrafted suit built to make him appear thinner and taller than reality. His highly stylized, black wavy hair topped a face that indicated an over-familiarity with strong whiskey and great food. The navy-blue suit, set off by a blue-and-white striped shirt with white collar, the bright yellow tie, and matching pocket square, were worn with the aplomb of a natural dandy. Lisa knew without looking that there would be a mirror shine on shoes that cost more than her monthly rent.

"Big day today, dear Lisa. We have pummeled the gangsters at Benevolent Insurance, and the final settlement has arrived. Another seven-figure day for G, H & B, and a happy client as well. Can you get with accounting and have them prepare a check for Tim so that we can present it with a flourish at lunch today?"

Lisa rose from her desk and, after straightening Giles's tie, slid past him, saying, "I better get going, then. Don't want to be late getting in line."

"Why don't you get one of the younger girls to go do that for you?"

"The weather is nice and I love standing in that line. Grace is meeting me early, so one of us will slip across the street for Bloody Marys. These are the best hours of the week for me: seeing the crazies on the street and finding out who is getting married in the bridal parties. I'll see you there after noon."

Patting her slender rear fondly, Giles said, "As the poets say: *A thing of beauty is a joy forever.* Try to get that first round table near the front window. That's where Tim loves to hold forth."

Grace Garland crossed Bourbon Street with two large plastic glasses full of Bloody Mary mix, straws, olives, celery stalks, and pickled green beans peering over the rim and threatening a spill on her pale blue silk dress. Her purse balanced on its strap over her shoulder as she wove her way through the mass of street musicians, hucksters, and pedestrians on both sidewalks and spilling into the street.

As she joined Lisa near the front of the line of people waiting outside Galatoire's, Lisa took one of the drinks from her hand, saying, "That dress is just stunning on you. You'll draw more attention than the boa ladies during lunch." With that, they both turned to the back of the line and gave finger waves to a group of women dressed immaculately with brightly colored feather boas wrapped around their necks. Some of the women were wearing fabulously ornate hats to match the boas. Laughter and loud conversation promised this large and attractive group of women would be in good form to draw attention from the men and provide entertainment all afternoon in the restaurant.

Turning back, Grace sighed and said, "Well, I guess I need to be ready to be out there again. Not really looking forward to lunch. I'm going to try to have a quiet word with Tim so there's no misunderstanding going forward. Don't think he'll take it badly, but I really want to remain friends."

As the door opened at eleven-thirty and the line of people walked through the door to secure tables, Grace said, "Hey, our music critic told me that Continental Drifters are at Tip's tomorrow night. There's supposed to be some hotshot studio musician opening. Let's make a weekend of it. Just like the old days, two New Orleans ladies sashaying, on the prowl again."

Clinking her cup with Lisa, Grace toasted with a grin, "Well, here's to those who love us, here's to those who don't, here's to those who fuck us, and fuck the ones that won't."

CHAPTER 23

Galatoire's main dining room had white starched cloths on each of its tables and was bright and cheerful. Black-and-white tiled floors lay between two walls predominated by mirrors. The wall facing Bourbon Street is filled with windows that provide much light and reverberant noise. During its long and boozy lunches, the walls encase and echo the sounds of jokes being told to raw laughter. Bons mots are highly prized and are told, then repeated for years. Shouts are heard and tears are often shed, but mostly the anger yields to remorse. More than one person realizes that alcohol is the fuel on which their anger burns, rather than some real or imagined slight or cutting remark. Apologies are made and accepted. Tears are wiped away and new toasts proposed. As with all life in New Orleans, the party continues.

The back of the room has two doors used by its waiters to enter and exit the kitchen. The buttery herb-filled smell of fresh bread and the fabulous cuisine exits the kitchen on each flap of the doors. Near those doors to the kitchen, there is a hallway and the men's room. Ladies are required to follow a stairway upstairs to attend to their makeup repair and other private matters.

Since Galatoire's does not take reservations, groups of people file into the small greeting area by the front door, where they are assigned a table. For those guests without what regulars think of as "My Waiter," a random waiter is assigned. The tables are continuously reorganized to accommodate a variety of numbers in the groups.

On most Fridays, the center of the room will be dominated by a table scrabbled together by smaller tables to banquet a large group of women celebrating an impending marriage, divorce, or sometimes the birth of a baby. Believing it their divine right, these women dominate the room, as they do all of New Orleans society. It is they who will provide the sexual tension and banter that is the centerpiece of a Galatoire's Friday afternoon. Trading comments with the denizens of this table is not for the faint of heart, which is why their primary suitors and antagonists are trial lawyers, writers, CEOs and others with more confidence than sense.

Grace and Lisa sat waiting for the others to join them at the round table immediately inside the room, next to the front windows. A short, stocky waiter with thinning hair and a tightly-trimmed mustache, dressed in standard waiter garb of white jacket, shirt, black pants, and tie, approached them with a wide grin on his face, and said, "Greetings, ladies. So nice to have you here with us again. How can I get you started? One to ten?"

John was Tim Noland's waiter and had been since Tim's father had first brought him to Galatoire's. John was famous in the city, known for first offering to tell what he called his "little stories", a number one you could share with your grandmother, while the number ten would embarrass most of the men at a duck camp deep in the marsh late at night.

Lisa replied, "Ah, hello, John, what a beautiful day. How about a five? And then, I'll have a Cosmo straight up. How about you, Grace?"

"Cosmopolitan sounds perfect, same for me. Okay, John, let's hear a number five," she said with a grin.

John leaned in between the ladies, as if to whisper, but in a normal voice, modified to take on a Cajun accent, he began, "You hear about how Boudreaux got lost in da Pacific Bayou? After six months, he finally landed in San Francisco. And, man, he was horny. So he got him a little gal at the cathouse. And he's going at it." With this, John made short punching motions with his fist, before continuing, "He looks up and says, 'Honey, how am I doing? Am I going too fast?' And the gal says, 'You doing about three knots.' Now Boudreaux scratch his head and say, 'What you mean I'm doing three knots?'" At this point in his story, John leant back, took the two napkins off the table, and with a flourish handed one each to Grace and Lisa, saying loudly, "And the gal looks him right in the eyes and says, 'It's not hard, it's not in, and you not getting your money back.'"

The ladies groaned and John whirled away, saying over his shoulder, "Back with the drinks in a minute."

Moments later, while placing an icy martini glass filled with pink almost-clear liquid with a floating lime peel in front of each of the ladies, John said, "So, Mr Noland is coming today? I can get a special order in for some nice appetizers that he likes so much. The crabmeat look really nice today."

"Ah, whatever you think, John, you know him better than me," said Grace.

The clicking of multiple high-heels on the tiled floor announced the arrival of the feather boa brigade, as the group of fifteen or so ladies entered the main room. One of the women peeled off from the main crowd and sat next to Grace, throwing her arms around her neck, and saying, "Gracie, I'm finally getting married! Can you believe it?" It was apparent that Sophie had already been celebrating prior to her arrival, so the words emerged with a slight slur.

"Oh, Sophie, I couldn't be happier for you. Phillip is such a lucky guy. You two will be the best-looking couple," Grace gushed while extracting herself from the death grip, and then added, "You know Lisa, don't you?"

"Oh, sure. Hey, Lisa, so nice to see you."

Lisa nodded as Sophie turned back to Grace, saying, "When are you and Tim going to tie the knot, Gracie?"

"Well, not today, Sophie. Oh, look. Mrs Peters is waving you over. Congrats again."

As Sophie moved back to the center of the room, Grace shook her head and looked at Lisa, saying, "Well, there's one benefit of the break. I won't have to answer that question for much longer."

Looking toward the door, Grace and Lisa saw a gnome-like man peering around the corner of the doorframe. "Oh, shit," said Lisa, "I should have known Jay would be bringing Norman."

Grace looked quizzically at Lisa, saying, "I thought his name was Milton?"

"Well, it is, but we've been calling him Norman ever since Tim told him that he reminded him of Norman Mushari, the sleazy lawyer from that Kurt Vonnegut book. Tim said Milton was the first lawyer he'd ever met who was of the same standard. Milton took it as a compliment, but, of course, he's never read a book outside of the law. A thoroughly disgusting creature is our Milton, but his lack of remorse and civility make him very effective in negotiations. He was born to play bad cop. You know how lots of lawyers volunteer to do pro bono criminal work?"

Grace nodded.

"Milton works for the prosecution in rural parishes on death penalty cases. Claims he's never lost."

The pear-shaped, extremely short man, with long greasy hair in a pony tail, rounded the frame of the door. He was wearing a white linen suit that looked as though it had been bought pre-wrinkled. He was trailed by Jay, whose loud voice heralded his arrival. Milton's feral eyes scanned the room, stopping for an unsettling look at the boa brigade. Jay gave the ladies only a brief glance and settled into a chair next to Lisa, saying, "In a garden full of flowers, you two are the brightest blooms." Turning to give Lisa a kiss on the cheek, he continued, "And you, dear, are the loveliest of all."

Norman settled in a chair with his back toward the room, which meant that he would have to spend most of the afternoon turning to ogle the boa brigade.

"Jay, you are so full of shit, but that is nice to hear. We ordered some appetizers. What time are we expecting Tim?" Lisa asked.

"Apparently he's got a sentencing hearing with Judge O'Neil this morning. Some pro bono work. Murder trial, which of course ended in a guilty verdict for the two knucklehead defendants. They shot poor Victor D'Allesandro on Canal Street in broad daylight in front of witnesses. Not much that could be done about that."

John arrived and placed a large, old-fashioned glass, filled with ice, clear liquid, and two olives in front of Jay. He turned to Milton and asked, "What can I get for you, sir?"

"I'll have the same," Milton said, to which John asked with mirth,

"Same as the ladies, or Mr Giles's choice?"

"Just bring me the gin, and you can leave out the wisecracks," Milton responded with a grimace.

Lisa turned to Jay and quietly asked, "Jay, can we go outside for a minute? I have something I need to tell you."

Hesitating only briefly, Jay said, "Certainly, love."

He stood and pulled out her chair, and they walked back through the door to the street. Grace couldn't hear what they were saying, but could see them through the window and guessed what was being discussed. It looked to her like she and Lisa would both, once again, be "Single and ready to flamingle", as the flamingo-embossed T-shirt sold on Bourbon Street advertised.

As she was reaching that conclusion, Milton turned back from staring at the boa brigade, which was now emitting laughter at steadily increasing decibels. He looked at her with contempt, saying, "So, I hear you're one of the hacks down at the paper? You enjoy that shit? Making everything about New Orleans so terrible."

Her voice laced with sarcasm, Grace responded, "Well, Milton, yes, I am a journalist and proud to be one. We don't make things about New Orleans terrible. We just report about facts and people. Some of the facts and some of the people, such as yourself, *are* terrible. So why don't you just fuck off and leave me the hell alone? Sit there and pretend to be a decent human being for as long as you can pull it off." With that, she sipped her drink, staring at him as his face turned scarlet.

Finally, he uttered a guttural grunt, then turned to look back at the boa brigade.

Grace sat quietly sipping her drink, watching Lisa and Jay through the window. Their conversation was becoming more animated as Jay appeared to be arguing in the same style he used in court: part pleading, part haughty lecture. Lisa appeared firm in her responses. Watching the discussion, Grace realized that, though it would be no real surprise to Tim, she would shortly be having a similar encounter. A part of her wanted Tim to resist and fight to stay together. Sadly, she knew he would not.

CHAPTER 24

Most of Galatoire's memories are of the conversations that take place, the laughter that flows, and the tears that fall. To Jay Giles's table on that day, their first memory would be of silent sadness in a room filled with happiness. Only a late turn of events and the inclusion of unexpected participants made it truly memorable.

Once Lisa and Jay returned, Grace walked outside to wait and meet Tim to discuss her decision before they joined the others for the meal. The realization that this group of people were going their separate ways cast a pall on the lunch. Stilted conversation, punctuated by rude remarks that bore no mirth from Milton, threatened to break up the lunch early. The presentation of the settlement check to Tim for his participation, which normally would have been a triumphant moment for all, did little to lift their spirits.

Tim Noland realized that Grace was making the right decision. Her fierce ambition and his distance and sadness was not a base on which to build a lasting relationship. There was so much of him hidden from view and he seemed incapable of bringing those feelings to the surface. Today was especially sad because he felt that he had failed both Grace and his morning's clients at the same time.

Jay appeared to be intent on quietly drinking his way to oblivion, finishing his fifth cocktail and signaling for more. He hardly ate a bite of the appetizers. Lisa and Grace chatted with each other, and Milton continued to stare in creepy fashion at the increasingly boisterous ladies at center table.

Finally, Jay turned toward Tim and asked, "So, Tim, what happened in court this morning? Did the sentencing go as you expected?"

Tim gave a big sigh, "Unfortunately, it went exactly as expected. Sometime in the next few years I'll be going up to Angola penitentiary to witness two truly stupid lives ending with a jolt of electricity. Jesus, the stupid bastards passed up thirty years to life that I had negotiated with the DA. He didn't want to press for the death penalty, but knew public opinion would be overwhelming once we went to trial. We could have gotten them put away, and if they had agreed, perhaps they would be out in twenty-five years or so."

Milton snorted. "Well, I for one am glad they get what they deserve. Evil little fucks."

Tim turned to Milton and said, "I'm sure that's how you would feel. I guess lots of people feel that way. They did something truly terrible, but they are so stupid. I can't help but think they had no more chance at life than they gave D'Allesandro."

Grace leaned over and put her hand on Tim's neck and rubbed it gently, "Ah, I'm sorry, Tim. You're such a good guy."

"Well, not good enough, apparently. I couldn't convince these two shitheads to plead. I told them that thirty years was the best they could ever hope to get." Tim shook his head side to side, then continued, "Listen to this. They convinced each other that they couldn't be convicted, because the cops never found the gun. 'No gun, not guilty,' they kept saying over and over to each other. Wouldn't listen to a word I told them. Finally, I got their momma to come sit with me to try and convince them to accept the plea deal. She cried; she pleaded. They finally snapped at her, 'Momma, no gun not guilty.' She got up and left without looking back."

Tim sat quietly sipping on his gin and picking in the bottom for the olive. He looked up and admitted, "I couldn't even get her to come to the pre-sentencing phase of the trial. When I called to ask her to come, she told me, 'I know you tried, Mr Tim. I tried, too. But dem boys just too stupid.

Like they daddy.' Turns out they will be joining their father up at Angola. It's a footrace with him to see who gets the chair first. This morning at the sentencing, the truly, truly stupid older brother stands up and yells at Judge O'Neil, 'You think you a badass, you white-headed bitch in your black dress' ... Unbelievable." Tim shook his head.

Once again, the table fell silent as John approached with three plates stacked down his arm and two in one hand. "Okay, how about some wine to go with this fish?" he asked, while elegantly placing the plates.

Tim said, "That'll be fine, John, but let's also keep the cocktails coming. Just pick out a wine for us." He turned his attention to the speckled trout almandine and placed a bite in this mouth. Looking up, he stood, patting his mouth with his napkin, and said, "Hello, Judge." Everyone at the table stood and turned to say hello to Judge Lawrence Emerson O'Neil, who was accompanied by a tall, powerful-looking man with a kind smile and penetrating eyes.

Judge O'Neil looked at Tim with sadness in his eyes and said, "Tim, terrible thing this morning, but justice requires us to occasionally do distasteful acts. Those times are what make me look forward to retirement." Turning to the man accompanying him, he said, "Let me introduce you to my friend, Theodore Dawes."

Greetings, introductions, and handshakes were exchanged, as Judge O'Neil and Doc Dawes moved toward the table set for two between Tim's large round table and another large table closer to the far wall. That table was occupied by a group of what appeared to be younger lawyers. They also stood and welcomed Judge O'Neil, who continued to exchange greetings with them, leaving his guest next to Tim's table.

Tim remained standing, and, grasping Dawes arm, asked him, "Are you from Mobile by any chance?"

Dawes said, "Well, yes. Why do you ask?"

Tim swept his arm over his group and said, "Ladies and gents we are in the presence of greatness."

Turning from Dawes to face the table, he recited from memory:

"The end of seasons,
stealing light, color, life,
yet providing serenity, knowing
life will change once more,
if not for me then for the seeds I planted—"

Dawes, with a broad smile finished the poem:

"I'm haunted by the question:
Did I plant the right seeds?

"I'm very pleased to meet you, Tim. Call me Doc," he said to the group. "All my friends call me Doc."

Reaching up to put an arm around Doc's shoulder, Tim said, "I love that poem, "A Glimpse of Winter", one of my favorites. I've only seen one or two others by you, have you published more?"

With a broad grin, Doc sat in the chair next to their table, leaning back, and said, "Well, Tim, I'm afraid that my family and profession leave me little time to write and I waste most of it on political writing. I have written one or two more, mostly dealing with what we all face, the absolute terror of life ending without knowing why or finishing what we set out to do. Whatever the hell that is for most of us."

"What are you doing in town today?" asked Tim.

"Deposition. My day job is that I'm a psychiatrist, and so I occasionally do expert witness testimony. I finished up this morning. Good chance to catch up with Lawrence. Also, a good excuse to come visit my daughter and grandchildren. Patty and I are also going to see one of my proteges at Tipitina's tomorrow night. Have you heard of Rob Coogan?"

"The soccer coach at Jesuit?" asked Milton. "God, I hate soccer—give me real football anytime. What's a soccer coach doing at Tipitina's?"

Appraising Milton momentarily, Doc dismissed him and turned to the rest of the table and replied, "One of the best musicians you'll ever see—brilliant melodies and completely poetic in his lyrics. He lived with us for a few years and was our club soccer coach. I do miss hearing him on the back porch at night, creating those wonderful songs."

"Yeah, so how come we never heard of him?" said Milton.

"Well, I could attribute that to a lack of knowledge on your part, but more likely it's because he's primarily a songwriter and studio musician. His choice, by the way." Looking with disdain at Milton, he continued, "I will say that anyone who has written and performed on more than a dozen top ten hits is someone you would know if you have any knowledge of music."

Lisa jumped in, saying "Doc, we are going to Tips, too. I thought the Continental Drifters were playing tomorrow."

As she said this, both Jay and Tim turned to look at the ladies, Jay saying, "We are?" With little hesitation, Lisa said, "Ah … no. I meant that Grace and I are going."

Both Jay and Tim looked crestfallen as Doc continued:

"Yes, Rob will be opening for them, so get there early. You know the Drifters are studio musicians mostly, so they know Rob well. I'm also trying to get Larry to come out of his shell for an evening. A chance to get that 'badass, white-haired bitch in the black dress' out for some fun."

With that, Doc's laughter began deep in his chest and grew in volume to dominate the main room of Galatoire's. Even Judge O'Neil smiled at this use of what would soon become his new moniker among members of the

New Orleans Bar. The name fit perfectly with his stern demeanor and tough sentencing reputation. Neither Tim nor Jay had ever fared particularly well in Judge O'Neil's courtroom.

CHAPTER 25

As often happens on these Friday afternoons, hours passed and the conversation at Jay's table seemed to merge with that of Judge O'Neil and Doc Dawes, who became part of the group. Grace caught herself staring at Judge O'Neil, after he insisted she call him Lawrence. Grace thought that he looked like what a Hollywood director would pick to play a serious and scholarly judge. His flowing white hair, aquiline nose, square jaw and deep tan set off his light blue eyes in an attractive way. Tall and thin, he had the erect posture of a man who took pride in how he presented himself to the world.

Grace knew she was feeling a strong attraction to this man and wondered if this would be another example where she was attracted to the mixture of sadness and kindness in others. That seemed to be a repeating pattern in her relationships.

In the midst of a boisterous argument at the other end of the table, O'Neil leaned into Grace and whispered, "Maybe we will see you at the show tomorrow. I've really enjoyed meeting you."

Grace surprised herself by responding without hesitation, "That would be wonderful—another reason to look forward to the show."

Nearing five o'clock, as the boa brigade left to seek more adventures elsewhere, John approached Judge O'Neil's table and asked, "Judge, we are doing the fried chicken in the back, you and Doctor Dawes want some?"

Every afternoon after four, as the lunch crowd thinned out, the staff fried chicken for themselves. They often offered it to the preferred and regular guests who were likely to stay for a while. Most of the serious drinkers would leave the restaurant as late as six or seven o'clock.

Standing up, Judge O'Neil said, "Sorry, John, not today. If I don't get Teddy back to meet Patty soon, she will skin us both." Turning to Doc, he said, "Perhaps we should go?"

Doc turned to Larry, saying, "Maybe just one more drink, Lawrence. Tim was asking me about a new bit of poetry I'm struggling with right now."

Pulling his chair between Grace and Doc, Judge O'Neil said, "Okay, John, you heard my friend. One more, but I'm cutting us off after that."

Settling back in his chair, Doc began, "So Tim, 'A Glimpse of Winter' is my weak effort at one of the pervading questions that trouble most of us later in life: Did I plant the right seeds? Did I affirmatively do those things that will bear fruit in a positive way for those I left behind? You'll recall the beginning of that poem is set in my garden." He began to recite in his deep and dramatic voice:

"Pondering my garden, as it reaches splendor,
sun shining, glistening, penetrating light
illuminating calla reds, iris yellows, hyacinth blues,
backdrop of many hued greens and clear sky,

rocks amid flowing and still waters,
air filled with impending summer,
yearning to see fall,
perhaps a glimpse of winter
that soon will envelope my garden.

The end of seasons,
stealing light, color, life,
yet providing serenity, knowing

life will change once more—

if not for me then for the seeds I planted.

I'm haunted by the question:

Did I plant the right seeds?"

There was sincere applause at Jay and Tim's table, joined by several of the men and women at other tables who overheard Doc's presentation. Grinning, he dramatically bowed and sat down, saying, "I have been thinking of the counterpoint to that question for a long while. Will we leave behind threats or problems we might have dealt with that will grow and threaten those we love? And perhaps that's a more important responsibility? What gave me the metaphor to ask this question is a problem I heard recently from a patient. A lovely, elderly woman recently widowed by a truly loving husband. He did everything right. Solid man, great reputation, left plenty of money and a lovely home. They had wonderful children. But he mishandled a problem that has come to haunt her. The woman who filled his life with such joy, now elderly, frail and terrified. You see, together they built and maintained a truly spectacular garden behind their home. It was off the back porch where they loved to sit and share conversations and cocktails each evening. Sometimes with friends, but mostly just the two of them. Those small moments that make life special and give it meaning. The garden was much better than my own, which was the inspiration for 'A Glimpse of Winter'. The centerpiece of their garden is an enormous and intricate Koi pond. It has a beautiful waterfall, rock islands and many, many floating lilies of yellows and pinks. For years her husband had become increasingly frustrated by the repeated incursion into the pond of a rather large cottonmouth water moccasin. The snake was ravenously eating the Koi fish, one day even waving a large silver gold beauty in the air above the water. That fish was his pride and joy. Finally, he had had enough of buying these expensive koi and began replacing them with regular, inexpensive goldfish. A reasonable solution. Of course, what he should have done was kill the snake and any others who wandered into his garden.

But he was a kind and gentle man, who thought that all of God's creatures should be allowed to live, no matter how deadly they are. Because the goldfish reproduce so rapidly, they provided the snake with a steady diet and it grew enormous over time. Quite a threatening creature, and for good reason. The air in the garden became redolent of cucumbers which is the odor given off by this type of deadly snake. The last time my patient visited her garden and looked at her koi pond, the snake was sunning on some rocks and bared its fangs to her. Of course, my patient was terrified. She abandoned her back porch and garden. She began to have nightmares that the snake was somehow entering her house and slithering under her bed late at night. Her husband's gentleness led him to leave behind a problem that filled his widow, a woman he cared for more than his own life, with terror. As my mother would say, kindness is a lovely attribute, but no virtue."

Doc shook the ice cubes in his glass and drained its contents, then said to Judge O'Neil, "Now, we must go, because Patty can occasionally fill me with as much terror as the snake when I misbehave."

Tim stood and addressed Doc, "Great meeting you. But hey, Doc, did you resolve that poor woman's problem?"

"Ah, that. Well, the last time Rob Coogan came over to visit I told him the story. Later that day Rob went by her house, found the snake and killed it. Told her that it was ancient tradition that when an Irishman got rid of snakes they never come back. Left her a St Patrick's medal to hang on the patio door."

Doc swirled the ice in his old-fashioned glass, picked the cherry from the bottom and popped it in his mouth, giving a satisfied smack of the lips. Then he laughed and said, "I called her when she missed her next appointment. She told me what Rob had done. Very politely told me everything was fine and I wasn't needed any more."

CHAPTER 26

Rob Coogan sat on a rather shabby leather chair, softly strumming his guitar in the dimly lit, small room that served as a green room for artists waiting to perform at Tipitina's. By the mid 1990s, the iconic New Orleans music venue had gone through many periods of uncertainty and changes of ownership. Named for Professor Longhair's iconic song, "Tipitina", the club regularly hosted music shows of up-and-coming musicians, many of whom returned after achieving fame throughout the world. It served as a home away from home for local college students, many of whom remained loyal to the club after graduating and beginning their careers in Louisiana.

Tonight's show would welcome an older crowd that might best be described as aging hippies gone mainstream. Lawyers, doctors, and professors at Tulane, mixed with the usual younger crowd of music fans, had come to see the Continental Drifters. The Drifters were comprised of fabulous musicians, most of whom were session players in the recording studios of Los Angeles. They had recently relocated from Los Angeles thanks to New Orleans natives Carlo Nuccio on drums and Ray Ganucheau on guitar and banjo. Tonight, they were expected to be joined by Peter Holsapple on keyboards and Mark Walton on bass, with Susan Cowsill and Vicki Peterson on vocals. This mix of talent had the anticipation levels of those filing into Tipitina's at a high level.

Rob was surrounded by several other musicians warming voices, and backstage folks tuning instruments and chattering about local music industry gossip and Louisiana politics. He was making notes and mentally working through the set list he would use for his performance tonight, but his mind kept wandering to last night, when he had been visited by Caoimhe.

Since he'd left Mobile, Rob had been visited by Caoimhe seven times. In her brief visits, she had told him what needed to be done. She advised him how to perfect a system to accomplish his work while escaping detection.

The palms of his hands had scars cut through the pads of each hand, reminding him of those times when he had failed to use gloves—a mistake he no longer made, though he continued to pray the rosary and then use it on each of his visits on behalf of The Children.

Last night was the first time that Caoimhe had come to see Rob without setting in motion something for him to accomplish on behalf of The Children.

He had awakened to her sitting on the side of his bed, running her fingers through his hair and gently singing what sounded to him like a Gaelic lullaby.

"Rob, I have a confession to make to ya. I must admit now that I have done wrong, something entirely selfish and only for myself. I wanted something that we faeries aren't permitted to have. When I saw you on that step, playing your music, I wanted you—to be mine and mine alone."

"Ah, Caoimhe, that's what I want myself. To be with you, to have children with you, to raise a family."

Caoimhe looked at Rob with a trembling lip and pools of tears in her ocean blue eyes. "And that, Rob, is my real shame. I put you under a spell, using my power to keep you safe, but also to keep you as mine alone. Even knowing that could never be." With that the tears fell onto Rob's hands, which held Caoimhe's face tenderly as he looked deeply into her eyes, seeking grace.

Caoimhe continued, "It is the work that matters, Rob. The Children. You and I cannot be; we never could. We live in different aspects of the same world. Even the timelines along which we live are vastly different. I'm not the same age as you. I am much, much older. Older even than your parents." Placing her hands on his forehead, she gently moved her hands to close his eyes, saying, "When you sleep tonight, you will no longer feel the same for me, and despite how I will continue to feel, you will never again sense that feeling from me. It is time for you to have your own life—the one you are entitled to have, with a family of your own. There is more risk in this, Rob, as you will no longer be as protected as you are right now. Only those times when we ask for your help will our protection from harm and capture be with you. If you take action on your own, you must be very, very careful."

Rob was surprised that after Caoimhe's visit he did not have a job to do on behalf of The Children. His vague recollection of the visit felt unusual, but comforting in a way he couldn't explain, even to himself.

He set about getting ready for his performance with a newly found enthusiasm. He knew that Doc and Patty would be at the show, and hoped that Marcelle and some of the boys would be there as well. He was thrilled to be ending his set in a combination with the Drifters as they were all fabulous musicians.

Tipitina's sound man, Nelson, and Rob had earlier finished the sound check for Rob's portion of the show. Nelson then turned to the mixer and outboard gear plan for the Drifters.

Most of the Drifters had just left after their sound check, but promised to be back in time to join Rob for his last two numbers, as he opened the show. Nelson sat in the corner of the room and lit a joint. The sweet smell filled the room until Nelson turned on a fan set up to pull the sweat-filled humid atmosphere from the room.

Though he didn't do a lot of pubic shows, Rob had remained busy writing songs for others and helping producers and musicians in their studio work. Royalties from his writing continued to provide him more resources than he had ever thought possible. His part-time work at Jesuit High School, with its soccer team and its budding musicians, balanced his life well. Rob felt that the last fifteen years, living first in Mobile and then in New Orleans, had been time well spent, but he now realized that the loneliness he felt would only be helped if he could find someone to share his life.

Walking past a small table covered with whiskey bottles, Popeye's fried chicken, grocery store potato salad, coleslaw, fruit and several sandwich trays intended to provide some nourishment to the performers, Rob left to enter the main room to see if the Dawes family had arrived. He stopped briefly at the bar near the back of the room and asked the pretty tattooed bartender for a beer. Looking at the stage with the backdrop mural of Professor Longhair hanging at the back of the stage, he felt at peace. Tip's had become a real substitute for his days at the Three Horses.

"Rob, you look good, dude, but you just got kind of a sad look on your face," said Julie, as she placed a beer on the countertop. "Anything wrong?"

"Ah, Julie, just thinking about my dad. We used to play together when I was a lad and I miss him every time I play."

"Is he back home in Ireland?" she asked.

"No, I'm afraid we lost him a few years ago. I was lucky enough to be with him when he passed away, though."

"I'm sorry to hear that. How about the rest of your family?" Julie asked as she leaned over the bar with a flirtatious look.

"Just me ma left back home. Don't see her much, not since the funeral. That was the last time I went home. She doesn't have much interest in coming over here." He laughed. "Told me last time we spoke that, other than me, America is of no interest to her."

"Rob, you mind if I ask you a personal question?" Julie said.

"Well, I'm not promising to answer, but go ahead."

After hesitating briefly, Julie leaned toward him and said in a whisper, "Are you gay?"

Rob looked startled, then laughed and said, "Now why would you be asking me that? What makes you think I might be?"

"Well, I've never seen you with a girl and you don't seem to respond to the girls here who flirt with you pretty shamelessly."

Rob laughed again. "So you're referring to yourself, are ya?"

Julie laughed out loud and said, "Well, I'm one of 'em, but there's plenty more I've seen over the last couple of years in here. So, are you? What's the deal?"

"Well first, no, not gay. But fair question. I guess I got stuck on someone back in Ireland and since then no one has seemed to measure up. I guess I hope to find someone, but it just hasn't happened."

Julie looked at Rob wistfully and said, "Rob, you have to look. Might be closer than you think." With that, she turned back to arrange bottles along the bar and gave a wriggle in her tight black jeans. She then turned her head and grinned, looking over her shoulder at Rob.

CHAPTER 27

Rob would usually focus on one woman in the audience when he was playing a love song and pretended he was singing to Caoimhe. Tonight, however, his eyes wandered through the crowd as he played his most famous song, "True". He grinned when he spotted Doc flirting with two young women standing next to him near the bar close to the entrance to Tip's. Patty punched Doc on the arm and Doc feigned innocence. Rob laughed along with the group standing near Doc.

"Eyes front, Theodore," said Patty to laughter from their small group. "It's bad enough that poor Grace has to be respectful to Lawrence and his foolishness, the girls shouldn't have to fend off both of you idiots."

Doc leaned down and reached his massive arms around Patty and said in his booming voice, "Ah Patty, I'm only practicing my sweet nothings for when I get you alone tonight." He added with a grin, "Besides, the white-haired, badass bitch is at a disadvantage without his black dress."

Grace and Lisa laughed out loud at Doc's comment.

"I'm sure glad we came tonight. This guy is fabulous. I don't think either Lawrence or Doc could drag her attention from the stage," Grace said to Patty, indicating Lisa standing near her side.

Lisa was transfixed by Rob on stage. His voice and lyrics had her spell-bound. She disengaged from the small group and asked, "I'm gonna go to the front bar and get some drinks. Anyone want anything?"

After rounding up an order, she slowly meandered toward the front, threading her way carefully through a packed crowd and never taking her eyes off Rob. *God, that man is beautiful*, she thought, wondering if Patty's description of what he was like in person could possibly be true.

Arriving at the packed back bar, Lisa nodded through the crowd at Julie, "Hey, Julie, this show is smokin'!"

Julie was scrambling around filling orders and yelled over the crowd lining the bar, "Hey, girl, that dude is so hot. I'm loving it. What do you need?"

"Take your time, JuJu, I'm gonna watch from here for a while."

Grace was listening carefully to the song and, when it ended, she turned to Patty and said, "I like that better than the original."

Patty nodded her agreement and said, "He wrote that song. He went to the same school as the band who first recorded it back in Boston."

Surprised, Grace said, "So he's from Boston? What's he's doing down here?"

"No, he's Irish. Some small town in Ireland, came over to go to music school and stayed. Coaches at Jesuit and works on a lot of recordings. He was my boy's soccer coach when he was going to Spring Hill to get an education degree so he could teach. He lived with us for a few years. Like one of my sons now," Patty said with a smile.

O'Neil arrived in the group carrying drinks in each hand, saying, "Gave up on Lisa and got us a new round." Handing out the drinks, he asked Grace, "You having fun?"

Grace planted a moist kiss on his cheek and whispered in his ear, "Fantastic, maybe you and I can have a quieter evening together?"

O'Neil whispered back, "That sounds wonderful. Soon?"

As he was handing out the rest of the drinks, Jay Giles unexpectedly joined the group. His face was sweating profusely and tinted red. His voice carried the thickness of drink when he said, "Good evening, Judge. Hi, Grace. Where's Lisa?" He nodded to Doc who introduced him to Patty.

Grace turned to O'Neil and said, "Soon."

To the rest of the group she said, "I'm going to find Lisa. Be back in a few."

Jay began to walk with her and said, "I'll go with you."

Placing her hand on Jay's chest and pushing slightly, she said, "No, I'll find her." Pushing him more firmly, she said loudly, "Jay, go home to your wife", and began winding her way through the crowd.

Arriving at the back bar, she nodded to Julie and leaned against the bar, watching Lisa. The band joined Rob and started a raucous rock number. Then they reached a point in the song where Rob took over with a solo guitar riff.

His face was luminous, sweat rolling down his cheeks. He seemed to have melded with his guitar, fingers flying, bending notes and creating sounds that wailed and cried with a passion and underlying sadness that transfixed the audience.

Looking around, Grace saw expressions of awe in almost every face in the audience, which had fallen almost silent, but was bouncing and swaying to the sound. As she turned back to watch the performance, she noticed that even the band members were shaking their heads in disbelief. Then she saw Lisa.

Standing next to the apron of the stage, she was looking almost straight up at Rob as he finished his solo, turned his back and slowly walked back to sit on the edge of the stool on stage. Lisa had tears streaming from her eyes.

As the band finished its song and Rob thanked the audience, Grace walked next to Lisa and said, "Come on, let's go."

Lisa appeared stunned and her look said *Are you kidding?*

“Jay just showed up, looks loaded. Let’s get out of here,” Grace said as she was dragging Lisa and walking over to the bar. “Hey JuJu, okay for us to slip out the side door? Some asshole at the front we don’t want to see.”

As she was placing beers on the bar, Julie said, “Been there, done that. Just tell Bobby I said it’s okay if he gives you any hassle.”

CHAPTER 28

October can produce days that seem like small miracles to New Orleans residents and visitors. The summer's oppressive humidity disappears and though the sun is bright in crystal blue skies, the air is cool and clears the senses. Even the post party odors of the French Quarter had receded on this Sunday morning in Jackson Square.

Wrapping her arm through Lisa's and leaning into her as they navigated through the crowd heading toward the Cathedral on the Square, Grace's voice was scratchy and deep, "Oh, God, girl. What the effen hell were we thinking? Do we think we're still twenty?"

Glancing at the Cathedral entrance, Grace made a Sign of the Cross and said, "Jesus forgive us for we know not what we do." She hesitated, then added, "But I know one thing. We violated Grace's first law of a night out drinking."

Lisa responded with a half groan and half laugh, "Ah, Lisa's First Law: Whenever shots seem like a good idea, it's time to go home. But no, of course, not us. What the hell were we doing? Sambuca? Seriously?"

"And it all started with your toast to our sudden escape from coupledom," Lisa continued, "but thank you for the save, an amazing escape."

Grace slipped her arm out of Lisa's, grabbed her hand and started skipping toward the smell of coffee and beignets drifting toward them from the Café Du Monde.

Arriving in the small line by the entrance, Grace turned to watch the small street band playing in a very lively fashion. Trumpets, trombones, guitars, a single snare drum, and a bass drum for emphasis allowed the instruments to blend into an uplifting melody that was the essence of New Orleans music. The singer's raspy voice, strongly reminiscent of Louis Armstrong, carried the tune along nicely.

As they were seated in the outside area under the green canvas awning, they settled into a small table facing both Jackson Square and the band, with several tables between them and the wrought iron fence that defined the seating area.

"Perfect," said Grace. "Two cups of café au lait and a large order of beignets," she said to the waiter, dressed in the Café du Monde's required white coat and shirt with a black bow tie.

"Ya'll want more sugar on the beignets?" the waiter asked.

"Oh God, yes!" Grace nodded her assent.

After the waiter brought their coffee, Lisa sprinkled the beignets with additional powdered sugar. They powdered their shirtfronts almost as liberally, as they ate the beignets and watched the band play.

The band began the song "It's a Wonderful World," and they sat quietly, appreciating the day, the beautiful weather and the sounds and words of the song. The combination began to lift their spirits and reduce the effects of the previous night's excess.

"Finally," Lisa said, raising her coffee cup to toast, "How does it go again?"

Grace grinned, clinked her cup to Lisa's and began:

"Here's to the men that we love. Here's to the men who love us.

But the men that we love

aren't the men that love us.

So fuck the men and

here's to us."

The women laughed as the waiter returned to refill the coffee.

The outside area of Café Du Monde filled, emptied, and refilled with people enjoying the idyllic day and the music accompanying coffee and beignets. Only the table next to theirs, closer to the band and the Square, was currently empty.

As they started their second cup of coffee, a man with a bright red face, rusty thinning hair, who appeared to be carrying two hundred and fifty pounds on a five-foot-six-inch frame, sat at the table with his back to them. The man was loudly humming the song being played by the band. He was dressed in absurdly large red soccer shorts, white jersey with a blue number nine on the back and wore knee-length blue socks with Adidas sandals. The most unlikely figure of a soccer player the women had ever seen.

When the waitress returned with his coffee and a large plastic glass of water, the man drank the entire glass of water in one gulp. He poured sugar seemingly endlessly into his coffee cup, stirred it and drank a sip with a delicate smack of the lips.

Adjusting his chair to turn so that he could face the women, he peered at them, leaned back in his chair, and, with a twinkle in his eye, said, "I know what it is you're thinking, you know."

Grace took the bait and said, "Oh, and what is it we are thinking?"

"You took one look at me and you started wondering: *How does that magnificent son of bitch get around a soccer field?* Now go on, admit it. Admit it and I'll tell you something you don't expect. Oh, and I'll address one of you by name."

"You will, will you? All right, you got us, that's exactly what we were thinking. We can't see you running around a soccer field," Grace said with a puzzled half smile on her face, while Lisa laughed out loud.

The man turned his chair to face them fully, sipping his coffee. "Well, Grace," he said, smiling and emphasizing her name, "I don't. Run that is. None, no running for me. My running days are behind me, though they grow in legend, like my ass." He laughed, pointed his finger skyward to emphasize his point, took a bow and said, "However, I remain a scoring machine. Which is why my over-forty team continues to put up with me. I stand in the penalty area, and if my teammates get the ball anywhere near me, I score. Goaaal!" He laughed out loud and stood, waving his hands in the air and doing a small dance. Sitting back in his chair, he continued, "They get especially angry because I refuse to play defense altogether. Makes the game a real joy for me." He slid his chair over to their table, reached out his hand to Grace and said, "Smile, Doucet."

"Dammit," Grace said, "I should have recognized you. Lisa, this is one of New Orleans' finest. Detective Doucet, this is my friend, Lisa Sanders."

"Nice to meet you, Smiley."

"Ah, no, Lisa, not Smiley, Smile. No Y. Got two sisters, Cheer and Joy, one brother, Grin. Oh, and a slightly mad mum and dad." He laughed again. "I see you girls have one beignet left. You planning to eat it? Or can I add it to my pregame meal," he said as he snared the last beignet off the white saucer, jammed it into his mouth, smacked his lips and licked his fingers, his jaw, neck and the front of his jersey covered in powdered sugar. "Grace, you're not always appreciated among my fellow officers, but it seems to me you seem to keep most of your stories pretty close to true. At least the ones I know about. That's pretty rare for our esteemed local news coverage. I met you very briefly at the press conference the Mayor had last year on that child murder. Terrible thing any time a child gets killed. Especially like that. Pretty cool, though, that the murderer ended up getting some of his own medicine."

Grace asked, "Did y'all ever figure out who killed the murderer? He gets bail, which was an outrage, then killed two days later. That was pretty big news for a while. Seems like it just faded away."

"Ah, always looking for a story, eh? We looked into it pretty hard for a while. Not much evidence. No prints, no other real evidence. Looked like he was garroted in a kneeling position, neck sliced through to the vocal cords, although we never shared that with the public. The official position is that it's still considered an open case. I'd be lying if I told you anyone gave a shit whether we find his killer or not. See what the mayor didn't tell the public is that we are pretty sure this wasn't the first kid that bastard killed. We suspected him of at least two others. Whoever killed him did all of us a favor."

Lisa looked at Smile curiously and asked, "Where you from? You've got sort of an accent I can't place."

Smile laughed. "Born in Houma, raised in Scotland. My dad was oil field trash and proud of it as they say on the bumper stickers. He worked off shore oil rigs in the Irish Sea. I grew up along the northern coast of Scotland. Bitter fucking cold. Wonderful people. Playing soccer was what we did all the time while I was growing up. Nothing much else to do. I'm a guy from Houma, Louisiana, who doesn't understand American football and could care less. And that, ladies, is why I'm so frickin' awesome." He laughed. "Hey, you girls married, engaged, or anything?"

Both women giggled and gave each other a look, before Grace answered, "Not currently, why? Are You?"

"Oh, yeah. I've got the old ball and chain firmly attached. No, no, I've got a friend meeting me here. Pretty good guy. He's at mass over at the Cathedral and should be along shortly. I'm just trying to help him, you know, maybe find somebody?"

Lisa and Grace hesitated, and finally Lisa responded, "Well, Smile, thanks, but that kind of thing doesn't really work very often, does it? Thanks, though, but I think we are going to shove off in a few."

"Oh, okay. We are heading to our match out at the park in a bit, so he should be along shortly. Maybe you can just say hello."

Over the coming years, they would all think back to this conversation and this moment. What began on a pleasant Sunday morning as an ordinary conversation over a cup of coffee suddenly became the kind of glue that binds people together over a lifetime.

Almost as one, the people in the Café Du Monde and the Plaza heard, then saw, a screaming terrified woman. She was being pushed down a walkway from the Riverwalk to the level of the Café and the Plaza. The Riverwalk runs along to the top of the levee, parallel to the Mississippi River. The woman had a baby in her arms and she was being pushed and prodded down the ramp by a man holding what looked like a double barrel shotgun.

Band instruments stopped playing one by one as recognition spread, with the song becoming unrecognizable. Finally, there was just the one snare drum beating a few extra beats, then it, too, stopped.

The enraged man's screams were nightmarish in their intensity and his rage aimed at the woman was terrifying to all who watched. Later, people would recall feeling frozen in place. Sick. Filled with terror.

Smile surveyed the scene, looking for other police officers and spotted two horseback officers on the far side of the Plaza. *Thank God. Someone will call this in over radio*, he thought as he turned back toward the scene.

While turning, he saw a figure he recognized running through the Plaza at top speed toward the perpetrator holding the shotgun. It appeared the runner was partially hidden by a large oak tree between the ramp and the plaza as he sped toward the couple.

When the runner finally rounded the tree and was five or six feet away from the couple, the man holding the gun pushed the woman and baby to the ground, then turned to face him. The runner launched in the air toward the shooter as he swung the shotgun toward him in the air.

CHAPTER 29

As the shotgun blast reverberated, people scattered, dove under tables, crouched, and lay down in the crowd. Smile climbed over the wrought iron fencing and took off at surprising speed toward where the gun had gone off during the collision.

He arrived to find the shotgun had been knocked from the madman's hands in the collision. The gun lay on the sidewalk. Smile picked it up, opened the breech and removed the last shell, then tossed the gun back to the sidewalk.

Reaching down to the dazed perp lying on the ground, Smile bent his arm behind him, placed him face down and put one foot on his hand behind his back. Two other police officers arrived, and one used his hand cuffs to finish securing the perpetrator. One cop held the perpetrator, while the other knelt next to the woman who had been terrorized and talked to her quietly as she clutched the baby tightly to her chest and cried.

Smile turned to his friend, who was lying supine on the ground. He turned him over and looked for any damage, saying, "Rob, you crazy bastard. That was truly stupid. Are you okay?"

Rob Coogan opened his eyes slowly, rubbed his head gently, and pulled back his hand to reveal blood that was leaking from his scalp. He smiled and said, "Good thing he's not a better shot, although he did manage to clip me head with the shotgun."

Smile reached down and grabbed Rob's hand and helped him to his feet. "Looks like no game for us today. We can't be having you get blood all over the ball. Come on, we'll go sit down for a bit. We can have someone patch up your head. Then I'm sure that someone from the district will want to interview you."

As Rob and Smile approached the table where Smile had been seated, Lisa turned to Grace and said, "Oh my God. That's him."

Grace turned to look, asking, "Who?" As recognition hit her she said, "The guitar guy from last night."

As Smile and Rob sat at the table, Smile said, "Now, ladies, I promise that we did not prepare that entrance, but this is the friend I mentioned. Rob Coogan."

Rob winced as Lisa sat next to him and placed a water-soaked napkin to his scalp and patted blood out of his curly black hair.

"Does it hurt?" Lisa asked.

Rob took in Lisa's wavy lustrous black hair and magnetic blue-green eyes, and said, "I saw you last night."

"Yeah, I was there. Love the songs and the way you play is amazing. I'm Lisa. Lisa Sanders."

"Well now, Lisa Sanders, I'm Rob Coogan. I appreciate the compliments and all, and thanks for working on me noggin."

Grace sat next to Lisa and said, "Hi Rob, I'm Grace. Do you mind if I ask you a few questions?"

"Careful, Rob, she's a reporter," joked Smile.

"Rob, I think we all want to know this. I know my readers will. What were you thinking? What caused you to rush in and tackle that man?"

Rob responded, "I wasn't thinking at all. Just reacted to what I saw."

"Did you know he had a gun?"

"Well, sure, I saw it, but the tree afforded me some cover, so I figured I had the best chance of helping. He didn't see me 'til I was almost on top of him. I was worried about the baby getting hurt."

“Me ma always told us, ‘Run from a knife, but toward a gun.’ You can avoid a gun if you’re quick enough and agile in your approach. Fella can always nick you with a knife, no matter how crafty you are. Besides, that fellow wasn’t right in the head. He sure looked to be killin’ that baby and the woman holding him. Someone had to do something. It just fell to me, is all.”

Grace said, “Rob, I’m going to go inside and call the paper and ask them to send a photographer over. Would that be okay, to take your picture?”

“Well now, Grace, I’m not sure that’s necessary—you’ll just be making something bigger than it really should be.”

Grace grabbed Rob’s hand and said, “Rob, it’ll help me out at the paper. I can get a good byline with this story and it’ll be featured more prominently with a good picture of you and perhaps the woman and her baby. Can you sit here for a bit with Smile and Lisa?”

Rob looked once again at Lisa and his face seemed to light up with a glow. “Well, sure then. That’ll be lovely,” he said as Lisa held the wet napkin to the wound on top of his head and wiped his face with another. Rob and Lisa appeared to be lost in an exchange of looks between them.

Grace looked across them to Smile and traded grins with him to acknowledge that they could both see what was underway.

CHAPTER 30

Rob's eyes opened when he heard the first set of knocks on his front door. Now, by his count, the knocks had been repeated five times and they weren't lessening in their intensity. Rolling his feet to the floor, he started to stand, then turned to look at Lisa laying in the bed, her blue-green eyes with a smile on her face as she gazed into his eyes. She raised her arms above her head, grasping her hands together, then languidly stretched her lithe, body in the bed next to him.

Rob pulled back the sheets then lay back down and began kissing her neck. He moved downward between her small but perfectly formed breasts, the nipples taunt with excitement, and gently kissed her with soft butterfly kisses. The front door knocking had stopped and Rob was caressing Lisa and lightly tracing along the contours of her stomach with the back of his fingers, when the taps on the bedroom windowpane started, and were followed by a man yelling, "Rob, I know you're in there. Come to the front door."

Groaning, Rob stopped his ministrations and said quietly to Lisa, "I'll be right back." Pulling on a pair of jeans and a T-shirt, he padded to the front door, removed the chain, and pulled it open.

Smile Doucet, dressed in soccer gear, walked through the doorway and said, "Where in the hell have you been? No one has seen you in over a week."

Laughing, Rob said, "Well, strictly speaking that's not true. *You* haven't seen me, sure, but I've been seen."

"Rob, I called Father Billy at the school on Thursday and he said you hadn't been there for either your music halls or soccer practices this week.

He told me you'd called in and couldn't make it this week. I've been pretty worried. Is your head all right?"

"Oh sure, it's fine and all. I've just had some things to deal with this week."

"Okay, good then, come on, get ready. Our match starts in an hour." He grinned. "You know you need to think about someone other than yourself. I need you to get me the ball. If you don't show, I may have to run and that won't work at all for me."

Hesitating, Rob stammered, "Ah, maybe I ought to sit out this week. My head and all."

"What are you? A pussy? Come on, get dressed and let's go! We have to get out to the park."

Rob walked into the kitchen area off the living room and said, "You want some tea or a bit of coffee?"

Lisa, walking out of the bedroom hallway in a pair of shorts and a T-shirt, with bare feet said, "Yeah, some coffee sounds good. How about you, Smile?"

Recognition showed in Smile's face and he said, "Oh, okay. Now I get it. You two have been banging each other's brains out? Is that right?" Without waiting for an answer, he continued, "Does that mean you can't play today? No break from the business at hand? Jesus, you'll probably be worthless anyway. I don't think you can play with that shit eating grin on your face."

Smile sat at the small round table in the center of the breakfast area and said, "I guess I'm out today, too, then."

Lisa walked over and sat in the chair next to Smile and said, "Aw, come on, big man, let's get going. I bet Rob will go if you ask him sweetly."

"You ask him sweetly, Lisa. It looks like he'll do whatever you want," he said, looking directly at Lisa as Rob put two cups of coffee in front of them. "The detective in me is dying to know something."

Looking from Rob to Lisa and back, he asked, "Did you come straight here last Sunday?"

Lisa said, "Well sure—we had to get Rob's head cleaned out and a bandage on it."

Turning to Rob, he said, "What day did you leave the house after that?"

Rob's face turned red and he shuffled about the kitchen, fussing with the cups, the hot milk pan, and the hot water pot with which he made tea for himself. Turning back to face Smile, he said, "Well, I'm not sure about that."

"Not sure what day? Did you see Tuesday's paper?" Turning to Lisa, he said, "Your girl, Grace, is a hell of a writer. She got the atmosphere and the events just right. Don't often see that in stories here locally. Big story, our boy here features prominently. 'Local Hero Saves the Day', or some bullshit like that."

Lisa laughed so abruptly it appeared to Smile that coffee might come shooting out of her nose. Then she said to him, "Well, strictly speaking, it's not that we can't remember what day we left the house."

Turning to Rob, Smile had a look of incredulity on his face. "You … You … For a guy that I can hardly ever remember having a date, now you lure some beautiful woman to your house and you don't let her out for a week?"

Lisa put her hands on her hips and gave Smile a saucy grin. "Smile, I was hardly captive and, as folks on the bayou say, you've stopped preaching and gone to meddling now. Let's go to the park so I can see whether either one of you lives up to your vaunted reputations. Maybe I'll call Grace and see if she wants to meet us there."

CHAPTER 31

Lisa and Grace had never been to Lafreniere Park, as it was out of their usual haunts. The park was surrounded by commercial strip malls and suburbs in Jefferson Parish, a bedroom community of New Orleans. Driving into the park, they had been surprised by its enormous size. There appeared to be dozens of baseball, softball and soccer fields, ponds and walking areas. On a beautiful Sunday in October the park was filled to capacity.

Families were picnicking on every piece of open grass, people were walking dogs, pushing children in carriages and sitting on benches reading the Sunday Times Picayune. The weather was spectacularly cooperative as a cool breeze offset the bright sun.

After consulting a map at the entrance, Grace wound her car to a lot near the back of the park, where they parked. They grabbed a blanket and two grocery bags with their own picnic supplies and walked past a small pond filled with geese and ducks surrounded by people feeding them bits of bread. The geese were so tame that they often came close enough to the children who would squeal with delight as the birds took the food from their hands.

Winding their way among several soccer fields, they found a spot next to the field where Rob and Smile's team, wearing their bright red shorts and white jerseys, were playing. They spread the blanket and each got a beer from one of the bags and settled down to watch.

Within minutes later, a woman walked up next to them with two young boys tugging at her shorts. The thin woman, her dark hair cut short, was wiping something from her blue T-shirt. She looked at them and tentatively said, “Lisa? Grace?” When they nodded, she said, “Hey, I’m Smile’s wife, Billie Jean.” As she continued to wipe her shirt, she saw the two looking at her, and said, “Aw, don’t mind that, it’s just vomit. Boys, ugh.” Indicating the two, she said, “Zeke and Zach. Boys, say hello.”

As the boys dipped their heads and mumbled a greeting, Grace jumped up and said, “Nice to meet you. We love us some Smile. Want to sit with us?”

Billie Jean turned to the boys and said, “You guys go play, but stay in sight. Mommy’s going to visit with these ladies. Don’t go too far.”

The boys took their soccer ball and walked behind the goal, where they mixed with others of similar age in a cluster of activity that resembled a scrum more than soccer.

Lisa cleared a space and patted it for Billie Jean to sit. “Hey, you want a beer?”

“God, yes,” said Billie Jean, as she sat, “I usually stop and get a daquiri from the to-go place out front of the park, but the boys were being a pain. Thanks. Not quite as exciting as last Sunday, but it’s fun watching these idiots pretend they are boys again.”

“Are they any good?” asked Lisa.

“Well, I’m no expert, but Rob is fantastic according to everyone. And my Smile can score goals, but he’s so frustrating to everyone. He won’t run more than five yards. In truth, Smile won’t do anything he doesn’t want to do. I just hope they don’t get hurt; these old folks leagues sometimes have guys dropping like flies. They may think they’re kids, but their bodies know better.”

Grace saw that Lisa’s full attention was on the field, watching Rob.

Rob had the ball at his feet and seemed to be slaloming through a group of opponents from midfield toward goal. As he approached the goal, he veered right toward the corner of the field. Just as he was nearing the end line, with a defender between him and the goal, he stopped, stepped over the ball, which stopped the defender, then continued toward the end line. He quickly chipped the ball toward the middle of the penalty area. Smile took two quick steps to lose his defender, then met the ball with his chest. The ball dropped to the ground and on the bounce, he struck it fiercely into the top roof of the net.

Smile jogged briefly around the field, waving his hands in the air as if hearing the applause of thousands. Rob gave him a high five as they trotted back toward the middle of the field.

"And that's why his team puts up with Smile's bullshit," said Billie Jean. "Kinda like at home. Just when I get fed up completely, he does something that makes me realize." She hesitated and looked at Lisa and Grace. "Well, just that he makes me know … Ah, if you need someone when it really counts then you won't find a better man than him."

Grace realized that she had never had someone like that in her life and that she couldn't see anything happening in her life that would change that any time soon. O'Neil was interesting, but it didn't look like that would last long. Her breakup with Tim, still fresh in her mind, had rekindled thoughts that her career would have to suffice. Thus far, no one in her life had offered that kind of love and security. She wasn't sure that any relationship would ever take precedence over her career. Or if she wanted it to. She thought of herself primarily as a reporter—that was her measure of herself. She was driven by the need to succeed and to achieve recognition for her success.

Looking at Lisa, she realized that a good professional life might not be what her friend wanted. Even after leaving Jay Giles practice and becoming a paralegal for Tim Noland, it appeared it was a job, not a career, for Lisa. She had never before seen the look in Lisa's eyes. *So that's what happy looks like*, thought Grace.

Lisa was on her feet, yelling for Smile, who took a bow and blew a kiss toward Billie Jean. He trotted over to the sideline and said, "That was for my bride. The Eighth Wonder of the World." Laughing, he walked back to the center of the field.

Rob was watching Smile, and he saw the interaction with Billie Jean and laughed out loud. He looked back again at Lisa and smiled.

CHAPTER 32

After returning from the park and one of the best days he could remember, Rob leaned over to remove his sandals and socks and he laughed out loud. The first sustained joyous laughter he could remember. It got him thinking that the last week had brought him more happiness than he had ever known in his adult life.

Then his gaze caught the nearly black stone top reflecting the table lamp's image and glow, causing the guitar string rosary to sparkle. The view made him realize that abandoning his other responsibility, to serve God and protect children, was something that he could not contemplate and would never do. He knew that he had made a vow that he could never abandon but couldn't he be happy too?

He knew that to be fair to Lisa would require complete honesty on his part. He wondered whether he could do that, to share those parts of his life that he had hidden from everyone else? He wanted to but he realized that if he couldn't now he might never do so.

His mind drifted back to Caoimhe's visit the night he played at Tipitina's. He had wondered why she had come to him that night leaving no direction for his work on behalf of the Children. Then her words from that night became clear. He was free and yet no longer as protected.

Rob knew that his obligation to God to help Children created a conflicting priority with having a true and lasting relationship which would increase the risk to him.

It would likely be difficult for Lisa to understand his motivation but he knew he had to try.

He began hesitantly, "Lisa, I have this feeling … and I know it's going to sound crazy … or too soon … but I hope, no, I feel, that you are going to be a special part of my life. Please know that it isn't easy for me to share who I am with anyone. I've been on my own for so long. I generally hide me feelings in the words of my songs. With you I want to be different, to be a better man. I know we must share with each other our deepest fears and feelings if we want to build a lasting relationship. And I do want that. So, I really want to get to know you and for you to get to know me. I want you to know who I really am and what is important to me. I want to know what means the most to you. I've seen in me own parents that people don't always get that right, owing to never really knowing what was in the heart of the other person."

Lisa walked over to Rob sitting on the sofa and slid into his lap. "Rob, what I know is that you are really sweaty." She smiled, wrapping his neck with both arms, and continued, "This week has been amazing, but it's not real."

Rob looked at her, humiliated, she giggled and continued, "Don't get me wrong, I like everything I know about you so far, and I love jumping your bones." She laughed out loud, then said, "But it will take time to know each other or whether this is just chemistry, the heat of the moment." She nibbled on Rob's neck. "Tell me about your family," she said. She immediately felt Rob's body stiffen as if in pain.

"There is only me and me mum. She lives in Ireland still. I'll probably never get her to visit here and I've only seen her once in the last twenty years. At me da's funeral. That was the last time I went home. While I was in school back in Boston."

"You don't want to go back to Ireland, at least to visit?"

Rob looked away, "No, there's nothing for me there. Sure, I'd like to talk to me maw and see how she is getting on, but that doesn't seem to be something she would be looking for from me. We write every once in a while. My ma has spent her life involved in the Republican cause, you know."

"Republican? Like the party here?"

Rob's grimaced, "No. Not at all like here. It's all part of the cause to unify Ireland with the North. Bitter, hateful conflict that's been festering for years. You've probably heard it called 'the Troubles'?"

"Sure, I think so."

"Well, that's been me ma's life really. Her bitterness traces back for centuries in our family. You've heard of the IRA?"

Lisa said, "Oh, that's the terrorist group, right? The ones with the bombs?"

"Ah, therein lies the rub, to quote the Bard."

Lisa looked confused.

"Well, you see, Lisa, a conflict like the Troubles is viewed by different people in different ways. I wouldn't really consider me ma a terrorist, but most on the other side would. From her perspective she is a patriot. She's a Provo."

"A Provo?"

"Provisional wing of the Irish Republican Army. The ones with the bombs and the guns. Now not meaning to take a side by that description, as I know that both of me grandfathers were shot by British troops in cold blood. No cause other than they wanted to practice their religion, and the Brits wanted their land. At least that's what was told to me. I always heard that mum taught firearms and bomb construction to the Provos. I know she used to hide and train troops that came in from the North. A fierce warrior me mum. Scary really."

Rob seemed lost in thought, a troubled look on his face. He lifted Lisa gently and slid her over onto the sofa, then stood and stretched, paddling across to sit facing her from a leather chair, before continuing, "About a year after me father died, I really hadn't heard much from her. Then one day I got a fat envelope from her. I ignored it for a day or so, but then finally, one evening, I had a couple of beers and a shot or two of the Jameson and sat in this chair to read the letter. See, I was hoping she would tell me more about me dad. All boys want to know about their father's history, what kind of man he was before he was being their father.

"Well, the letter started brilliantly, '*He was a great man. One of the greatest that Ireland has ever produced and they will be singing his name forever.*' It took me only a few more lines to realize that she wasn't writing to describe me father. It was a ten-page letter to describe to me the sacrifice, deeds, and death of a man named Bobby Sands." slumped forward. "You know who Bobby Sands was, Lisa?"

When Lisa shook her head, he continued.

"To be fair, he was a great man. Went on a hunger strike in Prison Maze and starved to death some sixty days later or so. Sometime in May back in 1981. About the time me own dad died." Rob hung his head, shaking it gently. "One of my own heroes, in fact. As a young lad, I briefly met him when he came by the house to meet with my mum. At the time he starved himself, in prison, he was elected as an MP."

Lisa asked, "MP?"

"Member of Parliament, House of Commons. After he died, the British Prime Minister said that Bobby was a criminal and had chosen to take his own life. A choice his group didn't give others. So that's how both sides viewed each other. Both thinking right was on their side. Hardened in their positions. While he was in prison, Bobby wrote a poem that I admire greatly." Rob then spoke from memory:

"*Oh, and I wish I were with the gentle folk,*
around a heathened fire, where the faeries dance unseen,
away from the black devils of H-Block hell,
who torture my heart and haunt my dream."

Lisa murmured, "Yeah, that will stay with you."

"I first read that during a really dark period in my own life and it made me realize that all of us have our own H-Block hell that occupies part of our mind. At least I do."

He stood up, as if lost in thought and wandered toward the kitchen. "Would you like a beer or something?" he asked Lisa.

"Sure, whatever you're having is fine,"

Rob returned with two bottles. Twisting the top off one, he handed it to Lisa and walked through the living room to the broad bookcase that covered most of the wall.

A small wooden desk and chair sat under the window next to the bookcase. An intricately carved, narrow wooden prayer kneeling bench with a wooden rosary hanging from its ledge rested in a corner on the other side of the bookcase. Its faded mustard pad displayed regular use through the indentations on both sides of the pad. Rob stood, looking through the tall wooden bookcase, pulling out and looking at several volumes, before finally removing a small leather-bound book. He then searched through the book, obviously looking for something specific.

He opened his beer and took a long draught, then put the bottle on one of the shelves and turned to Lisa, opening the book to the passage he had sought.

"This Bobby Sands's poem, 'The Rhythm of Time'—goes a long way toward understanding me mum and dad." He started to read:

"There's an inner thing in every man.

Do you know this thing my friend?

It has withstood the blows of a million years,

and will do so to the end."

He said, "There are other passages that give historical reference and the universality of these feelings that you might want to read later, but I'll skip to the last:

"It lights the dark of this prison cell.

It thunders forth its might.

It is 'the undauntable thought', my friend,

that thought that says 'I'm right!'."

Closing the book and returning it to its shelf, he moved to the sofa and sat, putting his arm around Lisa. "When I got that letter, I was bitter for a long time. What I wanted was my mother to comfort me with memories of my father. What she sent me instead was an admonition that, as St Ignatius Loyola of the Jesuits said, we are called by God to be a Man for Others. So, my parents didn't always give me what I wanted, but they gave me what they thought I needed."

He put his hand under her chin, lifted her face and kissed her gently. "Both my ma and da believed that they put God's will above their own. They were devout Catholics and tried to live that faith. But each, in their own, though entirely different ways, were committed to stepping over established lines to bring what they thought as justice to an unjust world. That is something that is at the core of who I am as well."

Hoping to keep his recollection of family going, Lisa asked, "No brothers or sisters then?"

Rob's eyes filled with pain, clouding, then changing their color from deep, clear blue to a darkness built of pain, tears and un-reflected light. Lisa put her arms around him as he sobbed uncontrollably. She held his head and smoothed his hair with her fingers, kissing him gently on his cheek and forehead.

He told her more.

HIDING IN A BOTTLE

More than seven years have passed since I first read her note. The paper is now brown with age, edges frayed. At night I often retrieve it from the top drawer of my nightstand. It seems that each time I read the note its paper feels more fragile. As do I. I realize that the note which tethers me to my past is disintegrating at the same rate as am I.

Laying in my bed before my whiskey sleep, I pray for whippoorwills. Tormented by their absence. Each night they fail to appear and to sing and offer me a vision of a peaceful life. The life she sought but failed to find. The peaceful life that seems beyond my reach.

I have done therapy. Counseling helps me to understand what is happening to me and why. I have studied the literature about abuse. The known consequences on family members of the abused is well documented.

My days are increasingly filled with madness and driven by fury.

I am filled with shame.

Where I once was welcomed happily by others in normal social exchanges, some people now approach me with caution. Unwittingly, I sometimes unleash myself on others in my path. These events fill me with more shame.

Many friends attribute this to a life of working in criminal law. Association with so many truly evil people daily. Long-time friends urged me to change direction in my profession or to abandon it altogether. I can see in their eyes that they are concerned for me and want me to recover. I don't know how or even if it is possible, but I give more and more thought to their advice.

The social life I maintain is damaged by my history, my inability to forget and my focus on revenge. I am on a first name basis with every bartender and every maître d' in most bars and upscale restaurants in New Orleans. There have been a few incidents which have reflected poorly on my public reputation.

I tend to date younger women for brief periods of time. They all want to fix me. When women want to get close to me, I push them away or treat them badly enough that they leave me. I don't know which humiliates me more.

Despite these problems, or perhaps because detachment is better suited to my profession, my career flourishes. Gifts I once had now gone and no longer able to provide me with the tools to go on in a normal way. My new characteristics serve me well in my life at law.

In my mind, I know that what I spend my time planning will not bring what I most desire, a peaceful life. Yet my planning continues.

It has now been nearly a year since I found out where the Dentist's Wife now lives. After divorcing her dentist husband and taking half his fortune, she moved to a coastal city in California. It is a beautiful, serene village with oceanside homes and peaceful parks and schools.

I know this because last month I traveled there. For several days I sat outside her home in a rental car.

One afternoon while I sat there she brought a young girl into her home. The girl appeared to be four or five years old but walked with her body bent as though she were an old woman. She appeared terrified and the Dentist's Wife appeared to delight in her terror.

Through the open car window, I heard the maniacal laughter that Bird had described so well. It made my nightmares come to life and I knew. Her evil continues. More children hurt, more families destroyed.

The next day, the local police stopped and asked me what my business was and why I was sitting there in the car. They let me go when I told them I was lost and consulting my map. They appeared doubtful, but they let me go.

Back in my hotel room, I called the local child protective services anonymously. While the person who answered the phone seemed sympathetic, her questions let me know that she thought I was someone with a grudge against the woman based on other disagreements we might have had.

She asked me to provide credible evidence so that they could open an investigation. When I told them I had nothing that would be legally valuable, the conversation ground to a halt. I was told that for them to move forward evidence would have to be provided.

Then she told me that the office was closing soon and perhaps I could call them back with evidence at another time. My rage boiled over and I used intemperate words in response to her comments. She hung up.

After two more days, I woke to a blackness clouding my thoughts. My last coherent memory was of the phone clicking in my ear. My room looked like a hurricane had blown through the window leaving a trail of broken glass and whiskey bottles strewn throughout the room.

It was then I recognized that my anger was misplaced. I realized that what angered me so mightily was my own failure. As much as I wanted to take revenge, to end this woman's life, and stop her evil deeds, I could not face the actual act of taking revenge.

I am a coward. I hide in bottles and plot fantasies that I am incapable of accomplishing.

NEW ORLEANS

2005

"We must see our present fight
right through to the very end.

Our revenge will be the laughter of our children."

– Bobby Sands

CHAPTER 33

Jules Jensen unfolded her slender muscular frame from the 1991 Silver 280Z in the basement of the parking garage next to the New Orleans police headquarters. Retrieving a hot cup of coffee from the car, she removed the napkin and lovingly used it to polish a spot on the driver side roof of the car. The twelve-year-old car was her pride and joy. She and her former boyfriend had restored it completely and its appearance and performance reflected the effort.

When the relationship fell apart, she traded for the car, leaving behind the small house in Mid City with her ex. A good trade in her mind. The car was fully restored and the house, like most in Mid City, seemed more a money pit than a single New Orleans detective could afford.

She had quite happily settled into an attached apartment in the rear of a large house on Phillip Street near the Irish Channel. It was a short drive from Police Headquarters and the Warehouse District. The one-bedroom apartment had a small kitchen, combined living and dining area and, most important to Jules, a covered parking spot off the street with an automated gate. The family in the main house was quite happy to have a New Orleans police officer as a tenant and kept the rent quite reasonable.

Jensen was a detective first and foremost, though most people would mistake her for an elite athlete. Her tall physique was distinctly feminine in a powerful way. Her dark eyes and long black hair pulled into a ponytail gave her face a mix of strength and beauty. As the first female homicide detective in New Orleans Police Department, she had been known for her intelligence, toughness and no-nonsense approach for the past fifteen years. The small crow's feet surrounding her deep black eyes were the only sign of the demands her job had placed on her during her long career on the force.

She walked through the garage to the main police headquarters building next door. Entering the elevator at the rear of the building for the ride to the third floor, she was joined by Assistant Chief Bensen who headed up the Criminal Investigation Division of which Homicide was the most important section. Bensen was known to the troops as one of the good guys in the hierarchy of the New Orleans Police Department.

Chief Bensen nodded at Jules, and as the door closed, he seemed to remember something. "Hey, I heard you guys think we might have a serial killer out there."

Jules responded, "Don't know about that, Chief, couple of killings going back a ways that appear to have some similarities. Three that we know of appear to involve garroting the vic. We haven't been able to resolve any of the three cases, but we can't seem to find anything to tie them together either."

As the elevator arrived, they exited and stood outside in the third-floor hallway.

"How far apart were the three killings?"

"First was over four years ago. Then again in late 2002. The latest we just got onto last year. None of the three look like any attempt was made to hide the bodies. The victims were on their knees with what looked like their hands folded in prayer. Of course, anyone being garroted is likely to be praying." Jules laughed.

"What's your plan?" asked Bensen.

"Chief, we don't have much info on the old cases, so we plan to work this new case hard. We've done the door-to-door and no one has turned up that saw or heard anything. The vic would probably still be there, except he had a cleaning service scheduled that used the key he left and they found the body. The good news is they say they backed right out of the scene and called us. The bad news is we didn't find any prints or anything that will yield any real evidence.

"Don't forget to check out the ViCAP stuff."

"I've put a couple of administrative folks working on filing reports with the FBI Behavioral Unit and we hope to get some feedback from them soon."

"Jules, for the love of God, please try keep a lid on this serial killer talk, would you? Last thing we need is to worry the public until we know for sure that's what we have."

"Okay, Chief, but I got a message this morning from Grace Garland over at the *Picayune*. She wants a call back. You want to handle that?"

Chief Bensen appeared to consider her comment, then finally, he said, "Naw, probably just raise her interest level if I call her."

As Jules walked past him, he grabbed her by the forearm and said, "Isn't she a buddy of Smile's?"

"I think he knows her. Maybe I'll let him call."

"Good, handle it," he said as the elevator doors opened again and they went their separate ways on the third floor.

As she entered the Homicide Division's bullpen area, Jules thought about the need to keep quiet the potential for the public hearing about a possible serial killer. She knew that such a disclosure would be exactly what they didn't need at this stage of an investigation. Public disclosure would bring the politicians and all other manner of crazies into an investigation. Time wasted with politicians and their demands for regular updates, most of which they would end up leaking to the news people, would further waste time in the process.

News of a serial killer would bring all of the nut jobs out of the woodwork, all of them looking for some reward or leverage with their own legal problems. Each would have to be worked and that would add a significant amount of work for the investigators.

The circus that would follow would be the worst possible environment in which to conduct an investigation. She hoped that Smile could head that off with Garland and so she went straight to his desk.

Smile was hunched over his computer and was squinting into the screen and pecking at the keyboard keys with a combination of two fingers on each hand, using the same method he'd used with a typewriter before the computers.

"What's up?" Jules said, tapping Smile on the back.

He spun in his chair and laughed, "Just realizing once again that I should have taken typing back in high school. This freaking machine has it in for me. If I ever break the backspace key I'm in a world of hurt."

Jules knew that she was lucky to have Smile as her partner. Smile's easy manner allowed him to get folks to talk more freely than most cops. He had the knack of putting them at ease. They had been paired up five years earlier and were known throughout the department as one of the most successful homicide teams that New Orleans Police Department had ever had.

The conventional wisdom in the department held that if "Boris and Natasha" couldn't solve a murder, it probably wasn't going to be solved.

While Jules appreciated the nickname, Smile bucked every time he heard its use. "These fuckers can't tell the difference between a Scottish Cajun accent and Russian—no wonder we have to solve half their cases," he'd say.

"The Chief wants to you to return the call for me to Grace Garland. He's nervous about it becoming known that we are looking at a potential serial killer."

"You convinced that's what we are looking at?"

Jules perched on the edge of Smile's desk and said, "Not yet, but it's starting to feel that way. Weird though. Doesn't seem to be the usual patterns and connections. We have two males and a female vic. Can't see how that fits the normal pattern. The spacing on the murders doesn't fit. No increase in how often, so it's unlikely to be sexual. So what's the connection?"

"I'm gonna call the Behavioral Unit at the FBI and see if they got the info we sent them and see what they think."

"Why don't you call Garland and see what she wants. Tell her I'm doing interviews and asked you to call, since you know her. Be good if we can head her off on this."

Turning to her own desk, Jules settled into her chair, opened her desk drawer, and withdrew a brush. Removing the rubber band, she ran the brush through her hair and replaced the band holding the ponytail, then picked up her phone.

CHAPTER 34

Grace Garland held her head in her hands, shading her eyes from the bright sunlight coming through the large windows facing Loyola Avenue. Her head was pounding with the two extra-strength Tylenol yet to work their magic. Last night had ended way too late for a work night and now she was paying a huge price. Perhaps O'Neil wasn't a good influence, as she had thought. He seemingly could drink all night without effect.

The newsroom was noisy with people moving and talking over and at each other at breakneck speed. Grace knew that she needed to at least pick up the phone and pretend to be busy or her editor would have something derogatory to say in short order.

Her phone rang just as she was reaching to pretend to make a call.

In a gravelly voice, she answered, "Grace Garland."

"Well, who the hell else would it be? You have a secretary now that you're a big shot reporter with her own Sunday column?"

"Smile, not today okay?"

"Ah, someone has been a bad, bad girl. As they say in the homeland, you sound like wan o'clock half struck. I can hear it in your growl," Smile said, using a clipped Scottish accent.

"What do you want, Smile?" Grace responded with her phone in one hand and the other hand continuing to cover her eyes.

"Just checking on my buddy. Can't a friend check in with a friend?"

Grace shifted in her chair, cradling the phone between her shoulder and her ear. She took a large swallow of the coffee in front of her and said, "Official business, Smile. You're on the record as of now. I'm gonna assume that Jensen asked you to call me so that you could abuse our friendship to put me off."

Smile laughed out loud. "God, you're good. Now that's it exactly. What can the NOPD do for the fourth estate?"

"I have it on good authority that you guys are looking at a *series*," she emphasized the word, "of murders that appear to have been committed in the same manner. Is my source correct?"

After a brief pause, Smile said in an overly officious tone, "If you are looking for confirmation on the record, then the answer is no, we are not looking at a series of murders and we are not sure why someone would suggest that we are. I could only speculate on why someone would say something like this to you, but I'd be happy to go off the record," he added in a much friendlier tone.

Grace sat silently hoping Smile would fill the silence. Finally, she said, "And if we went off the record would you be more willing to tell me why I'm hearing this from someone in your department?"

"Off the record is good," said Smile quickly.

Too quickly, thought Grace. *I've got to get more.*

Grace hesitated. She had the names of three victims going back three years and had been told there were similarities in the method of the killings. Her source had told her that but no more. She knew Smile would try to keep this from going public as long as possible.

"Okay, Smile, here is where I abuse our friendship. We go off the record, you give me what you've got, and I agree to hold all of this until you give me the okay. But … I get a complete exclusive when we go public. No bullshit. No, 'Aw the brass let it go, sorry'. Nothing like that happens. Understood?"

"I'll tell you what, Grace. You get the paper to buy me lunch and we can have a very broad off-the-record discussion that I know you will find interesting and useful in your pursuit of that first Pulitzer." Smile laughed. "Mandina's? Twelve o'clock?"

Smile walked up and leaned over the top of the partition separating Jules's work area from the rest of the bullpen. His elbow was resting on the top edge of a large ornate plaque that read, "Jules Jensen—2, Perps—0" in gold lettering. While many police officers can go an entire career without using their weapon, Jules was very different than most police officers.

The plaque had been presented to her by fellow detectives six months earlier. It was on the occasion of the second time Jules had been forced to use her gun on a perpetrator. In both cases she had been underestimated mightily.

Early in her career as a patrol officer, Jules encountered a PCP-crazed man who was able to pick up a loose railroad tie and attempted to swing it into her head during a drug arrest. She dropped him with one bullet to the chest. As she said: "He hit the ground faster than the railroad tie."

The perp later credited Jules with saving his life after he recovered from his wound and got through rehab. She had packed the wound with her uniform shirt until an ambulance arrived. Jules attributed it to her failure to shoot as accurately as normal. In her defense, she said, "I've never practiced with a railroad tie swung at my head by some drug enabled asshole, so being off by three inches wasn't too bad under the circumstances."

Six months ago, she had stopped for a red light under the Mississippi River bridge ramp on her way out to meet some friends and listen to some music in the Warehouse District. She was looking into her purse for her phone when she heard a metallic tapping sound on her window. Turning to the sound, she was looking into the barrel of what appeared to be a nine-millimeter pistol held by a dirt-covered, skinny white man with a bandana tied around his face. He looked to have the shakes brought on by his need to fix, and soon.

"Gimme your purse, bitch," the man had said, "or I'm gonna fuck you up."

Thinking quickly, Jules said, "This window doesn't work." She rolled down the passenger side window and said, "go over to the other window and I'll hand it to you through there."

Panic and confusion filled the eyes of the junkie. Finally, he said, "Hold up the purse and I wanna see both your hands and the purse while I go around."

As if to comply, Jules picked up her purse and held it toward the open window of the passenger door. The junkie seemed to crab walk around of the front of the car, never taking his eye off the purse or Jules. As he approached the window, he reached his left arm through the window to grab her purse.

Jules fired her weapon from inside the purse, the bullet went through her purse, through the open window and hit the junkie in the right shoulder, spinning him to the ground. She was quickly out of her car, around to the other side, and putting handcuffs on the junkie, who lay moaning on the sidewalk.

"Aw, shit. Shit, shit, shit. You didn't have to shoot me. Goddamn, I just wanted money."

"Now listen, you little turd. You were gonna take my car, too, weren't you, asshole?"

As she later told the story: "It was bad enough the shithead got blood all over my car—I wasn't gonna let him take it. Took almost a week to get it cleaned up. Plus, the purse was ruined, and I loved that purse."

Smile tried to never underestimate his partner. He knew she was smarter and tougher than he was, so he constantly sought her input on his activities and ideas.

He'd had an idea while talking to Grace, but wanted to run it by Jules before lunch.

CHAPTER 35

Smile placed the blue magnetic bubble light on top of the department Ford and bounced the siren a couple of times while he maneuvered through a U-turn on Canal Street. He pulled up in front of Mandina's restaurant and parked in the red zone within steps of the front door. Grace was standing at the front door in the corner of the building and shook her head as Smile walked toward her with a grin on his face.

"Jesus, Smile, you don't even pretend to care about how people view the department, do you?" Grace said. She was dressed in jeans and a form-fitting blue jumper that highlighted her eyes and made her look glamorous and casual at the same time.

"Grace, my girl, of course I do, but truly not enough to change who I am. Despite what many say, I think people really like the authentic me." He grabbed the door and held it for her as she walked into the crowded room and snaked her way to the bar that ran along the left side of the room.

The noise in the room was loud and boisterous. Grace gave a friendly smile and a nod to the man behind the bar talking to the bartender. She held up two fingers. He pointed to the front room corner and she shook her head and pointed to the back side of the bar. He walked through the bar to its end where Grace and Smile followed him into the room behind the bar. Grace hoped it would be a little quieter and less hectic than the front room.

The maître d' pulled out a chair for Grace and said, "You know he's not allowed in here without his wife and kids."

"Ah, Leo, just a wee misunderstanding, that's all that was. I was certain I'd been forgiven by now."

"Smile, two things. If you weren't married to a Saint, and if you weren't police, you'd never get in here again."

"Ah, Leo, what about your godson? Zeke didn't deserve what happened, did he? Don't I get some benefit for being such a good father to the boys? Wasn't I protecting the youngsters?"

Ignoring the last remark, Leo asked Grace, "What can I get you, girl?"

"Bloody Mary. Double."

"I'll have the same, Leo," said Smile to his back as Leo returned to the bar, ignoring him completely.

"You're a real fuck up, aren't you, Smile? You gonna tell me why you were banned?" asked Grace.

"Like I said, a bit of a misunderstanding. We were sitting out front and some clown at the bar kept backing into Billie Jean and bumping her chair. Uptown asshole who thought he was important, some associate at a big law firm downtown. Kind of guy who is born on third base and thinks he hit a triple. Then he spilled his drink on Zeke. Sort of apologized, but then he had a right good laugh about it."

"And?"

"Bit of ruckus, but, well, we all settled down. A bit later I noticed him go into the back to use the can and I followed him in there. Handcuffed him to the urinal and stuffed his mouth with paper towels. Hell, I told him I'd come get him when we finished our meal. That he needed to learn manners before he'd be allowed back in public."

"Jesus, Smile, you're lucky he didn't file a complaint with the Department. You could have been in serious trouble." Grace couldn't believe that Smile would do something so rash.

"Nah, he's a pussy. I went back after a few minutes and let him go. I told him that he was old enough to know that messing with police seldom went well in New Orleans over the long term."

Leo returned to their table and placed drinks in front of them. He said, "Y'all want to order now, or wait a few minutes?"

Grace said, "I'll have a shrimp romaine salad. How about you, Smile?"

"A meal on the newspaper, I ought to order a big, fat, juicy steak, but I'll go for the softshell crab po-boy. Can't pass that up. You got the softshells today, Leo?"

"Yeah, sure. We got 'em," Leo grunted and left to put in the order.

Smile looked around the small room, trying to determine if there were any folks nearby whom he would not want to overhear the next part of the conversation.

"So all this is off the record for now, okay?" Smile said to Grace with a look that let her know that this was going to be the serious part of their discussion.

"Smile, I got to get something good or I'm going with what I got," Grace replied.

"Sure, sure, I get that. What I got is way better that some bullshit 'maybe' serial murders. For one thing, we don't even know that there is a serial killer out there. We know two things about that. First, they don't tie together like most serials other than the method is similar."

"Meaning what?"

"Three victims years apart with no time pattern. All garroted. The problem is, there doesn't appear to be anything else about it that says serial killer. Victims don't tie together. They aren't all the same sex, two male, one female. Second thing, we are going to deny it, and all you are going to do by coming out with this now is muck up our investigation. We will end up chasing a bunch of bullshit leads that don't amount to anything but overtime for us working stiffs."

An older waiter arrived with their lunch and they paused to allow him to place the plates in front of them. Smile loaded his po-boy with cocktail sauce and took a huge bite that left juice dripping down his chin. While still chewing, he said, "God, this is heaven right here at Mandina's."

As the waiter was leaving the room, Smile yelled, "Hey, podnuh, bring me a Carona, would you?"

As they continued to eat, Grace thought about what Smile had told her and realized that she didn't have much of a story, especially as the department was prepared to officially deny the rumor. Perhaps she could parley it into something else. "So what else you got for me?" she asked.

"Grace, darlin', I've got a potential story as juicy as this po-boy and the details are as messy as the legs of this crab dangling off the edges of this heavenly bread. Yours exclusively, courtesy of your best friends on the force, Jules and myself. Not only are you going to get this exclusively, but you and a photographer of your choice get to be there when we make the arrest."

Grace sighed and said, "Come on, Smile, the last thing I want is pictures of some drug bust going down. Those are a dime a dozen."

Smile's grin spread from ear to ear and lit up his entire face. "Ah, now Gracie, I wouldn't do you that way. I'm talking about the arrest of the CEO of a local financial institution in the early morning outside his palace on St Charles Avenue."

Grace sat up straight and placed her fork on her plate, took a large sip of her Bloody Mary and thought for a moment. This was definitely worth holding off on the possible serial killer. "I thought those bank cases were mostly federal? What are you guys doing involved in that?"

"Well, the bank is where he works, but not where he is committing his evil deeds," said Smile.

"My pal in the child abuse section tells me they are about a week away from having him dead bang on serial child abuse. Nasty stuff, too, not just your wag and diddle. If ever someone deserved to fry in public, it's this bastard. That's why my buds are looking for me to be the cutout between them and the leak to you guys in the press. That way they keep their hands clean if there's any blowback on the fifth floor."

"Well, Smile, I knew there was a reason I liked you despite all your obvious flaws," Grace said, laughing quietly. "Who is this prick?"

"All in due time, Gracie. Best I'll be able to give you a twenty-four-hour notice, with the address and name, so you can do some background on the perv in question."

When the waiter showed up with the Corona beer, Smile waved it away and said, "I think we'll have two more Bloody Marys instead. And make mine a double without any Bloody Mary mix, would ya?"

CHAPTER 36

Winston Butler admired himself in the full-length mirror. He gazed at the muscles that rippled throughout his shoulders and the flat stomach that emphasized his six pack. His regular workouts on the weights had produced exaggerated musculature that looked one step from a steroid user.

As he admired his body, he dressed in the powder blue linen shirt and white slacks he had selected, offset by the soft yellow sweater he carefully wrapped around his shoulders to look casual and carefree. Glancing again at the mirror, he thought that his ensemble was perfect for a day on his sailboat. *That should make the best impression on the bank clients he was scheduled to entertain*, he thought with a self-satisfied smile.

He examined his white teeth for any stray remains of the breakfast Lily had delivered to his bedroom when she had woken him for his early day at the yacht club. He brushed his long blond hair until it grew soft enough for him to flick his long bangs to one side with a quick turn of his head.

Thoughts of the prior evening were briefly unsettling. "Damn that kid," he muttered to himself. "I am going to have to insist that he be more careful who he is bringing with him." The fun may not be worth having anyone else involved. It had amused him when the very young child had left the house with terror on his face and tears running down his face. It was the part he liked best. The terror following the pain he inflicted. Butler especially loved hurting them young, the younger the better. The street child last night couldn't have been older than eight.

Crossing to his enormous four-poster bed, Winston pulled back the covers and looked at the bloodstains on the sheets and the cover itself. Stripping the bed, he wrapped the sheets inside the cover, intending to get the maid to dispose of them later.

Winston knew that his position in the community afforded him protection. No one would believe any accusation of some street urchin over that of a bank CEO known for his generosity to charities throughout the city. Still, it paid to be careful …

Crossing his large, second-story bedroom he looked out the window onto St Charles Avenue. The shadows cast by the enormous oak trees along the boulevard were beginning to shorten as the sun rose higher in the sky. The passing streetcar was filled with people on their way downtown to work. Winston saw the limo that the bank sent to pick him up every day pulling up to the curb. His driver stepped out of the limo, lit a cigarette, and leaned back against the driver's door.

When he reached the bottom of the winding staircase, Winston dropped the bundle next to the stairs as his maid emerged from the kitchen. "Lily, please put this in a trash bag and throw it away. I cut my hand last night and got blood all over the bedcover and sheets."

Lily picked up the pile and returned to the kitchen, thinking that this wasn't the first time she'd had to replace stained bed linens. She pulled the bundle apart and looked at the sheets and cover more closely. Taking a garbage bag out of the laundry cabinet, she began to stuff the material in the bag when she heard loud yelling and noises coming from the front door. She rushed into the entry area to see two police officers placing handcuffs on Butler, who was yelling at the policemen, "Wait until I get the Superintendent on the phone. I'll have your asses, you worthless bastards."

A tall black man dressed in jeans and a sport coat with a tie half-tied was holding a card and reading the warning that Lily recognized from her favorite police shows on TV. When he finished, the policeman asked with a tone that matched the sneer on his gaunt face, "Do you understand the rights I've just read to you?"

"I understand that I'm going to have your badge. Wait until I get the Superintendent on the phone." Butler's face was bright red; it looked to Lily like he would explode at any moment.

He turned to Lily and barked, "Lily, pick up my cell phone off the floor. Call Mr Greene. Tell him there is some terrible misunderstanding and I need him to meet me right away."

"What's the number for Mr Greene?"

"Look in the goddamn directory. Hurry."

"Yes sir, Mr Winston, where d'you want him to meet you?" Lily asked as she picked up the phone from the floor and scrolled through its directory.

Turning back to face the officer with the card in his hand, Butler asked, "Where are you taking me?"

"Police Headquarters. Tell the lawyer either the first floor, Child Abuse Division, or the third floor, Sex Crimes. It appears that we have enough to convict your sorry ass on multiple counts in both areas. Tell him to ask for Detective Decker."

Lily put the phone to her head, spoke briefly, and then called out, "Mr Butler, Mr Greene say he ain't criminal, but he gonna find you one and they both meet you there."

The policemen turned Butler and pushed him roughly. Lily hung up the phone and put it on the entry area table.

Detective Decker continued walking behind Butler, pushing him toward the front door. As they emerged onto the brick portiere landing, there were clicks and the flashes of a camera pointing at him. Glaring at the photographer, he yelled, "Who the hell are you? What are you doing on my property? Get the hell out of here!"

Grace Garland stepped around the lanky, disheveled photographer and faced Butler with a recorder in her hand. "Mr Butler, I'm Grace Garland with the *Picayune*. I understand that you are being arrested of multiple counts of child abuse, sex with minors, and rape. Do you want to comment?"

Butler took his time to compose himself before saying, "Ms Garland, I am certain that this is some terrible mistake, perhaps one of mistaken identity or an accusation by a disgruntled employee or customer of the bank who blames me for their own trouble. This is the kind of nightmare you read about. I only hope that when this is straightened out, your paper will print the correction that I'm sure is due."

Grace moved quickly to position herself to keep him rooted on the bottom step of the stairs, while Decker held him so that she could continue her questioning. "So, you deny the charges?"

"Certainly. Any accusation is false on its face," Butler replied with a withering look.

"I'm told that the police have videos and voice recordings of horrific acts on very young boys," Grace said, watching as Butler's face went white and his lips drew tight in a misshapen snarl. His head went down and it appeared that he finally understood the trouble he faced.

"I have no further comment," he grunted.

As the police officers were placing Butler into the police cruiser, his sweater slipped from his shoulders and landed in the road. Grace watched Smile emerge from around the back side of the car. He picked up the sweater and bundled it between his hands, before wrapping the sweater around Butler's neck. As he pulled the sweater knot a bit too tight, Smile looked him in the eye and said something softly in his ear which Grace couldn't hear. But Butler suddenly had a look of terror on his face. Then the detective put his hand on his head and pushed him roughly into the back seat of the cruiser.

Smile seemed to skip toward Grace with a large grin on his face. “Well, now, Gracie dear, who’s your best friend?” he laughed as he joined Grace on the steps and Detective Decker walked up to the steps to join them.

“Thanks, Billy,” said Grace. “I owe you one.”

CHAPTER 37

Central Lockup in New Orleans is a nightmare for its many visitors. Cacophonous noise, God-awful odors, blending feces, urine, and fear sweat, amid constant surges of the New Orleans population made the entry room closely resemble a nightmare scene from Dante's *Inferno*. The picture was completed by the splotched institutional green paint on all of the walls, including those in the cage that sat in one corner of the entryway, with four people sitting on steel benches attached to the concrete floor.

Sergeant McNulty, in charge of the booking desk, considered it his castle.

Here, as opposed to at his home, he was king. More important than his longstanding service as the Sergeant in charge of Central Lockup booking, his wife, Marge, was the oldest and favorite sister of the Sheriff of Orleans Parish. In his home, McNulty was beholden to Queen Marge, as she was known. He often brought the animosity of the subservient to work with him. Victims of his anger were numerous and legendary.

Lawyers who had constant business in Central Lockup regularly genuflected at the altar of King Mac. The smart ones brought donuts and po-boys and those gifts were reflected in his girth. Christmas brought enough top shelf alcohol to stock his bar year-round. His cheeks and jowls looked the prototype for Hollywood depictions of southern cops. His bright red face and thinning hair completed the picture.

King Mac didn't even care much for the cops who brought him new prisoners as they added to a workload that never ended. Most of the prisoners were drunks, petty thieves, hookers, and other lowlifes—or "wastes of sperm", in King Mac's vernacular.

The King was looking at three men approaching the desk with equal parts indifference and disdain. All three were clearly lawyers, but only the one he knew looked comfortable enough with the surroundings to identify him as a criminal lawyer. The other two were clearly not dealing well with being in Central Lockup amidst the regular denizens of that netherworld.

McNulty studiously avoided looking at them while he shuffled papers around on the desk to ensure that their discomfort continued. Finally, he looked up and asked, "What can I do for you, Freddy?"

Placing a brown paper bag on the desk, the small rather feral looking lawyer said, "Sergeant, it's a glorious day outside and I thought perhaps you might enjoy an oyster po-boy for your lunch today. Perhaps you can take it outside and bask in the sun."

McNulty grunted and opened the bag. "Did you bring any cocktail sauce?" he said as he rooted around in the bag. "I don't see any in here."

Clearly anxious, the lawyer said, "Didn't they put that in there? Incompetent bastards. I'll have my girl pick some up and drop it to you in a few minutes."

"By which time the oysters will be a soggy mess." McNulty glared at him. "But I suppose you think it's the thought that counts. What can I do for you?"

At that moment, the phone on the desk rang. McNulty picked it up and said, "McNulty here."

McNulty noticeably sat up straighter. Whoever was on the other end of the phone could be heard by the three lawyers giving directions to McNulty, though the directions weren't audible enough to understand who was giving them or what was being said. When McNulty turned in his chair and looked at the picture of the Orleans Parish Sheriff, it became clear who was on the other end of the line. He pointed at the picture and then to his phone.

The two lawyers, in three-thousand-dollar suits with crisp shirts and perfectly knotted ties, waited. They whispered into the ear of the criminal lawyer, Freddy, whose sharkskin suit and frayed collar shirt marked him as belonging in this environment. Then they stood waiting for the call to end.

"Yes, sir. I understand," said McNulty as he hung up the phone. "Your will be done," he muttered under his breath. He addressed the two corporate lawyers: "Okay, gents. I understand that you have engaged young Freddy here to handle the Butler case for him. My understanding is that he is due to have a hearing sometime this afternoon or early morning at the latest." With a wave of his hand, he indicated the cage. "As you can see, he is currently in the cage with a few other fine folks where he will remain until the hearing. If the hearing isn't scheduled until tomorrow, the Sheriff has asked me to make sure that he remains here rather than be transported to Parish Prison at the end of the day."

Freddy said nervously, "That's great, Sergeant. We hope to have a hearing scheduled sometime in the next couple of hours. May we have a word with him now so that we can prepare?"

"Of course. Help yourselves."

The more senior of the two corporate lawyer types said, "Is there somewhere we can meet that's more private?"

McNulty looked amused and said, "Well, normally we would be pleased to share our conference room with you, but since we don't have one, you'll just have to whisper through the bars like all the other asshole lawyers who come here every day. Freddy knows the drill." With that, he opened the brown paper bag, unwrapped the po-boy, and took an enormous bite. Flakes of bread crumbs, mayonnaise, lettuce and small bits of tomato spilled onto the front of his uniform. Chewing happily, he indicated they could begin their visit by waving the sandwich in the direction of the cage.

Watching them from a corner of the cage, Winston Butler was terrified. His blue linen shirt was misshapen and large sweat blotches ran from under each arm and down the middle of his chest. His white linen pants had streaks of what looked like dirt mixed with an oily substance. The powerful odor of urine grew stronger as they approached the cage.

Butler leapt from the bench and met them, staring through the bars. "Jesus, Bill, when am I getting out of here?" His voice had a peculiar pitch and his eyes darted from lawyer to lawyer, seeking answers.

Bill Greene, the senior of the two corporate lawyers, said, "Here's what we've done and where we are. This is Freddy Mouton. We've engaged him to handle your case for now, at least through an arraignment. Freddy is quite familiar with all of the procedures used in criminal cases. I've reached out to the Sheriff and he has agreed to make sure that you aren't transferred to Parish Prison before we get you a bail hearing, which we hope will be this afternoon, but may take until tomorrow. In the meantime, you will remain here."

Butler appeared to lose all blood in his face and it turned from bright red to pale. "Are you kidding? I have to stay in here because of these trumped up charges? This is insane." He looked around the cage at the three other occupants and whispered, "These people are dangerous. I'm not safe in here."

Freddy spoke up with more force than his appearance indicated, "Look, Mr Butler, these charges are severe. Right now, you are charged with rape of a minor and assault. If you are denied bail, which is possible, you are going to be in Parish Prison pending trial. Trust me, that's way worse than here."

"But these charges are preposterous. Why would I do such a thing? What kind of evidence could they have to back up these claims?"

Freddy looked Butler in the eye and said, "Doesn't matter. I'm going to do my best to get you out on bail. I just want you to know what may happen. Worst case: you stay in Parish Prison. It will all depend on the judge. Right now, we are looking at who we will go before to see how to handle this problem."

"Now, how quickly can you put together cash for bail? I'm guessing that if we proffer a million dollars, we can get you out, but you'll also have to surrender your passport and agree not to travel out of state." Freddy peered over Hilton's shoulder at the other three occupants of the cell. Two of them looked to be sleeping and the third was leaning against the back wall of the cell. He appeared to have urine running down his pants legs and puddling on the floor.

"I can handle that," said Butler. "Bill, call Juanita in my office and she will arrange for whatever the amount is for bail."

Freddy said, "Well, as long as she is doing that, have her put a check together for a hundred thousand dollars, which is my retainer in a case of this magnitude. We can discuss the full cost once we have a clearer handle on the facts of the case."

Freddy's cellphone rang and he looked at it, then flipped it open. "What you got?" He listened and nodded several times, then smiled and said, "See you there."

Turning back to Butler, he said, "Mr Butler, you are a lucky man. First, you got me to represent you, for which you can thank Mr Greene. Then, we drew the right judge, and finally," he looked at his wristwatch, "the preliminary hearing is scheduled at four-thirty today. I should know more by then what we are facing and hopefully the judge will set bail. You could be back at home tonight."

Turning to Greene, he said, "Mr Greene, you need to arrange the cash for Mr Butler's bail and let me know those arrangements. I'll send over my girl later today to pick up my retainer as well."

CHAPTER 38

Rob peeked through the branches of wax myrtle brush that were trimmed and strapped to the wooden structure and used to cover the duck blind. He shivered from the cold as he looked out over the acre-sized pond in the middle of the south Louisiana marsh. Enough light was beginning to filter over the horizon and reflect off the pond so he could see the decoys he and Smile had tossed from the boat on their way to the blind. He sat on the bench that ran along the side of the blind, facing away from the sun, petting a yellow Labrador retriever with one hand, and had his rosary working through the fingers in his other hand.

Inhaling the primordial, fetid odors, he heard sounds of the marsh coming to life. The rustle of birds getting off the water, frogs croaking, and nutria screaming made what had been eerily quiet just moments before spring to a noisy life. Once again, Rob realized what a complicated and beautiful place God had created in Louisiana. Thanking God for this miracle, he finished his prayers and put his guitar string rosary into a plastic container and slipped them into his pockets by reaching down the inside front of his chest-high waders, placing them into his jeans pocket.

In a few more minutes the rising sun would begin to produce radiant patterns in the sky, coloring the pockets of water set among the rushes and grasses of the marsh. The combination of the decoys and calls that mimicked the ducks resting on the water would attract the ducks to fly into danger. At least that's what Rob and Smile hoped.

Rob heard the sloshing sound of Smile wading through the thigh-deep waters of the marsh, returning to the blind after hiding the boat in brush a hundred yards away. Smile was carrying on a running commentary to accompany his heavy breathing. Reaching down to pet the yellow Labrador retriever sitting next to him in the blind, Rob laughed and said, "Well, Cu', there's a surprise, more complaining from Smile. That fellow can't keep his mouth shut for even a bit."

Smile climbed into the blind by leaning against the wooden floor that sat almost level with the water and hefted himself, push up fashion, crawling into the blind. Cu' licked his face the entire time he was attempting to lift himself. That set him off, first complaining and then laughing so hard he fell back on his stomach in the bottom of the blind.

Rob grabbed the back of Smile's waders, and helped him to his feet. "Now then, Smile, do you think you could be a bit quieter? The feckin' noise you make sounds like a water buffalo coming through the marsh. You'll scare all the birds away."

Smile sat on the wooden bench in the blind and didn't respond as he breathed so deeply it appeared he'd just completed a marathon. He removed his hat and steam rose from his head as he wiped his face to remove the sweat flowing down his face. After a few minutes, his gasps subsided and he reached under the bench and pulled out a camouflaged floating gun case. He unzipped the case and pulled out a Remington twelve-gauge shotgun. He checked the safety before loading three shells into the chamber. Then he took a string of duck calls out and hung them around his neck. "How long 'til shooting time?" he asked.

Rob looked at his watch and said, "Two minutes."

Smile grunted, stood up, leaned his gun against the blind, and said, "Perfect." He moved to the open end of the blind and pulled his waders off his shoulders and down below his knees, then reached inside his heavy coat, and, struggling a bit, said, "Ah, the peeing-while-duck-hunting dilemma.

Six inches of clothing and four inches of dick." He laughed while bending and reaching and finally began to pee into the water off the edge of the blind.

As he finished and was adjusting his clothes, he heard two loud blasts of Rob's shotgun behind him, followed seconds later by the sound of two splashes thirty yards out in the decoys. Turning, he looked at Rob, who laughed and said, "Well, I'm done. Can we go in now?"

Making room for Cu' to pass him in the narrow blind, Smile shouted, "Cu'!", and the dog leapt into the water and swam toward the decoys. He found one of the ducks quickly and returned to the blind. "Drop!" Smile told him as he entered the blind with the duck in his mouth.

Dropping the duck into Smile's hand, Cu' turned and leapt into the water, once again returning shortly with a duck and placing it into Smile's hand.

The next hour passed quickly as the blind was regularly dive-bombed by flocks of teal. The occasional pintail circled and circled then landed too far away to shoot. Smile was on his game that day, and the pile of ducks grew to nearly match the legal limit imposed on the two hunters. Rob did not shoot after his early-morning exploits, preferring to watch Cu' work and Smile shoot. Smile did a count and realized they had only one duck left to achieve two legal limits. Cu' was lying down in the bottom of the blind. As the sun reached in to warm him, he appeared to be asleep.

"Hey, let's watch them fly for a while. I'd like to get a green head to finish up. We're loaded up with teal," said Smile.

"Yah, let's do that. Such a glorious day, we don't want to go in too soon," said Rob. He looked around the marsh and indeed it was one of the rare late winter days where the weather was spectacular. The air was cold, crisp and bathed in sunlight promising spring was just around the corner. They sat in silence and watched a nutria swimming through the decoys, then finally disappearing into the grasses that lined the pond. Edges of the pond were filled with coots, their pointed beaks rocking back and forth like metronomes.

Finally, Smile broke the silence. "When are you going to marry that girl, Rob? You let her get away and I will personally make it my mission in life to kick your ass."

Rob looked sorrowful, saying quietly, "I've asked her, Smile. I'm afraid she won't have me. Can't say I blame her."

Smile looked stunned. "She turned you down?"

"More than once," Rob replied.

"But she's crazy about you—anyone can see that. What the hell? Are you really going to escape the torment of marriage?"

Rob stood in the blind and leaned away from Smile, his voice taking on an Irish flair that was more pronounced than normal. "Fair play to her, there're bits about me that I cannot force myself to share. She knows in her heart that a marriage can only succeed with complete honesty. Let the other into the places they hide from the world in the main. I love her more than my own life, but I cannot seem to get myself to do what needs doing."

Smile said, "Rob, what the hell could you be hiding? You're without doubt the best person I know."

Sitting quietly without responding, Rob thought about the bodies that he had brought to this marsh. Both times were during the heat of the summer. He had tied a concrete block to each leg and lowered the bodies into a deeper pond at the far edges of the hunting lease. Before the duck season, he had checked the pond and found only the concrete blocks, the rope ends frayed from the ravages of the elements and the animals that had carried the evidence of his actions away.

The week before when she had last visited Rob, Caoimhe had warned him that he must be increasingly careful as she could foresee danger in his future. Her voice trembled with trepidation and her face was filled with fear. She suggested that perhaps it was time to stop, to put aside his mission. She told him that he had already done more than most toward helping The Children.

Rob was intrigued by this suggestion. Perhaps abandoning this work would allow him to build the relationship with Lisa based on greater trust.

He had awakened later that night, sweating and shaking and remembering the day he had learned of the explosion that killed Padraig and Caroline. The event that continued to haunt him as if it had just happened. The explosion had made him feel his connection to God had been permanently severed. He knew in his heart the sin which he continued to feel was unforgivable. Both by God but more by himself. He knew he was beyond redemption. Perhaps Lisa remaining so close and yet so out of reach was more punishment for his sin.

Lisa had sat up in bed and put her arms around him, seeking to comfort him. "What is it, Robby?" she asked, looking equal measures frightened and concerned.

"Ah, just a bad dream. Nothing, really. Go back to sleep," he had said and turned away from her and curled up as if returning to sleep himself. He hadn't seen the hurt and disappointment in Lisa's eyes and the tears that ran quietly down her cheeks.

Returning from his daydream, Rob sat back on the bench and opened the breech of his shotgun. He put one shell in and closed it firmly. He pointed out into the open air above the decoys and said, "There's your mallard, Smile. Take him."

Smile crouched down behind the brush to avoid detection by the duck as it slowly began its decent into the decoys. As the bird set its wings for its final glide into the decoys for a landing, he stood and aimed briefly before pulling the trigger. Then he watched with satisfaction as the bird crumpled and landed in the water. Just as he was turning in triumph, he saw Rob shoot. He yelled, "Rob, we've already got all our ducks, that'll put us over the limit."

Rob turned to Smile and said, "You see, Smile, there's always something out there that most aren't aware of. That's not a duck. It's a speckle-belly goose and doesn't count toward the limit. Something for the Easter table coming up."

CHAPTER 39

Billie Jean Doucet loved these nights at home with her friends and her family. She stared out the window over her kitchen sink into the small grassy back yard surrounded by the wooden privacy fence. Zeke, Zach, and Rob were kicking a football at the small PVC goal in the corner of the back yard and she laughed out loud when Zeke smashed one into the goal and threw his arms in the air then wriggled as though dancing.

Smile was fussing while lighting the propane burner and placing a stainless pot on top of the burner. He held a hose to fill the pot in which he would boil the crawfish he and Rob had picked up on the way home from the duck camp. He balanced the hose in the pot to keep it filling, while he added a bag of seasoning to the water. Then he turned to the small propane pit and lit the gas to get the coals ready to cook the appetizers. Sweat was running down his face despite the cold weather.

Billie Jean finished wrapping bacon around the sliced duck and goose breasts filled with jalapeño peppers and cream cheese and dropped them into a bowl of marinade. She put the bowl into the refrigerator. Turning back to the sink, she tapped on the window until she got Smile's attention and waved him to come inside. Then she finished washing the lettuce in the sink and turned to the small center isle to begin to chop other vegetables to complete the salad. The smell of baking brownies in the oven filled the kitchen with what Billie Jean thought of as the smell of a happy family.

Lisa and Grace were sitting at a small Formica breakfast table in the far corner of the room next to the back door. As they were talking, Rob came into the kitchen and said to Billie Jean, "I've been sent on a mission by the chef. I'm here for the poppers." He leaned over and kissed Lisa on the top of her head, reached around her and took a long pull from the bottle of beer that he took from her hand by slowly intertwining his fingers through hers.

Lisa smiled and turned back to Grace. "Who is the dude they arrested?"

"The CEO of a bank. Apparently the man is an animal. He gets these young street kids and brings them to his house on St Charles. Molests them and physically tortures them. His public reputation is that he is a charitable guy, giving to lots of causes. My story ran on him when he was arrested—did you see it? I think he thinks his public reputation will save him in a 'he said; he said' situation."

Rob walked over and opened the refrigerator, then said, "Billie Jean, are these the poppers in this bowl?"

Billie jean reached in the refrigerator and handed Rob the bowl. "Tell Smile not to burn them again," she said, and handed him the bowl.

"Are you serious?" Lisa asked Grace as Billie Jean joined them at the table. "Did you see the videos?"

Grace looked at both Billie Jean and Lisa and said, "No, but I'll bet that Smile has. Not that he will tell me. Billy Decker, the detective who made the arrest, told me they made him puke. Apparently, this guy really hurts these kids. Decker says that any juror that sees these videos will bury the guy."

Billie Jean looked doubtful. "Smile says they are worried about being able to get the videos admitted. Apparently some other kid helped them to get the videos and maybe a judge doesn't let them into evidence. Then it's a street kid's word against a pillar of the community that's really worrying those guys. Billy Decker said if this dude gets off this time, he's the type who will go to Thailand for his sick thrills and will be out of their range forever."

Rob leaned over on his way out the door and kissed Lisa again on the top of the head. As the door closed, Grace shook her head and said, "You're crazy to keep turning that guy down. If you're not going to marry him, maybe

I will," she said, laughing. "Although he'll probably drop me like all the rest. I think my love life may be jinxed."

Billie Jean turned and asked, "I thought you and the judge were going strong? Is that over?"

Grace stood up and walked to the refrigerator. Looking inside, she took a long neck bottle and waved it at Lisa and Billie Jean. "Y'all want one? It's kind of an involved story."

Lisa nodded and Billie Jean said, "Okay, time for a break." She grabbed a bottle from the refrigerator as Grace handed one to Lisa and sat back at the table.

"Yeah, we've been done for a long time, couple of years, really. Now, he just escorts me if I need someone for an event and vice versa. He's turned into a really good friend, someone I can rely on and I try to repay the favor."

Billie Jean snorted and said, "Well, that's the kiss of death. Good friends, ouch. Don't you worry that other guys will get it wrong like I did?"

Grace shrugged her shoulders and said, "What other guys?" She looked at Lisa. "You remember we met Lawrence at Galatoire's and saw him the next night at Tip's? The weekend you met Rob. The weekend we met Smile. A great weekend, one of our best. I got that story on Rob saving that woman and kid. It really gave my career a big push at the paper. Judge took me out to dinner a couple of weeks later. We talked for hours. At the time, I realized he was too old, like he's almost thirty years older than me. But I enjoyed his company and I found him really sexy. Sophisticated, extremely intelligent and a genuinely kind and thoughtful guy. Not at all like the obnoxious, arrogant assholes our age that you and I were dating at the time."

"I remember thinking you were head over heels," Lisa said.

"Yeah, I kinda was. He seemed tormented, carrying a lot of misery, and I've always been attracted to melancholy. But we talked all the time by phone. Late at night. I guess we are both insomniacs. I think he was going through some stuff but I never really figured out what it was. You know, he's the kind of guy that asks a lot about you and doesn't really open up. I loved it. He gave me good insight into local politics and advice on my career."

Lisa looked at Grace and said, "Okay, you don't have to answer this, but how about sex? Were you sleeping together? Is it true what they say about older guys?"

Grace didn't answer. She looked down as if in deep thought and finally said, "Well, for the longest time it just didn't seem to happen. He's a great kisser and you can tell he would be tender and loving in the right circumstance, but the time never seemed right. I was dating other guys and he was dating other women and he always told me he was too old for me and I could do a lot better. Truth be told, I could tell he really wanted to, but something was holding him back."

Turing to Billie Jean, Grace continued, "Billie Jean, you don't know this about me, but I was adopted at birth. Typical Catholic adoption here in New Orleans at the time. Nuns came to Baptist Hospital and took me straight to my adoptive parents. I never knew my natural mother and father." Grace walked to the refrigerator and took out a bottle. She waved it at Lisa and Billie Jean as if to ask if they wanted one. Both declined so Grace opened hers and took a long draught. "Look, I was lucky. I had the best parents, the people who raised me were wonderful. I still miss them terribly. But like most adopted children, I became curious about my natural parents when I was a teenager. Then I felt like it hurt their feelings, so I never pushed it. Then they went through a divorce and it never seemed right to ask. Before she died a few years ago, my mom finally told me that my natural father was a politician and my birth mother was eighteen when I was born. She never told the father; she just chose to put me up for adoption because she knew she couldn't give me what a child needed. I still didn't know who either of them were."

Sitting down at the table with them, Grace felt warm and comfortable in sharing what for her was a very intimate confession.

"The night Lawrence celebrated twenty years on the bench, he asked me to go with him to the big wingding celebration. It was a great party, lots of stories about the 'big white-haired bitch in his black dress'. Remember that, Lisa? There were people laughing, great food, and the was booze flowing. It was late when we grabbed a cab back to my place and I asked him to come up with me. I remember thinking it was now or never.

"We talked and he opened himself up to me in a way that he hadn't done before. Told me stories of his professional triumphs and disasters. That's when I told him the story of my adoption. A few minutes later, when I leaned over to kiss him, he hesitated, excused himself and went to the bathroom."

Grace started crying and used the paper napkin around her beer to dry her eyes. "When he came out of the bathroom, he said that he hadn't realized how late it was and he needed to go home. Kissed me on the cheek and left. I didn't hear from him for more than a month."

Silence filled the kitchen as Grace's shoulders shook to accompany her silent tears. Finally, Billie Jean said, "Jesus. What the hell?"

Grace's voice became wistful and despondent. "Yeah. I was pretty shook up. Angry, bitter, feeling totally worthless and rejected. Lisa, you know that's not me, but it was hard."

Grace sat quietly remembering that it was during that month that she decided that her career as a reporter would be it for her. If love wasn't in the cards for her, she would dedicate herself to her career and vowed never to let her personal feelings get in the way of a story. It was as if she'd grown a shell that cut her off from a connection to her own emotions.

In a sense that was when she became better at her craft. Totally objective, no room for personal feelings. A killer, they called her in the newsroom. Now her sights were totally set on professional goals. Even Lisa had noticed the change in her and their relationship had cooled, become more distant.

Finally, Billie Jean broke the silence. Looking hard at Grace, she said, "So, that's the guy who's your friend? I'm not sure how that works."

Grace grumbled. "So a month or so later he started calling. I wouldn't take his calls. Every day for two weeks he called. Left messages. I could tell he was drinking when he called. Then the calls stopped. I thought he had given up. I was relieved, ready to move on.

"I get home one night late from work and he's sitting on my stoop. Again, I could tell he'd been drinking and thought that I was going to be in for some pathetic bullshit. He looked old. In a sad voice, he said that he was there to offer an apology, not in an attempt to be with me, but to explain why that night it had become apparent to him that he couldn't. So I sat down next to him on the step and listened."

Judge O'Neil sat on the stoop of the walk-up townhouse in the Warehouse District. A restored building that housed four condominiums, each with its own street-level entrance that gave the buildings the look of a brownstone in New York. The breeze washed the humidity quickly and the air held a pretense of cooler weather on the way. Not that he noticed. Once again, he had hurt someone and he wanted to make this right.

He watched Grace walking toward him on the sidewalk. Her confident stride lent an air of style to her walk through the dappled light cast by the faux antique streetlights that lined the sidewalk. When she spotted him, she hesitated briefly before continuing toward him at a rapid clip.

He stood up as she reached him and held his hands up in front of him, saying, "I won't take long. I realize that you don't owe me the time to explain, but I'd be very grateful if you let me do so." He indicated the step and sat down.

After hesitating for a moment, she sat and said, "I don't have much time, so what is it you want?"

"Grace, I like you. I know I hurt you. I simply didn't know how to tell you what happened." He sat with his elbows balanced on each knee and his head hung between his shoulders. He looked once at Grace and then continued without looking directly at her again.

"So the night of my party I was very, very happy you were with me. A night like that generally has both wonderful feelings and a sense of melancholy about it. With retirement soon, I will have more time to do other things, but you have to recognize that age is catching up with you. I've always had an amazing ability to mess up my personal life. That night I realized that is what you're left with when your professional life is over for the most part.

"I was worried that our relationship wasn't fair to you, given our age difference. Then I realized that was up to you. If you wanted to be with me despite those differences, then who was I to complain? So I was quite happy.

"Then, when you told me about your adoption it startled me.

"I thought about what I'd been up to as a person and as a politician when you were born. I realized that I might actually be your father. The man who was described to you.

"I wasn't on my best behavior back in those days and sex was pretty casual in my crowd. I remembered a girl I had been with that had just disappeared on me at some point. I saw her a year later and she said that she'd gone traipsing through Europe with a girlfriend for a year. When you told me your story, she sounded a lot like the woman you described as your natural mother. So I bolted." O'Neil lifted his head and looked Grace in the eyes. He had tears welling in his eyes as he said, "Grace, I'm sorry I hurt you."

Grace's lip was quivering and her voice was quietly raspy when she said, "So, you're my father?"

Billie Jean looked at Grace, startled. "He's your father?"

Grace laughed and said, "Actually, no. He said he worried for a week or so, then hired a private investigator to figure it out. The night he started calling he wanted to apologize and tell me what he'd found out. Turns out he knows who my father was but my natural father died several years ago. My natural mother is a prominent uptowner. Lawrence offered to tell me who, but I told him I didn't want to know. I had a great mom, the woman who raised me."

CHAPTER 40

Rob, Smile, and the boys were gathered around the large stainless-steel crawfish cooker and were using tongs to pull individual crawfish from the strainer basket in the steaming, boiling pot. Smile held one aloft and blew on it to cool it enough to test. Juggling the crawfish briefly to avoid its boiling heat, Smile finally peeled the tail and squeezed the meat into his mouth. He continued to blow around the tail in his mouth and finally chewed the tail, following it quickly with a pull on his longneck beer. With a grin, he nodded approval and indicated they could remove the strainer from the pot to drain.

Lisa and Grace were spreading newspapers on the picnic table in the back yard, getting the table ready to receive the crawfish. Lisa leaned in close to Grace and said, "That was quite a story. Why didn't you tell me that when it happened?"

Grace sat on the bench attached to the table and looked at Lisa for several moments before saying, "Lisa, it made me feel so alone that I thought that I would never be able to tell anyone. Have you ever had a conversation that made you realize that your life had changed forever? That's what that night felt like. I was in a daze for a couple of weeks. I wasn't ready to share it with anyone. And you and I had been drifting apart for a while. Hell, Lisa, it hasn't been a year, more like two, since we spent time together regularly. I didn't want …" She hesitated. "… your pity. You've been so happy with Rob that it made me feel even more alone." Turning to Lisa, she looked in her eyes and said, "I'm glad that we talked about it. I miss seeing you and having someone I can really rely on to listen."

Lisa sat down next to Grace on the bench, put her arm around her shoulder as if to protect her from the cold, and whispered to her, "Well, here's a curve ball—I'm pregnant. Rob doesn't know. I think I'm going to have to tell him tonight."

"That's wonderful!" said Grace. "I couldn't be happier for you and Rob." She wrapped her arms around Lisa's neck and buried her in a bear hug.

When Lisa emerged from the hug, Rob was standing there smiling and said, "You're finally going to say yes? I've been asking long enough. Sweet darling, you're well worth the wait."

Smile walked over with a sizzling plate of hot poppers, which he placed on the table, "Ah, so Lisa, gonna make an honest man out of Rob, are ya?"

Lisa and Grace realized that Rob and Smile had confused the news they overheard completely. Instead of the announcement of her pregnancy, they assumed Lisa was finally agreeing to marry Rob. Lisa looked from Rob to Smile with a look of confusion and anxiety on her face. She shook her head as if to say no, then stammered, but was unable to say anything coherent.

Rob sat on the bench next to Lisa and put his arm around her shoulders and drew her close. He could see from her reaction that something was wrong and that they had misread Lisa and Grace's interaction. He also realized that the time wasn't right to have this conversation, so he jumped up from the bench and said, "Now then, Smile, let's get those crawfish on the table before they get overcooked."

Lisa and Grace finished covering the table with newspapers and walked into the kitchen to help Billie Jean.

Smile had a look of consternation on his face and asked Rob, "Well, what the hell is that all about? Is she gonna say yes or not? It looked like she was mad at you or something."

Rob shook his head sadly, slumped back down onto the bench and said, "Smile, I love that woman with all my heart, but she's right in how she feels. If I cannot be the open person that she deserves, that I should be to treat her right, then I don't deserve her."

Lisa, Grace, and Billie Jean rejoined them at the picnic table, placing a bowl of salad that would be mostly ignored in the middle of the table. Smile made sure that they each had a cold beer and that Zeke and Zack had a Barq's root beer. The table was covered with a steaming mound of glistening red crawfish, mixed with small potatoes, artichoke hearts and slices of smoked sausage.

The steam rising in the night air carried the smell of crab boil seasoning, adding a spicy edge to the atmosphere. Elbows propped on the table, hands covered with seasoning and dripping the detritus of peeled crawfish, the group was quiet while quickly peeling and eating the crawfish in the South Louisiana ritual.

After years of living in Louisiana, Rob felt at home, peeling and sucking the crawfish meat from the tail in one motion. He paused to look longingly at Lisa, who studiously avoided returning his glance.

Conversation picked up slowly, with Grace asking Smile about the Winston Butler case and Smile indicating he was worried about whether the videos that were the heart of the case would be allowed by the judge. Apparently, the judge chosen to oversee the case had a strong and favorable relationship with the Defense Bar forged over long boozy lunches at Capital Steak House on Broad Street. Smile was convinced that, if the videos were disallowed, Butler would walk on the charges.

For reasons that only Lisa could fully understand, they did not return to the discussion of either her pregnancy or the wedding that all hoped would happen between Rob and Lisa. As he often did, Smile was playing a compilation tape of Rob's music through his outdoor speakers and the songs lent an air of melancholy to an evening which had started out so festively.

Rob lay on the bed, staring up into the darkness. He knew that Lisa was awake and she knew that he was as well. Upon returning from Smile's at the end of the evening, they went through the end of the day rituals robotically with very little interaction. When Rob emerged from the shower, Lisa was already in bed with the lights off. He crawled into bed and kissed her cheek, then lay on his back with his hands folded on his chest. Sleep would not come.

Rob could not balance his love for Lisa with what he felt was his overriding duty to God—to help save children from evil.

He remembered his conversations with Doc Dawes years ago. Based on those conversations, he knew that if he shared what he did with Lisa, she could become legally complicit with his actions. He simply could not make himself share what he was doing if that would be the result. He would not put her life at risk to the kind of legal trouble he would face if his work came to light.

Rob lay in the bed and fingered his rosary. As it often did, this triggered a silent conversation with God as much as actual prayers. He started by asking God to forgive him for the terrible deed he had committed that ended Padraig and Caroline's life. He thought back to his conversation with Padraig and tears filled his eyes when he remembered the look and sound of Padraig's last few words to him. "Dear God, is there no way for me to continue redeeming myself by saving the children and to also be honest with Lisa? Please help me to continue this important work which I will never abandon. Help me to find a way to share with Lisa what she needs to know about me so that we can marry."

The question emerged from the darkness like an arrow: "Who is Caoimhe?"

Rob was startled. He felt the adrenaline rush through his body, a physical reaction that accompanied his emotional response of confusion and fear.

“This woman you speak with in your sleep? Who is she? What is she to you?”

Lisa sat up in the bed, turned on the bedside lamp and looked at Rob with a quiet resolve. “I’m pretty sure you aren’t cheating on me. There may be a reason that I have to share our life with someone else. You should trust me to share that with me. I think I’m entitled to know who she is and why she is so important to you.”

Rob hesitated, struggling to find the words to begin explaining this secret to Lisa in a way that was honest, but did not endanger her by revealing too much.

Before he could begin, Lisa continued, “Rob, I recognize the name from your song, ‘True’. The girl who came out of the mist. The girl from the Irish Sea island. What is she to you now all of these years later? Is she the reason you cannot open up to me? Did something happen in your past?”

As he rose from the bed, Rob unconsciously grabbed his rosary tightly and began pressing his fingers into the barbs made by the twisted steel guitar strings. The sting of those barbs brought a comfort to him and allowed him to steady his breathing. Sliding into the barrel chair next to the bedside table, he turned to Lisa and sighed.

“Lisa, there is both a simple answer and a complicated answer to that question. Maybe to help you understand, I ought to give you bits of both.”

CHAPTER 41

Lisa had seen Rob disintegrate before. The night she had asked him about siblings he had told her that his brother and sister had been killed by a bomb set off in his hometown. They were carrying a song that he had written to a local pub owner when the explosion instantly killed them both. She thought that his asking them to bring the song had left him with a feeling of responsibility for their deaths and that it haunted him.

Although she did not know the full truth of his responsibility and the life-long consequences it had brought, she had always thought that there was more to Rob's pain than what he had shared with her.

Lisa had described Rob's disintegration to her mother as the moment she knew there would never be another man for her, but that he might never be right for her as well.

She had held him in her arms while he cried and described the horror and aftermath of the explosion. He told her of the years in Boston when he wandered aimlessly and felt completely lost.

Yet he had not shared the true consequences of his actions with her. How it left him bereft, feeling unredeemable and isolated from his deepest faith: yes; but not how it left him open to what he now considered his mission in life.

Like many mothers and daughters in the South, college had transported Lisa and her mother, Rosy, from mortal enemies when Lisa was a teenager, to best friends and true confidants as Lisa became an adult. Lisa had shared her concerns with Rosy when her mother had pressed her on why she continued to reject marriage.

At first, Rosy had worried that Rob might be too emotional for Lisa and would become too reliant on her for comfort. Rosy knew that Lisa would only respect what she considered a real man. After meeting Rob and getting to know him, Rosy knew he would always be a man others could rely on and that gave her great comfort. She became Rob's biggest fan and constantly pushed Lisa to agree to marry him.

Lisa loved Rob and loved his music which seemed a great gift to her. She knew he was kind and gentle as few men were, yet he was still respected by other men. The boys on his high school soccer teams appeared to think that he walked on water. He had friends throughout the city and was much in demand for work in the music industry. The lyrics and melodies he wrote in his songs seemed to speak directly to her heart.

Sitting cross-legged in the bed and facing Rob, Lisa decided that tonight she would listen but would also ask the questions that had lingered in her for the past few years.

"Rob, all of the music you write, that you listen to, maybe all you can hear, are sad songs. I know that only a soul as beautiful as yours could hold on to all that pain. I also know that there is something in there that you won't share. I need you to, because I don't think that is enough for me to just let it go. I wish that I could, but if I'm to give you everything in me, I'll expect the same from you. Will you do that for me? I so want to marry you and be with you forever, but if we have secrets that we aren't willing to share then it just won't work. At least not for me."

Rob sat quietly, as if contemplating what to say and rejecting each of several starts. Finally, he sighed, as if realizing that he only had one choice, and said, "Lisa, the simple answer is that Caoimhe is a faery. You may not know this, but we Irish believe, no we *know*, that every time a baby laughs for the first time, a faery is born. That is where the natural affinity between the faeries and human children comes from and why faeries spend so much of their life on the condition of human children.

"So Caoimhe is a faery whom I met as a young man. She has given me spiritual advice, as well as encouragement to use the gifts that God gives us all."

"But you recognize that she's not real, right?"

"Well, she's real enough to me."

Incredulity spread across Lisa's face. "Seriously?"

Rob stood up and paced throughout the room, his rosary tethering him to the conversation, as he felt the pain of the barbs that brought him a small sense of reality. Otherwise he felt like he was suspended between that reality and the world in his head that he occupied most of the time. He rarely tried to connect the two worlds he occupied, primarily because he was not sure that could be done or which was more important to him.

"This is the most serious I can be." He hesitated briefly, then continued: "I am very different to most people you know in an important way. Catholic people today go to church and they try to live a good life. They also want to define what that means. They do not follow what they view as ancient, otherworldly rules. I'd describe most people today as cafeteria Catholic. They go through life and pick and choose those parts that they consider important and they ignore those rules that are inconvenient or socially embarrassing.

"My folks brought us up as real believers. We took on board all of the Catholic rules. I still think that we are better for it. I still believe. I know that I do. So many of the people my age have taken the freedom of the sixties and seventies and turned it into a way to deal with all of life's ills. Not that that has worked well. Not for society or for themselves. Still, they're good-hearted people in the main.

"Look, I recognize that my being here with you and our physical life is outside the bounds of Catholic teaching. So I'm not saying I'm perfect or that I don't have a fair amount of guilt and hypocrisy in me. As the man said, if hypocrisy was helium we'd all float off into the sunset on occasion."

Rob reached out and took both of Lisa's hands in his own. Looking deeply into her eyes, he said quietly, "I want to set that part right. To be man and wife with you before God." Sitting in the chair and leaning his head back, he said, "See, one of the gifts of having such rigid beliefs is that we are more open to the possibility of miracles." Rob smiled, then said, "Or the miracle of possibilities. So I see Caoimhe as very real. She helped me set my moral compass at a time when it was very difficult for me to even think clearly. What I do, what she helps me with you may not understand or even believe. I believe in her and help her and the faeries protect children from harm."

Lisa listened with a confused but open heart. She found it difficult to believe Rob's statement on its face. A faery? And what did he mean by "protecting children"?

CHAPTER 42

The moon hanging close to the horizon cast rippling lights stretching nearly a mile on Lake Pontchartrain toward the yacht club nestled on its shore. It danced among each slip of the marina, many of which were occupied by sailboats speaking of freedom from the tethers of ordinary life. Magnificent craft, some capable of sailing around the world, all providing a place of solitude and freedom from the day-to-day realities of mortal men.

Rob surveyed the marina from a crouched position on the dock near the yacht club building. It appeared that none of the boats was occupied save one. The one which was the reason for his visit. His position on the slip near where that boat rocked gently on the waves gave him a clear view into the sailboat.

That afternoon, Smile had come by to visit Rob and he had been furious. In the course of blowing off steam he told Rob and Lisa that Winston Butler had been released on bail and appeared likely to skate on the charges. The only witness to corroborate the charges had appeared shaky to the detectives who were now saying their best hope was to strike a plea bargain on lesser charges.

Smile admitted to Rob and Lisa that he had followed Butler to his boat after his release and had threatened him. "Which is really stupid. I can't do anything and that prick knows it. It didn't even make me feel better," Smile had said.

Rob was able to enter Pier Two of the marina by climbing around the extended fencing that spread from the metal gate. The sailboat in the first slip was tied close enough that Rob was able to climb from outside the gate onto the boat and back onto the pier on the other side of the cast iron gate.

Moving soundlessly, he traversed the walkway and crouched down behind a wooden storage box next to Butler's sailboat.

Nearing midnight, the only sound competing with the lapping water striking the sides of the yachts was a grunting noise made by Winston Butler each time he performed a sit-up. The moonlight glistened off the sweat accumulating on his chest and abs as he continued to work furiously and with apparent anger. His multimillion-dollar sailboat stood out for its magnificence among the other boats tethered nearby.

When his cellphone rang, he stopped his sit-ups and stood, retrieving his phone and snapping his answer: "About fucking time you called me."

After listening briefly, he said, "Mouton, listen carefully you shithead. You didn't get me out on bail, my million bucks got me out. And for what? My goddamn board has suspended me, pending, and I quote, 'resolution of the matter'. I can't go to the bank, and now can't even go to my house, as it's surrounded by the fucking press. I'm stuck on my boat, at least until the cops tell the press I'm out here. That crazy cop who threatened me this afternoon, he told me he had his eye on me. So you tell me, what happens now?"

Butler listened, becoming increasingly antsy in his behavior. He paced back and forth on the yacht, only occasionally interrupting with brief questions. Finally, he said, "Six months? What the hell I am supposed to do for six months? Can't we get to that kid who is the witness and get him to recant? If he recants, won't they have to drop the charges?"

He listened again for several minutes, before seemingly calming down and saying, "Okay, get him to talk to the kid. I know he will respond to money. See what can be done. Let me know. I'm willing to pay what's necessary."

Butler hung up his phone and threw it into the cushion of the captain's chair behind the large metal steering wheel. He walked to the port side of his boat and stared out into the marina and into the lake through the opening to Lake Pontchartrain, used by all the boats when exiting the marina. His silhouette was motionless as his breath cast a steamy shadow that highlighted the glow of the moon off the water.

Rob watched him carefully, knowing he would have to surprise Butler when he made his move. Looking at his silhouette, it was apparent to Rob that Butler was extremely fit and that subduing him would be a challenge. The technique that Rob had used over the years involved an approach from behind and surprising his victims. The position of the dock and the boat and the small opening to enter the boat appeared to make that difficult at best.

Butler remained motionless for several minutes, staring out into the lake. Finally, he turned back toward the yacht club building, picked up his phone, and dialed. After several minutes, he snapped the phone closed and set it back on the Captain's chair.

He grabbed the large steering wheel and playfully steered the boat as if the sailboat was racing through the water. Releasing the wheel, he walked toward the back of the boat, checking lines of rope connected with the moorings on the dock. Finally, he sat on the dock side of the boat and stared at the lake with his back toward the dock.

Realizing that this was his best opportunity, Rob stood quietly, stretched and reached inside his pocket and retrieved his rosary. He adjusted his grip on the rosary through the yellow deer skin gloves he had used now for several years to keep the rosary from cutting into his hands.

Rob walked quietly but quickly down the walkway toward Butler's back. Just as he reached Butler sitting on the side of his boat, the dock rocked in the water and scratched against the boat, alerting Butler. He glanced over his shoulder just as Rob was placing the rosary around his neck. Before Rob could tighten this grip, Butler was able to put his left hand between the rosary and his neck.

The boat separated slightly from the dock and Butler pulled Rob over the side and into the boat. Together, they collapsed into the bottom of the sailboat in a heap. Rob was on top of Butler who was faced down in the bottom of the boat. Butler was bucking like a bull coming out of the chute.

Rob pulled back on the rosary and tightened it around Butler's neck. Butler's left hand remained lodged between the rosary and his neck. As Butler wildly twisted and fought him, Rob hung on and pulled as tightly as he could. Butler was able to get to a kneeling position and crawled toward the far side of the boat, all while resisting Rob's tightening of the rosary. Butler crawled toward, then grabbed, the railing along the far side gunwale of the boat facing the lake. As he began to rise with Rob on his back, Rob was able to get his left knee centered in Butler's back.

The combination of Rob's pull on the rosary and the knee pressure now arched Butler's back. Finally, Butler began to emit choking sounds and he filled the air with spittle. His head briefly twisted toward Rob, who saw Butler's eyes bulge and crimson splotches fill the whites of his eyes. Rob finally felt him weaken. Then Butler's knees collapsed and he lay face down on the deck of the boat.

Rob continued his pressure, twisting the rosary in his right hand to tighten it even more. Butler's breath became more labored and shallower and finally stopped. At the same time, his body released a foul odor as he defecated on himself.

Rob continued to pull the rosary tight as he prayed for him.

Finally, he unwound his right hand from the rosary and lifted Butler from the deck.

Butler's body now hung over the lake side of the boat. His waist was slightly above the top of the gunnel of the boat so only the pressure of Rob's knee had kept him from falling into the lake. As Rob continued to pray for him, he realized that the rosary was deeply imbedded in Butler's hand and that he would have to remove his left glove to get free of his grip on the rosary and on Butler.

Just as he managed to unwind his glove and released his hand from the rosary, he heard a noise from the water that startled him and caused him to lose his leverage on Butler's body. He tried to grab Butler but the body gained momentum and slid overboard and into the marina's dark waters. As Butler slid overboard, Rob saw that his rosary was still embedded in Butler's left hand and his left glove remained in Butler's grasp.

Rob carefully looked around the yacht club marina, peering into all of the boat houses that had lights shining and showed signs they might be occupied. He saw nothing which gave him pause or indicated the presence of any other occupants. Then he searched the dashboard in front of the Captain's chair where he found a flashlight.

Walking quickly back to the side of the boat, he leaned over its edge. Using the flashlight to scan the waters, he spotted Butler floating next to the boat. He was face up looking directly at Rob, his eyes still wide, bulging and speckled with tiny red explosions throughout.

The waves gently pushed Butler's head into the side of the boat, the banging sound reminiscent of the drum in a mournful funeral march. His left hand's fingers still grasped the rosary and Rob's glove was caught in the metal of the rosary's decades.

Rob was turning to leave when he realized he had seen something else in the dark water. He leaned over the side again, using his flashlight to scan the surface of the water. Then he saw them. The glowing orange eyes of a large alligator whose head was nudging Butler's arm.

CHAPTER 43

The phone rang before dawn. On its third or fourth ring, Jules Jensen rolled over in her bed and, placing the phone to her ear, clicked the button and said, "Jensen".

"Detective, this is Lou on the desk. You up yet?"

Sitting up in the bed, Jensen looked at the phone and realized it was not yet five in the morning and said, "Well, I guess I am now, Lou. What you got?"

"We got a floater out at the municipal marina near the yacht club. How soon can you get there?"

"I guess I can be there in about twenty, Lou. Have you called Smile yet? He's closer than me."

Jensen could hear the hesitation on Lou's part. "What?" She asked.

"Did you hear that your knucklehead partner went out and threatened that banker yesterday after he got released? His lawyer was on the phone to the Lieutenant before Smile got back in his car. Well, that's who the floater is—that pedophile banker. Lieutenant don't want Smile anywhere near the scene. So that leaves you to handle it solo. You good?"

Jensen slid her legs off the edge of the bed and said, "Sure, sure, got it. Tell them to give me twenty, I'm on the way."

Jensen got dressed quickly, putting on yesterday's blue jeans and a dark blue t-shirt with Police printed in yellow on the back. She clipped her badge to her belt, put her backup 9mm in her ankle holster and her service weapon in the holster clipped to her belt.

She set a Styrofoam cup in her one cup coffeemaker and hit the button to make a French roast coffee. While it was brewing, she walked into her bathroom, brushed her teeth and make a few quick passes on her face with some foundation. Picking up the coffee, she closed and locked her door, got into her Z and took a sip as the gate opened slowly.

Pressing the pedal, she looked at the phone which told her she had taken seven minutes to get ready and leave. *Not bad*, she thought. Then she started thinking about Smile and wondering if he was really as dumb as the powers that be thought he must be. Nah, he's a dumbass sometimes, she thought, but he'd never put his anger above his family.

This side story was definitely going to complicate the investigation, because someone that Smile had offended somewhere along the line would use the opportunity to feed the press and cause trouble. She knew that there was no shortage of fellow officers that Smile had offended over the years.

Reaching into her glove box, she retrieved a blue bubble light and placed it on the roof of the Z. As it began casting the warning flashes, she turned onto St Charles Avenue from Phillip Street and punched it. The car leapt to speed quickly and Jensen realized that these next few moments behind the wheel were going to be the highlight of what could turn out to be a long day. The roads were empty and she quickly flew up West End Boulevard toward the marina.

Jules arrived at the municipal marina near the yacht club as the sun began to provide first light of day. She saw a small group of people on the Pier Two walkway in the marina. They were standing near one of the larger sailboats. After she parked and opened her door, the wailing hit her full force.

"He eatin' dat dude! He eatin' dat dude! Somebody stop him! Aw, sweet Jesus! Dat man arm gone. Somebody stop him, he eatin' dat dude!"

Jules jogged over to a group of five people, including a heavy-set older man whose name-tag identified him as the harbor master. Along with several men who looked like maintenance workers, they were staring at a woman of indeterminate age and race who was wailing over and over. The woman looked wide-eyed at the rest of the people gathered, as if pleading with someone to do something. The crowd avoided eye contact with the woman, seemingly in fear they might actually have to help.

Jules spotted the body drifting face up near the bow of the sailboat. It appeared to her that an extremely large alligator was attempting to grasp the man's left arm in its mouth. Then she realized that the man's arm was in the alligator's mouth but it was no longer attached to his body. She leapt into the sailboat and worked her way to the front of the boat.

She dialed her cell phone as she retrieved her pistol from her holster. "Come on, come on, answer the fucking phone." Finally, she spoke into the phone, "Smile, where is it I'm supposed to shoot an alligator? No, I'm not joking, goddamn it, you told me once where you have to shoot a gator to kill it."

Jules listened for a minute. "I'll call you back," she said, then hung up the phone. Walking to the front of the sailboat's bow, she leaned over, and, aiming carefully, shot the alligator through the top of its head immediately behind its eyes in front of the v-shaped brow of the alligator's skull. The gator released the arm in its mouth, rolled over several times and then slowly sank below the surface of the water.

The body of the floater continued to bob face down with its arm floating separately a few feet from the body. Still grasped in the hand was what looked like a crudely made rosary with a yellow glove hooked into one of its barbs.

Oh, shit. That's Smile's rosary, Jules thought. She retrieved her cellphone and dialed quickly. "Lou, this could be bad. You need to get the Lieutenant to call me. He's gonna want to get out here real quick."

She walked down the dock to two EMS workers who were arriving with a stretcher between them, and said, "No need for that, boys. We just will need to get him out of the water and then wait for the coroner."

After taking a few steps on the walkway, she turned back to the harbor master and said, "Let's wait for the photo guy to take some pictures before we remove the body from the water. Make sure they get pictures of his arm and that no one touches the glove or the rosary. Let the evidence guys take care of that. I'd also like to get the alligator if we can get a diver out here to retrieve its body."

Jules walked back to her car and grabbed the remains of her coffee. Sipping the lukewarm brew, she thought about the rosary and the glove. Her experience as a homicide detective told her that those two items would tell the tale on Smile's future and there was not a damn thing he or she could do about that either way. Reaching into her car, she dialed Smile's number and waited for him to answer, thinking, *At least I can give him a head's up as to what's coming at him.*

CHAPTER 44

"Come on. Come on. Answer, goddammit." Smile tapped his fingers impatiently on the steering wheel, waiting for the phone to be answered. When the light changed, he took an illegal left turn off Carrolton Avenue onto Banks Street. Finally, his call was answered and he said, "This is Smile. I need him to meet me at McCool's."

He listened a moment, then said, "Well, wake his ass up. This is important. Yeah, like life-or-death important."

Once again, he listened, becoming more agitated, and finally interrupted, "Millie, I need you to understand that this isn't a joke." He paused, then said, "Okay, right away. Now, if possible."

Barely slowing down, he made a U-turn and drifted in front of Finn McCool's on Bank Street. He parked his car and walked to the door, finding it was locked. Banging on the door loudly, he waited until he heard a voice from inside saying, "We ain't open yet."

"You think I don't know that?" Smile shouted. "It's Smile, Malcom, let me in, goddammit."

The door opened briefly and Smile heard the lock click as it was closed behind him. An overpowering odor of stale beer and cigarette smoke welcomed him into the dark low bar. The walls were covered with a mixture of beer advertisements, posters, jerseys, and badges from soccer clubs and matches around the world.

A thin, scruffy man wearing baggy jeans, flip-flops, and an Arsenal jersey shook his head and said, "Smile, you ever consider that a man who needs a drink this badly this early in the morning might have a problem?"

"I'm not here for the drink, asshole. I'm meeting Rob here on his lunch break at school," Smile said as he walked through the darkened space to the end of the bar, took a left under the Slaite sign, and went into the bathroom.

When he emerged from the bathroom. he found a stool midway down the bar and sat, thinking. Jules's call had sent him spinning. Right now, his fellow detectives thought he had killed Butler. As Jules said, she'd had to identify the rosary as Smile's. It was that or be part of a coverup and she wasn't willing to do that, even for Smile. He had promised her that he would be at the office right after lunch and would clear this up.

"Smile, how can you clear this up?" Jules asked.

"Because I didn't do it, Jules," he hesitated, "but I know who did."

Now Smile faced the same dilemma. He knew that he hadn't killed Butler, as much as he would have liked to do so. If he hadn't killed Butler with the rosary, that meant that Rob had, since the rosary that Jules had seen him carry had been a gift from Rob and an almost exact duplicate of the one that Rob made and carried himself.

What really worried Smile was that he recognized the similarities to the other murders that they were thinking might be linked to one killer. Smile was trying to remember the photos from the recent killings where the victims had been garroted. When he got back to the office he would have to compare those to photos of Butler.

"Malcom, give me a shot of Jameson and a chaser."

"Jeez, Smile, you sure? It's pretty early."

"Yea, Malcom, I'm sure. I'm gonna need it."

Malcom poured the shot and was drawing a draft when the pounding started on the front door. "I got it, Malcom," said Smile as he peered through and then opened the door.

Tim Noland, dressed in khakis and polo shirt, looking like he was still half asleep, walked straight to the bar, took the shot of Jameson in one gulp, and started drinking the draft. "Malcom, draw one of these for my friend here and fix me a Bloody Mary. Strain the ice and put in an egg if you will." Turning back to Smile, he said, "Millie said you made her get me up for some urgent matter, so what's on your mind? Just so you are aware, I'm not feeling my best this morning, so try to keep it simple."

"Malcom, bring that next round over here, would ya?" Smile walked over to the far corner of the room and sat at a wooden high-top table for four, indicating that Tim should join him. He sat there looking so glum that Tim finally realized something serious was to be discussed.

He sat and stared with a quietly expectant look at Smile. Putting his hand on Smile's forearm gently, he said, "Hey, man, what is it? You look like you've lost your best friend."

"Ah, Tim, you've put your fucking finger right on it. I feel like I'm about to do just that." He drank the shot in one gulp and took a long sip of the draft beer. Wiping his lip with his sleeve, he looked at Tim with mournful eyes. "You heard about that asshole Butler getting killed last night?"

"No. Really? Well, good riddance. I couldn't stand that guy even when I thought he was just an egomaniac. Is it true what they are saying he was doing to all those kids?"

"Yeah, true. Worse than you've heard. A real piece of shit."

"So what's the problem?"

Smile lifted the glass and finished the beer in one long draught. Tilting the glass toward Malcom at the bar, he indicated he wanted another.

"To start with, when I go back to headquarters, there's a good chance I may be arrested for his murder. At the very least, I'll be questioned extensively. They think I did it."

"And why would they think that?" asked Tim.

"Yesterday when he was released on bail I followed Butler out to the yacht club and threatened to kill him. Which he promptly reported to his lawyer. This morning they found him floating next to his boat."

Tim was stunned. As much as he thought Smile was a hothead, there was no way that he would have thought him capable of murder. Unfortunately, his law practice had taught him that people are often not exactly what they seem.

"Go on," he said.

"Apparently they found the murder weapon. A rosary was used to garrote him, deep enough to put a second smile on his face. The rosary was hand-made out of steel guitar strings. Looks exactly just like this one," he said, reaching in his pocket and removing a rosary and placing it on the table. "Oh, and did I mention we've been investigating three other murders that have a very similar MO."

"Jesus, Smile," Tim said. His face took on a pinched look as if his hangover was emerging through his eyes and he was trying to keep it locked inside. "Just so you know, I never ask a client whether they did it or not. Don't want to know and it gets in the way sometimes."

For the first time since sitting down, Smile looked relaxed, and said, "Well, just so you know, I didn't do it, but I'm pretty sure I know who did. Anyway, I'm not gonna be your client, but he's on his way to meet us now."

Once again, there was a pounding on the locked front door of Finn McCool's bar. Smile got up from the table, walked to the front door. He unlatched the dead bolt and opened the door. Rob Coogan was standing there with a quizzical look on his face. He peered into the darkened bar and spotted Tim Noland. Then he turned and saw the serious look on Smile's face.

Smile put his finger to his lips and made a shushing sound, then said, "Rob, whatever you do, you go sit and listen to Tim and you do exactly as he says. Don't say anything to anyone, especially me or any other cop. When you are through talking to Tim, you need to call Father Phil at Jesuit and tell him you won't be back for a while. Then go home and talk to Lisa. I'll call Tim later and arrange for you to surrender yourself later today, but understand, you won't be going home any time soon. Maybe never."

With tears in his eyes, he hugged Rob and walked out the door of Finn McCool's.

CHAPTER 45

After waking up late, Grace cleaned her apartment and went through the tall stack of mail which she had ignored for days. Only on her drive to the newsroom did she remember that she was "King for the Day".

She wasn't a fan of the tradition, but she knew that it wasn't worth the squabble that would ensue in the newsroom if she failed to arrive with a new King Cake today. Having eaten a piece the prior day, and having discovered the "baby" hidden inside, made it her obligation to bring a King Cake to work today.

Grace was a huge fan of a more traditional French King Cake. She was daydreaming of the Galette des Rois she'd had two days earlier. Prepared as a dessert by Billie Jean, it was crusty and flaky and filled with frangipane almond cream. Just remembering it made Grace's mouth water.

Her thoughts drifted to visiting with Lisa at the Doucet's the night before last. She was sad, realizing the differences in their lives now diminished the closeness they'd once felt. Although Grace still enjoyed being in Lisa's company, she no longer felt the same connection that had once made them inseparable, almost like sisters.

She was waiting patiently in the line at Gambino's Bakery on Washington when she felt a tap on her shoulder. She heard, "Let me guess, you got the baby?" and turned to see a tall, dark-haired and very attractive black man speaking to her. She quickly realized it was Detective Billy Decker. She gave him a smile.

Grace liked Decker; he'd always been straight with her and she owed him for the Butler tip. She said, "My sweet tooth always gets me in trouble. Seems like I always get stuck with the baby. Same with you?"

Decker looked bemused and said, "Naw, I'm just here in my traditional cop role: donuts and a coffee. I love their café au lait here." He quietly added, "Hell of a story on Butler, huh?"

Grace was confused, but said, "Yeah, crazy they let him out on bail. You guys worried about interference with his trial?"

Decker snorted. "Well, not anymore." He smiled, gave her a sly look, and asked, "You didn't hear? I thought you guys had a pipeline into the department."

When Grace shook her head, Decker said, "He's dead."

"Dead?"

"The proverbial doornail," said Decker. "Jules found him floating next to his boat this morning out at the lake. Apparently a friend of Smile's garroted him on the boat and left him floating as alligator bait. We thought for a while that it was Smile that done it, as that knucklehead threatened the guy last night. Apparently Smile's in the office now clearing it up. He told the Captain that he knows who did it. The guy's supposed to turn himself in later today."

Grace was startled. "You said a friend of Smile's? Can you tell me who? He might be a friend of mine, too."

Decker hesitated and lowered his voice to a whisper. "I really shouldn't. He hasn't been arrested yet and if it came out that I somehow screwed up his surrender, I'd be toast."

Grace replied, "Yeah, I get that, but by any chance is this guy a musician who plays on Smile's soccer team?"

Decker hesitated and cast his eyes toward the floor. "I never told you nothing, right?"

Grace said, “Right,” and gave him a grateful pat on the shoulder. She turned and started to leave the store, the King Cake forgotten in her rush.

Before she had taken a few steps, Decker whispered, with his head down, “There's more.”

Turning back to Decker, she looked expectantly and waited. Like many detectives, Decker apparently realized that sharing information with a reporter could occasionally prove useful and he said, “Same MO as three other killings in the area over the past few years.”

Grace could feel her body sagging from the shock. Her face lost all of its color and her voice became hoarse. “Jesus. Ah, Jesus … the serial killer.” She turned to walk out the door.

Leaving Gambino's, she got in her car and sat thinking about what to do next. She knew she wanted this story. It would be sensational in New Orleans and to a wider audience that would bring her the professional accolades she badly needed. At the very least, front page news for the next week or more. Follow-up stories would continue for months, including a trial if it went forward. It was the kind of story that had legs and could lead to journalistic accolades.

In order to put herself first in line to take the lead on this story she knew she would have to return to the newsroom and make her case with her editor, Tillie Wilson. As she started the car and put it in gear to head to the office, a thought occurred to her. Instead of heading to the office, she turned her car away from the newspaper office and headed for Esplanade Avenue.

Pulling up in front of Rob's house on Esplanade, Grace parked on the street and sat staring at the house. She remembered the many nights she had spent there with Lisa and Rob. Those had been joyful times.

She had met many of Rob's musician friends and spent time with them in his home. People she supposed she would have to interview in pursuit of this story. Quiet nights listening to Lisa talk about her future with Rob. Rob playing and singing beautifully. Often, Grace had wished she had Rob's way with words. Those nights were peaceful and had been special to Grace.

Now she realized those times were forever in the past. Her intended actions would seal off her friendship with Lisa forever. A feeling of sadness swept over her.

She wondered why she was prepared to sacrifice those tender connections to her ambitions. Whether her willingness to do so stemmed from ambition or to her envy of her friend, Lisa.

She supposed it didn't matter now. She knew that she was willing to sacrifice whatever was necessary to be at the center of this story.

Reaching into the glove box, she retrieved a digital camera and a small digital recorder. Putting them in her purse, she opened her car door and set out to do her job.

CHAPTER 46

Lisa had spent the past two days at her Mother's house near the small shrimping village of Dulac. Last night she had slept in her old bedroom in what seemed a memorial to her high school days. Pictures of Lisa in cheerleader costumes, group photos of her high school crew, stuffed animals and other familiar objects provided a comforting atmosphere for making the difficult decision she faced.

She planned to meet Rob for dinner at home for the discussion both wanted, though for different reasons. For the past week they had each been trying to find time to have a serious discussion. Rob had said he wanted to tell Lisa what he had not shared with her yet about his life and to be closer to her as they approached marriage.

Sitting in the kitchen with her mother, Rosy, talking through her thoughts and concerns about Rob had been very helpful. She was now prepared to tell Rob that they were expecting a child and she had decided that she would marry Rob. She had gone to see her mother to make sure that she was reaching the right decision. Her mother had reinforced her choice that afternoon.

Putting her arms around Lisa and holding her close, Rosy had whispered softly into her hair and kissed her forehead, "Look, hon, none of us is perfect. I can see that Rob loves you and that you love him. Whatever he is holding back from you. I understand why you feel the way you do. It's important that people in a marriage share everything. That's what your daddy and I have always done. I am so happy for you that Rob has agreed to open himself up and share with you."

Releasing Lisa from the hug, she leaned back and looked directly in her eyes. Brushing her hair gently with her fingers, she said, "You and Rob are more complicated than your daddy and I were. You won't have the simple life we've had. Rob is not suited to simple as he is a such a complicated man. His talent and his heart will take him, and you with him, places we could never have imagined. Honey, you need to tell him how important this is to you that he shares everything in his history and his heart with you. You also need to be prepared to have whatever it is make a difference in how you feel if he does choose to share something buried so deep."

Her mother had rocked her as if she was a child, and with tears of joy told her, "Whatever you both decide to do, remember that this child must come first now. You will always be parents together. I hope you do that as a married couple, but we will love you and care for you and the baby no matter what."

As she hugged Rosy and said goodbye, Lisa looked around the only home she had known growing up. She hoped that she and Rob could provide as warm and comforting a home to their child as she had been lucky enough to have growing up.

Rob rested his head on the writing area of his small desk next to his bed. In his left hand he held a rosary similar to the one he had used on Butler the previous evening. He felt no guilt for his actions, only a deep measure of sorrow that his arrest would bring pain to Lisa.

He looked over the letter he had written to Lisa once again, hoping that she would arrive home soon enough that he could tell her in person what he had done rather than leaving it to the letter.

He needed to leave soon to meet Tim at Central Lockup in time to surrender. Smile had been very specific that if Rob did not surrender by three o'clock, the police would arrive to forcibly take him to be arrested. It left him less than half an hour before he had to meet Tim Noland at Central Lockup.

As he rested his head, he heard a knock on the front door, then the doorbell rang. He folded the letter and put it in this front shirt pocket. Leaving the bedroom, he walked to the front door, and, looking through a side panel of glass saw Grace standing on the front porch.

Opening the door, he said, "Grace? You looking for Lisa? She isn't here right now and might not be back for a while."

Grace seemed to straighten her shoulders, as if steeling herself for battle. "Actually, Rob, I've come to see you. Do you mind if I come it for a minute?"

Rob stepped back from the door and waved Grace into the front hall, saying, "Sure Grace, come on in."

She followed him into the living room area where Grace saw him take a folded piece of paper out of his pocket and slide it onto his desk before turning to face her. "Can I get you some coffee or something? I'm kind of in a rush, but what can I do?"

"Rob, I heard the news today about the Butler thing and I wanted to see if you have anything to say?" She took her recorder out of her purse, turned it on, and placed it near Rob's startled face, which now looked white and drawn.

If he had known Grace was there as a reporter he wouldn't have let her in the house. He'd already made up his mind that he intended to follow the advice of Tim to not make any comments to the press or to the police. "Sorry, Grace, Tim tells me that I shouldn't say anything. I'd like to talk with you, but I better listen to him for now."

Grace said, "Well Rob, can you at least tell me if you've been charged with anything?"

Rob hesitated, then said, "No, no I haven't. At least not yet."

"Do you expect to be?"

"I suppose so, I'm going down in a few minutes and meeting Tim there. I'm not sure about the full situation."

"Tim Noland is your lawyer?" Grace asked.

Rob nodded his head, said, "He is", then moved away from the desk and turned to face Grace, indicating that she should sit in one of the two facing chairs as he sat in the other.

"Right now I'm waiting for Lisa to get home. I was hoping to speak with her before I have to go meet Tim. Now it doesn't look like I can wait."

Grace thought briefly and said, "Well, Rob, I can stay and be here when Lisa gets home. You tell me what you want me to say when she gets here."

Rob stood and said, "Grace, that's very helpful. Just tell her what you know, that I've going to be charged and had to meet Tim at the police. Tim can fill in the gaps. He knows more about what's going to happen than I do."

"She still works for Tim, right?" Grace asked.

"Yes, she does. She's been there ever since she left working for that other fella, Jay Giles. She didn't care for him at all. Seems to adore Tim, though."

Grace stood and said, "Yeah, Tim's the best. I'll stay 'til Lisa arrives. You get going."

Rob looked around the house, as if he was trying to take a series of mental photographs, knowing that it might be a while before he returned. With a nod to Grace, he hurried out of the front door.

Grace collapsed into the chair. She glanced at the desk, her eyes resting briefly on the folded paper. Her mind wandered back to that afternoon in Jackson Square when she and Lisa had been inseparable friends. When they had met Smile and watched Rob's act of heroism. When her friendship with Lisa had been the most important part of her life.

Now I am about to betray that friend on the altar of my own ambition, she thought. I am not at all the person I thought I would be. I'm not even the kind of person I would want to have as a friend.

Taking the digital camera out of her purse, she walked to the desk, unfolded the white pages. After reading briefly, she snapped a photo of the first page of the letter. Then she turned over the first page and took a photo of the second page. Folding the pages back together, she returned the letter to the top of the desk. When folded, it showed the salutation, *My Dearest Lisa*, written in Rob's hand. She quickly snapped a final picture of the folded letter.

Grace reached for the phone and quickly dialed a number. Tapping her fingers while she waited, she tried to plan how she was going to handle the story. First, she had to make sure that it would be hers.

When the phone rang a final time and was answered by a gruff female voice, saying "What?"

Grace said, "Tillie, Grace here. Hey I want the Butler story and I think I'm owed. I'm the only one who knows the people involved. Plus, I broke the original arrest and I'm in a good place to provide info others can't get."

Grace heard the hesitation when Tillie didn't respond immediately. They both knew that this would be a huge story and would usually be covered by the crime bureau reporters. "I'm not sure I can do that Grace," Tillie said. "You're going to have to give me more of a reason to let you lead this story. Other people will have expectations as well."

Grace thought quickly. "Well, Tillie, I have something that they don't have. Something even the cops and the DA don't have."

"What's that?" asked Tillie.

Scrolling through the pictures on her digital camera, Gracie said, "How about a confession, does that help?"

NEW ORLEANS

PARISH PRISON

AUGUST, 2005

"Too long a sacrifice
Can make a stone of the heart
O when may it suffice?
That is heaven's part, our part"

"Easter, 1916" – WB Yeats

CHAPTER 47

Finally, Rob looked up and across his cell at the largest, blackest man he'd ever seen. Black Wilson looked like he had to be folded to enable him to sit on the lower bunk in the cell they now shared. His six feet, eight inches carried his three hundred and forty pounds almost gracefully. His skin was a shade of black that seemed to absorb all the light and which had resulted in his nickname. The name was given to him by the grandmother who took him in as a baby and raised him.

Over time, Ida Wilson's Sylvester "Little Black" Wilson had turned into "Black" to his family and friends as he grew to his enormous proportions. Black's pockmarked face and tight haircut gave him a fierce demeanor that would have been frightening even in a much smaller man. His coal black irises were surrounded by a bright white that seemed to give off light they contrasted so much with the rest of his face.

When Rob had first been placed in his cell, Black was sitting quietly on the bottom bunk, facing the small built-in bench next to the toilet in the corner of the cell. Rob walked to the bench and sat, placing his head in his hands.

Nothing was said for more than an hour. Rob was lost in his thoughts. He wondered when he would get to see Lisa and thought that he should let her know that while he still loved her, she should move on, as his future was so bleak.

In his deep gravelly voice, Black broke the silence by saying, "I know what you thinking."

Rob looked up and responded, "I'm sorry, what? You what?"

Mistaking his confusion, Black repeated, "What you thinking. I know what you thinking."

Rob looked curious, "What's that? What am I thinking?"

Black stood at full height, adjusted his white prison jumpsuit while towering over Rob. With a serious look on his face, he said, "You want to be de husband or de wife?" Black growled with a fierce look in his eye.

Rob bent from the waist with his hands locked in his lap. His head dipped low and his shoulders began to shake. His gasps for breath became more rapid until a full-blown laugh erupted and his head rocked back and laughter filled the cell.

"Smile," Rob said finally, with tears streaming from his eyes, standing and extending his hand toward Black. "He told me there would be someone in here I'd really like. He also told me that joke. I'm Rob."

Black laughingly said, "Well, come on then, husband, get over here and shake your wife's hand." His enormous belly shook with laughter as he reached for Rob's hand. "Tim and Smile told me you was coming and they gonna hold me responsible for you. They want me to explain some of the dos and don'ts of life in this place. My name is Sylvester, but people call me Black. Dat's right, Black. My maw maw named me and it stuck. Can't imagine why," he said with another belly laugh. "You definitely gonna want the top bunk, case it give way. I'm hoping to get my release sometime in September, but it could be late as Thanksgiving. I gotta get home to St Francisville for Christmas, 'cause I play in the band at the Sheriff's party and help give out all the gifts for the kids. We prolly gonna be in here together 'til about then anyway.

"So, listen up. Rule one in here is you don't tell me or anybody else nothing about what you did or did not do. I'm supposed to do the same, but I got a hard time with dat. Smile axed me to keep an eye out for you, said you were good people. Where you from, Rob?"

"Black, I'm originally from Ireland, but I've been here in New Orleans for years now. Tell me about your children."

"Oh, they ain't mine. Well, maybe some of 'em is, but I'm talking about the Sheriff's party where he give all the poor kids presents. Everybody come to the party and dance and sing and have a fine time. We got us a great Sheriff up in the 'Ville."

"The 'Ville?" Rob asked.

"St Francisville. Hill country. Most special place in Louisiana. When you cross Thompson Creek, you know you in a different place. White folk call it the Republic of West Florida and say it was a separate country for a while. They don't tell that the country only lasted for ninety days. I learnt that in school." Black's laugh started in his belly and shook his enormous body. He turned back to his bunk, sat, and mumbled, "Lots of stuff white folk don't say nothing about. Like don't get too drunk in N'awlins, and if you do, stay away from police, and if you can't do that, keep yo mouth shut.

"Rob, one of them told me you play music, guitar, writing songs and such. You play much blues? I can't play nothing but a blues harmonica, but they let me play for the Christmas party. Sheriff says I got to stay away from the sad stuff."

As Rob would come to realize in the coming months, Black did not care much for silence and filled it constantly with stories, jokes, and all manner of useless information. This suited Rob well, because Black did not insist on his audience paying close attention and Rob would spend most of his time lost in his thoughts.

He sat wondering whether his mission to help children would now come to an end, or whether it might continue in jail. Tim had not held out much hope that Rob could avoid conviction, which would bring serious time in prison to Rob's future. He advised Rob to stay quiet and follow his instructions to the letter. Rob had to fight himself and his pride in what he had done to protect the children. He needed to keep quiet and follow Tim's advice.

Rob was startled to realize that this was his first concern rather than what would happen to his relationship with Lisa. He had spent the last few months hoping that she would agree to marry, but that didn't appear likely now. The events of the last few days would increase her reluctance to marry. He knew she would be better off if they went their separate ways.

Rob felt lost once again. He fell to his knees and began praying looking for direction from God as to what his purpose was now:

"May Christ be with us!

May Christ be before us!

May Christ be in us,

Christ be over all!

May thy Salvation, Lord

Always be ours,

This day, O Lord, and evermore. Amen."

THE PATH BECOMES CLEAR

I have been handed a gift.

Despite my cowardice, I now have an opportunity to enlist someone with a much greater capacity for heroism than I will ever have myself. Someone to help me find the revenge that I need to soothe the pain raging inside me all these years.

This path is clear, yet difficult.

He must go free.

Free to once again be the neutral arbiter of true justice. The type of justice served by one person to another.

To protect those visited by evil abusive adults preying on children.

He knows, as I do, that they cannot be stopped, only eliminated.

If I had his courage, I would have already done what's needed.

He needs to be unencumbered by the constraints of a legal system that pretends justice is served when that seldom is the result.

I will bring my skill in that arena to serve the greater good. To enable the revenge I seek but lack the courage to enforce myself.

When he is free I will point him in the right direction.

Toward the Dentist's Wife.

CHAPTER 48

Unlike a normal summer where Millie would have moved Tim's household operations to his country home the week before Memorial Day, she remained stuck in uptown New Orleans. Moving to the country suited her well. Every year she looked forward to spending her summers there. Summer was her time to recharge for the demands of her managing Tim Noland's universe in uptown New Orleans.

In Millie's way of thinking, hers was a near perfect life. Tim's world was filled with interesting people, some old, some new, and a constant stream of events, large and small. Only the aura of his occasional sadness kept it from perfection.

Mondays in the country, she cooked Tim breakfast early, so that he could spend an hour and a half driving into the City to attend to his legal business. Often he would then stay in New Orleans for three or four days, leaving Millie to soak in the pool and relax in the sun unburdened by the normal flow of visitors in and out of his Henry Clay residence. He was known as a prodigious worker in the legal profession and those were days when he worked twelve hours, as he put it "becoming better prepared than the other guy's lawyer." It is why he won a lot of tossups.

Despite the arrival of the pervasive heat and cloying humidity, there had been no discussion of when or even if, they would be moving operations. Millie supposed it was due to his intense involvement in defending Lisa's boyfriend, Rob Coogan. Tim seemed more serious than Millie could ever remember. He worked incessantly. His demeanor was serious and he seemed sad most of the time. Today, his anger at Grace would be palpable.

When he'd come down to breakfast this morning, Millie had asked him whether they would be going to the country home and having their standard Fourth of July party. Tim had snapped at her. Something she could never remember him doing before. Then he had slammed the newspaper on the counter and left the house in a hurry.

When she glanced at the newspaper, she realized the cause of his anger. The headline screamed, "Coogan Admits Guilt", with a sub headline that read, "Multiple Murders?"

Millie filled her coffee cup with steaming hot milk topped off with thick black coffee. She poured a heaping teaspoon of condensed milk into the cup then sat down, slowly stirring her spoon to get the mix right. She noted that the byline on the story was Grace's and she shook her head in sorrow, thinking, *Well, baby girl, there's no coming back from this.*

COOGAN ADMITS GUILT

Multiple Murders?

By Grace Garland

Rob Coogan, well-known local coach and musician, admits his guilt in the killing of Winston Butler, in a letter to his fiancée exclusively obtained by this reporter. Butler was the banker charged earlier this year with child molestation and abuse. His body was found floating in the marina at the lakefront. In the letter, Coogan also alludes to his having a "standard of selection" and his involvement in several other murders over the years. He alleges that the murders were all performed on child abusers, though he fails to present evidence of this allegation in his letter.

Police have been unable to tie Coogan directly to those other murders, although police have noted there are "similarities in the acts that would lead one to assume they were committed by the same perpetrator," according to Detective Jules Jensen of the NOPD.

Tomorrow we begin a series of interviews with friends and acquaintances of Coogan, reaching back to his college days, which will cast a shadow over the wildly popular reputation of Rob Coogan.

Tim Noland, Coogan's attorney, when called for comment, responded, "There is no way that my client would admit to doing an act he did not commit. And certainly not in this manner. The paper should be ashamed to present this as fact. I am amazed that the newspaper is seeking to prejudice a potential jury in this manner. We will ask the court as soon as we can get a hearing to move this trial to a location where the news media is not seeking to act as judge, jury, and executioner."

Millie thought about the careful way that Tim Noland had framed his response and laughed out loud. *They won't get my slippery devil without a fight, and that's for sure*, she thought.

Millie liked Rob as much as any man she'd ever known, but she adored Lisa. Lisa had gone to work for Tim after leaving Jay Giles's firm for reasons that neither Tim nor Lisa had explained to her. Lisa was a quietly kind and beautiful young woman, whom Millie had briefly hoped Tim might latch onto. When she met Rob and saw Lisa and Rob together, she quickly realized that would never happen.

Millie spread the newspaper on the large kitchen table and was clipping coupons for her weekly visit to the grocery when the phone rang.

"Tim Noland's residence," she announced.

After a brief pause, she heard Tim's voice: "Ah, Millie. I'm so sorry about yelling at you this morning. I'm not sure what came over me, but I sincerely apologize for letting my anger spill onto your lovely countenance. I hope it didn't spoil your day."

"Now don't you worry, Tim. I saw the headlines and realized that it wasn't the most pleasant way to start your day. I'm surprised at Gracie. She and Lisa are such good friends."

"*Were good friends*, might be the operable phrase now, Millie. Apparently she stole pictures of a note Rob left for Lisa the day he had to turn himself in to the police … Anyway, its sneaking up on the fourth and I like the idea of having the big party anyway, so thanks for the reminder. I think people have come to expect it, so unless we've left it too late, let's get it going. I'll tell the office to mail you the invite list. See if the fireworks guys from Slidell can make it as well. Tell 'em we want a big show about eight-thirty pm on the far side of the pond. I'm gonna call the Mag and ask them if we can steal their house band to play that night. I'll leave the decisions about the barbeque and the rest of the food and booze to you. You okay with that?"

"Sure, Tim. I'll probably have to go up to St Francisville next week to get the house in order and ready to go. You gonna be okay on your own 'til after the party?"

"You bet. Next week I'll have to focus on trying to get a change of venue so we can get the trial moved out of town."

"Do you think a judge will let that happen?" Millie asked.

"No, probably not, but it doesn't matter much whether he moves the venue or not, we have to ask for it to get our side of the story out in public."

Tim was a serious proponent of the theory that any criminal defense had to have a simple and sympathetic theme to be successful winning over a jury. In order to do that for Rob, he had to have Butler's reprehensible behavior become a topic of conversation widely in the area that the jury pool would be drawn from when the trial started.

Tim realized that his case was precarious and presented difficulties that would be very hard to overcome. Prosecution disclosure in the preliminary hearing had revealed a claim by the prosecution that they had the murder weapon and had recovered a glove from which they expected to reveal DNA evidence. Judge O'Neil had refused bail, based on Rob's Irish roots and financial resources, so Rob would remain in jail until the trial.

Without asking him, Tim was filled with certainty that Rob had killed Butler, and in the words of Rob's note to Lisa, that Rob would "gladly do it again". That knowledge took Rob's testifying off the table. Tim couldn't allow Rob to lie and Rob's general unwillingness to dissemble or deflect the truth meant that should Rob testify, it would only seal his doom.

Tim said, "We are in a publicity war and Judge O'Neil has already told me that he will shut down the 'he needed killin" defense as soon as there is one utterance in court in front of the jury about the victim. He also said that I would be sanctioned for going in that direction after being admonished by the court."

Tim continued, "So a change of venue hearing will be the only chance I get to present the fact that Butler was a scummy child abuser into the storyline in the newspaper. My guess is that Grace is gonna milk this story between now and the trial. Once we place Butler's acts in the middle of the story, she'll have no reason not to include that every time."

"I didn't know that Judge O'Neil was assigned the case. That ought to be good—he's your buddy, right?" Millie asked.

"Millie, I admire Lawrence as much as any judge in New Orleans and we are a bit more than just acquaintances," said Tim. He hesitated, then continued, "But I respect him mostly because he would never let personality or friendship enter into his rulings. His warning on the jury nullification means he is going to run a very, very tight ship."

“You’ll figure out how to get around that, Tim. You always have. I’m guessing you’re the lucky guy whose luck never runs out. Least I hope not.” She laughed. “Fix supper for you tonight?”

“Not for tonight, thanks. But hey, fix me a big pot of red beans and rice you can leave for me while you’re gone.”

“I’m going to get Lisa working on a plea for a change of venue. Then I gotta go by and visit Rob to bring him up to date. I’ll see you in the morning before you leave for the Country.”

As he was about to hang up, Millie heard him pull the phone tight and say, “Oh, and Millie, I’m *really* sorry about snapping at you this morning.” Then the phone clicked and he was gone.

CHAPTER 49

Tim Noland's law office was not standard fare for the office of a successful criminal lawyer. Instead of a wall full of photos of politicians, the main wall behind his desk was covered with Tim's extensive collection of guitars.

Another wall was covered with album covers, including Motown, Funk and Rock from the sixties, seventies and eighties. The wall facing the front of the building had two floor-to-ceiling windows that filled the office with light.

The massive partner's desk, which Tim had inherited from his father, dominated the middle of the room. Matching leather desk chairs at each end of the desk also matched the inlay of leather in the broad desk. The chair Tim used faced the office door and looked considerably more worn than the chair facing him from the other side.

The other walls were surprisingly bare, with no great show of bookcases filled with law books typical of most law offices. The portable computer facing Tim's chair was both a connection to the outside and the source of whatever legal research was required by his practice.

A sideboard held a CD player and stereo speakers along with a fairly large screened television and various bottles of liquor and glasses. Next to the wall with the album covers was a small seating area with a large sofa, coffee table and two comfortable chairs. Al Green was playing over the speakers and Tim Noland appeared lost in the song, "Let's Stay Together", as he stared at the keyboard in search of something in his research.

Lisa knocked briefly and stuck her head around the door, asking, "You ready? Want some coffee?"

“Two minutes,” said Tim, looking up. “Coffee sounds great.”

Lisa closed the door quietly and walked down the hall to the kitchen.

Tim was having an exceptionally hard time with the Coogan case. Lisa’s sorrow tore at his heart every day.

One of his strengths in criminal law was his ability to maintain distance from his clients. That distance helped him to recognize the strength of the prosecutor’s case with a clear eye. It also enabled him to occasionally recommend taking a risk to the client. As important, it allowed him to keep his perspective on the possibility of success or failure without being weighed down by the negatives that invariably come out in a criminal trial.

When Lisa returned to the office, balancing two cups of coffee and a notepad, Tim saw that the light from the floor length window outlined her slender body underneath the thin cotton dress. Quite noticeable was the bulge in her midsection and he realized she was pregnant. He thought carefully about how to raise this with Lisa and came to the conclusion that he would have to wait for her to say something first.

“Lisa, you ready to get started? We need to file a motion today to ask for a hearing on a change of venue. I’d like to have it in Judge O’Neil’s hands tomorrow afternoon. I put the research and a rough outline on your desk last night. Let’s work up a draft together that we can take a look at as soon as possible.” Tim directed.

Lisa placed Tim’s coffee in front of him, then sat in the chair facing his partner’s desk. She opened her stenographer’s notebook and started taking notes. They worked for a while, with Tim dictating the various elements of the filing. When he was finished dictating, Tim leaned back in his chair and spoke quietly: “Lisa, I’m going to see Rob this afternoon to bring him up to date. Is there anything you want me to tell him for you?”

Lisa looked up from her notes, and, looking quite pained, asked, “Tim, is there any chance I can get in to see Rob? I have something I’d like to tell him face to face. I haven't seen him since his arrest and I don't want him to think I've abandoned him."

Her face held an expectant look that was almost painful for Tim to see. "Lisa, you can certainly go see Rob for a visit, but you aren't covered by privilege, so it's going to be important that you stay away from anything that could be said that might cause a problem. That's why we haven't even let you see the letter he left you on his way to be arrested."

Lisa said quickly, "Oh, no, nothing like that, it's a, uh, well a personal matter. Can I go with you today and spend a few minutes alone with Rob?"

Tim stood and leaned over his desk, "Lisa, Sergeant McNulty helped me to arrange Rob's cell assignment so that he'd be safer and we don't want to mess that up, but if you ride over there with me later we can ask him if it's okay for you to have a visit."

With tears welling in her eyes, Lisa said, "Thank you, Tim. I don't know how Rob and I will ever be able to thank you enough."

"Call Millie and ask her to get a gallon of her seafood gumbo ready for us to bring to Sergeant McNulty. That always puts him in a good mood."

CHAPTER 50

A small group of cops and lawyers was gathered in front of Sergeant McNulty's command post, waiting patiently for him to turn and face them. He was leaning back in his chair and facing directly away from the supplicants with his fingers interlocked and appearing to hold his head steady from behind. No one could determine whether he was asleep or awake. None was willing to risk facing his ire, so a standstill had ensued.

Tim Noland strode across the room and directly into the group. He placed a gallon plastic ice cream container, now filled with gumbo, on the desk. Then he tapped on the desk, announcing, "Well, now this gumbo isn't gonna eat itself."

McNulty turned with a look of anger on his face that quickly turned into a broad smile upon spotting Tim. He lifted one edge of the plastic top and took a deep inhale, using his other hand to wave the smell toward his red bulbous nose, saying, "That fucking Millie is a genius. You know, Tim, when I have a good night's sleep, I know it's because I was dreaming of that Christmas Party at your house every year."

"Sarge, it's a bit of a drive, but you should plan on bringing the family to my place in the country for the Fourth of July party. Millie outdoes herself."

"How about if I come without the family?" McNulty said with a laugh.

"Well that'll be on you, then, Sarge. Far be it for me to give advice to a man such as yourself who is still married to his high school sweetheart."

He continued, "Let me introduce my assistant, Lisa. We have a bit of a favor to ask, if you can help us. In addition to being my assistant, this young lady is Rob Coogan's friend. Do you think it would be possible to arrange for her to spend a few minutes with Rob? She hasn't seen him since his arrest."

McNulty looked at Lisa with some sympathy in his eyes, but said, "Well, now, Tim, how could we do that? I'd have to bring him over from his cell at the Parish Prison and then they would have to meet here in the intake cell. That would take quite a bit to arrange. I'd have to have all the folks in there now moved out."

Tim decided to just play the conversation as though McNulty had agreed. "Wow, Sarge, that is so kind of you to offer to do that. If you think it will take some time, why don't Lisa and I leave you to it as we are heading to court for a motion to change the venue. We could be back here around four. She'd only need a few minutes." Tim walked around the desk, and, leaning in, spoke quietly behind his hand placed near McNulty's ear: "I believe she needs to tell him that she is expecting. Not exactly the best place to find out, but I think you'll agree he needs to know."

Realizing that he'd boxed himself in, McNulty responded, "Sure then, Tim. Come back a little before four and I'll have it arranged. And please thank Millie once again. Tell her I'm gonna bring my whole tribe to the fourth, so she better put in extra provisions." McNulty laughed and turned to the other people waiting, immediately assuming his more natural frown.

CHAPTER 51

Despite her promise to herself, tears leaked from Lisa's eyes as she stared through the bars of the cell at Rob. He stood in his orange jumpsuit with "OPP Prison" printed on the back in black letters. He looked very pale and thin, as though the sun had not seen his face in months.

His mournful gaze added to her misery. "Lisa, dear, you shouldn't be here. In fact, you should forget about me altogether," Rob said quietly.

"Now you hush, Rob, and listen to me carefully. I love you. I will always love you, no matter what. As to why you're in here, we can't discuss that, because I'm not covered by immunity, so I could be called to testify as to what we have discussed about what happened."

"Just let me say that I understand why you might have done what they say you've done. It doesn't matter to me at all … in a way … it makes me proud. I think you are one of the finest men I've ever met."

Lisa looked at Rob and grabbed his hand. "Last weekend my dad told me that it didn't surprise him a bit, because he knew from the first that you were a man who knew that people have to sometimes do the right thing, even if it's against the law." She laughed. "He told me that apparently the Irish are like Cajuns—they know nothing is more important than children and family … But, Rob, now you have to do your best to get out. That means you have to listen to Tim and follow his instructions to the letter. No talking about what happened and especially no talking about doing it again. I need you to get out and Tim's the way to get out."

She gripped the bars fiercely and pushed her face between two bars. She reached with her hand and pulled Rob's face to meet hers and kissed him, tenderly at first, then with a fierceness that surprised them both.

From across the room, Sergeant McNulty harrumphed and said, "Now, Lisa, there can be none of that. Just tell the boy the good news, as you've only a few minutes left."

Rob looked quizzical and asked, "What good news is he talking about?"

"The day they arrested you I was visiting my mother, you remember?"

"Sure, I was waiting for you. I had come to realize that I had to share that part of my life with you if you were ever going to agree to marry me. I was hoping to discuss it with you when you got home from your ma's. Of course then it all changed. I only had a few hours and so I had to write the notes. Apparently Grace got her hands on them and they were in the paper. I was trying to explain why I had done what I'd done and why I would likely keep doing it if I can. I had come to realize that I had to share that part of my life with you, if you were ever going to agree to marry me. You needed to know everything about me and who I am. So I set about to do that. Now I realize it's too late." His eyes filled with tears and his head dropped toward his chest.

Lisa placed her hand on Rob's face and lifted it to look in his eyes. Using her thumb, she wiped his tears, while cupping his face tenderly. "It's not too late, Rob. I so want to marry you." She laughed, "Some would say I have to."

Rob frowned and said, "Have to … ?" Then recognition broke and he smiled more broadly than Lisa had ever seen on his face. "Oh, Sweet Jesus," said Rob. "We are going to have a child." He reached through the bars and hugged her, leaned back, and looked her over from top to bottom and said, "Well, you can't be very far along you're thin as a rail."

Tim walked up to the cell and said, "Rob, I hope you're motivated to listen to me." Rob nodded and Tim continued, "You will remember that at the preliminary hearing the prosecution said that they have the weapon, and expect to have DNA evidence tying you to the crime. The good news is that thus far we know of no witnesses." Placing both hands on the bars, he said, "So it's going to be tough. I really think that our best chance is to use this change of venue hearing to bring out what a horrible, evil person Butler was. Potential jurors need to hear that now. That hearing is when we will be playing to the press to get that word out on Butler. Judge O'Neil won't let me use a jury nullification strategy during the trial, but there is no way he will allow your notes to Lisa into the court record either. So your role in all this is to do and say nothing. Not to Lisa, not to me, and not to anyone. Can you do that?"

For the first time since his arrest, Rob felt vaguely hopeful. He realized that he now cared about whether he would be convicted. "A child. God is blessing us with a child," Rob cried, realizing he needed to do whatever he could do to make sure he could be there for Lisa and for their child.

CHAPTER 52

Tim Noland leaned over the railing of the back porch of his country home. The view during his Fourth of July party at his home was his favorite and made him glad he had put the party in motion with Millie in time to pull it off.

Along the banks of the pond in the distance, kids with fishing poles were keeping their fathers occupied trying to get crickets on the hooks and removing tiny bream, then returning them to the pond. Every once in a while, a fish would be of sufficient size to put in a small ice chest for tending to later. Those catches came with happy shouts of joy.

Young couples had spread blankets on the grass between the pond and the pool and were taking in the sun. More kids were in the pool immediately behind the back porch being watched over by moms with frozen daquiris, their legs dangling in the pool. Laughter filled air redolent with the smell of sunscreen and barbeque.

Now that the sun was beginning to hide behind the trees in the distance, the band was setting up. Soon they would start playing from the porch of the pool house and the music would go late into the evening pausing only for a fireworks show to celebrate the holiday.

Millie was holding forth next to the tables around the pool. Running back and forth between the kitchen inside and the barbeque pit off to the side, she had tables filled with an food. Sergeant McNulty was loading a paper plate so full it was bending in the middle.

The desert table was devoted exclusively to home-made ice cream in multiple flavors and five or six blueberry pies made from fruit Tim and Millie had picked together the day before.

"Well, there's a man who looks like he should be on top of the world."

Tim turned to see Doc Dawes wearing outlandish orange Bermuda shorts and a garish Hawaiian shirt carrying a large daquiri as he sidled up to Tim and leaned against the railing next to him.

"And yet he's not." Doc patted Tim on the back and asked him quietly, "You all right, Tim? You look kind of troubled."

"Oh, hey, Doc. Naw, just daydreaming. You doing ok? I thought I saw Patty out there with the ladies."

"Fine, Tim. Beautiful day. What a fabulous place you have here."

"I guess I'm a lucky guy, Doc." Tim turned to face Doc directly and said, "Well, you know, Doc, I was just looking across the way at Lisa. She's over there helping the band get set up. She really didn't want to come to the party, but I convinced her that moping around their house wasn't going to do Rob any good."

Doc's eyes clouded and he bent his head as if he wanted to say something, but refrained from doing so. Finally, he said, "Do you think Rob has a chance when this goes to trial? It seems that he hasn't gotten much of a break with the media. I guess this week, you did lay down a good marker that the guy he is supposed to have killed was a really terrible person. Do you think that helped?"

"Who knows. You take your best shot. Those articles of Grace's were really, really bad for Rob. The line she quoted from his note to Lisa that keeps getting repeated is bound to stick in people's minds: "Yes I did it and I'm glad. I'll do it again if I get the chance."

Doc sighed deeply. "Tim, I thought about calling you, offering to testify for Rob. I dunno, character witness of whatever. Honestly, though, I don't think I could do that. I love that boy. I think of him as my son, but I know too much to be of much use. I'm afraid all I could do is make it worse."

"Know too much?" asked Tim.

Doc ignored he question and walked over to the cushioned sofa that faced an outdoor fireplace near the back of the porch. He sat, then patted the sofa, indicating Tim should join him. "You know that Rob can't testify, don't you, Tim?"

Tim shrugged his agreement, then asked, "Because … ?"

"As he did once with me, he'd tell the truth and that would be the end of him. That boy is capable of a lot, but telling a lie isn't in his repertoire." Doc continued, "I hear that my friend Lawrence has warned you about putting the victim on trial. Is that true?"

Tim sat next to Doc on the sofa and took a long drink, finishing the dark beer he was carrying. "I am afraid so, Doc. He's a good judge, so he recognizes that strategy isn't permitted. He won't allow it. He did give me great leeway in the hearing this week when I sought to move the trial out of town. So I got a few shots in about the sleazebag that got killed. I think Grace felt enough guilt to lay that on thick in her coverage of the hearing. Unfortunately, Lawrence ruled against me yesterday on changing the venue. We are scheduled to go to trial in September "right here in river city." He gave a big sigh and rubbed the glass against his forehead. "I have to admit that wasn't unexpected as its really difficult to move a venue under Louisiana law."

"If you can't put the victim on trial, then I guess you'll look for another culprit?"

"What do you mean, Doc?"

"Is it true that there are no witnesses?"

"They haven't found any so far."

"Really? I thought witnesses say they saw Smile down there threatening the victim that afternoon. Has no one shown up to say they saw Rob there?

Didn't I hear that the main physical evidence is that they found a rosary made from guitar strings?"

"Yea, that's right."

Reaching into his pocket, Doc pulled out a rosary made from guitar strings and held it in his hand toward Tim. "Look like this one? Or like the one Smile carries?"

Standing and looking like he had completed his mission, Doc said to Tim, "Seems like a good lawyer could make a good case of reasonable doubt on that alone."

"Love the party, Tim. Thanks for the invite." Doc walked off the porch and out among the crowd of adults watching the small kids frolicking in the pool. He leaned down and put his massive arm around Patty. Kissing her on the top of her head, he whispered in her ear and laughed so loud Tim could hear him through the crowd.

NEW ORLEANS

2005

"An event like Katrina leaves you feeling
like you may have reached the End of Time.
At least the end of your own time.
It's only later that you realize
that it will be a new beginning.
Whether you want one or not.
Whether you are ready or not."

– Theodore Dawes, M.D.

The ADVOCATE

Monday August 29, 2005

KATRINA'S WRATH NEARS

New Orleans in crosshairs: BR expects a blow

Category 5 at 10 pm

LOCATION: 27.5 degrees N 89.4 degrees W

MOVEMENT: NNW at 10pm

MAXIMUM SUSTAINED WIND: 160mph

The ADVOCATE

Tuesday August 30, 2005

BIG BLOW

Katrina swamps New Orleans;

Four dead in LA.

The ADVOCATE

Thursday September 1, 2005

PLEADING FOR HELP

....

Page 5

The state Department of Corrections Secretary Richard Stalder said Wednesday that his office began moving the inmates from the Orleans Parish jail, as well as those in Jefferson Parish, around 1am.

CHAPTER 53

Black continued to joke, despite the conditions.

"I done disappeared," he mumbled. "It's so dark in here that I can't even see myself." He laughed in a voice grown raspy from lack of water to drink, despite the two feet of putrid water that covered the floor of the cell and lapped against the bottom bunk.

The combination of the darkness and the oppressive heat that had descended after Katrina had departed made the cell they occupied in the Old Parish Prison feel like a stop on the road to hell not far from the destination.

"Damn, if it wasn't for the greasy shit smell floating out of that water down there I'd probably get down there and drink a gallon off the floor," he croaked, and poked Rob in the ribs with his elbow. "You think this bunk can hold us both much longer?" When Rob didn't answer, he continued, "You think anyone is going to bring us something to eat or at least some water? We ain't seen nobody since they handcuffed our cell door yesterday. We should've broke out like them other motherfuckers did."

The prior day they had watched several inmates break the locks on their cell doors and appear to wander away. After that, guards came back and had looped handcuffs through the bars to offset the weakness of the cell door locks.

A day after it appeared, the storm had passed, they had begun to believe that they had made it through unscathed. Then the water had begun to creep into the first-floor cell area. Shortly thereafter the guards had disappeared. The water had started rising fairly rapidly in the cell late Tuesday.

Now it was late Wednesday, and Rob and Black sat next to each other on the top bunk of the cell they had shared in Old Parish Prison for the last several months. The water lapping over the bottom bunk was continuing to rise slowly.

Their last contact with those outside the prison had been a call Rob and Lisa had on Saturday. Rob was surrounded by prisoners waiting for their turn to call and check on their families. The phone in the common area had suddenly gone dead. Rob had just finished telling Lisa she needed to evacuate New Orleans. Lisa was hesitant to leave and told Rob that she had a contingent plan in case the storm damaged the home on Esplanade.

Rob was worried about Lisa and hoped she had listened and gotten out of New Orleans. She had told him that her Mom and Dad were planning to go to Lafayette to stay with her Mother's sister. Rob had encouraged her to join them. Unfortunately, all communication was now cut off, so all he could do was hope that she had listened.

It was clear to Rob that the Orleans Parish Prison had descended into chaos. The guards looked more frightened than the prisoners and it appeared that no one was in charge. It was Wednesday now and the prisoners had not been fed since they had each had a sandwich thrown to them through the cell bars on Saturday.

At first the guards had brought bags of ice which they had used for water, but that had stopped the prior day when Katrina arrived in full force. The wind and rain had battered the buildings and finally the electricity had failed and the prison had turned dark.

In the darkness it was difficult to keep track of time. Rob thought that it might be nearing dawn as the prior day he could see some light leaking under the door to the guard's area where there was a window to the outside. Now it appeared that a faint light was beginning to show.

Suddenly that door opened and through the darkness Rob saw the beam of a flashlight shining down the corridor. A large bald-headed guard, sweat streaming off his face, stepped through the door and in a loud commanding voice said, "Listen up. One cell at a time we are going to open up and the two prisoners are to gather your shit and form a line in the hall. When you are all out of your cells we will proceed outside."

Prisoners began to mumble and complain and reveal how scared they were. The prisoner in the cell next to Rob and Black started shouting, "I can't swim. I can't, please, I'll drown!"

The guard walked over to the cell pointed his flashlight in the face of the prisoner and told the prisoner, "You don't have to swim. Just stand upright. If you fall over I'll pull you up."

"I can't do it. Please don't make me."

"Okay, here's your choice, asshole. Do what I say and you'll get out of this. Keep complaining and I'll lock your ass in here and you will drown." The guard turned to Rob and Black's cell and unlatched the hand cuffs, tucking them in his back pocket. "Out, get your shit and wait here in the hall."

Rob climbed down into the water carefully. He reached back up to top bunk and grabbed his few personal effects, including a picture of Lisa which he had placed in an ice bag and tied up to keep dry. Black slid off the top bunk and landed in the water with a splash. They walked carefully through the thigh-high water into the hallway.

Prisoners began to fill the hall. In the light of the flashlights held by the guards, the water reflected an oily sheen that reinforced the smell of diesel mixed with the rancid smells of the overflow from all of the toilets in the cells.

Black continued to mumble and complain, while Rob stood stoically waiting for instructions. He was thinking of Lisa and hoping that she had listened to his admonition to get out of New Orleans before the storm. As strange as it might appear to others, Rob felt happier than he had in years after finding out that Lisa would marry him and they would have a child. *Now I just have to listen to Tim and hope that he can keep me from spending me life in prison*, he thought.

The prisoners were marched down the hall and through the guard's tiny office. The light was provided by two guards' flashlights and the window, so the prisoners were bumping into furniture and each other setting off arguments and complaints in equal measure.

After passing through the guard's office, the line continued down a long hallway, ending at a door with light beginning to shine through from the outside. It appeared dawn was breaking.

"All right. Stop here. You are to remain in the hall until we bring you out through the door. Once out of the door, you will be loaded into a boat. Follow instructions and you will be okay. If you attempt to run, you will be shot."

When their turn to climb into the boat came, Black nearly tipped the boat over when his bulk hit the side of the boat. As the boat began to take on water, Rob and several other prisoners still in the now waist-deep water lifted the boat's side to help offset Black's bulk. Climbing into the bottom of the boat, Rob settled in and wondered where they were heading and whether there would be water to drink when they arrived.

As the boat began to move slowly through the gate, Rob began to pray about what to do with Lisa. He knew that his future was bleak. Tim had been honest—it was likely that he would be convicted given the strength of the evidence that the police had. Despite her protestations of love and her intent to marry Rob, he knew that the only way that could ever happen is if he was able to reach a not guilty verdict in his impending trial.

CHAPTER 54

The sun was rising over the Mississippi River and glaring directly in their eyes through the massive bridge when their boat bumped onto the Broad Street overpass. The fierce shards of sunlight promised unbearable heat would soon be added to the already humid atmosphere. The boat faced onto the overpass and Black exited first, then held the boat in place for the others to climb out and walk up the ramp.

The overpass was almost covered with prisoners lined up back-to-back in rows. Almost all had a look of total misery, Despite the early hour, most of the men were covered in sweat and looked desperate for something to ease their thirst.

Black walked over to a group of prisoners sitting on the riser of the roadway, staring without expression at him as he arrived.

"Wassup. You dudes know where we can get some water?" Black asked.

The question was met with derision from the group, one of whom responded with a growl, "Shit no. They ain't give us no water to drink since yesterday."

This set off grumbling among the prisoners, who nodded in agreement.

"Do y'all know how we getting out of here?" Black asked.

"They gone put us in that line over there. Right now we gots to sit down back-to-back in these lines. When the time come, you climb down and get a bus the fuck out of here."

"Where the buses go?" Black asked.

The only reply he got was a shrug of the shoulders and then the prisoner he had been talking to turned away as if to dismiss any more questions.

Black and Rob walked over to survey the line. When they reached the starting point of the line on the far side of the overpass, they saw men speaking to a guard who made notes on a clipboard and then the prisoners climbed over the edge.

Leaning out, they realized the men were climbing on to a scaffold and down to the interstate highway that crossed underneath the overpass. Both ends of the overpass were in water. The interstate highway was on risers so that the end heading in the direction of the Mississippi River Bridge remained above the flood waters. The top of the interstate was covered with school buses and guards and prisoners scrambling to load the buses.

Black looked at Rob with fear in his eyes and said, "I don't know about climbing down that rack. Looks mighty light to me. My fat ass might fall straight through that thing. I'd end up busting my head and drown in that nasty water."

Rob put his arm on Black's shoulder and said, "Look, I'll go down in front of you. That way I'll be there if you fall."

"So you gone catch me?" asked Black.

Rob grinned, "Probably not, but I'll wave as you go by. Seriously, man, we can do this. We really don't have a choice. This is the path home for you and for me to see Lisa again. Besides, it looks like there are some really bad guys around here and not nearly enough guards. It could get dangerous if we are still out here tonight after it gets dark. Let's go get in the line."

After nearly five hours in the line, with the sun at its full baking power, Black and Rob were at the front of the line and began their descent toward the gathering of busses on the interstate. Rob climbed easily down the scaffold and waited for Black, who was taking his time.

Finally, they were pushed by guards into a line and loaded onto a school bus. The bus was built for forty children, but was packed with over sixty prisoners by the time it began to move out. Each prisoner was handed a bottle of water which most gulped in an instant.

"Hey, Guard, where we going to?" asked Black.

The guards in the front of the bus glared at him briefly and turned away without answer. The bus crossed the Mississippi Bridge and went north on the West Bank Expressway.

Time passed slowly as the bus became less and less habitable. The stench of the men's odors became unbearable. Finally, the guards had answered the pleas for a stop with, "We ain't stopping until we get there, so y'all quit axing."

Eventually, Black leaned over and told Rob, "Looks like we heading to my neck of the woods."

"Where is that?" Rob asked.

"North of Baton Rouge. Could be they taking us to Angola," he said with a pained look on his face. "You better hope we turn off on Highway 68. Then we ain't going to Angola but to Dixon."

"Is Dixon better?"

"Ain't none of 'em good, but my cousin in Angola say it's like scary dangerous. Fellows always getting killed in there. No matter where we go, just make sure you don't look nobody in the face."

Several minutes later, the bus turned right onto a two-lane road and Black said, "Whoo. Look like we going to Dixon."

The bus wound through several large curves and up and down hills, finally slowing down to enter a prison that looked like it had been built in the middle of a massive pecan orchard. The prison fences were topped by razor wire and several towers loomed over the facility. The facility was surrounded by hundreds of acres of pecan trees in precise rows and tightly mowed grass that gave the area a manicured look.

Once the bus was inside the prison, the guards told the prisoners to form a single file and follow them to the designated area outside. Each prisoner was required to tell the guard filling out paperwork their name, offense and the name and phone number of their lawyer if they had one. Then they were walked to a corner of the fenced area that looked like a well-used exercise yard and told to find a place to sit.

They were allowed to get water from coolers that were placed around the sides of the area. After an hour or so a golf cart came out to the area and the two guards on the cart handed out boxes of food for each of the prisoners.

Black finished his meal in seconds. He drank his water as if he'd just arrived at an oasis in the desert, gulping and allowing it to run down the side of his face.

Rob sat with his back to the interior fence of the exercise yard and wondered how Lisa and the baby were doing. He realized that he was already thinking about them as one: Lisa and the baby. It made him happy in the hell pit to think of that.

Black looked at him and said, "Man, you crazy. We sittin' here in a prison yard surrounded by angry bad dudes lookin' to stick somebody with a shank and you grinning like you won the fucking lottery."

Rob looked at Black with a sense of satisfaction that was the impetus behind the look on his face. "Well, Sylvester, knowing Lisa and I are going to have a child feels like that to me."

The midday sun at Dixon Correctional was baking Black and Rob as they sat back to back in the yard next to the wire interior fencing of the prison. Black was constantly mumbling and wondered aloud whether they would get out the formerly relatively safe prison alive. Rob sat quietly wondering when he would hear from Lisa.

The prison administrators and guards were confused about who each of the prisoners were and what offenses they had committed to put them in prison. This confusion had led to prisoners being placed together despite warring gang affiliations.

As the gangs began to coalesce and reform, violence became rampant, as the gangs sought to gain alpha status. Each day had brought multiple stabbings. The violence had gotten worse daily, with the nighttime filled with moans, screams and other sounds of madness.

Even more frightening, former snitches and others who had testified to receive reduced sentences had been placed in the open yard serving as a holding area. In some instances, in the same confines as those they snitched on to get reduced sentences.

Most of the prisoners' attorneys were difficult to reach as they were also from Orleans Parish and had scattered to Houston, Lafayette and as far away as Dallas. Contact with prisoners' families was nearly impossible.

As a local, Black had an advantage no one else seemed to have. By promising to get his attorney to find a gang leader's attorney, he had been able to take his place at the head of the line to the one phone in the prison courtyard

Then he was able to call Tim Noland at his weekend home in St. Francisville. Tim's home was thirty miles west of Dixon Correctional. Black told Tim where he and Rob were being held and asked him to see what could be done to help them. He also asked Tim to see if there was a number where Rob could call Lisa.

When he returned to his seat, he was once again confronted by "Tee" Williams, the head of the fiercest gang in the Ninth Ward that had moved from the New Orleans Parish Prison. Williams was establishing his control over Dixon. His bald head and light black skin looked like an ax had traversed his face, a deep crease ran from his forehead down through his chin to his chest into his white coveralls. The coveralls were bulging with muscle covered with tattoos.

"Nigger, you best tell me that you got ahold of my lawyer," Tee growled.

Black stood up to his full height and, despite his fear, looked Tee in the eye and said, "I did what I told you I would do." He hesitated, then continued, "My dude said that he did not know your lawyer, but knew of him. He would reach out and try to find him and get him in touch with you."

Williams glared at him. "He better, 'cause if I don't hear from him today, you gonna pay." With that, he turned and walked back to rejoin his gang that idled throughout the outdoor weight lifting area.

Black settled back next to Rob and said, "Shit, a man can't even get a rest here in prison from all these fools." Elbowing Rob, he pointed to the entrance road that wound through the pecan orchard toward the prison. "Hey, look." There was a police vehicle making its way toward the prison.

Rob looked and said, "A police car? What about it?"

"That ain't just a cop car, Rob. That's Sherriff Petrie hisself. He's my homie from St Francisville. We played football together at Wes Fel. I bet he come to see us. Ole Tim the man. You know what, Rob? We may be on our ass in prison but we ain't forgot."

Twenty minutes later Rob and Black spotted a group of prisoners hanging around the yard gate separate and two prison guards enter, followed by the Warden escorting a tall white man dressed in khakis and a white polo shirt with a badge pinned over his heart.

Black elbowed Rob again. "I told you. That's my Sheriff." He jumped to his feet as the Sheriff approached and said, "Sheriff, you a sight for sore eyes."

The Sheriff stopped just short of Black and said, "Sylvester, I told you not to go down to New Orleans and get liquored up. But no, you don't listen to nobody. How did that turn out? You were in Parish Prison for how long?"

"Way too long, Sherriff. I know you was right. Ain't never going back to N'awlins. Never again. Sheriff, this my friend, Rob Coogan. I'll bet Tim Noland called you about us? That right?"

"Sylvester, you still have some time to serve, but the warden here is looking to reduce population, so he released you to finish up in the St Francisville jail." He laughed. "That's kinda like your second home anyway. You come along with me." He turned to leave, then said over his shoulder, "Tell your friend to come along, too. Seems if we take you we get a two for one special today only from the warden."

CHAPTER 55

Sitting on the picnic bench in the exercise area at the St Francisville Jail, Rob watched tourists walk down Ferdinand Street. He wondered where they came from to this small town in the deep south. They appeared unaffected by Katrina, the hurricane that had disrupted so many lives and left devastation in its wake only days before. Rob felt as though Katrina had swept him into its powerful winds and carried him to St Francisville.

Ferdinand was just a short block away from the small cul de sac where the Parish jail sits in the middle of town. It winds through St Francisville from its intersection with Commerce Street past historical houses, Grace Episcopal Church, then down Catholic Hill to the ferry landing on the Mississippi River. The ferry landing is where riverboats regularly unload tourists drawn to the beauty and history of the town.

Often the tourists stopped to use the rest room at the end of the block near the jail. Then they walked across Ferdinand to rest near the fountain that marked the center of the Historical District. Rob envied their countenance and seeming lack of worry and concern.

Six of Rob's fellow inmates were playing a low-key game of basketball in the yard, spending most of their time complaining that it was cheating for Black to get every rebound. It infuriated them even more when Black laughed and said loudly, "One mo rebound." Then waved each rebound he grabbed as if he was holding an orange in one hand. Then he would pirouette gracefully and jam the ball through the hoop and rattle the metal netting as the ball rocketed through. "Two mo points."

Since his arrival in the St Francisville jail, Rob had come to realize how lucky he was to have moved out of the prison environment in New Orleans. Most of the prisoners in the town jail seemed low key and non-threatening. Having Black as his cell mate afforded him even more protection. Black knew the guards as well as most of the other prisoners who gave him wide berth because of his size.

Despite this bucolic setting for his incarceration, Rob was increasingly worried, because he had not yet heard from Lisa. By his count the hurricane had passed over a week ago and there was still no word.

The Sherriff had dropped them at the jail after a ride over from Dixon four days ago.

During the ride over from Dixon Correctional, they had found out that the Sherriff loved all kinds of music and he admitted to being a fan of Rob's. He said that he had danced with his wife to the song "True", in his words, "back when I was in the ninth grade and courting the most beautiful girl in West Feliciana Parish." He got a wistful look as he told Rob, "I probably did better with her than I deserved thanks to you."

Tim had come by the jail the afternoon they arrived and told Rob that he hadn't heard from Lisa, but not to worry, as most of the phone systems in South Louisiana were down and he was certain that they would hear shortly. He would be staying at his home in West Feliciana and would let him know as soon as he heard from Lisa.

Rob watched the Sherriff's car round the corner onto the side street where the jail sat, and cruise into a parking spot marked "Sherriff Only". The Sheriff jumped out of his vehicle and, carrying a guitar, walked into the jail building.

Several minutes later, the Sheriff and the warden walked into the exercise yard. The Sheriff handed the guitar to Rob and said, "Okay, here's the deal. You can use this guitar until they transfer you wherever your trial is going to be. No playing past lights out. Play quietly. If anyone complains we will have to give it up. You good with that?"

Rob shook his head as if he couldn't believe it, "Yeah, sure, thank you. I don't know what to say."

The Sherriff responded, "Just hold on a minute." He dialed his phone and after a moment said, "Hon, do you remember our first date to the dance at Jackson Hall back in high school?" He listened for a moment then turned to Rob. "Play 'True', Rob," he said.

It took a few moments for Rob to adjust the tuning on the guitar, then he began the song softly. It reminded him on that night in Galway when he and Caoimhe had created the song together outside that pub. As Rob sang the chorus, he looked up to see moisture glistening in the Sherriff's eyes.

When Rob finished singing, the Sherriff turned away, whispered something quietly into his phone, disconnected, looked Rob in the eye and said, "Damn, boy, you really something."

With that comment, the Sheriff walked into the jail building, leaving Rob surrounded by the other prisoners, including Black, all asking for Rob to play more tunes.

Black and Rob had walked from Highway 61 down Highway 966 past the old Star Hill Cemetery and were approaching the intersection with Audubon Lane when they saw a purple and orange Ford F-150 that looked decades old turn into Audubon Lane and screech to a halt.

Black turned to Rob with terror in his eyes, "Oh, shit, Rob. Here she come."

Rob responded, "What are you talking about, Black?"

"My baby momma. That's one scary woman and she looking to kill me. I ain't seen her since I left for N'awlins."

Rob, Black, and two other prisoners were carrying large garbage bags. Each of them held a mechanical pick stick used to help them pick up garbage along the highway.

Five days a week, prisoners walked the tree canopied roads of West Feliciana Parish, picking up trash. They were alternately followed or led by a Sheriff's Deputy driving a white Sheriff's Department van pulling a trailer carrying a portable toilet and the bags of trash that they accumulated.

When the F-150 pulled to a stop at the entrance to Audubon Lane, Deputy Clinton Williams opened his door and casually stood outside his vehicle. He had a broad grin on his cherry red face framed by bright yellow hair cut in a 1960s flat top. Twisting his stocky body, he turned and looked at Black with an expression that said, "This is gonna be fun to watch."

The truck door flew open and a short, round, light-skinned African American woman dressed in a long flowing colorful dress and a black tank top shirt flew out of the vehicle with her eyes flashing and venom in her voice and said, "Sylvester, you low life, sorry, motherfucker. I don't know why you bother coming home, you ain't welcome here no more."

She marched across the highway and began to walk past Deputy Williams without acknowledging him in any way. The Deputy tried to stop her by putting his hand gently on her arm as she passed. She shrugged off his grip and continued walking directly up to Black. She hissed, "Don't you dare touch me, Clinton." Recognizing the wisdom of her warning, he leaned back against his car and put a toothpick back in his mouth.

Standing within inches of Black, she provided a stark contrast. The top of her tight afro barely reached his chest, which she proceeded to smash with each of her hands repeatedly as if beating on a door to gain entrance.

Black stood with a helpless expression on his face. He finally dropped his bag and stick and put a massive hand on each of her shoulders and pulled her closer to him. As they fell into an embrace, he whispered repeatedly, "I'm sorry, baby. I'm so sorry. I'm coming home soon. I'm gonna talk to Tim," enveloping her in his massive arms.

Finally, Deputy Williams approached the two and said, "Lulu, ya'll finish up. I can't allow this physical contact. If the Sheriff comes by and sees this, I'll lose my job."

Sniffling, Lulu moved back a step, "Thank you, Clinton."

Turning to Black, she poked him in the chest repeatedly, saying, "We ain't done with this. I'm still mad, but I'm glad you back and didn't get caught up in that Katrina down there. Your babies need you here, fool."

"Oh, we did, Lulu baby, we got caught bad. It was terrible. I almost drowned up in there. Snakes everywhere, floating dead bodies, toilets flushing right out into the water. That stinky water got so high we had to wade out with it up to our necks. Then we got made to climb some jungle gyms like back in grade school and then took a boat ride and you know I can't swim. We coulda died all manner of ways. And all I could think about was you, my Lulu baby."

Deputy Clinton started walking back toward his vehicle and said over his shoulder, "Y'all finish up now, Lulu, you going to have to visit Black at the jail. We done here. Okay?"

Black bent from the waist and kissed Lulu gently on the lips, "I'm so sorry, baby. It ain't never going to happen again."

With that, Lulu flashed anger once again, saying "Don't lie to me, Black. You ain't out of this ditch yet, not with me."

Turing to Rob, who had watched the whole confrontation in amazement, she said, "What you looking at, white boy?"

"Whoa, Lulu. That's my friend, Rob. You gonna like him a lot."

"Look like jail trash to me. What you in fo?" she asked.

Rob didn't answer. He turned and looked helplessly at Black.

Black finally spoke, "They say he killed some low life that was hurtin' kids."

Lulu looked at Rob and said, "That's against the law? We supposed to help kids, keep 'em safe, ain't we. Plus, you kinda a handsome devil. Okay, I'm pleased to have met you."

She patted Rob on the arm, crossed the road and got in her truck. The truck blew a cloud of smoke as she drove away down Audubon Lane without once looking back.

"All right, breaks over. Let's get moving," said Deputy Williams as he got back in the van and started up the engine. He pulled forward a hundred yards and pulled over to the side.

Black, Rob, and the two other prisoners began walking on both sides of Highway 966, looking for the bits of paper, beer cans and other items that provided them an opportunity to walk in the shade along the beautiful road.

Rob finally asked, "Black, you described her as your baby's mama. Is that what she is? Or are you married?"

Black laughed heartily, "Oh, yea, Rob, we got married last day of high school."

"She seems like a very strong woman. Does she keep you in line?"

"She tries, Rob, but I got a bit of ramblin man in me." He laughed again. "I come by it honestly. My daddy was a cowboy. He had what he called fourteen head of kids, four different women. Ain't never married none of 'em."

"My two kids different 'cause of their momma. My oldest girl top of her class at West Fel. Smart like her momma. My son … well, he a good boy, plays basketball. Tenth grade. He already six-ten. Hardworking boy. His grades okay. That's mostly his momma, too.

"You know, Rob, I don't know a whole lot, but you want good kids, you got to pick the right woman. Now she caught up with me I gotta get home.

Imma get Tim to get me out. I'll be sorry to leave you by yourself, but Lulu want me home."

As the morning grew warmer and they continued their work along Highway 966, Rob thought about Black and Lulu's marriage and the children that had come from that union. He did a quick prayer for them, that their happiness would continue and that the children would remain safe.

His thoughts turned to Lisa, the baby and their future. His purpose in life had always been clear to him. To serve God and to make amends for the terrible sin he had committed. He remained driven to continue to rid the world of evil people. He viewed his relationship with Lisa as proof of God's love for even someone like himself that had committed such a terrible sin.

He marveled at how simply, yet how clearly, Lulu had articulated his life-long mission. To help kids and keep them safe. All of a sudden, the thought of spending the rest of his life in jail filled him with dread.

CHAPTER 56

One way to tell the New Courthouse from the Old Courthouse in the middle of St Francisville is that almost nothing works in the New Courthouse.

Its air conditioner intake was built immediately adjacent to the exhaust and thus came perilously close to poisoning all of the Parish employees with carbon monoxide when the building first opened. Electric plugs built into the floors and walls were never completely wired so they have open spaces where electrical plugs are supposed to reside. One of the corners of the New Courthouse cracked and sank when the water system continuously dripped massive amounts of water and over time the footings collapsed.

The Old Courthouse was a solid building that was built in the early 1900s. Its construction was surrounded by much controversy, as it was built on the site of the original Courthouse destroyed by fire.

Some of the locals argued vociferously that it should be restored rather than razed and a new structure built. People marched and protested.

Controversy has been a cornerstone of St Francisville life ever since.

The Old Courthouse is topped with a beautiful white cupola with four sides. Each side has a clock face that points due east, west, north or south. Every few years the Parish makes an effort to repair the clock and get it running again, but those efforts have seldom lasted long.

It is now permanently four twenty-three in St Francisville and it appears that the ladies of the Historical Society intend to keep it that way. The last time the Parish was looking for bidders to work on the clock, the Society submitted a comment in the Parish meeting requesting that the clock be left alone. After due consideration, the motion to submit for bids was tabled on a vote of five to one.

The New Courthouse is home to the Sheriff and Assessor on the first floor, the Clerk of Court is in the basement, and it has a second floor where there are two small but modern courtrooms and a chamber used by the Parish Council for its meetings.

The Old Courthouse has a traditional courtroom built of carved maple railings and furniture, tall wooden windows, and a large audience section that lends a somber appearance to the venue. Surrounding the Courthouse square are houses now converted into lawyers' offices mixed with beautiful and historic residences still in active use. Across Ferdinand Street is the Grace Episcopal Church with its oak grove cemetery out front.

Tim Noland parked his car along the street facing the Courthouses and walked through the entrance of the New Courthouse. He put his briefcase and cell phone on the metal detector and noticed the slender, bald-headed Deputy laughing when he did so. "I'm sorry, but did I do something?"

The Deputy stood, offering his hand and said, "Naw, that thing ain't worked since we moved over here. That's why any time we got any real controversy we use the Old Courthouse. They got a metal detector that can actually spot some metal. I'm Deputy Griffin. Who you here to see? And please go ahead and fill out the log," he said, turning a log booklet with an attached pen to face Nolan.

"I'm Tim Noland. I represent both Sylvester Wilson and Rob Coogan and I'm here to see the Sheriff."

Deputy Griffin laughed out loud and said, "Them two are something. You got yo hands full with that pair. That boy can sing though, we go over and listen to him play some afternoons at the jail."

Confused, Tim said, "The Sheriff?"

Deputy Griffin hooked a thumb over his shoulder and said, "Back that way. Right through that door. I guess he expecting you?"

Tim loved St Francisville, but it always left him feeling slightly confused when he dealt with its residents. It was like each one of them was extremely eccentric, whereas the people of New Orleans were collectively, yet only slightly, insane. He always felt off balance in St Francisville.

Like most people who had moved to West Feliciana or found a weekend home there, Tim wanted to be the last person to cross Thompson Creek and hoped it would remain small and eccentric forever. When he first bought his place the real estate agent had given him some advice: "Don't ever talk about anyone here to someone you don't know. Everybody here seems to be related in some way and word will get back to them." It had turned out to be good advice.

As he entered the Sheriff's office suite, he spotted Sheriff Petrie through the door to his office off the reception area. He had a book balanced on his left knee and was twirling the chamber on a .38 and pretending to quick draw with the right.

His secretary, Barbara, looked up at Tim and said, "He said to go on in when you got here."

"Oh, and Tim, I sure did enjoy that fourth of July party. That Millie is probably the best cook I ever seen. Please don't tell my mama I said that."

"Your secrets are safe with me, Barb."

Tim walked into the Sheriff's office and said, "I sure hope that .38 isn't loaded."

The Sheriff turned back, placed the gun on his desk and said, "Tim, you gotta treat 'em all like they loaded. Man have a seat. It's great to see you. I guess you escaped Katrina okay. Any flooding at your house?"

They continued talking about how desperate New Orleans was and how grateful Tim was to have his place in West Feliciana to get away from the devastation. Finally, Tim said, "I do have a couple of items of business. First, I reached out and got a release order for Sylvester Wilson. The judge agreed to let him go early, believing that having to go through that ordeal was sufficient punishment for a drunk and disorderly."

He handed the paperwork to Sheriff Petrie, who shuffled the papers and pretended to read them, then called Barbara on the intercom, "Barb, call over to the jail and tell them to release Black. Ask him to come see me after he gets released. Tell him I might have some work for him out at the farm."

Tim hesitated, then said, "I have a personal favor to ask. My paralegal is a young woman named Lisa Sanders. She is engaged to your other prisoner, Rob Coogan. When the hurricane was approaching, she decided to stay behind at Rob's house on Esplanade. Apparently, the house had no flooding and only minor damage, but we haven't heard from her. I'm quite worried."

Petrie closed the book, a well-worn copy of *Lonesome Dove* that he placed on a shelf next to his desk. The entire shelf was filled with Larry McMurtry novels. He picked up a small calendar, and, as he turned back, he looked quite serious. "Tim, by my count that's been nearly two weeks. Have you checked with her family?"

Tim's face was pale, "I have. They are out of their minds with worry."

Petrie looked at Tim with concern, "Let's get all her information and I'll put out word through the system to look for her. I'll also reach out directly to the State Police and file a report."

CHAPTER 57

As he drove up the asphalt single lane driveway to Tim Noland's summer house, Sheriff Petrie realized he was going slower and slower as he neared the house. This was one of the duties of a Sheriff that required more emotional control than Petrie was comfortable being assured he possessed.

As he rounded the last bend of the driveway and emerged from tree cover to the front of the house, two black Labradors yipped and barked a welcome. After parking his car, he walked slowly toward the front porch, petting the labs as he approached.

Before Sheriff Petrie reached the porch, Tim opened the front door and stood staring at the Sheriff. He was looking for a positive answer he could tell would not be forthcoming by the look on Petrie's face.

"Tim, I'm afraid ..." Petrie's voice broke.

"She's gone?"

Petrie nodded and Tim broke down and sobbed.

They moved to two rocking chairs on the porch and sat side by side. Tim cried quietly and Petrie cleared his throat repeatedly to keep from joining him. Neither said anything as time seemed frozen. The two labs walked up on to the porch and both leaned against Tim's legs, as if to give him comfort.

Finally, Tim stopped sniffling and asked, "What happened?"

"Tim, the best we can piece it together, she got through the storm fine. We had some troopers who went through the house and they saw what they called evidence she had been there during the storm. They couldn't figure out where she went, though. Apparently all cell communication was down and the landline wasn't working.

"Later that day they got a report of a car near one of the underpasses that looked like a wall of water had hit it full force. The car had been moved by the flood into a small canal and sank. Apparently no one noticed or paid any attention to it until the water receded and they saw the top of a car in the water. When they dragged it out of the canal, they found her in the front seat, still in her seat belt. The backseat was apparently filled with new baby gear. Car seat, bassinet and so forth."

Tim's shoulders sagged and his sobs became louder and more powerful.

Petrie stood up and patted Tim's back hesitantly. "They've notified her parents. Her parents are going to retrieve the body. Don't know about a service." He paused, then said, "I thought maybe you would want to ride into town and tell Rob yourself later today."

Tim looked at Petrie, his eyes clouded with emotion. "Yeah, sure. I'll do that in a while. I think I need some time to process this."

Petrie started down the stairs of the porch and turned back, "Oh, one more bit of news you won't want to hear."

Tim looked up.

"Judge O'Neil called looking for permission to use the Old Courtroom. Apparently he is going to move the trial for Rob here to St Francisville. He told me he wants to get it going soon, because he plans to retire when it's over. He's got that place at the Bluffs and wants to settle in there and play golf."

"So the local DA will be the prosecutor? What's he like?"

"Uh, no. More bad news. The New Orleans DA has hired a guy by the name of Milton Bensen. Supposed to be some hotshot prosecutor for hire."

Tim groaned and put his head in his hands.

"One of my buddies who's a Sheriff in North Louisiana said to me that in Louisiana there are supposed to be seven poisonous snakes, most of which will leave you be if you don't disturb them. My buddy says that there's actually eight when you count Bensen. He described him as the most poisonous of all the snakes, says he goes looking for something to hurt."

Tim looked up slowly. "Yeah, I know Bensen. Terrible person, but unfortunately for us a great lawyer."

ST. FRANCISVILLE

2006

"You, Your Honor, are a judge. I am the supposed culprit. I am a man. You are a man, also. By a revolution of power, we may change places, though we could never change character. If I stand at the bar of this court and dare not vindicate my character, how dare you calumniate it?"

– Robert Emmet

"Speech from the Dock"

Dublin, Ireland

September 19, 1803

CHAPTER 58

Rob drifted between sleep and wakefulness, his jail cell quieter now in the months since Black had been released. Yet seldom was his sleep undisturbed.

In the morning his trial would begin. That was only a minor factor in his lack of rest. His prayers were seldom complete when sadness would overcome him and his mind would wander through a torturous review of his life. He renewed his prayers over and over, yet no peace came to his heart or his mind.

After lying in the dark in his confused state for what seemed like hours, he abruptly sat up, twisted his legs on his thin mattress and reached his bare feet to feel the cool concrete floor of his cell.

Seated next to him, his mother, Maeve, looking elderly and frail, shook him by the shoulders and admonished him to live up to his promise to God: "Live your life as a man, Rob. Do what is needed in this trial you face so that you may continue to have purpose until God is finished with you and releases you from that purpose."

Rob shrugged his shoulders away from her, and turned away to face Caoimhe. Her long black hair framed her cerulean eyes, which were creased with worry. She stroked his cheek and whispered quietly in his ear, "The Children still need you, Rob. You do them no good here. I know that the loss of Lisa tears away at your humanity, but the children still need you."

Rob closed his eyes and placed his head in his hands. When he opened his eyes, Black was standing in the corner of the cell. He was dressed in an immaculate dark blue suit with a crisp white shirt and a red tie matching his red pocket square. His shoes were buffed to a patent leather shine. "They right, you know. You can't do nobody no good up in here. I know you sad. You deserve to be sad. You lost you a good woman. But she gone, bro."

Rob lay down and pulled the thin blanket over his body and closed his eyes. He turned toward the wall. When he opened his eyes, he was looking at Lisa. "Please rest, my darling Rob," she said to him. "We will be together again when your work here is done."

Tim Noland finished his coffee, placed his folder holding a legal pad on the table. He looked around the Bird Man Coffee shop that was the social center of St Francisville. The room was filled with tables of various sizes. Almost all were filled with what looked to be mothers having dropped kids at school and now on their way to play tennis. The largest table near the front had older patrons who were deciding the fate of the world.

Tim had stacked his briefcase and two boxes of documents on one of the chairs. The other chair was occupied by Michael Harvey, his co-counsel for the trial that was scheduled to start that morning.

Harvey was a thin wisp of an older, meticulous lawyer. He was well known and highly regarded in West Feliciana Parish. His slight body and ascetic demeanor was non-threatening to all and he was highly respected by both those who practiced in the local courts and those who came to those courts seeking justice. Like many rural lawyers, his principal business was drawing up wills, divorces and real estate purchases. Thus, he had wide knowledge of the people of West Feliciana that Tim knew would be valuable throughout the trial.

Harvey was wearing a tweed jacket, dark pants and a rumpled blue shirt with a non-descript tie. He was hunched over a yellow legal pad and making notes rapidly next to the list of names on the pad. The names represented the pool of potential jurors that would be put through their paces today in seeking the jury that would determine Rob Coogan's fate.

“So we agree? We want mostly women, right?” asked Tim.

The Parish had once been named as one of the five best places in the country for single women in a national magazine article. The article cited the census, which showed twice as many men as women lived in West Feliciana. Locals laughed, knowing that of sixteen thousand total population in the parish, six thousand of the men lived in the parish only because they were incarcerated in Angola Prison.

The prison also meant that there were a disproportionate portion of the population aligned with law enforcement and were more likely to side with any prosecution.

“Sure, mostly women, but I think that the notes I’ve made should be helpful. We definitely don’t want the men or the women I have scratched off here,” said Harvey. “I know most of them would hang anyone on suspicion of crossing the street against a light.”

“What I don’t understand is why Bensen seems so intent on seeking the death penalty. This isn’t a death penalty case,” said Harvey.

“I agree. You’d have to know him better. First, he’s very good. Second, he thinks it’s his mission to send people to the death penalty. Third … well, he’s an evil little dweeb and sending people to the death penalty is the only thing he has that makes him feel special.”

“What worries me more is that Judge O’Neil has sent folks to death row before, including two of my knucklehead clients.”

As he rose to go to the check-out and pay his bill, he bumped into someone rushing through the coffee shop and stopped to look. “Grace? What are you doing here?” he asked.

Grace Garland stood with a hand on her hip and flirtatiously said, “Well, I’m actually looking for a good-looking lawyer from New Orleans by the name of Tim Noland.”

Tim turned and handed his credit card and bill to the young girl behind the cash register. "Grace, I'm not talking to the press. I'm focused on the trial right now."

"Not even for me?" Grace said with a sly smile.

"Especially not for you," said Tim, signing his receipt. He walked over to the table and loaded his boxes and his files and started for the door.

"Let's go, Michael."

CHAPTER 59

The courtroom in the Old Courthouse was packed. In addition to the local media and one or two reporters from the New Orleans and Baton Rouge newspapers, there was a smattering of national reporters, there for the opening of the trial.

Television reporters and their cameras had greeted Tim Noland and Harvey as they walked past the Confederate Statue and up the walk to the side entrance to the Old Courthouse. The kabuki theatre of lawyers ignoring shouted questions set the stage for what the neutral observers hoped would be an exciting trial.

Upon arrival at the courthouse, Judge O'Neil had asked them into his chambers. He first asked them to estimate the amount of time they would require to put forward their defense. He showed his surprise when Tim told him he thought it would take less than a day.

Bensen, on the other hand, had told Judge O'Neil, "We plan to put on a comprehensive prosecution, Your Honor. The sacred responsibility of the State in a Capital Murder case to is to carefully present compelling evidence that does not allow doubt to linger. I believe we can do so in three full days after opening arguments."

Judge O'Neil said, "Gentlemen, today is Tuesday. I suggest we get jury selection completed today through Thursday and on Friday you can each make your opening arguments. Mr Bensen, you can begin presentation of your case in full on Monday. Now, do you have anything else?"

Milton Bensen stood, and, reaching into his briefcase, removed a sheaf of papers and said, "Judge, I am requesting again that the prosecution be permitted to present to the jury an article in the New Orleans paper that reveals the defendant's confession of the crimes to his fiancé."

Before Tim could raise an objection, Judge O'Neil said, "Denied, Mr Bensen. I've ruled on this previously and I have no reason to change my opinion. Let's move on."

Bensen remained standing and said in a forceful manner, "Judge, I repeat my request and ask that you reject my petition formally and in writing so that I may bring it for an appeal prior to the beginning of the trial. I will be seeking an emergency ruling of the circuit this weekend."

Reaching across to pick up the filing, Judge O'Neil glanced through it and reviewed it before signing his rejection of the motion. Returning it to Bensen, he said, "Milton, do not ask for an extension of time to await this ruling. If you haven't received a reply by the end of the trial we will not wait or delay. Is that clear?"

Reaching across, grabbing the motion, and putting it in his briefcase, Bensen said, "Yes, Your Honor. Now I have a request to amend my proposed witness list to include Grace Garland, who may be called to testify as to the contents of the notes she reported on in the paper."

Tim threw his hands in the air and in an exasperated voice said, "Your Honor, these supposed notes have no validity. If they exist at all, which I doubt, then they are, by Ms Garland's own admission, stolen property. You cannot permit them, or her, to be relied on in this case."

Michael Harvey stood up and said, "Judge, please let me add that this last-minute appeal of this unreliable witness leaves the defense no time to prepare for the witness. If the prosecution was going to bring this witness forward, they have had plenty of time to do so in a manner that would allow us to prepare properly."

"I'm going to withhold judgement on that question to consider it more fully. Mr Bensen, do you have any supporting briefs?"

Reaching into his briefcase once again, Bensen handed Judge O'Neil a file folder with a thick brief tucked inside.

"Your Honor, if you permit the witness to testify, will you place limitations on what she may testify to with regard to this case?" asked Tim.

"Please clarify, Mr Noland."

"Well, Your Honor, if she is permitted to testify with respect to the intent of the defendant and actions purported to have resulted in Mr Butler's demise, will testimony be permitted as to why Mr Coogan decided to take the actions that he is alleged to have taken?"

Judge O'Neil grimaced, then said, "I told you that you would not be permitted to put the victim on trial here, Mr Noland."

"Nor would I seek to, Your Honor. After all, it is the prosecution who is seeking to put Mr Coogan's thoughts and words before the jury. Surely, Mr Coogan is entitled to have his defense do the same."

"If you and Mr Harvey would like to submit briefs on this issue, I will be happy to review them prior to ruling. Okay, let's go back inside and pick a jury. I'll give my instructions to the entire pool; they will be dismissed and then we can begin. We will bring them up in lots of fourteen. You will each have ten peremptory dismissals and may challenge for cause."

Tim and Michael huddled at their table in quiet conversation, while waiting for jury selection to begin. Tim told Michael that he believed that the trial would be won or lost in picking the jury and that Michael should speak to the potential jurors. Both of them agreed that this would give prospective jurors a local connection to their defense. Now that the trial was beginning, the reality of a death penalty case weighed heavily on Tim.

Rob Coogan, dressed in a blue blazer, gray pants and a white shirt with a narrow blue tie, sat looking like a statue of a man in agony. He had lost significant weight and his suit hung so loosely he appeared to be ill, though his face remained tanned from his daily walks picking up trash along the road. That solitary exercise had quieted, but not removed, the sadness that pervaded his life since he had been told of Lisa's death. He rarely spoke and then only if someone spoke to him.

Tim had spent time with Rob preparing him for what was to come in the trial. Early on, Rob had discussed that he might want to testify. When Tim had finally presented him formally with the choice, Rob remembered what Lisa had said and reluctantly agreed that in his present state he would likely do more harm than good. He knew that the only value left for him in his life was to continue what he saw as his life-long work helping children.

After considerable research and a deep review of the evidence and list of witnesses that had been provided them by the prosecutor, Tim and Harvey had reluctantly reached agreement on a defense strategy. Tim knew that it was risky and that its success depended on Milton Bensen's arrogance leading him down paths on which Tim could spring a trap or two.

After two days of discussion and time spent looking for other options, Michael had agreed with the strategy, saying, "The truth is we cannot put Rob on the stand, so we have very little else."

A Deputy Sheriff serving as bailiff walked in from the judge's chambers and spoke to the assembled crowd. When he finished his brief oratory and the crowd stood up, Judge O'Neil entered the courtroom from his chambers and strode across the raised dais and took a seat behind a massive desk with the seal of the State of Louisiana carved in its face.

Seated in front of the judge were Lois Lemle, the Clerk of Court, and the court's stenographer, Lois's cousin, Ruth Lemle. Immediately behind Ruth was the raised jury box with twelve seats in two rows of six and another two seats behind the second row, reserved for two alternates. Small pools of

Deputies, court workers, and others spoke quietly while waiting for court to begin.

As a capital murder case, the jury would have twelve members with the two alternates poised to step in if any individual juror was unable to finish. In Louisiana, only ten of the jurors are required to find a defendant guilty. This made the burden on the defense even greater than in other states, where unanimity was required to convict on a capital murder.

In front of the rail that separated the raised dais from the courtroom, two tables faced the judge. On the right side, Rob, Tim and Michael sat quietly, huddling together occasionally as a thought occurred to one or the other.

At the left table, surrounded by large stacks of paper, file folders, books and documents, sat Milton Bensen. Moments earlier, to the staccato sound of her high-heels tapping on the wooden floors and echoing off the twenty-foot ceilings, he had been joined by his co-counsel, Betty Leach.

Leach was an assistant attorney in the Criminal Division of the New Orleans DA's office. In her blue business dress, she exuded graceful elegance. Although she was sharp and well-versed in the law, her role on the team was primarily to present a less threatening visage than Bensen was capable of exhibiting.

The prosecution, too, had a list of the prospective jurors, notes written throughout the list. Bensen was bent to the task of a final review of the information they had on the jurors. Leach would question the jurors so that Bensen could study their demeanor and reactions.

Every seat in the courtroom was taken. The first row had been reserved for members of the media, with Grace Garland front and center, flanked by local and national reporters.

The rest of the courtroom was filled with nearly one hundred prospective jurors, ordered by subpoena to appear that morning at nine. They were waiting patiently to be called. The vast majority were hoping to be excused, as the service worked a hardship on their family or work life.

After checking his watch, Sheriff Petrie, dressed in a dark blue suit with his badge clipped to the jacket pocket, tapped the bailiff on the shoulder and indicated he should announce the Judge.

After entering the courtroom promptly at nine-thirty, Judge O'Neil spent a few minutes thanking the prospective jurors for their service, "despite that service being involuntary," which drew a laugh from those assembled. He then looked at the Sheriff and the Clerk of Court and thanked them for "their kindness and hospitality in allowing the court to be used for a trial originally scheduled in Orleans Parish".

"As you all know," Judge O'Neil continued, "New Orleans has been devastated by Katrina and we aren't clear when normal court schedules will resume."

Judge O'Neil then indicated that the clerk should call a roll of prospective jurors. The Clerk asked that each person whose name was called to indicate that they were present and how far they had to drive to the courthouse from their home. This was so that they could get the mileage they were entitled to be paid during their jury service.

Judge O'Neil instructed the potential jurors that they had to be US Citizens, be at least eighteen, able to read and write and not under indictment in the previous five years. "If you don't meet those requirements, or you have another reason why you may not be able to serve, please step forward and speak to me."

One by one, eight people filed up, spoke quietly to Judge O'Neil, and were dismissed.

The clerk then drew fourteen names from a small bucket of the jury pool. Those fourteen prospective jurors were seated in the jury box. Each of them swore or affirmed to do their duty, and selection began.

CHAPTER 60

By the end of the day on Thursday, the jury was seated. Twelve residents of West Feliciana Parish—farmers, teachers, housewives, two small business owners, and three prison guards—would be the ones to decide Rob's fate. Whether he was guilty or not, and, if so, whether he should be sentenced to death or not.

Tim viewed them as a good mix. The three prison guards would likely give greater credence to law enforcement than an ordinary person, but Tim hoped that would be offset by the four African Americans who might lean the other way.

Judge O'Neil thanked the jury and warned them not to discuss the case or watch any news reports concerning the trial. Both the prosecution and the defense realized that the jury would likely not heed that warning. Tim hoped that any news reports would highlight the reason that Butler had been arrested.

Having spent the last few months in preparation, Tim thought that Rob was likely to be convicted. The prosecution had the murder weapon, and would carefully weave that evidence into the story they were prepared to tell. The only weaknesses in their case were that they had yet to produce a witness and they would be reluctant to discuss the motive.

If Judge O'Neil ruled that the prosecution could call Grace to testify, then her testimony would provide the jury with a confession on which they could hang a guilty verdict. Even worse, if Bensen's appeal was returned and it allowed him to produce the news articles Grace had written, then the jury would have both a confession and a motive laid out in writing. While Tim thought that the Appeals Court was unlikely to produce an opinion that allowed what he viewed as hearsay evidence, he wanted to spend much of the weekend building a plan to refute that testimony.

Tonight, Tim would work on his opening statement. As a defense attorney, he always tried to avoid the temptation to overthink an opening. What had worked successfully for him in the past was to simply and without flourish take apart the theory presented by the prosecution.

Judge O'Neil concluded his remarks to the jury by letting them know the schedule they could expect and when their service might conclude: "So tomorrow we will hear from the prosecution in their opening, then the defense will respond. Bear in mind that what they say is not evidence; it is generally an outline of what they hope to prove.

"While it may be helpful in organizing their presentation, evidence is what you should rely on when reaching a verdict, not theories or conjecture. Since tomorrow is Friday, we will recess after lunch and come back on Monday when the trial will commence.

"Let me thank you once again on behalf of your fellow citizens for your service. We are dismissed." O'Neil tapped his gavel and stood to leave.

The following morning, Judge O'Neil sat behind the cheap wooden desk that served the judge in the small office off the main courtroom. Betty Leach sat in one of the chairs facing him, while Milton Bensen gripped the back of the chair in which she sat. Tim faced the judge from a wooden chair next to Betty Leach and Michael Harvey stood behind him in the tiny space.

"So, Milton, any word from the Appeals Court?"

"Not yet, Your Honor."

"Okay, then. I am going to wait to hear their decision before I rule on whether Ms Garland may be called to testify. I will say that it's difficult to see how you get her testimony by the Hearsay Rules, but I'm willing to listen to arguments here in chambers." He turned and looked fiercely at Bensen. "Just so we are clear, any reference to those news articles and their contents will result in severe censure from the bench." Judge O'Neil then turned to Tim. "As for you, Mr Noland, you are well known for hijinks in the courtrooms of South Louisiana. Please be aware that you will be treated just as harshly.

"Now, you're both excused."

As they walked through the door to the courtroom, Tim turned to Bensen and asked, "Do you think he means it, Milton?" He laughed to show Bensen a confidence he didn't feel.

After seating the jury and instructing them once again as to the purpose of opening remarks, Judge O'Neil said, "Mr Bensen, you may begin."

One of the reasons that Bensen had been so successful in securing guilty verdicts was that he recognized that most jurors take the responsibility very seriously. He never cut corners in presenting a case. He was so thorough that many thought he bored a jury into a conviction.

He knew that if you left something out that a juror thought important, doubt would creep into that space. His battle was with doubt and he entered the fray with doubt in his opening remarks.

"Ladies and gentlemen of the jury, I'm Milton Bensen. I am here representing the State, in the matter of the State of Louisiana versus Robert Emmet Coogan. Mr Coogan is charged with the most serious of all crimes: felony murder with special circumstances. As such, should you convict him, he is subject to the death penalty." Raising his voice slightly, he pointed at Rob and paused dramatically before continuing, "Which he deserves, for committing this terrible crime." Bensen rocked back and forward from heel to toe as he looked at each member of the jury. "This is a solemn responsibility that you and I share. I want you to know that in the course of this trial, we will present evidence and testimony that will prove beyond a doubt that Robert Emmet Coogan did 'lay in wait' with the full intention of murdering Hilton

Butler on his boat on April 4th of last year. I mention the term 'lay in wait' because that is the special circumstance of this heinous crime that makes it punishable by death.

"This wasn't a crime of anger or passion. Crimes which you and I might condemn but understand on some emotional level. Mr Coogan decided to kill Winston Butler. He made a choice; then he made a plan. He hid himself and his intentions. He watched and waited for the right moment. The moment when he had maximum advantage, and then he leapt out of the dark, seized Winston Butler around the neck with a homemade weapon, a rosary, and choked the life out of him.

"So my job is important, but simple. We will present evidence that will prove that Mr Coogan made the device used to kill Winston Butler. We will hear how the police came to suspect Mr Coogan and we will hear medical evidence of how Winston Butler died at the hands of Mr Coogan."

With that, Bensen returned to his seat, and returned the stares of the jury who appeared to be wrapped up in his remarks, including two jurors who appeared to nod as if in agreement.

Tim stood next to his table, cleared his throat and began: "What we know is that Winston Butler died. By the end of this trial we are likely to hear testimony as to how he died. What we won't be any closer to is the answer to the most important question: 'Who killed Winston Butler?'

"Because Rob Coogan didn't kill him. In fact, he wasn't even the first person that the police suspected of murdering Winston Butler. That suspect had a much better motive for killing Winston Butler. That suspect was seen at Butler's boat the afternoon Butler died.

"As this case moves along, I want to ask each of you to keep in mind that the prosecution will not present any evidence or testimony that ties Rob Coogan to this murder. Zero. Nada. Zilch." Tim waited and looked at each juror one by one. "Their entire case is built on speculation. And that's not enough to convict beyond a reasonable doubt."

CHAPTER 61

The first witness Bensen called was Jerry Wittle, the harbor master of the New Orleans Yacht Club marina. After taking the oath, he settled his large body, wrapped in an ancient polo-style shirt that barely covered his protruding stomach into the witness chair. He was clearly uncomfortable in the formal atmosphere of the courtroom, shifting his body from side to side and rotating his head as if his neck were stiffening as he sat.

He was introduced by Bensen, who asked him about the morning he found the body floating in the harbor. Wittle told the jury that his maintenance crew had spotted the body floating next to Butler's boat: "He appeared to have been wrestling with an alligator and he had lost badly. Poor Lea, the cleaning lady, was freaking out. I have to say it was a pretty awful sight."

"Did you know Mr Butler? Is that why you were able to identify him at the scene?" asked Bensen.

"Oh, sure. I knew him okay. He'd kept his boat at the marina for a few years. He was demanding and pretty full of himself."

"So you were able to identify him?" Bensen repeated.

"Oh, yeah, the alligator bit off his arm, not his head. I knew it was him once they pulled him out of the water."

"Okay. Then you identified him for the detective?"

"Yeah, it was awful. Some alligator was chomping on the arm of Mr Butler when we found him. Took his arm clean off, it was sticking out of the gator's mouth."

"So you identified the body for the detective?" Bensen asked again.

"Yeah, I did. It was a mess."

"Thank you, that's all," said Bensen.

Tim Noland passed on the witness, believing that the quicker they got through the particulars of the crime, the better.

After Bensen excused the witness, he called Dr Neibe Osterhaus to the stand. Dr Osterhaus was tall, appearing to be over six foot. His shoulders were slightly slumped and his hair was thinning. His handsome face, however, appeared assured, as if little would disturb him.

"Dr Osterhaus, can you tell us a bit about your background and where you presently serve?"

"I'm currently assistant coroner for the Parish of Orleans. I've been on the job there since 1998. I was trained at the New York University School of Medicine. While there, I worked for the New York City Coroner's Office. When I married a woman from New Orleans in 1998, she didn't give me a choice where we were going to live. I was hired by the coroner in New Orleans and I've been in that office ever since."

"And since 1998, how many autopsies have you performed?"

"On average two to three per week so approximately a hundred to a hundred and fifty per year. All told, I suppose well over a thousand."

"So, Dr Osterhaus, did you perform the autopsy on Winston Butler?"

"I did."

"Was there anything unusual about the autopsy?"

After a brief hesitation, Osterhaus responded with a smile, "Well, the arm of the deceased had been bitten off by an alligator. In fact, we recovered the murder weapon from the stomach of the alligator. You don't see that often, although it's not unheard of here in Louisiana."

"So, given the attack by the alligator, can you tell us whether that attack was what you identified as the cause of death?"

"No, absolutely not. Our testing showed that the alligator attack was post mortem. We identified the cause of death as murder: murder by strangulation."

"Thank you. Can you describe for the jury what you believe happened to cause Mr Butler's death."

"Strangulation is described in the literature as the utilization of pressure on the throat by hand or with an object that results in the cutting off of oxygen. Strangulation will generally result in a fracture of the hypoid bone which proved to be the case here. In this case, the victim appeared to have been garroted with a wire object."

"And was that object recovered at the scene?"

"Yes."

"Can you describe it to me?"

"It was a religious object, a rosary that had been hand-shaped using guitar strings to create the beads constituting the decades of the rosary as well as its cross."

"The rosary in question, do you have it with you today?" Bensen asked.

"No, I'm sorry but I do not," Dr Osterhaus responded, clearly chagrined.

Bensen looked puzzled and against all of his training asked a question to which he did not already know the answer: "If you don't have it, where is it?"

"I'm sorry, but we don't know."

"Meaning what?"

"It, along with all of the other evidence for this case, was stored on shelves in the evidence cages in the basement of police headquarters. The basement went under water during the Katrina flood and remained flooded for several weeks. Most of the evidence was stored in grocery bags or paper file boxes. As you might imagine, neither of those survived the flooding. When we tried to prepare yesterday, we discovered the evidence for this case was missing. I do have pictures of the rosary." He reached inside a folder he was carrying and handed several ten-by-twelve-inch black-and-white photographs to Bensen.

Tim Noland and Michael Harvey rose simultaneously and as they began speaking, Harvey acceded to Tim, who stated, "Your Honor, may we approach?"

Judge O'Neil said, "I'm going to excuse the jury for a few moments."

The Bailiff opened the door to the jury room and the jurors filed out in single line fashion.

After the jury left, Judge O'Neil stood, looked at the four lawyers, and said, "Please join me in chambers."

CHAPTER 62

Judge O'Neil had removed his robes and sat with the fingers on each of his hands pressed together, his elbows on the desk and looked at Bensen who was standing in front of him. "How did you come in my courtroom this morning not knowing that you no longer had possession of the murder weapon?"

"Apparently Dr Osterhaus has been trying to reach me since yesterday. At least that's what he just told me. I've been here preparing, so I'm not sure why he wasn't able to do so."

Bensen continued, "Your honor I admit this is embarrassing." Michael Harvey snorted out loud, then swiftly smothered his grin. "But we will have the testimony of both Dr Osterhaus and Detective Jensen that the weapon we can identify in the picture was the one used to commit the murder. As you know, appellate courts have ruled that pictures of a weapon can be submitted as evidence."

Judge O'Neil said, "Yes, but those rulings assert that you cannot represent that it is the murder weapon, merely an image of what you believe the murder weapon looked like at the time it was used."

Bensen suddenly had the suspicion that he was being sandbagged by one or both of the detectives in the case. But he had no evidence to prove that either. The witness following Dr Osterhaus was the lead detective, Jules Jensen. Milton had spent considerable time preparing her testimony, during which time she had been thoroughly professional. Bensen had even questioned her about whether Butler's alleged crimes had influenced her willingness to testify against Rob Coogan. "Mr Bensen," she'd said, "it's not my job to sort out the good folks from the bad. Everybody who is a victim of a crime deserves my best."

Thinking back on that, he surmised perhaps it was simply a coroner's office that had been overwhelmed by effects of the storm and were yet to recover their operating equilibrium.

Judge O'Neil considered Bensen's comment, then asked, "Was there any other physical evidence in this case?"

Bensen consulted his notes. "Yes, Your Honor. There was a glove found in the alligator's stomach. We had hoped to have the glove checked for DNA, but the acids in the alligator's stomach apparently destroyed any chance of that."

"So that had limited value for you anyway." Judge O'Neil thought some more. "Let's go back in there and continue." He started to stand, then sat again and asked, "Mr Bensen, have you heard from the Court of Appeals? Any word at all?"

"No, Your Honor, we have not."

When the courtroom reconvened, Bensen sought to rehabilitate Dr Osterhaus's testimony: "So, is it your testimony, Dr Osterhaus, that this picture shows the weapon used in this case to murder Winston Butler?"

"It is."

"And how are you so sure that the rosary was the weapon?"

"We examined the neck of the deceased. There were tears in the flesh along the neck that matched the small beads made from the guitar strings."

"Thank you." Bensen sat down, strumming his fingers nervously on the table.

Tim Noland stood and walked halfway to the witness stand. "Dr Osterhaus, is it your testimony that the rosary in question was used to murder Mr Butler?"

"Yes. I'm certain of that."

"You're certain?"

Bensen objected: "Asked and answered."

"But you don't know where it is?" said Tim.

"That's correct."

"So we cannot examine the so-called murder weapon?

"Unfortunately not."

"And you don't know whom it belonged to, do you?"

"That is correct," said Osterhaus.

As Tim walked back toward the desk, he turned and asked, "Dr Osterhaus, have you ever seen another rosary similar to the one you say was used as the murder weapon?"

Osterhaus looked startled, as if he had not thought about that possibility. "No, I don't believe I have ever seen a similar rosary."

Turning to face the bench, Tim said, "We are finished with the witness for now but want to reserve the right to recall him for further testimony."

CHAPTER 63

Detective Julie Jensen towered over Milton Bensen as he accompanied her to the witness stand. She wore blue jeans, cowboy boots, and a blue blazer with a black shirt, her badge tucked into her blazer pocket. Her hair was pulled back into a ponytail and, even with very little makeup, she looked stunning.

The bailiff administering the oath was clearly smitten with Jensen. When she had finished taking the oath, she winked at him and his face turned beet red. She sat in the witness chair with the comfort of someone used to testifying, used to being challenged by defense lawyers seeking to create doubt.

After she described her current assignment and background with the New Orleans Police Department, Bensen began his questions. He started by asking her to describe the morning the investigation began.

"Well, I got a call from the desk sergeant. Actually, he woke me up. He told me there had been an incident out at the municipal marina at the lake and told me that I would be lead on the investigation. I got dressed and headed out there in my personal vehicle. It was very early, so there was almost no traffic and I made it there in short order.'

"Can you describe the scene when you arrived?"

"Well, there was a lot of whooping and hollering going on. Four people were standing on the dock and this cleaning lady was screaming," She consulted her notebook, "*He eating him*, over and over so I double-timed over to see. Sure enough, they were watching this fairly large alligator who appeared to be carrying off the deceased's arm."

"What did you do next?"

"Well, I made a phone call to my partner, Detective Doucet. He told me how to take care of the alligator."

"And how was that?"

"There's a V-shaped bone structure on the head of an alligator. If you shoot them in that spot, they die pretty quickly. I figured we had to kill the alligator to be able to retrieve the body so we could determine what had happened."

"Detective, I understand that the alligator had two items in his mouth when you first saw him."

"Yes, sir, that's correct."

"Please, describe the items for the jury."

"There was a rosary made out of guitar wire that was half in the gator's mouth hanging from what looked like a yellow leather work glove. Before we could get to them, the alligator took them wholly into its mouth."

"So then you killed the alligator."

"Yes, sir. We had to autopsy the gator to examine the contents of his stomach."

"Please continue describing the rest of the morning's investigation."

"Well, we roped off the scene, interviewed everyone present. Then we retrieved the body that was floating next to the boat. Mr Butler's body was missing the left arm which was floating nearby. We retrieved that as well. Later that morning, divers brought up the alligator and we turned that over to the coroner."

"Detective, how did you come to believe that the murderer was Rob Coogan?"

"Actually, that wasn't me. As I was returning to the station, I called Detective Doucet and when I described the rosary, he said that he was certain he knew who it belonged to and that he would get the person to surrender that afternoon."

"Which he did?"

"Yes, sir—later that afternoon, Rob Coogan surrendered."

"Could you identify the man who surrendered that afternoon?"

Jensen pointed at Rob, sitting stoically at the defense table, and said, "That's him right there."

Tim Noland was having a difficult time keeping the exultation off his face. The loss of evidence had clearly knocked Milton Bensen off his game. Then he had compounded his error by the manner in which he had examined Detective Jensen.

As Bensen tendered the witness to the defense, Tim and Michael Harvey consulted quietly and quickly agreed that there was little reason to wait until it was the defense's turn to go in for the kill. Harvey walked over to the small room off the side of the courtroom and returned with four easels and several large photographs. He set them up where they were visible to the jury and Detective Jensen.

Tim Noland stood and began: "Detective Jensen, after examining the four photos, marked as defense exhibit A, we are showing to you and the jury, would you agree that these photos represent images that one would see from the dock next to where Mr Butler's boat was tied up and where Mr Butler's body was placed when he was brought out of the water?"

Jensen looked briefly at them and then said, "Yes, they do."

"Almost all of the boat docks have a structure to provide cover for the boats. Is that correct?

"Yes."

"On top of most of those structures are what appear to be small apartments where the boat owner can spend the night. Is that correct?"

"That's correct."

"In the course of your investigation, did you interview all or most of the owners, over seventy-five of them, if my math is correct.

"Yes. We did."

"All of whom had a view of the boat where Mr Butler was killed. Correct?"

"Yes. That's correct."

"How many of those you and your team interviewed reported seeing Mr Coogan kill Mr Butler?"

"Many, no, most of them weren't there at the time of the murder."

"Of the ones who were there, how many reported seeing the murder?"

"None."

"Did any of those boat owners make a complaint that day to the NOPD?"

"Not about the murder, no, sir."

Tim turned away as if he were finished, then turned back with a quizzical look on his face. "So there were calls that day?"

"Yes, sir. Earlier that afternoon the department received some complaints."

"What was the nature of those complaints?"

"Apparently Detective Doucet was in an altercation with Mr Butler."

"What kind of altercation? What was reported to the police?"

"The reports say that residents heard Detective Doucet threatened Mr Butler."

"Threatened to do what?"

"I'm not clear on what the threats were."

"I suppose that's why you never considered Detective Doucet as a potential suspect in the murder of Mr Butler?"

Bensen was on his feet immediately. "Objection, Your Honor, leading the witness."

"I'm going to sustain that, Mr Noland. The jury is instructed to ignore that statement."

Tim bowed his head quickly to the judge. "My apologies, Your Honor. I thought we were here looking for the truth."

Judge O'Neil hit his gavel several times and glared at Noland. "Mr Noland, I'm not going to warn you again."

"Sorry, Your Honor," Tim said, and sat at the defense table to look through his notes.

After several minutes, the judge asked, "Are you finished with this witness, Mr Noland?"

"Just a few more questions." Tim stood and asked, "May I approach the witness, Your Honor?"

Judge O'Neil said, "You may."

As he walked to the witness stand, Tim removed something from his pocket and slowly released a rosary made from guitar strings which he held out toward Detective Jensen.

"Have you ever seen these before, Detective?"

Jensen's brow was squeezed together as if she were looking at a very small object too far way to see. Finally, she said, "I can't be certain, but that looks like the rosary that we recovered from the alligator."

"The murder weapon?"

"Yes."

"Have you ever seen a rosary that looked like this before you discovered it at the murder scene?"

"I have."

With raised brows, Tim asked, "And where did you see that rosary?"

“My partner, Detective Doucet, carries one just like it. I believe Mr Coogan made it for him.”

Tim turned and faced the jury, then turned back to Doucet and asked, “Is that why the first person you thought had killed Mr Butler was your partner, Detective Doucet?”

CHAPTER 64

Milton Bensen was frantic. He had barely slept following the nightmare in court the previous day. His room at the Best Western in St Francisville looked like it had been destroyed by Katrina, with documents and books stacked on every flat surface in the room.

"Cut your losses, Milton," said Betty. She was anxious to finish the case and leave town. It was clear to her that they had bungled the prosecution. Bensen had spent the night trying to make an argument that the two detectives had colluded to free Coogan.

"Even if that's true, and I don't think so, Milton, then they did one hell of a job. Christ, I'm your co-counsel and I wouldn't vote to convict."

Bensen stopped pacing for a brief moment. "We get Grace Garland's testimony, we will be able to have a virtual confession. That might not get us the death penalty, but I'm pretty sure we get a conviction."

"That's a big if, Milton. Judge O has already said he's not waiting for the Appeals Court to act on your writ, and we have to go in there this morning and resume our case. We have no momentum. More important, we have no additional evidence or facts. Our case is finished."

When the phone rang, they both looked at it as if it were a foreign object. Milton finally answered and listened for a few minutes. Smiling, he said, "Thank you, can you fax that to me here and also to Judge O'Neil?" He hung up the phone, turned to Betty, and said, holding his hand up for a high-five, "Back from the dead. The Appeals Court just ruled that Grace Garland can testify. Limited what she can say, but we will get that confession on the record in some fashion. Later this morning."

Judge O'Neil sat quietly, listening to the arguments of the two lawyers. He noted the look of concern on Tim Noland's face. Finally, he said, "Okay, folks, let me summarize where we are at this moment. Mr Bensen produced the ruling of the Appeals Court earlier this morning and we went into recess to allow him to produce Ms Garland as his witness. Mr Noland objected."

"I have already ruled that Mr Bensen may call her and, under very tight constraints, question Ms Garland. Mr Noland, you have objected."

Tim responded, "Judge, I have no objection to Ms Garland testifying per se, my objection is to her being asked to put in evidence a supposed confession that she has written was taken from Mr Coogan's residence without his permission. It is now nearing the end of the day and Mr Bensen hasn't produced Ms Garland to testify."

Bensen said, "Judge, Ms Garland has attended the entirety of this trial, yet today she is nowhere to be found."

"Judge, that's hardly our problem," said Tim. "I do think we are entitled to get on with the trial. The jury has been sitting in a small room all day wondering what is going on, and now so am I."

Bensen then says, "Judge, what we could do is wait until tomorrow and give me a chance to continue to look for Ms Garland."

Judge O'Neil contemplated the dynamics. Finally, he said, "Mr Bensen, you made an excellent point and one I hadn't considered until now when you mentioned Ms Garland's continued presence in the courtroom.

"I am going to rule that Ms Garland still cannot testify because she has been present in the courtroom every day of this trial. The sequestration order that precluded witnesses from watching others testify should have included her if you intended to call her as a witness."

"But, Judge—" Milton started.

"I don't want to hear it, Mr Milton. It's not this court's fault that you did not think through the requirements on sequestration put in place to restrict witnesses from hearing the testimony of other witnesses."

Tim had a hard time not looking gleeful as he stood up and handed Judge O'Neil a document. "Judge, I'm going to suggest that Milton rest his case now. I request that you rule on our motion for a Directed Verdict. This case clearly meets the test for a Judgement of Acquittal, as the evidence presented is insufficient to sustain a conviction."

JUSTICE IS SERVED

As I have done most mornings since the trial ended a couple of weeks ago, I sit on the outside patio area of the Bird Man Coffee Shop sipping tea and eating a Glorious Morning muffin.

The proprietress, June, named her shop after her father—the original Bird Man. He carved authentic-looking birds of all types that sit on pedestals and hang from wires throughout the shop. In the right light, it sometimes appears as though flocks of birds are flying through the store hovering near the ceiling to avoid the people below.

Today I was drawn to a new replica of a whippoorwill. Apparently it was placed above the cash register yesterday afternoon. When I asked about buying it, I was told that it wasn't for sale.

It's the last bird the Bird Man carved before he passed away late last year. June had finally brought it to the store to serve as a daily reminder of her father while she was at work. Since I couldn't buy it, I was happy to know that it would remain in the shop for me to see whenever I visited St Francisville. Most mornings I sit quietly outside, read the paper, and listen to the other customers who gather to discuss the news of the day and the goings-on about town.

Although I now own a home here in West Feliciana, I remain a perpetual outsider since I did not grow up here. Nor do I have ancestors whose heritage would allow me to claim that I am a local. Yet the people are nice to me, often asking for my opinion on a legal matter or a statewide political issue. There is live music at the Bird Man and I go to those lovely events occasionally.

Almost no one has asked about the trial. I suppose it is now yesterday's news. Like the paper in the bottom of a bird cage, no longer the story of the day. For that I am grateful.

As the locals begin to wander off in pursuit of their daily responsibilities this morning, I find myself alone, listening to the birds. I watch the occasional vehicle meander down Commerce Street. The cool breeze is offset by the sun creeping through the ivy-covered arbor, warming me to the edge of slumber. When the door to the shop opens behind me, I turn and look over my shoulder to see who is coming out to join me.

With coffee in a paper cup in one hand and a guitar case in the other, Rob Coogan uses one foot to push through the door and walks quickly to my table under the overhanging ivy winding through the arbor above the patio. He pulls out a metal patio chair, then puts his guitar on top of the table. He sits and looks at me with a blank expression.

After taking a sip of his coffee, he puts the cup on the table. Then he opens the guitar case and removes the manila envelope I gave him the afternoon the trial ended weeks ago.

The folder is now slightly stained, as if someone used it as a coaster. He slides it across the table and says to me quietly, "Judge O'Neil, I was surprised when you gave me this information."

I look at the small letters written in my handwriting that read, "The Dentist's Wife" The folder contains all of the information telling the story that broke my heart.

He leans forward in his chair, his intense blue eyes showing curiosity without judgement. "Judge, why did ask me to do this for you? Why didn't you take care of this yourself?" He hesitates for a moment, then continues, "I'm pretty sure that you've sentenced men to death. How is this different?"

It takes a moment for me to gather my thoughts. While I am doing so, Rob removes his guitar from its case. He holds it lovingly, then adjusts the tuning carefully, before strumming a sweet melody.

After a few moments, he looks at me very directly, stops playing, and asks once again, "What makes this different?"

"Two things," I whisper, not able to hold it back any longer. "First—the institutional nature of my job has always allowed me to set aside individual guilt, at least in my own mind. Mostly, I lack the courage to act as an individual."

" I hide behind a glib intellectual construct—one that allows, no encourages me to believe that society doesn't need individual strength or discipline to do the difficult things ourselves."

"Then one day you came along. You appear to have no choices to make, all your decisions locked in place by a rigid moral code that's so admirable to me but is foreign to most people today. I thought that perhaps you would do what I could not. At least I had hoped so."

I pick up the manila folder and stand up to leave. "Thank you for at least considering …" I say, my words trailing off in disappointment.

His head is bent down and I can tell he doesn't want to look at me as he speaks: "What we learned in Ireland is that justice systems are more often about revenge than justice. What I do is different."

"I will always be certain."

"I try to make sure we pray together first. I want to help them save their souls. I recognize that they cannot stop what they are doing. So I stop them because children must come first."

Then he told me this: "When I asked her if she remembered little Bird, she laughed and said, 'Oh my, that was a lively one.'"

Rob looks up at me, his strength shining forth. "And of course then I knew. I always have to be sure, but then I knew. So I prayed with her and sought absolution from her sins … and mine. She will harm no more children."

With those words reverberating in my mind, my heart begins to beat again.

I go inside the shop and stand in front of the cash register to pay, lost in thought, staring at the whippoorwill hanging from a wire. It is spinning colorfully in the spring light coming through the stained-glass window behind the register. I can almost hear it sing.

CHAPTER 65

Smile rode in the passenger seat of the Ford Explorer as it meandered up the driveway. He helped the children scramble out of the car. Billie Jean was left to carry the beach bags and towels. Smile made the boys scream with joy by spraying them with a large and powerful water gun.

The boys ran dodging and weaving all the way to the swimming pool behind Tim Noland's country home. Some of them jumped in the pool fully dressed in their shorts and T-shirts, including Smile, who did an enormous cannonball which threatened to empty the pool.

Billie Jean set about organizing the towels and other clothing for the children. She waited for Smile to emerge from the water. He finally surfaced and, swinging his head from side to side, emitted a sound that mimicked a seal bellow exactly. The boys, having waited for this moment, squealed in delight.

Millie poked her head out the back door and yelled to Billie Jean, "If those brats can all swim, come on inside. I'm fixing cocktails. If you have to keep an eye on them, I'll bring you one."

"Oh, hell no. Smile can watch them. I'm coming in to get a break from the madness if you don't mind."

Millie laughed, then waved for Billie Jean to follow her and walked through the back porch and into the great room and kitchen.

Tim and Grace sat at the breakfast bar that separated the massive kitchen from an equally impressive great room with bookshelves on one wall, a large screen television surrounded by cabinets on another wall and a large fireplace facing into the room. The windows facing the porch and pool area covered the entire wall in both the great room and the kitchen dining area. The view of the pool, pool house, and the pond and forest behind the pond set an idyllic backdrop for the dining area and the great room.

"God, I love your house, Tim," said Billie Jean. "We really appreciate your asking us to come up for the day."

"I'm glad you guys could make it. We've been enjoying some down time since Rob's trial ended. I'm hoping he's coming out to join us. He's been so down for so long and he doesn't appear to be recovering from Lisa's death. Maybe we can cheer him up at least a little."

Millie looked at Billie Jean and asked, "You want some coffee, or are you more interested in a cocktail?"

"Bloody Mary if you've got one."

"You kidding? We keep a pitcher in the refrigerator on weekends," Millie said as she reached in and pulled out a large pitcher. Grabbing a glass from a cabinet, she filled it with ice, measured a shot of vodka, smiled at Billie Jean, and added another shot, before pouring the Bloody Mary mix into the glass. With a piece of celery, she stirred the drink briskly. Then she plopped an olive into the glass and handed it to her. "Voila" she said.

Billie Jean took a long sip, and said, "You mind putting one of those in a plastic cup so I could bring it to Smile out by the pool?"

As Millie set about the task, Billie Jean turned to Tim and Grace. "So, you two back together? Watching from afar, it looked like the trial and all that publicity had you on different sides."

Grace sighed, then said, "Well, I … We were both hoping Rob's situation would turn out okay. I don't think Tim particularly liked me doing my job the way I did. But I'm a reporter—that's what I do."

Tim said, "It was just putting that letter from Rob to Lisa in the paper that pissed me off, it really made it hard to get a fair trial, especially in New

Orleans. If that had been allowed to be presented to the jury, it would have put Rob away for life."

"Tim," said Grace, "I've told you that I consulted with someone in the legal profession about that prior to publication. He told me there would be no way that it would ever be allowed in the trial if it came to that. He also told me that it would allow me to continue telling the story about Butler and what a terrible piece of human waste he was."

"What if Judge O'Neil had allowed it into the trial? He certainly had that power to do so."

"There's no way he was going to allow that," said Grace.

"How do you know that?" Tim asked.

"Let's just say, I knew. For absolute certain," Grace said and looked away.

Tim's red face gave away the level of anger he still held about what Grace had done. "The only way you could know that with absolute certainty is if..." His face relaxed and his eyes started to crinkle as it suddenly occurred to him how Grace knew. "He—"

Grace held up her hand. "Let's just leave it alone, Tim."

Billie Jean said, "That reinforces what Smile told me during the trial, he said: *Judge O'Neil is never gonna allow a jury to convict Rob.* He didn't know why, but he said, and I quote, "The judge is in the bag on this deal."

"When Millie asked me out that day to go fishing," said Grace, "it really surprised me, particularly as the trial was coming to an end. Then I realized you guys were up to something and I wanted to know what it was. My editor was pissed that I wasn't there for the last day of the trial, but I got all the details so the story didn't suffer. I guess I owe you, Tim, for letting me interview Rob that day. That put me back in my editor's good graces." Grace snorted with laughter. "Laurence told me later that Milton was very angry and he couldn't understand why I wasn't in court that day."

“That night was the best fish fry we’ve ever had here,” said Millie, “and we only caught one fish. I guess we were just busy celebrating the one that got away!” She was laughing so hard, she had tears in her eyes. Millie handed Billie Jean the red plastic cup with a celery stalk sticking out of the top and Billie Jean went outside to check on the kids and give Smile his drink.

Looking out of the windows as the setting sun cast a warm glow and looming shadows over the children still playing in the pool, Sheriff Petrie said, “Jesus, those kids must be freezing.”

Tim laughed and said, “Smile makes those kids go swimming on New Year’s Day every year—I think they’ll survive. He says it’s not as good as growing up in Scotland, but it’s the best he can do.”

They both looked at Rob and Smile sitting by the pool with their heads bowed and their arms on their knees as if they were huddling against being overheard, or the cold, perhaps both. Billie Jean sat on the opposite side of the pool, watching the boys, sipping her drink and dangling her hand in the pool.

“You think the judge got it right, Sheriff?” Tim asked with a serious look.

Petrie looked thoughtful, then responded as if he wanted to get the answer exactly right. “Tim, the world is a better place with Rob out there in it and that bastard he killed gone. I think we had a damn good judge who found something to hang his hat on and who was damn glad to do it.”

EPILOGUE

The old woman sat smoking at a table near the full-length set of windows overlooking the parking area outside the restaurant. The restaurant was highly regarded locally for both the quality of its servings and the atmosphere. The bucolic setting was two kilometers into Northern Ireland but was easily accessible from Belturbet.

She was approached by a young waitress dressed in knee-length socks, a short green skirt, and tight silver bodice over a white shirt that was intended to make her look Swiss, in keeping with the theme of the restaurant.

"I'm sorry, ma'am, but there's no smoking allowed in the restaurant," the waitress said with a cheerful lilt to her voice as she placed a glass ashtray in front of the old woman, then turned and walked back toward the kitchen.

The woman watched the waitress walk away with eyes that lacked empathy or interest. She placed her cigarette to her lips, drew deeply, and released a large cloud of smoke. She turned her gaze back toward the window.

The smoke curling around her gnarled fingers reminded me of the fog in the tree roots near Glen Car Falls the day I watched Rob and Father Mulkey those many years ago. I thought back to the bridge and little Peter Keane. I remembered Padraig and Caroline, Tim Tanner and so many more.

She was waiting for Rob, as was I. She hadn't seen him in over thirty years, yet she showed no excitement or even interest. Her slightly hunched shoulders, and her legs and arms were neatly crossed making her appear tightly wound. The cigarette remained perched on the end of her fingertips, smoke curling into the air as if the burning started in her body and exited through the tip of her fingers.

When I saw the young waitress look out from the kitchen and stare at Maeve, I hoped that she would pretend not to notice the cigarette still burning and go back into the kitchen. Unfortunately, the waitress strode across the dining area and said, hands on hips, "Madam, I told you there is no smoking allowed in the restaurant."

Maeve looked at her with a vacant expression one might use in confronting a fly or another annoying insect. She placed the cigarette in her mouth and pulled the smoke slowly and deeply into her lungs. Then she exhaled, blowing a plume of smoke in the direction of the waitress.

"Fuck Off," she said, and flicked the ash on the ground before turning to gaze out the window once again.

It was apparent that the waitress had no backup plan and, after standing awkwardly for several minutes, she turned and headed back toward the kitchen. A moment later, she had the chef by the arm, dragging him out of the kitchen and pointing to Maeve. He appeared to recognize Maeve and started shaking his head at the waitress, clearly expressing he was uninterested in intervening.

Rob opened the door to the restaurant and looked inside. It seemed he had hoped he would have arrived before his mother. She had been strangely reluctant to have him come to their old home, insisting he meet her here for lunch instead. It was a building of stone and timber, the interior was furnished elegantly. Far above the old places he remembered from his youth in Belturbet. Apparently there was something to this Celtic Miracle people went on about at every turn.

"Mum, I'm so happy to see you," Rob said as he reached the table.

Maeve put out the cigarette and stood to greet Rob. "Don't you look grand, Robby? I can see your father's lovely eyes on ya." The hug she gave Rob was somewhat stilted, but he made up for it with his own fierce grip.

They stood holding each other for several minutes. Finally, Maeve pushed back and sat, patting the table. "Sit, Robby. Let me just look at you for a bit."

The young waitress came over to the table and gave menus to Rob and Maeve. She stood waiting, then finally asked, "Would you like a drink before or do you want to order now?"

As the waitress prepared to take their order, both Rob and Maeve heard the sounds of singing, flutes, and accordions playing nearby. Looking out the window, they saw men of all ages dressed in dark suits, many carrying umbrellas with v-shaped orange collarettes hanging around their shoulders. Some of the men wore bowler hats. The men looked solemn as they turned the corner around the restaurant building. In lines of four or five wide and nearly twenty deep, they marched through the parking lot before rounding the corner and disappearing from view.

"Jesus, do they still do that now, Mum?" said Rob. He was surprised by the appearance of the parade though he had seen them often as a young man. Nominally, the men were celebrating the victory at the Battle of the Boyne when England's William of Orange gained ascendancy over Ireland. The parades were now viewed as a symbol of Protestant control of Northern Ireland despite the majority of the population being Catholic.

"I thought that would all be behind us now that The Troubles are over."

The waitress continued to stand next to the table looking impatiently at Rob and Maeve.

"We aren't ready to order yet. Bring us each a Jameson neat with a beer back and come back later," Maeve told the waitress in an impatient tone. Turning to Rob, she said, "No, Rob, they are still lording it over us, vicious bastards that they are."

"But, Mum, I keep reading how things are settled now. Didn't it all get put aside back in '98? That's what the local papers reported in the States."

Maeve grunted a brief laugh. "Well, the papers here said you were guilty as sin and sure to go to the death chamber. Yet here you sit with your old mum whom I'm sure you think wasted her life on a cause that's still unsettled."

Rob hesitated briefly and looked to me like the young man talking to his mother back when he had been trying to decide what his future would be—footballer or musician. But he spoke with the quiet determination of an adult. "Mum, I know that life doesn't turn out the way we plan. I've spent most of my life trying to help children. To protect them from damage caused by adults. That is a never-ending job. When I was sitting in that jail in the States, I thought about each step I'd taken along the way. How I came to be where I was and facing the possible consequences of my actions.

"Then life changed for me when the hurricane struck. I lost a woman I loved deeply … And I lost the life she was carrying inside of her. It was the woman and our baby who gave me hope of a more normal life. Now that's gone.

"I imagine it's the same for you. I'm proud of what you did for our country and our people, Mum. I wish it had turned out better than it has, but it's better than it was. Maybe that's all any of us can do—our best."

The waitress returned and placed a shot of Jameson and a draft beer in front of each of them. She stood waiting with her order pad looking from Maeve to Rob. Waving the back of her hand, Maeve said, "Shoo. We'll call for you when we are ready … So where are we then, Robby? Are we finished? Is our work done?"

Maeve and Rob toasted with the shot glasses clinking. Rob took a sip of his drink and Maeve finished hers in one swallow.

From my place nearby, I heard him say, "Mum, the one thing I know with absolute certainty is that my work isn't done."

I knew then that I could leave them to finish their meal alone. Our journey together was not over and we would be seeing each other again.

Soon.